THE TWISTED LEGACY OF

LADY OF WIGI

Best Wishes
from Norton

THE TWISTED LEGACY OF MAUD DE BRAOSE

LADY OF WIGMORE

FRAN NORTON

YOUCAXTON PUBLICATIONS

OXFORD & SHREWSBURY

Other books in this series:
In the Shadow of a Tainted Crown
Throne of Shame

Copyright © Fran Norton 2016

The Author asserts the moral right to
be identified as the author of this work.

ISBN 978-191117-536-0
Printed and bound in Great Britain.
Published by YouCaxton Publications 2016

DEDICATION

In memory of

Lady Eileen Buckworth Herne Soame,

sadly missed by her family and friends

FOREWORD

As anyone interested in researching events in our rich history will know, there are frequently a number of differing accounts of events and descriptions of people which only adds to the fascination of the medieval period. In trying to maintain a balanced view I endeavour to lean towards some favoured chroniclers and respected historians plus adding my own interpretation in an effort to bring to life the characters portrayed.

Fran Norton

PREFACE

The reign of Henry III, son of the hated King John, is deemed to be one of the most disastrous in English history. Faced with the simmering resentment of his nobles and magnates for refusing to uphold the laws laid down in the Magna Carta. Henry further infuriates his native born nobility by endowing his half brothers, the Lusignans, with titles and lands. Their lawless reign of terror is ignored by Henry thus enraging his magnates even further. Added to this tinderbox of resentment is the volatile relationship Henry has with his brother-in-law, Simon de Montfort, Earl of Leicester, who becomes the leader of the Barons Party and the scene is set for England to enter into a period of civil wars. Throughout this period the wars with Wales have also continued against Llywelyn ap Iowerth, Prince of Wales, his armies held at bay by the Welsh Marcher barons, a breed of independent, warring families who have proved effective against the Welsh insurgents.

This is the England into which Maud, daughter to one such Marcher baron, William de Braose, Lord of Abergavenny, is born and the events which unfold within these pages are based on fact. The consequences of her father's actions are part of 'The Twisted Legacy' of pride and shame Maud and her sisters inherit.

William's wife, Eva Marshal, one of five daughters of the legendary knight, William Marshal, Earl of Pembroke, is left with her four young daughters, Isabella, Maud, Eleanor and Eve, to bear the shameful circumstances surrounding her husband's death, but it does not preclude the girls from making prestigious marriages, due to their wealthy dowries of the lands and estates of the de Braose, Brewer and Marshal families.

The betrothal of Maud to young Roger Mortimer, heir to the Marcher Lordship of Wigmore, is the beginning of a significant change to the Mortimer fortunes. Maud grows up to be a strong willed feisty young woman, who proves to be more than a match for her husband but the bitter lessons she suffered through her childhood stand her in good stead to face the dangers during one of the most turbulent periods in English history.

Through the years, Maud de Braose, Lady of Wigmore, demonstrates her courage throughout the troubled years of wars. The code of loyalty and honour, she endeavours to uphold in an effort to expunge the shame of her father's sins. Love, duty, courage and sadness, are all ingredients woven into the tale where loyalty and friendship can change overnight during the period of civil strife. Maud embodies all the attributes of the doughty wives, mothers and daughters of the Welsh Marches, women whose unbowed spirit is rarely acknowledged by the historians and chroniclers of the age. Within these pages I have tried make amends for their oversight.

Now come, let us join Maud de Braose, and journey back into the thirteenth century.

ACKNOWLEDGEMENTS

My sincere thanks go to the following people who have given their unstinting help with the research of the Mortimer family: to Dr. Ian Mortimer, President of the Mortimer History Society, Dr. Paul Dryburgh President of the Society; to Barbara Wright for the valuable details from her Mortimer Cartulary, to John Grove founder of the Mortimer History Society, to Hugh Wood and Dr. Martin Toms and, to Dr. Emma Cavell, from the Department of History and Classics at Swansea University, for her generous help over the months. I would also like to add Colin and Ina Taylor, formerly of Ellingham Press and to Bob Fowke, of YouCaxton for his invaluable advice.

Fran Norton

CONTENTS

DRAMATIS PERSONAE

Actual Historical Characters

William de Braose Lord of Abergavenny, Gwilym Ddu [Black William]

Eva Marshal wife of William, Daughter of William Marshal

Isabella [Izzy] de Braose, Oldest daughter of their four daughters and later marries Dafydd ap Llywelyn [Prince of Wales]

Maud de Braose, Second daughter of William de Braose and Eva Marshal later wife of Roger Mortimer

Eleanor [Nell] de Braose, Third daughter who married Humphrey de Bohun heir to the earldom of Hereford

Eve de Braose, Youngest daughter who married William Cantelupe

Isabel de Clare, Sister to Eva Marshal - first husband Gilbert de Clare Earl of Hertford her second husband is Richard Plantagenet Earl of Cornwall brother to Henry III

Richard de Clare, Son of Isabel de Clare later inherits the titles of Earl of Hertford and Gloucester; cousin to Maud

William de Clare, Second son of Isabel and Gilbert de Clare

Agnes de Clare, Daughter of Isabel and Gilbert de Clare

Amice [Amy], Youngest daughter of Isabel and Gilbert de Clare

Gilbert de Clare [Red Gilbert], Son of Richard de Clare who later becomes Earl of Gloucester

Henry III, King of England reigned 1216-1274

Eleanor of Provence, Queen of England 1223 - 1291

Lord Edward Plantagenet, Heir to the throne reigned as Edward I from 1274-1307

Eleanor of Castile, Wife of Lord Edward 1241 – 1290

Edmund Plantagenet, Second of Henry III's sons and brother to Edward

Robert Burnell, Later to become Bishop of Bath & Wells & Chancellor of England b: 1239–1292 friend of Edward

Sir Ralph Mortimer, Lord of Wigmore b: 1190 – 1246 father to Roger Mortimer Maud's husband

Gwladus Ddu, Daughter of Llywelyn ap Iowerth and wife to Ralph Mortimer

Roger Mortimer [Lord of Wigmore], Eldest son to Ralph and Gwladus Ddu husband to Maud de Braose

Ralph Mortimer, Son and heir of Maud and Roger

Edmund Mortimer, Second son to Maud and Roger later inherits the title of Lord of Wigmore

Isabella [Bella], Eldest daughter to Maud and Roger who marries John FitzAlan heir to the earldom of Arundel

Roger [Lord of Chirk], Third son of Maud and Roger Third son later to become the Lord of Chirk

Margaret [Meg], Second daughter to Maud and Roger who marries Robert de Vere Earl of Oxford

Richard FitzAlan, Son of Isabella and John FitzAlan – and Maud's grandson – inherits the title Earl of Arundel

Maud [Maudie] FitzAlan, Daughter of Isabella and John FitzAlan and Maud's granddaughter

Humphrey de Bohun [Earl of Hereford],

Simon de Montfort [Earl of Leicester], Brother-in-law to Henry III

Eleanor de Montfort, Widow of William Marshal Earl of Pembroke who was Maud's uncle; later marries Simon de Montfort

Llywelyn ap Iowerth [Prince of Wales], Also known as Llywelyn Fawr [Great]

Dafydd ap Llywelyn, Son and heir to Llywelyn who marries Isabella de Braose

John Giffard, Marcher baron

William Devereax, Marcher baron

Llywelyn ap Gruffydd, Nephew of Llywelyn ap Iowerth who later becomes Prince of Wales

Dafydd ap Gruffydd, Younger brother to the above later inherits the title of Prince of Wales

Fictional Characters

Guy de Longeville
Comte Etienne de Vivonne
Lord Rhys ap Ioin
Hal, Carys, Jane, Martha Ela and Rufus.
Errol, the servants and the young squires, Richard, Arthur
 and Edwin

LINEAGE OF MAUD DE BRAOSE

MATERNAL

Richard de Clare [Strongbow] [1130 – 1176] - m: Aoife [Eva] [The Red] McMorrough

Isabel de Clare [Countess of Pembroke] [1172 – 1220] m: William Marshal [1147 – 1219]

Sons: [5]

William [1190-1231] m: Alice de Bethune-- Richard [1191-1234] m: Gervase de Dinant ----Gilbert [1197-1241] m: Marjorie of Scotland--Walter [1199-1245] m: Margaret de Quincy--Anselm [1208-1245] m: Maud de Bohun

None of the Sons had any legitimate issue.

Daughters: [5]

Maud [1194-1248] m: Hugh Bigod--Isabel [1200-1240] m: Gilbert de Clare--Sibyl [1201-1245] m: William de Ferrers--Eva Marshal [1203-1246] m: William de Braose - Joan [1210-1234] m: Warin de Munchensi
[Earl of Norfolk]   [Earl of Hertford]   [Earl of Derby]   [Lord of Abergavenny]   [Lord of Swanscombe]

Isabella [1222- ?] m: Dafydd ap Llywelyn Prince of Wales - Maud [1224-1301] m: Roger Mortimer - Eve [1227-1255] m: William de Cantelupe - Eleanor [1228-1251] m: Humphrey de Bohun

*Isabella[ ] - Ralph[d:1274] - Edmund[[1251-1304] m: Margaret Fiennes - Margaret[-1297] m: Robert de Vere - Roger of Chirk[-1326] Geoffrey [-1282] William m: Hawise de Muscegros
(1) m: John Fiztalan   [Earl of Oxford]
[2]m: Robert de Hastang[Hastings]

*NB: Isabella Mortimer has been recorded as being married three times but Dr. Emma Cavell of Swansea University has recently found evidence to disprove the marriage to Ralph d'Arderne
Also, Isabella never held the title of Countess.

PATERNAL

William de Braose [III] d :1211

William [IV] d:1210   Giles [Bishop of Hereford] d: 1215   Reginald de Braose d: 1228 m: Gracia Brewer

William [V] ex: 1230 m: Eva Marshal

BOOK ONE

SHADOW OF SHAME

CHAPTER I

Late March
1230 Hay Castle

'No! No! I will not drink that foul potion'. The words were spat out in a high piping tone.

'Maud, the curative is merely feverfew and will help with your.............' Lady Eva Marshal's words were cut short, 'I care nothing for your physic I would rather die than drink it!' The little girl turned on her heels and ran from the chamber her hair flying out like a flaming pennant.

'You really should take that child in hand and teach her manners.' Isabel de Clare, Countess of Hertford, looked hard at her sister as she spoke.

'I know, but it is not so easily done.' Eva spoke in hushed tones, 'she is her father's favourite, and he sees no wrong in her actions describing them as high spirits.'

'Pah!' Isabel looked askance 'does he not realise that the child will find life in the future all the harder when she marries and comes under her husband's rule?'

Eva shrugged she was well aware of her daughter's shortcomings but Isabel also failed to understand no-one dared to oppose her husband William de Braose, Lord of Abergavenny, whose fearsome reputation was no exaggeration for, he was renowned for harsh punishments inflicted on those unfortunate enough to gain his displeasure; these did not stop at his own household's door. Instead, she smiled with an expression of resignation on her pale, handsome features.

'Maud will pay the high price for her father's indulgence I fear, leaving me to feel I have failed my own daughter.'

'Send her to me for awhile she will quickly learn how to

behave. Agnes, Amice, and Richard, are old enough to keep their cousin in check; children often find their own ways of dealing with unruly peers.'

'You would have me go against my husband?' Eva looked questioningly at her sister, 'the bond between them is too strong, and I would not dare to anger him. I pray you do not speak of this matter again for my sake.'

Isabel noted the fear in her sister's eyes as she spoke of William de Braose.

'It saddens me to learn that you must suffer the tantrums of a spoiled child out of fear of your own husband. At least Isabella and little Eleanor have more pleasing natures.'

Eva's expression softened and she became visibly more relaxed, 'indeed they are bright, cheerful and healthy such a boon when there are so many childish ailments to lay them low. Now, tell me what news of your brood? You mentioned Agnes, how does she fare, and what of your husband, have you heard from him of late?'

Gilbert de Clare, Earl of Hertford had accompanied the king to Brittany. 'I miss him desperately' Isabel's voice was full of emotion as she spoke of her beloved husband. Eva could only feel somewhat envious of her sister's marriage. The two women quickly fell into an easier topic of family affairs giving little thought to the dramatic departure of Eva's fractious daughter.

Maud meantime, had run back to her own chamber slamming doors behind her and leaping onto her bed still in high dudgeon.

'Mistress Maud you know your mother has your welfare at heart.' The nursemaid tried to comfort her charge but to no avail, when Maud de Braose was in a temper, then only time would slacken its heat.

Gwenlyn busied herself collecting the discarded clothing and shoes, for Maud was as untidy as she was temperamental. So many nursemaids had come and gone in recent years due to the child's volatile temper. A whisper to her father brought swift retribution on the heads of those Maud felt had given her grievance whether the slight was true or invented. She delighted in the power she held over those around her which included her sisters who, did not escape her tantrums and were often found weeping after Maud had pinched them, for it was her favourite torment.

When William de Braose was at home Maud's behaviour improve dramatically, she would accompany her father when he inspected the troops and knew by name his captains, lieutenants and sergeants; she also knew who were the finest archers, the best swordsmen and the swiftest destriers and the best chargers. Only among her father's men-at-arms, squires, and knights did Maud feel really comfortable, in turn she was prized as their mascot. It pleased William that his daughter – whom he felt should have been born a boy, took so much interest in his world of warfare. He had fallen into the habit of talking to her of tactics, though there significance was frequently lost on the little girl; she still smiled and pranced along chattering away to the man who was the scourge of the Welsh and was feared and hated in equal measure throughout the Marches.

When Isabel de Clare kissed her sister farewell neither women had any premonition of the dramatic changes the year would bring to them both. Eva had felt a deep sadness as she watched the colourful retinue trot briskly out of sight. She sighed and returned to the pressing matters of the day.

A few days later a messenger rode into the courtyard his tabard denoted he was one of the de Braose troop. He brought word that the Lord of Abergavenny would be arriving before nightfall and with this news the castle staff hurriedly began to prepare for their lord's homecoming. The fires in the kitchens were stoked – to bake or steam the fish pies, or some were prepared for poaching, likewise – vegetables roasted, or boiled in readiness to feed the hungry mouths even though it was still Lent. The urgency amongst the servants was tinged with fear for, if William de Braose was not satisfied with what he found upon his return, then those he felt had failed in their duties, would be painfully punished.

Eva felt a knot in her stomach knowing the demands her husband placed on her not only with regard to the household but, also for his carnal appetites and she shuddered involuntarily at the thought. William's requirements in their marriage bed were ones she felt sullied by and made the sign of the cross in resignation for what she knew lay before her that night.

However, on this occasion, the visit was to be but a brief one as William had urgent business which required his immediate return to Wales. The recent treaty with Llywelyn, had yet to be formalised which, included the betrothal of his oldest daughter Isabella, to Llywelyn's only legitimate son, Dafydd. Although Isabella was not quite eight years old, it followed the age old custom of arranged marriages. Plus, the annoying fact, he had yet to make the final payment of the huge ransom still outstanding for his freedom agreed after his capture in 1228, something which irked the Lord of Abergavenny more than a little.

As blustery winds heralded in the first days of April, buffeting the grey walls of Hay Castle, William de Braose made ready to depart with a party of heavily armed troops, together with his scribes and clergy. This betrothal would ostensibly, forge closer links with Llywelyn ap Ioewerth, and bring about a cessation of hostilities, which at least for the time being, would ensure safe trading between the former protagonists.

Maud stood beside the burly figure of her father; she was filled with pride at the sight of his fine armour and prancing destrier, her feelings of admiration offset with sadness at the thought of his departure, especially as he had been at home less than a sennight.

'You will come home soon Papa?' She looked up at him her dark green-grey eyes filled with tears. 'Don't weep Maud you know that is a sign of weakness. I hate the sound of wailing women.'

'I am *not* weeping' her voice was filled with defiance as she brushed away the tell tale tears. 'You have been back for such a short time – that is all.'

'Never fear, I will be riding back through those gates err long and then we can go to Radnor Castle for awhile' he smiled down at her as he spoke, 'you always enjoy your time there.'

Maud's tears melted, replaced by a cheery grin of anticipation. It was true Radnor was such a busy place, what had Hywel the steward called it, *'the gateway to the Marches.'* She loved watching the shepherds herding the sheep on the way to the markets in Shropshire, and listening to the many voices and dialects of merchants, drovers, pedlars, and travellers. Troops, constantly marched back and forth bringing with them tales of skirmishes - of victories and defeats - it was a place of excitement and urgency and Maud revelled in its exhilarating atmosphere.

As William stooped to lift his little daughter for a kiss of farewell she clung to his neck.

'I love you best of all, Papa!' He roared with laughter but kissed her soundly on the lips.

'And I love you my dearest Maud. Promise you will take care of your mother and sisters until my return.' The child nodded for words would no longer come as she choked back her childish emotions.

'I have tarried too long and we have many miles to travel err nightfall.' He lowered Maud to a waiting attendant and swiftly mounted his steed, raised his arm to signal his troops before he looked back at the castle and saluted towards the window where his wife stood; blew a kiss to Maud, then spurred his horse forward through the mighty gates of Hay Castle.

As swift as an arrow Maud ran back to the castle and breathlessly, raced up to the battlements to watch her father's departure. She stood until the last banner dipped from view then let the tears flow unchecked. It was so unfair; women were always left behind to do the mundane tasks. She vowed not be like them when she grew up, she would ride to war with her father and have her own standard. Needlecraft, spinning and weaving, were for others, *not* Maud de Braose.

Whilst her daughter stood on the battlements watching the last of the riders, Eva Marshal moved from her window with very different emotions at her husband's departure to the ones felt by the little girl. She called for hot water and sweet smelling oils, Eva needed to wash away the memories of the past nights. Her body was covered in bruises and teeth marks, her breasts were sore and tender but although she hated the coupling she longed for a son and prayed constantly that her next pregnancy would produce the longed for male heir. Maybe then her husband would begin to treat her with proper respect. Maybe then she would find personal satisfaction and fulfilment. As Eva lay immersed in the warm bath she allowed herself the luxury of dreams.

As the days of April passed the buds and leaves on the trees and bushes began to fill and burst with colour. Bird song filled the Early mornings as work in the fields began the yEarly routine in earnest, seeds sown, cattle and sheep were moved out onto summer pastures and new born lambs could be seen skipping and bleating for their mother's milk. It was the time of year Maud loved best of all. The days were growing longer as the sun gained strength; skeins of geese and swans flew back to their summer breeding grounds as the bees buzzed amongst the flowers searching for the sweet nectar, the sounds adding to Spring's chorus.

'Do you think Papa will return soon?' Maud sat winding a skein of wool as she spoke. Eva looked across at her daughter's outline in the window, the sunlight turning the thick curling tresses to flame, framing her pale oval face. Eva recognised the early promise of beauty - for once, Maud was so engaged in her task all thoughts of mischief and temper forgotten and with the normal defiant expression absent, she looked quite enchanting.

'His last letter said he expected to be home by early May no later but, it appears that lord Llywelyn has been detained elsewhere, therefore it has delayed everything.'

Maud flashed a rare smile, 'Good, I have almost finished stitching my sampler – that is when I can unravel this wretched yarn.' Eva sensed a change in mood so she leaned over.

'Do you wish me to help you?' Maud was just about to throw the work to the ground but hesitated.

'Would you?'

Eva smiled at her: 'of course I will, you only have to ask I am always here to help.' Then in a flash Maud threw the needlework at her mother and said spitefully

'Here, I am done with the wretched threads.' And without further ado she ran from the solar. Eva sighed, for just a fleeting moment she had hoped her daughter was finally beginning to conquer her anger. She turned to Isabella who had been quietly working on a framed tapestry.

'Your sister's temper is overworked is it not?' Isabella stopped and moved round to where her mother was seated she put her arm around her mother's shoulders.

'One day I hope to learn what moves Maud to anger and maybe then she will begin to accept her lot in life.' Eva turned and kissed her eldest daughter's cheek, 'At least I am blessed with my other daughters who, thankfully are sweet natured.'

As Maud ran from her mother's chamber she felt frustrated, she so wanted to finish her sampler, which had taken her so long as she found any task with a needle difficult, but had been determined to show her father her efforts and gain his praise. Now she could not go back without losing face. She slowed to a walk as she continued along the shadowy passages of the castle, until she reached the gardens. A gardener and a boy were busily weeding the herb beds, but neither raised their heads as she passed by, and continued their work without speaking. Maud was not the most popular child of the family in fact, only her father superseded her in their dislike.

Seeing she was to be ignored, Maud made her way towards the kitchens; sometimes there were tasty titbits to be had and her mood began to lighten a little at the thought. As she neared the bake-house she saw a kitchen lad holding his ear.

'Mistress Bowdler is not to be trifled with today.' He muttered as he ran past her; touching his forehead as he went. But Maud feared no-one and continued until she stood at the heavily studded door that led into the hot interior of the castle's kitchens.

The place was a hive of activity and the cook, Mistress Bowdler was stirring a huge cauldron from which delicious aromas rose, to fill the air. Her face was red and sweaty and she frequently brushed her left arm across her brow, as she called for one of the kitchen maids to bring spices and salt.

'Have a care with the salt 'tis precious and Hawise, if you do not stop your dawdling ways I will box your ears!'

It was just then that the kitchen staff became aware of Maud's presence, and they all curtseyed. 'What smells so tasty Mistress Bowdler?'

''Tis but the final piece of last season's beef which needs a might more simmering I fear.' She continued with her stirring but shouted to a tiny girl not much older than Maud, 'fetch Mistress Maud one of the honeyed candies and be swift about it girl.' The maid scuttled away returning with shining treat holding out towards Maud with a look of expectation on her face. Maud took the candy, popped it into her mouth, and nodded her thanks to the red faced cook. With the fasting for Lent now over she savoured the delicacy with relish. She left the busy scene knowing the little servant girl would be licking her fingers, the only way she would share in the sweetness.

§

When William de Braose arrived at Llywelyn's heavily guarded stronghold he was escorted to an apartment which although comfortable was not elaborately furnished. He learned of Prince Llywelyn's absence and was informed the feast of welcome would now be hosted by the wife of his host. Lady Joan was a voluptuous woman with heavily hooded eyes and features which denoted her Plantagenet bloodline, albeit from the wrong side of King John's blanket. Their previous encounter had been brief but, both had felt a mutual attraction.

Easter's religious festivals had been observed and the time of fasting was now over. The heavy trestle tables groaned with mouth watering fare of venison, roast boar, suckling pigs, goose, and a variety of savoury pies. Trenchers were filled and the wine flowed in copious quantities, the atmosphere was filled with excitement and expectation. Minstrels strummed their lutes and harps filling the air with Welsh music as the guests made merry.

William de Braose found himself sharing his trencher with his hostess complimenting her on the fine table of food and heady wines. Lady Joan found the Lord of Abergavenny a most attentive guest and as the evening progressed and the festivities became louder and more uninhibited she felt his dark eyes watching her closely.

'Prince Llywelyn is indeed a most fortunate man to *possess* a wife as lovely as you, my lady.'

'Come my lord, your own wife is a noted beauty is she not?'

He smiled, a trickle of gravy running from the side of his mouth. Joan leaned forward to wipe it away,

'Therefore my judgement is not in doubt?' He noted the fullness of her breasts as she leaned towards him her mouth slightly open, her lips moist and inviting. She looked him full in the eyes.

'Have a care my lord we are being watched.' He began to smile.

'Danger adds spice does it not?'

'Be assured, my husband is a jealous man.'

'So would I be, if my wife possessed such a ripe body.' Joan demurred but the seductive glance she cast in his direction denoted her pleasure at his words.

The Hall became hotter as the dancers began to whirl to the hypnotic beat of drums and the throbbing of the reed instruments which had replaced the former gentle strings of the harp. Laughter echoed round the vaulted timbers as William drank deeply of the rich, red Gascon wine; his lust became ever more urgent. The Lady Joan was well aware the Marcher lord wanted her for she was no stranger to men's sexual desires. However, what was so different about de Braose was his blatant disregard to her warnings and as the heady wine began to flow through her veins, she felt her own desires become more acute. De Braose could in no way be described as handsome but his physical presence was overwhelming. She noted his hard muscular body and strong, scarred hands and found herself wondering what it would be like to have this lusty man in her bed. At first she dashed the thoughts quickly from her mind but as the evening wore on the urgency of her body would not be subdued. William was well aware of the mutual attraction and he grinned, 'Let me come to you tonight and I promise you a night of delight.'

Joan's eyelids closed for a second as though she had not heard then under the table her hand reached out and she touched his manhood her eyes opening wide on contact. She remained silent but inclined her head almost imperceptibly. A few moments later she rose, waved to the company to continue with their jollities, and left with her lady-in-waiting.

An hour later the door to her bedchamber opened slowly and the burly figure of de Braose entered.

'Are we alone?'

From deep under the fur coverlets Joan murmured, 'Quite alone my lord.' Quickly he discarded his garments and slid under the cover reaching across to where she was lying, his hands soon exploring the soft curves of Joan's body. William de Braose was no stranger to women and the delights and passions they aroused in him. Their coupling was neither gentle, nor romantic they both needed to assuage the burning lust they had for each other. Although Joan's body felt soft to his touch her desires were strong and it took his entire physical prowess to bring about her climax.

As they lay in the aftermath of their passion she stroked his thigh. 'You know how to *serve* a woman.' He grinned in the darkness.

'I will always be at your service.' She punched him gently on his chest.

'We both must seek forgiveness for this night.'

'I will do penance most willingly' he whispered with a chuckle then added 'and often.'

The rest of the night the couple satisfied each other many times and with the dawn they fell into a deep sleep totally unaware that Llywelyn, Prince of Wales, was only a few miles from home. The doughty warrior prince had woken in the night with an urgent presentiment that he had to get home as quickly as possible. Rising, he immediately ordered his horse whilst his men struck camp with the speed gained from many years of experience. As soon as they gained the road he urged his horse to a brisk canter.

'We shall break-fast at home Gethin?'

'Aye, my lord.' His servant was still half asleep. Even the horses knew they were not far from their own stables and quicken their pace. As servants, stable boys and grooms were just beginning to go about their daily duties, the Prince of Wales trotted into the courtyard. Dismounting, he put his fingers to his lips to indicate he did not wish his arrival to be heralded thus wakening the rest of the household.

Striding nimbly up the stone stairwell Llywelyn made for

his wife's bedchamber and upon opening the door found her
deep in slumber with the Lord of Abergavenny, their bodies
still entwined. The blow Llywelyn felt was physical, sharp,
deep; his roar of anguish filled the air and echoed around
the walls like a wounded bear. His servants and men-at-arms
came running thinking their lord had been attacked.

At the commotion the recumbent couple stirred to face
the wrath of the Welsh Prince. William was dragged naked
from the bed his arms held fast by the guards, who muttered
angrily in Welsh. Joan began to weep begging her husband's
forgiveness. Llywelyn stood stone faced his heart, his pride
dashed, by the woman he truly loved. Outwardly he now
appeared calm; some who witnessed the scene thought he
would be absolved from the sin of murder had he slain de
Braose there and then but the Prince of Wales was a man of
honour and therefore, would observe the laws of his realm.
However, the fate of William de Braose was sealed by members
of Llywelyn's council who had been hastily summoned for
the trial; without hesitation they ordered the death penalty,
the execution was to be carried out without delay.

The messenger sent by the Welsh Prince to inform Eva
Marshal, of her husband's death, passed the gibbet where
the body of the Lord of Abergavenny swung in the early
morning breeze. He would still be warm, but soon the crows
and ravens would peck out the eyes and pull at the soft flesh,
but Wyre knew his master to be merciful and have the body
taken down before nightfall. The man had paid for his sins;
the shame was his and not that of his family, a fact his master
had instilled on his followers.

The swift riding messenger reached Hay the following
day carrying the scandalous news. As Eva read the heavily
sealed letter, the words swam before her eyes; de Braose
hanged! The terms were apologetic in the phrasing, but as
she continued to read it was the crime of *adultery* which
leapt out at her. She sank down onto a seat - her husband
had been caught with the wife of the Prince of Wales! It
seemed like some strange nightmare from which she would
wake. The nightmare however, was real, the events, fact;
the sentence final.

Her first thought was for her little daughter Maud, this news would break the child's heart, but then, how was she going to tell his adoring daughter the ignominious manner of her father's death. The whole incident was unbelievable. The commandments broken, adultery was one of the seven deadly sins. The sentence had been brutal but what Eva felt most acutely was the betrayal, and the greatest betrayal was of his child, who idolised him.

Eva quickly gathered her wits and summoned the household together giving orders that the children should remain in their nursery for the time being. As she spoke to the gathered company, Eva did not immediately divulge the manner of her husband's death as she struggled to find the right words.

'Until I have spoken to my children I command all present to say naught of this matter.' She hesitated before continuing, 'I know you will understand my reasons. I will need the help of you all during these difficult times, you have served my husband most diligently therefore I look to each and everyone to continue in my service.' There was a murmuring and almost everyone in the room knelt and bowed their heads, they all respected the Lady Eva and by their unanimous response she knew there would be no problem in taking over complete control of the household.

The coming days were difficult for the Lady of Abergavenny, hours filled with arrangements for the impending funeral and the countless letters informing the king, her brother William Marshal, Earl of Pembroke and the rest of her family, together with all those who would be most affected by her husband's death, but she welcomed the diversion for she had no wish to dwell on Williams' shameful end. Eva had been all too aware that he had been a womaniser but to be so stupid! Other thoughts also crept into her head – *she was free,* she made the sign of the cross at such guilty thoughts nonetheless they were thoughts which she could not completely suppress.

Meantime, there were the children; the most difficult task of all lay ahead of her, how to break the news to Maud? What would be the girl's reaction be when she learned her father was dead? Eva had no notion but knew it would not be without tears and the inevitable tantrums. Eva took a deep breath, squared her shoulder and sent for her daughters.

Later that evening as Eva sat busily penning more personal letters to her sisters and brothers she placed the quill back in its tray as she recalled the aftermath of her dreadful news upon her children. Eve and Eleanor were too young to understand the implications. Isabella, had received the news with quiet acceptance; but the greatest reaction understandably had been Maud's stunned disbelief followed quickly by a rage filled outburst.

'He promised he would come home soon he cannot be dead. He promised! He promised!' The choking words had been followed by scalding tears and sobs which wracked the slight body so violently Eva thought her daughter would go into a convulsive fit. She gathered Maud in her arms rocking her gently, as she crooned softly trying to comfort the grieving child. Isabella looked on without a word. When Maud calmed down a little, Eva called for Gwenlyn to take the girls back to the nursery. She signalled a servant to carry Maud so she could be put to bed.

'Keep watch on her I think she will sleep now but let her weep - she needs to release her grief, better in tears than more tantrums.' Gwenlyn nodded. 'I will not leave her be assured of that my Lady' she said softly.

Eva picked up her quill once again and continued her letter urging her sister Isabel to take her two oldest daughters into her care for awhile although the request left her troubled, when her children needed her most she was bound by duty and all the legal matters of inheritance which her new position entailed, rather than fulfilling her role as mother. However, there was no time for self pity; issues raised by the death of her husband were more pressing. Isabel would understand her concern as Maud's fiery temperament needed special attention never more so than now during her time of mourning.

CHAPTER II

Countess, Isabel de Clare, sat at the large, ornately carved desk which her husband had brought back from France after one of his many visits. A frown creased her brow.

'Nan, I fear I am about to stretch your patience and understanding to its limit. My sister's daughters will be arriving err long but I fear the younger one, Maud, may prove more than a handful. She is possessed of a volatile temperament which has been allowed free rein by her misbegotten father. God rest his blighted soul' She added, the note of irony not lost on the listener. Isabel paused, searching for her words, 'the situation is not entirely straight forward due to the fact the child is grieving for a father whom she loved deeply. Even the circumstances of his death will be difficult for her to come to terms with however, I know if anyone can handle a troublesome child it would be you my dearest Nan.'

Mistress Nan Twemlowe nodded: 'As you say my lady, the poor maid will have a great deal of growing up to do being faced with the fact she is no longer a 'favourite' which will be a difficult situation for her to accept, without the added weight of grief.'

The Countess rose and moved round to stand in front of the sturdy figure of a woman she had known all her life and loved as dearly as anyone in her own family.

'With the Earl away, you know how busy I am with matters of his estates and therefore, have left the daily welfare of my children in your most capable hands, but I do feel guilty about heaping this extra burden upon you. I fear Maud needs to learn how to conduct herself in a more courtly manner.'

Nan nodded, 'I remember you were not always the meekest of children', and her eyes twinkled as she spoke. 'Hush, do not reveal my secrets.' Isabel smiled with relief. 'I knew I could rely on you in this matter therefore I give you full charge over the children, should you need to report any unpleasantness I promise to support you at every step; you have my complete confidence.'

Nan dropped a curtsey, 'Thank you my lady'. Isabel reached over and caught the hand of her former nursemaid. 'You have my deepest gratitude Nan.'

After the door closed Isabel returned to sit behind the great desk normally occupied by her husband. It was true, she did trust the abilities of her trusted servant, but she knew Maud's future would not prove easy over the coming months and how she would cope with life's new order, was in doubt. It may turn out the child would be even more troublesome than before, and that even the consummate skills of Nan Twemlowe, may be left wanting. She took a deep breath, said a silent prayer, and then called for her scribe to assist with the mountain of scrolls which never seemed to wane.

Mistress Nan Twemlowe walked briskly towards the apartments occupied by the de Clare children, her black kirtle brushing the grey flagged floor, she would have to make some changes to the sleeping quarters. However, whilst her mind was busy with the logistics which would be easily overcome, the matter of an unhappy child may prove a more difficult challenge but Nan had faith in her own abilities and felt confident she could bring about the changes which she knew were essential to Maud's future.

Two days later when the party arrived, the Countess called for her former nursemaid so she could be formally introduced to her two nieces'. As they entered, still wearing their travelling cloaks, Nan noted it was Maud who walked in first, the older girl making no protest at the lack of respect by her sibling.

Maud curtseyed to her aunt, although it was far from graceful, then promptly went, and sat down as her sister Isabella, made a much more ladylike attempt.

'How was your journey?' The Countess looked up as she spoke although the question was directed toward Isabella it was Maud who piped up,

'I am sore and hungry, and I swear my pony is lame!'

The Countess coughed back her annoyance, 'my question was to your sister Maud, it is impolite to speak before spoken to!' Maud was unfazed by her aunt's reproach.

'Well! If you wait for Izzy to reply we may die of old age and starvation before she finds her voice.'

'Maybe your sister is so used to you speaking for her; she no longer feels any urgency to reply. I believe you will find in the de Clare household, there is a very different order to which we all adhere to and one, my dearest Maud, you will have to quickly learn or fall foul of the consequences.'

'What consequences?' Maud sounded genuinely puzzled.

'All will be explained in time by Mistress Twemlowe, who will be in charge of your welfare throughout your visit. Now come and be introduced and then after you have freshened up I am certain your imminent starvation will be assuaged.'

Nan stepped forward as the Countess took Isabella's hand and placed it in the older woman's in a gesture of formal introduction; holding her right hand up to stop Maud from leaving her chair until signalled. Isabella noted the gesture; which she instinctively knew, marked an end to Maud's precocious reign. Although Isabella was aware of the change, as yet, Maud had no notion of how her life was about to be turned upside down.

The girls followed the imposing figure of Mistress Twemlowe to the part of the castle which was to be their quarters for the duration of their stay. Maud continued to voice her complaints, her clear tones echoing around the thick grey walls as they walked hurriedly down the long passageways.

Upon reaching the courtyard, they paused looking about them at the impressive walls, before entering the doorway which led into a small chamber; at its centre, stood a glowing brazier. Two white capped servants stepped forward to take their cloaks. Their guide indicated for the sisters to follow her through another door, revealing a larger chamber which was light and airy. At either end of the room were two tables with a variety of chairs, stools, and benches, which were dotted around, all covered with brightly coloured cushions, but Nan continued on through yet another door, which brought the girls to the foot of a winding stairwell. After mounting the worn steps they entered a heavily studded door which opened into a large bedchamber; two attractively covered beds stood on either side of the chamber; Maud ran and jumped on the first one.

'This is mine.'

'No Mistress Maud, this one is for your sister Isabella.'

Maud's face clouded for a moment.

'Oh! Izzy won't mind, will you Izzy? I always get what I want don't I?'

'Well, from this day forward Mistress Maud, your sister takes precedence. Remember, in a few weeks she will travel to the household of the Prince of Wales, where she will live until she is of an age to marry his son Dafydd. So you must now treat her with all the respect her new position as a future Princess dictates.'

Maud looked at Nan a frown creasing her brow, as she replied tartly, 'But Izzy can't marry him, his father murdered our father.'

Before Nan could speak, Isabella stepped forward and stood in front of her sister.

'It was our father who broke the commandments, dishonouring Prince Llywelyn .....' Maud launched herself at her sister with fists and feet but Nan was equally as quick and swept the bundle of fury off her feet.

'Now that is no way to behave, least of all towards your sister, who merely speaks the truth, and if you are unable to accept the truth you will find life a deal more difficult than you expect.'

Maud ceased struggling for an instant then turned her fury onto the speaker.

'You lie, he was murdered.' But her doughty captor continued across the chamber to the other bed and plopped Maud down with a bump.

'If you *move* without my permission there will be no supper – do you understand?' Without raising her voice she continued in an even tone: 'Now, whilst you both wash and change I will send for some food.' She looked down at Maud as she spoke, 'No-one has ever died of starvation in this household to my knowledge, which will be of some comfort to you Mistress Maud.' The younger girl glared at the speaker but remained silent.

Nan left the chamber but stopped outside the closed door and listened for moment.

'I wish to go home, I don't like it here.' The voice was unmistakably Maud's.

'Sadly your wishes are no longer of any importance and you, like the rest of us, must obey the dictates of our elders.' Isabella was at last taking charge after years of restraint; she had immediately grasped her position in the new hierarchy and was already beginning to act accordingly. Nan realised the coming weeks would be difficult for her but even more so for the little girl who had been so spoiled by a seemingly doting father.

CHAPTER III

As summer edged towards autumn Isabella's departure to Wales loomed ever closer. In her heart she was somewhat fearful of her future but outwardly her misgivings were well disguised from her siblings. However, Nan Twemlowe knew of her doubts and tried to reassure the quiet, dignified girl she had come to hold dear over the weeks since she had arrived.

'Have no fear Mistress Izzy, you have the makings of a great princess, and your Welsh family will soon come to love you.' The two were alone in the bedchamber. Isabella looked up into the eyes of the old nurse.

'Do you really think so?'

'Yes child, you have an endearing nature and will quickly captivate all you meet, of that I'm in no doubt.'

'Thank you Nan; I have been really happy during these past few months even though Maud has proved somewhat difficult at times.'

'Your sister is also experiencing a great challenge in her life which I foresee may prove more than a little difficult for her in the months to come, but I for one, believe there are the beginnings of a breakthrough in her attitude. We can at least pray there is!'

Isabella took Nan's hand 'I shall miss you, for you have proved the rock to which I have clung during my time here.'

Nan leaned forward and kissed Isabella's brow.

'May God travel with you through life my child?'

Just then the door flung open and in rushed Maud and Agnes their faces flushed with anger. Nan sighed; Maud's temper had obviously got the better of her again and so it proved.

'I tell you that it is mine!' Maud's irate voice was beginning to rise.

'No, it was given to me!' Agnes de Clare, not normally an emotional child, was quite adamant.

'Come, this behaviour is unacceptable to young ladies of breeding.' Nan stepped forward and held out her hand. At first Maud stood defiantly facing the speaker but it was the look of grim determination on the older woman's face which overcame her initial resistance. Reluctantly Maud handed over the bright blue ribbon.

'Where did you get this?' Nan's voice was stern and unremitting. The two girls looked sheepishly at each other, neither replied. 'I am waiting!' Still they remained silent. 'From your failure to reply I will give it to Isabella and that will be an end of the matter.' Without further ado Nan handed the pretty ribbon to the older girl who looked delighted at her unexpected acquisition.

Oddly enough the incident would prove to be a turning point in the younger girls' relationship which had to date, been somewhat at odds. In future the two became inseparable. Nan felt pleased, for she knew Isabella's departure would undoubtedly have a profound impact upon Maud.

The days before Isabella's departure were the most harmonious of their stay and Nan felt sad that just as the life of her young charges seemed to be more settled, they would once more suffer the pain of separation. She sighed; life was certainly not easy for the children of noblemen.

On the eve of Isabella's journey to Wales the sisters sat together in an awkward silence both lost in thought. Eventually Maud spoke, 'are you looking forward to being married and becoming a princess?'

Isabella looked up her face serious, 'No! But I know Mama believes it is my duty to fulfil the wishes of our family with this union therefore, I must abide by their wishes.' Again the room fell silent.

'Will you write and tell me all about your wedding day?' Maud's voice faltered.

'Oh! You goose, of course I will. Besides, you will probably be there! However, there is something I wish to impress upon you Maud before I leave, you really must learn to cage your temper. I have heard some husband's beat their wives if they defy them, even go so far as to use the scold's bridle.' Maud looked horrified.

'I would slit his throat if any husband of mine tried to lay hands on me!'

'Brave words but believe me, the world is ruled by men, a fact we must learn to accept or suffer the consequences. Any outward sign of defiance would be fruitless and we would lose far more therefore we must use the only weapons we possess - our wits and play their game.'

Maud sat deep in thought for a moment then with a winning smile she said artlessly, 'like a game of adults?'

'Exactly, like a game of adults.'

Although Isabella was secretly dreading her new life in Wales, she knew to disclose such fears to the younger girl would be unwise. However, it was her duty to warn her younger sister of the perils her wayward behaviour which could affect her life, and in turn may reflect on their family. If Maud did not yet know the whole truth about their father's execution, Isabella was in no doubt; the manner of his death would overshadow them for years to come.

'Promise me Maud; you will endeavour to control your temper for when I have found myself at odds with you in the past, you can utter some cruel words and a once a hasty word is spoken, it can never be recanted. Enemies are easily made by such utterances.'

The younger girl hesitated but noted the earnest expression on Isabella's face, and knew this to be important, she nodded, 'I will try, on that you have my word I know I do boil over at times and ....'

Isabella leaned over and caught her sister's hand.

'It pleases me to know at least you will try!' The two hugged and then made ready to go down to supper which was being held in the Great Hall to celebrate Isabella's forthcoming departure. During their stay with the de Clare's, Maud had come to realise how much she loved her older sister.

The following morning dawned chilly, heavy clouds threatened rain as the party rode through the gateway. Maud leaned forward at the window to catch the last glimpses of her sister and waved frantically, hoping she would be seen. In the last few weeks Maud had learned some difficult lessons but with the help of Isabella and her cousin Agnes, she had begun the road of self awareness. At times, life had seemed very hard. Soon after she had arrived, the two older de Clare children, Richard and Agnes, had quickly made it clear, she was their junior, and had treated her thus. But through the ensuing weeks Isabella and Agnes had shown their loyalty to her and had frequently come to her aid.

Within days of Isabella's departure a mud splattered messenger galloped his spent horse through the great gateway as the rider dismounted; he staggered with exhaustion but indicated his news was urgent and that an immediate audience with the Countess was imperative.

Apologising for the state of his apparel, and with shaking hands he delivered the sealed scroll to Isabel.

'Pray, be seated before you collapse.' The messenger nodded unable to speak and dropped onto a bench nearby. As Isabel broke the seal and began to read, a cry escaped her lips and she sank to her knees, tears streaming down her face. She remained for some moments before she regained her composure then turning to her attendants she said in a muffled sob, 'Our dearest lord is dead!'

Later, when she managed to finish reading the letter Isabel learned the Earl had died at Penrose, on his way home from Brittany. After her initial uncontrolled outburst of grief, Isabel regained her composure and began to make arrangements for her husband's funeral and send letters to the rest of their family. The outcome to this sad news was she felt that Maud should return to her mother's household and all the girl's cries of protest went unheeded. Once again Maud's young life was to be disrupted and Nan Twemlowe felt saddened, as she had witnessed the beginnings of a real change in the child. Now, with this further disruption she felt uncertain how the little girl would react and feared she may fall back into her belligerent ways.

CHAPTER IV

1236
Early January

Eva Marshall looked up as her daughter entered the solar.

'Mama, Father Sebastian gave me a penance of *five* novenas! Do you not think that excessive?'

Eva smiled 'So what pray, gave rise to such a harsh penance?'

Maud sighed heavily. 'I was late twice for Mass.'

'Oh! Dear an unforgivable sin in Father Sebastian's eyes.'

'He is such a dried up old stick....'

'Now Maud that is uncharitable Father Sebastian is nigh on three score years and of a different era; he merely seeks to safeguard your soul for God.'

Maud made a face. 'How can such an unworldly cleric judge my soul? Methinks the time is ripe for his retirement.'

Eva Marshal was struck by the changes wrought in her daughter during the past six years. In the months after Maud returned from the de Clare's, her moods had fluctuated between anger and sullen silences and the one who bore the brunt of it all, had been the luckless Gwenlyn. Until one day, the young servant had turned to face her tormentor.

'Well Mistress Maud, you can rail against the entire world if you wish, but the simple truth is the death of your father was never murder, he brought down the wrath of the Welsh Prince on himself by committing one of the seven deadly sins – adultery, with his wife.'

Maud had thrown herself at the speaker in a white hot fury but Gwenlyn, had captured her attacker and continued: 'that is the simple truth. It is no good blaming anyone else and the fact that Mistress Izzy has gone to Wales was to fulfil the promises given by your father. You know from her letters that she is well cared for and is treated with great respect. One day she will become Princess of Wales and rule over not only the household of her husband but also, its people. Remember, you and your sisters will also be expected to become ladies of great importance but if you continue to act like some virago, then it will bring shame on the name of Marshal and de Braose.'

Those fateful words had halted Maud's onslaught. Gwenlyn had realised that this was not the time to stop now she had the girl's undivided attention.

'Have you not noticed how different life is nowadays? Your Mama is respected and loved by all who work for her; they try to please, not out of fear but out of a wish to help her through this difficult time. She is the one who rises early and works without respite throughout the day, and even when she is weary, she always comes to the nursery and asks after the welfare of her daughters. You are all long asleep and believe she does not care. Believe me, Lady Eva cares most deeply about her girls; she made us all promise not to tell you the truth about your father until the time was right. Today, I deemed the time was right and I for one think you are old enough to understand and accept it, call it the will of God if you wish, but it is a fact you can never alter. Now you must concentrate on learning how you can apply yourself to ensure you are ready to fulfil your destiny and to be able to rule a large and busy household; but first, you must learn to control yourself. Accept what you cannot alter and look to how you can make changes for the better, within your abilities.'

The prophetic words had been the catalyst and from that day forward Maud had begun to change her attitude towards life. It had been a slow progress at first but nowadays, although Maud's infamous temper no longer erupted as frequently, it still flared on occasions, and Eva knew Father Sebastian could well be the spark to ignite the flame, the two had been at odds for years. Eva had no wish to see the re-emergence of the former wilful child, so different from the twelve year old girl who presently stood before her.

'I have decided that you shall accompany me to Canterbury to celebrate the king's wedding.' Eva paused, waiting for her daughter's reaction. Maud's expression was not of expectation or for that matter, excitement but quite the contrary; she wrinkled her nose before replying.

'The journey will be cold and miserable - do I have to go?'

'Maud you never cease to amaze me I thought you would be delighted to see the pageantry and the spectacle of the king and his courtiers, not to mention of meeting your cousins again!'

'W-e-l-l yes but, I really do not fancy the discomfort of all those miles in the saddle.'

'You can travel with me in my litter and we shall keep each other entertained on the way.' Eva said trying to hide her feelings for there was another reason she wished her daughter to accompany her to Canterbury a most important one; to meet Lord and Lady Mortimer, parents of Maud's future husband, Roger.

During the intervening years the relationship between mother and daughter had grown closer therefore it was with pangs of real regret Eva felt it was time to acquaint her daughter with plans affecting the girl's future.

'Come here my dear, sit with me, for I have news concerning a prospective husband, therefore the failings of Father Sebastian will have to wait for another day.'

Maud noted the serious expression on her mother's face. At thirty three Eva Marshal was still a handsome woman, but she had resisted the many offers of marriage, persuading her brother, Richard Marshal, Earl of Pembroke, not to press her into a second marriage due in part to the painful memories of her first husband, William de Braose. Another more important reason was land; much of which she had inherited from her father, William Marshal and her mother, Isabel, Countess of Pembroke. Marriage would affect the inheritance of her daughters, Isabella, Maud, Eve, and Eleanor and their futures were now her sole priority.

After the death of her oldest brother, William Marshal in 1231, only a year after her husband and her brother-in-law Gilbert de Clare; Richard, known to his family as Dickon, had been far more sympathetic to her request not to re-marry; too late for Isabel, who at William's insistence had married

Richard, Earl of Cornwall, the king's brother, in what Eva thought, unseemly haste. The union had brought with it many emotional problems for poor Isabel, who still mourned the loss of her beloved Gilbert.

The Welsh Marches, over many generations, was a restless, war torn region, not only with battles and skirmishes with the Welsh but also between some of the powerful barons whose borders were constantly altering due to death, marriage, and quarrels. The stubborn character of many of the warring barons proved the stumbling block to resolving disputes over possession of lands and properties.

Eva had proved an astute administrator since the death of her notorious husband, but it hadn't been easy and she had come to rely on her brother Dickon for support. Now she must apprise Maud of the plans which had been agreed for her future marriage.

'Maud, you know there have been negotiations for some while now with a number of our neighbours with regard to the boundaries of our estates within the Marches. The most important one being with our closest ally, Ralph Mortimer, Lord of Wigmore, which is nearing a conclusion; as you know he has a son and heir, Roger, who is but five years old. Nonetheless, age is no barrier to a betrothal.....'

'Mama, are you about to tell me I am to be betrothed to a boy of *five?*' The incredulity in Maud's voice was unmistakable. She failed to add that there was already a verbal agreement and had been since Roger had been a baby.

'My dear, the Mortimer's are a powerful and much respected family they have the wherewithal to protect you and your inheritance. Besides, they are related by blood to both the English and Welsh ruling houses and Lady Mortimer's first husband was Reginald de Braose.'

'I shall be *old* by the time the boy will be of an age to marry! Look at Amy and Richard, already married.'

'Oh! Maud my whole concern is for the well being and future of my beloved daughters. Marriage is the essential role for women is it not. Besides, the other alternative is the Church and we both know your nature is totally unsuited to the life of austerity and dedication to God.'

Maud nodded. 'I know Mama but *five!*'

They looked at each other and laughed out loud.

'Does this mean I shall have to go to Wigmore?'

'The details of your dowry are yet to be decided and agreed upon, so nothing will change for the time being. I merely wished to let you know where your future lies. Therefore I thought the ceremony at Canterbury would be an ideal place for you to become acquainted with the Mortimer's.'

Eva felt relieved that her news had not incited an outburst of anger or in fact any resistance in her daughter for although Maud was a much changed character, like a summer storm, there were still moments when the famous temper erupted.

'Mama, why have you never re-married?'

Eva rose and walked to the window she looked out over the scene below before answering.

'Unlike you Aunt Isabel, I escaped your late Uncle William's plans for my re-marriage and chose to remain a widow to ensure the future of my daughters. Poor Isabel on the other hand, had little choice and was urged into a royal marriage in the belief it would safeguard her children's future.' She paused before continuing, 'sadly, this second marriage has been far less successful than her first. But.....' Eva turned and walked back from her vantage point to sit beside her daughter 'it was a decision which brought her and her new husband, into conflict with the king.'

'Uncle Richard of Cornwall is after all the king's brother, and they did marry without royal consent, did they not?' Maud's words were nothing if not true.

'Indeed my dear, but that dispute has long been settled. However, poor Isabel has suffered so much since, what with losing two of her babies.' She omitted to mention Richard of Cornwall's lecherous tendencies, and the fact he refused to put aside his Mistress of many years, had only added to the rumours, if true, he had made many more conquests since his marriage.

'Aunt Isabel has young Henry now, who appears by all accounts hail and healthy.'

'We will pray that Henry remains thus.' Eva said thoughtfully.

'Now my dear, I must finish this endless correspondence or

will be working late into the night. Besides, you must choose your wardrobe for the king's wedding.' She smiled then added, 'as you leave, pray summon Master Edgar.'

Maud kissed her mother and left the solar which in winter Eva used as her study. After Maud sent word to her mother's scribe, she walked back to her own apartments her mind buzzing with thoughts of her forthcoming visit to Canterbury and the meeting with the Mortimer's. What did marriage really entail? More importantly, what did she feel about being married to the Mortimer boy? Questions she would put to Gwenlyn upon her next visit. Life had never been quite the same since her former burse-maid had left the de Braose service to marry a young silversmith and now lived in Hereford.

CHAPTER V

Canterbury
15ᵗʰ January 1236

'So-o what did you make of all the pomp and pageantry of the king's wedding?' Eva spoke softly and watched Maud, who sat on the edge of the bed, which was covered by a fur coverlet.

'Honestly, I thought Eleanor of Provence looked sick! She was so pale and walked as if she had a poker up her back.'

'The poor girl was probably scared out of her skin.'

'Fancy, being married to someone over twice your age!' Maud exclaimed.

'Unlike me, who is to be married to a Mortimer, seven years my junior!' Maud looked at her mother to see her response. Eva ignored her daughter's remark.

'Now the formal ceremony is over there will be sufficient time for an introduction to *your* future family and I want you to promise to be on your best behaviour.' Eva looked earnestly at the seated figure of her daughter. 'Their impression of you will count a great deal, especially with Lady Mortimer. Remember she is not only Lady of Wigmore but also a Welsh Princess'

'Like Izzy!'

'No, Maud, Izzy has married a future Prince; Lady Mortimer *is* a Princess by birth.' Eva's expression warned the girl not to be too pert with her mother.

'Worry not Mama, I shall not let you down.' Maud smiled disarmingly as she spoke.

'I cannot emphasise enough how important this marriage is and ....'

Maud rose and went and hugged her mother 'Have no fear my dearest mother, I promise I will play my part. Come, there are so many faces I do not recognize and would have you instruct me as to their names, titles and.....' she stopped looking mischievously at her mother, 'scandals.'

'You are too young to listen to gossip which often leads to trouble, mark my words.' Eva saw the twinkle in her daughter's dark green-grey eyes, 'Maud you are a minx and no mistake' but Eva laughed at the girl's words.

That evening, bedecked in their finest apparel, Lady Eva Marshal and her daughter Maud, sat at one of the many tables with Lord and Lady Mortimer. The girl was as good as her word and spoke only when spoken to, for she realised that this was her first formal step into adult life. At the outset it was the two older women who fell into conversation but Maud was aware she was being observed not only by the Mortimer's but also, by many in the Great Hall. The gathering was much larger than any she had previously attended and she was somewhat in awe of the whole occasion. Unlike earlier during the ceremony in the cathedral, all eyes had been focused on the royal couple, now she found many curious glances being cast in her direction and left her feeling a little uncomfortable.

'My dear you must be so proud of your daughter,' Lady Mortimer spoke in lilting tones. 'She is quite lovely.'

Eva Marshal smiled 'Of course, I am proud of all my daughters.'

'Quite so,' she leaned forward and spoke directly to Maud. 'Are you enjoying all the festivities?' Gwladus Ddu, Lady Mortimer, directed her question at the girl.

Maud studied the woman who would be her future mother-in-law; she noted the oval face with its high cheek bones and smooth olive skin, contrasted by a pair of golden hazel coloured eyes. She also noted the fine lines around the corners of those fascinating eyes; the only visible signs of age.

'Quite a spectacle is it not my lady?' she said in deferential tones.

'Indeed, a little too noisy for my taste these days, but it will be the topic of conversation for the rest of the season I'll warrant.'

Maud smiled shyly and nodded. Lady Mortimer had the innate air of a woman of breeding but the girl was aware she was also being assessed by the Lord of Wigmore, who spoke but little throughout the evening, she could but hope that she had met with the couple's approval.

After the first hour Maud relaxed a little and allowed herself to observe those who sat at the other trestle tables. She recognised many of the English Earls and some of their wives and daughters but it was to the members of the young queen's entourage that her eye was constantly drawn; amongst their number was one of the most handsome men she had ever set eyes upon. Comte Etienne de Vivonne was tall, fair, and perfectly aware of his affect upon women. His smile lit up his face, and his hands were used expressively as he spoke. There was much laughter at his table. Maud's gaze moved to the figure sitting next to the 'handsome one', who, in total contrast to his companion, was dark haired, and appeared somewhat aloof, but recognised he was a person of authority and no mere servant, by his rich, but unfussy apparel. There was an air of strength and confidence about him, but as she studied him, became aware that he in turn, was studying her, and she blushed and dropped her gaze. It was the words of Lord Ralph Mortimer which broke into her thoughts.

'I see the Savoyards are already making their presence felt, the Queen has wasted little time surrounding herself with family members, which will not sit lightly with many here tonight.' Although the Lord of Wigmore had whispered softly in his wife's ear, Maud had overheard. She looked down at her trencher, at the succulent meat, then popped a piece into her mouth hoping her face had not betrayed the fact she had overheard their private conversation.

Throughout the rest of the evening Maud continued to observe the colourful company. She would question her mother later as to the significance of Lord Mortimer's words but for now her attention was fully engaged with the spectacle before her, especially at the antics of the jesters.

As the evening progressed, voices became louder due to the vast quantities of wine consumed. The musicians played and minstrels sang many songs, which were mostly familiar but interlaced with new ones, composed especially for the occasion. Their voices rose high into the rafters, filling every corner of the Great Hall.

After the mummers, jugglers, and jesters, had finished their evening's entertainment, the dancing commenced and Maud was entranced by the swirling couples in their beautiful, colourful finery; the candle glow setting their jewels ablaze.

'The king and queen appear to be enjoying the revelry.' Lady Mortimer's voice broke in on Maud's concentration.

'I have been so engaged with watching everyone I have scarce paid any attention to the royal dais.' Maud smiled as she answered.

'If you wish to join in the dancing I will ask my kinsman to partner you!'

'Oh! No! Really I would much rather watch, but thank you!' Maud stammered her reply. However, just at that moment, to her delight, she spied her Aunt Isabel accompanied by her cousins Agnes, Amice, and Richard heading towards them. Maud noted the change to her aunt's appearance for she looked pale and heavy eyed so unlike the vibrant woman she remembered.

'Ah! Maud, you have grown into a budding beauty, no less.' Isabel, Countess of Cornwall, bent and kissed her niece, then nodded in friendly greeting to the Mortimer's.

'Children grow at such apace 'tis hard to keep track of the years is it not?'

Lady Mortimer smiled, 'Indeed, they have scant time to be children.'

Isabel turned to Maud, 'Pray where is your mother?'

'I believe she has gone to speak with Uncle Gilbert.' Maud scanned the Hall as she spoke.

'No matter, she will soon return no doubt.' Isabel sat down with a grateful sigh.

'I fear nowadays I tire so quickly.'

'Age is no friend to us Countess.' Lady Mortimer said sympathetically. The women were soon lost in conversation leaving Maud and her cousins to catch up with their own gossip.

'Have you seen the handsome Comte?' Agnes whispered to Maud.

'Oh! The vain popinjay who believes all women will faint at his feet. Yes I have seen him but would not trust him an inch.' Agnes smiled at Maud's words.

'You have not changed Maud, still as forthright as ever, cousin.'

Maud looked across at Richard de Clare who, at fourteen was quite tall for his age; he was standing beside his young wife, Megotta de Burgh. Their marriage had angered the king, as Hubert de Burgh, Megotta's father, had omitted to gain royal approval for the match and was currently in disgrace over the matter. The marriage had also caused anger amongst the Marshal family, as it had been a kinsman of de Burgh, who had helped to bring about the shameful 'murder' in 1234 in Ireland, of Richard Marshal, Earl of Pembroke, known by his family as Dickon. The treacherous act would have repercussions in the years to come.

'How do your knightly skills progress, cousin?' Maud studied the youth who was, by right of birth, the Earl of Hertford and Gloucester. He grinned

'Tis hard work and my bones are constantly aching – otherwise,' he paused; then a frown passed across his face, 'although I can never please my father-in-law or my step-father, however hard I try, can I Meg?'

Maud studied the dark eyed girl standing beside her cousin. 'My father is a hard task master.' She murmured nervously.

Agnes tugged at Maud's sleeve, and whispered. 'Poor Rich, it's true, he is always getting the sharp end of the Earl of Cornwall's tongue, and it grieves my mother so, but she can do naught to change the situation as she has learned to her cost.'

Maud looked enquiringly at her cousin 'How so?' But Agnes would say no more as her mother's gaze had fallen on the whispering pair.

'It is ill mannered to whisper in company you two!'

'They are merely gossiping much as we are doing.' Lady Mortimer said smiling at the girls.

As the evening continued Maud, Agnes, and Amice, more often called Amy, who had married Baldwin de Reviers, Earl of Devon, in the previous year, took their opportunity to apprise each other of events in their lives since last they had all been together. Amy, already pregnant, chatted companionably long into the night until finally Eva, who had long since returned to her place, indicated it was time to retire but the younger generation were unready to leave the noisy company. Unlike the Countess of Cornwall, who had left earlier to seek her bed exhausted by all the merriment?

'Are you aware the pretty French Comte, you so despise' Agnes whispered 'has been looking over at you all through the evening.'

'Rubbish!' exclaimed Maud.

'No! No! Really it is true Maud! I've watched his companion trying to distract him.'

'I am certain you are being fanciful.' Maud said thoughtfully. 'I have seen him dancing with a number of ladies throughout the evening.'

'Ah! His companion on the other hand, has been talking to that upstart, de Montfort and my step-father.' Agnes spoke softly not wishing to be overheard but her brother, interrupted.

'You mean Sir Guy de Longeville, the Comte's brother-in-law.' Rich whispered, and then continued, 'he must feel sad on such an occasion.'

'Why?' The question was uttered by Maud and Agnes in unison.

'He was married as a boy, then six months after the ceremony his bride caught a fever, which left her in a bizarre plight; the effect has left her locked in the age she was when she fell ill.'

'What! You mean she is still like a child?' Agnes said in amazement.

'Mmm!' Richard nodded.

'You five look like conspirators whispering over there.' Eva Marshal spoke without rancour. 'Pray, what are you gossiping about now?'

'Oh! Aunt, Rich was just telling us about Sir Guy de Longeville's tragic marriage.' Agnes's voice sounded wistful as she spoke.

'God tests us in many ways but he usually provides us with the necessary weapons to combat such trials.'

'Mama, what weapons did he give to the girl who will never grow up or, to her husband to whom she can be no comfort at all?' Maud's voice held a challenge in the tone. 'Besides, such a marriage could be annulled, surely?'

Eva sighed as she replied.

'The girl, whom I believe is named Celeste, is unaware of her malady and knows only the world of a child therefore; she knows naught of her true condition.'

Maud looked unconvinced. 'So Lord de Longeville, has a wife who is no wife, how does he come to terms with such a situation? But even more intriguing has to be why!'

'Maybe he sees it as God's will or, maybe he feels it his duty'. Eva's voice was clipped and sharp and she glared at her daughter as she spoke.

'I am not questioning God's will, merely questioning his reasoning Mama.'

'Which is not your place to do so, Maud? Now it is time for bed and the end of the matter.' Without a further word Eva turned on her heel and walked away her head held high, her shoulders rigid.

'Oh! Maud now you have upset your mother.' Agnes said 'run and ask for her forgiveness.'

'Come on Agnes, you know full well Maud would rather eat worms than beg for forgiveness even from her own mother.' Richard's voice rose and fell in an odd cadence as his voice had not fully broken making it sound quite odd under the circumstances. Agnes squeezed Maud's arm gently:

'God night, and do try and smooth matters over with your Mama before the morning.'

Maud followed her mother to their chamber knowing it would be a chilly encounter, but her mind was still too full of questions regarding the French noblemen, questions she was determined to find answers to on the morrow.

The following day was blustery and cold for the tournament; banners billowed and the flapping pavilions and marquees, tugged at their ropes in an effort to fly free. Heralds practiced their clarion calls; knights and their squires were busily preparing for the day's event. The royal servants were rendered desperate in their efforts to secure rugs and cushions to the seats on the dais. Hucksters, stall holders, pie sellers, all struggled with the conditions so too the grooms were finding the powerful destriers, skittish and fractious, as their caparisons blew, and flapped around their legs. Bellowing voices rose and fell in an effort to compete with the howling winter wind but to Maud, it only added to her excitement as the herald signalled for the start of the tournament, the first occasion where she would be seated in a place of importance.

The air was filled with tense anticipation as the combatants entered the arena mounted on their mighty destriers. Standards, so bright and garish, denoted the houses of the powerful nobles from England and the Continent. Maud had learned there was bad blood between the Pointevins, Savoyards, and the English, which would only add spice to the forthcoming event. The king and his young wife, flanked by his brother and his wife, the Earl and Countess of Cornwall, together with the Earls of Hereford, Gloucester, and Norfolk, who took their places in the front ranks of the marquee, whilst other members of their families sat further back.

Maud was glad of her thick, fur lined cloak with its deep hood, for the wind whistled unmercifully around the spectators. She noted how Eleanor of Provence, shivered from time to time, whether from cold or nerves, Maud was uncertain.

As the herald blew the summoning notes for the commencement of the joust, the crowds leaned forward to watch the parade, some placing wagers on the outcome of the day; some, merely to point out their favourites or, to see who would compete that afternoon. Whatever the outcome, no-one would go away without a lurid tale to tell.

For Maud de Braose, it denoted an exciting new period in her life; this visit to Canterbury, was the onset of adulthood. She watched intently as each round began, until she felt a nudge to her ribs and Amy's whispered voice.

'Look, it is Baldwin, see the extra piece of plate in his armoured' she giggled ......due to his growing girth. It is not only my belly which swells.'

Maud noted the nervousness in the giggle.

'Do you like married life Amy?' Maud waited for her cousin's reply.

'Not really!' Came the whispered reply but Amy's expression was unreadable as she watched the cumbersome figure of Baldwin de Reviers thunder along the lists. Even above the hoots from the crowd and the flapping of the pavilions, the crash of steel could be heard as de Reviers lance found its mark, his hapless opponent toppled to the ground. A great roar went up from the throng for he had beaten one of the queen's knights; Maud looked across to see the reaction from the queen but if she thought to witness any show of emotion, the face of Eleanor of Provence's remained impassive. A cold creature, England's new queen, was Maud's personal opinion.

With each bout the scores changed first, in favour of the French, then back to the English and the tension grew ever higher as the afternoon wore on. Maud's attention was captured, when she saw the black plumed figure riding a great black charger enter the arena and instantly recognised, Sir Guy de Longeville. But it was a loud whispered comment from someone seated in front of her which set her wondering about this enigmatic knight.

'What's an English knight doing in the service of the Frenchman? No wonder his family disowned him.'

The whole life of this tall, darkly handsome knight, she found intriguing and was determined to discover more. As she watched, she marvelled at the deftness and accuracy of his skill and the swift dispatch of his opponent to the roars of the crowd.

By the end of the afternoon however, the scores were even, which was judged a satisfactory outcome, at least for the royal party. After the congratulatory speeches and prizes had been presented the crowds drifted away to enjoy the other diversions of street entertainers, cock fighting, bear baiting, singers and musicians, whereas the nobility retired to rest and change, for yet more feasting and revelries to be enjoyed over the coming hours.

During the evening, Eva Marshal introduced Maud to the Earl of Hereford, Humphrey de Bohun the rancour of the previous evening forgotten.

'You are blessed with beauteous daughters my lady,' Humphrey smiled at Eva as he spoke, his appreciative gaze travelling over Maud. His craggy face was softened by a pair of twinkling blue eyes. Maud smiled demurely at his words.

'As you know, Eleanor will in time be married to the Earl's son, and we have been discussing arrangements for her to go and live with his family until such time she is old enough to become a wife. The Earl has suggested that you may like to accompany Nell to Hereford, it would be a satisfactory arrangement not only for your sister but also, for you, especially as young Mortimer will eventually join the Earl's household as a squire, making it easier over the coming years for you to become acquainted with your future husband.'

'If that is what you wish Mama!' Maud looked up at the Earl, 'I hope you do not regret your invitation.' She smiled roguishly as she spoke.

Eva sighed. 'Then that is settled. As for myself, I intend to spend more time in Devon this year. I have a number of projects I wish to carry out.'

'I look forward with interest to our future meetings.' The Earl said raising his goblet to Maud then excused himself when he noticed the king beckoning him to re-join the royal party; he bowed then made his way to the royal dais.

'I hope you can make a friend of the Earl and his family it could aid your husband's standing in the future. Besides, Nell will be old enough to go into the de Bohun household soon in readiness for her future marriage, a customary move under the circumstances.' Eva continued 'as Nell is of a more gentle disposition I will feel happier knowing you are there as her confidant and mentor.' Eva put her hand on Maud's shoulder. 'Remember, in the future, Nell will have the ear of one of England's most powerful Earl's and we can never have enough allies. You know the Marches are a complicated and troublesome region to rule and friends in high places are essential.' Eva's advice was not lost on her daughter; who recalled the words of her father's sergeant about having a trusted ally at your back.

'Besides, I rely on you Maud, for I know you possess the Marshal family's strength of character and wit, which will serve you well in the years to come.'

'I pray I may fulfil your faith in me Mama.' Maud said thoughtfully. Maud did not voice her fear she may also have inherited some of her father's faults. The acerbic words of Father Sebastian now rang in her head, *'the sins of the father.'* As a child she had failed to understand their meaning but now burgeoning on womanhood, the words often haunted her. It had been very difficult to accept the truth about her father, but over the years the true nature of his character had been revealed and even now, she felt shame at the mention of his name. Maud's childish, unconditional love, had been used as he had used everything and everyone, for his own gain or amusement. The hurt never healed, the shame never quite extinguished, the doubt about his true feelings for her, never quite resolved. Such dark thoughts dashed the feelings of euphoria she had felt earlier in the day.

Maud would long remember her first venture into court life and wrote to Izzy describing in detail the fine garments and jewels and the people she had met; she also described the Queen in somewhat unflattering terms. She recounted Amy's words regarding her marriage and how awkward Rich appeared to be with his young wife, but underlined her remarks on the dramatic change in their Aunt Isabel. She also wrote about the handsome French Comte and his companion. As Maud replaced the quill back on its stand, she re-read her letter and whispered to herself: 'The Game of Adults has begun in earnest methinks dearest Izzy!'

CHAPTER VI

Young Nell de Braose twirled in front of a long reflector, 'look Maud is it not the finest kirtle you have ever seen?'

'Indeed, quite the finest and the shade of green suits you well.' But Maud's words were somewhat distracted as the day of departure to their new life in the de Bohuns' household was drawing ever closer and it was a day Maud was dreading. For Nell, it was the first steps into adulthood even though she was but ten years old; in a few years she would marry the son and heir to one of England's most prestigious Earldoms, whereas she felt her own position was somewhat less defined.

At fourteen Maud felt quite grown up especially since her mother had allotted the responsibility for part of the household expenditure to her during the past two years. In future, she would be expected to play nursemaid to her sister and it was not a role she relished. Maud enjoyed being in control of the provisioning, although she had been guided by Edwin, one of her mother's stewards. She learned where to purchase the finest flour at the keenest prices; who was the most skilled butcher on the staff; who brewed the best small beer and cider; which orchards grew the sweetest apples; which hives had the richest honey and listened avidly to Edwin's knowledgeable advice.

Over the past year Maud's resourcefulness had saved the household coffers precious silver, gaining the praise of both Edwin and her mother. With the move to the Earl of Hereford's household, she would be relegated to the state of an ignominious attendant and her proud nature railed against this future role. It was the sound of the door latch which broke the train of Maud's thoughts. Eva entered the chamber to find her daughters surrounded by rolls of many coloured materials which were strewn haphazardly all over the floor. Picking her way carefully through the maze of colour she smiled at the chaos.

'My sweet Nell you look truly lovely does she not Maud?' Eva smiled indulgently at her youngest daughter. It was quite true the dark haired girl was as pretty as a picture but when there was no immediate response to her words from Maud Eva turned her gaze towards the older girl.

'Sorry Mama I was lost in thought. Yes, yes of course Nell looks lovely because Nell *is* lovely.' Maud smiled but Eva noted the trace of wistfulness in Maud's expression. She would miss her daughters but did not dwell on the thought of her own loss it was the normal sequence in the girls lives which was far more important than remaining as her companions; they were about to step onto the marital ladder, and by so doing, make their mark in society, a position to which they had been preparing for since birth.

'Have you chosen *your* new wardrobe of clothes yet?' Eva raised a questioning eyebrow at Maud.

'I need fewer garments for I shall be playing a subordinate part in the de Bohun household.' Maud hoped her words did not convey her true feelings.

'Nonsense, I urge you to alter your line of thinking, it is important you make a good impression, you will be meeting many important people in the coming months therefore I strongly advise you make an effort and concentrate on your wardrobe. Remember, it is imperative to leave no-one in doubt of your standing in society, which must be established from the onset. First introductions leave a lasting impression, therefore it is essential for you both, not to let our family down. One day you will play hostess for your husband's which will include royalty as well as other important dignitaries, so use your time well with the de Bohun's, and pray never forget' she hesitated, ' Maud de Lusignan, is a force to be reckoned with and I do not wish either of my daughters to be found wanting. Please the Countess and your lives will become easier, annoy her and .....' the de Braose sisters needed no further explanations.

'Will she put us in the dungeons if she is displeased?' Nell's voice trembled as she spoke.

Before Eva could answer Maud interrupted, 'No, but I would die before I let that happen to you Nell, so fear not.'

'Now girls this is *not* the attitude to take with you I merely give you warning of the nature of the Countess; forewarned is forearmed.'

Eva nodded to the seamstress who obediently brought forward rolls of expensive materials so Maud could choose some for her new kirtles but the more she thought of the coming months, the more Maud dreaded the future, she liked not the warning about her new chaperone – Maud de Lusignan. It was common knowledge that there was great resentment in the ranks of the nobility against the king's half brothers, the de Lusignans, as Henry had promoted them into lands, titles, and marriages, without considering the consequences. But she had to put such thoughts aside for now and concentrate on the matter of fashion.

During the days which followed, the busy seamstress stitched and embroidered the girls' garments. The days lengthened and the sun gathered strength; the sisters consoled themselves knowing that at least they would be together in their new life. As June waned arrangements were made for Nell and Maud to leave for Huntingdon, Maud thought it ironic going to the castle which had once been in the hands of the de Braose family. It was a tearful parting as they rode out of the gates of Totnes Castle. Eva had entrusted her children to the captain of her guards, Hywel, who had remained in her service after the execution of her husband. She felt confident that he would never let any harm befall the girls.

The party trotted out with the pale morning sun glinting on the weapons and armour of their escort. Eva wiped a tear from the corner of her eye made the sign of the cross, then turned and went back into the cool walls of the place she had made her refuge.

CHAPTER VII

Maud de Lusignan, Countess of Hereford, frowned as she watched the riders enter the gates of Huntington castle she had been against this marriage from the onset. The daughter of William de Braose was not a match she would have made willingly however much land was involved, she felt her son deserved better. Her arguments had been ignored by her husband who stated quite forcefully, that the arrangements had been made with Eleanor's uncle, the late Richard Marshal, Earl of Pembroke, who had been hailed as one of the finest knight's of the age and he refused to break the alliance as a mark of respect. Besides, he was proud to be associated with the Marshal family through his son's impending marriage.

Thwarted by her husband's words, the Countess had begrudgingly agreed to allow Eleanor's sister to accompany her, merely to allay further arguments with the Earl. Humphrey de Bohun, who was normally of an equable temperament, could on occasions be the most stubborn of men, a fact his wife had learned quite early in their marriage, much to her chagrin.

As the girls entered the chamber the Countess was struck by the difference in their appearances. The younger child was dark, and pretty, she stood shuffling her feet in her nervousness. Not so the older girl, Maud. She stood, straight and proud, her hair gleaming like the colour of autumn leaves and her dark green-grey eyes did not flinch under the gaze of her host and hostess. The Earl moved forward his hands outstretched in greeting.

'Welcome! I hope your journey was not too arduous.' He smiled as he spoke.

'Thank you my lord, we were fortunate with the weather, therefore made good time.' Maud extended her hand in greeting.

'Come meet my wife and family' he half turned and beckoned to where Maud de Lusignan stood stiffly beside the great fireplace, her hands clenched in front of her; Maud saw the tension in the shoulders of the Countess of Hereford, this woman may prove problematic as predicted by her mother and she felt glad that Nell would not be alone, for Maud could envisage trouble in the future in the guise of the de Lusignan woman.

With great dignity the Countess came and stood beside her husband, the de Braose girls curtsied. However, the Countess noted there was nothing deferential in the older girl's action.

'You must be tired? I will have you shown to your apartments where you can rest and freshen up before dinner.' Although the words in themselves were welcoming enough, the clipped, stilted tones were cold and anything but welcoming. Maud smiled beguilingly hiding her true emotions behind a mask of civility.

As they reached their chamber the servant smiled shyly, 'the water is nice and hot and I have put some sweet smelling lotions for your use.' She hesitated, 'my name is Jane, and I shall be at your service.' She bobbed a curtsy, 'do you wish me to help you?'

Maud shook her head, 'thank you Jane, I think we will manage. We need to rest awhile once we have washed off the dirt from the journey. Pray come back in an hour then we will be glad of your help to dress.' She smiled at the young woman who curtseyed again and hastened from the chamber.

'Our hostess greeting was nothing if not chilly, Mama was right, we must be ever watchful of that one.'

Maud grinned at her sister. 'Have no fear Nell; it is fortuitous that I am here to protect you from her acid tongue.'

'Oh! Maud I wish we could go home.' Nell's voice sounded thin and fearful.

'Come, Nell are we not granddaughters of the great William Marshal who fought his way from obscurity to the highest position in the kingdom? We will not allow a peevish woman to prove too difficult an opponent will we? Trust me Nell, let us meet the challenge, and find ways to overcome our adversary! Maybe we judge her too harshly and she is not as bad as we fear.

Now let us wash and rest before our next encounter with Lady Lusignan.' Maud grinned impishly at her young sister who was in no doubt that Maud's courage was a match for anyone and sounded as though she even relished the idea of future verbal exchanges with the Countess.

Maud realised that Nell would take the lead from her and therefore she must tread with caution and do nothing to jeopardise her sister's future. Should the Countess prove hostile, and given the iciness of her greeting, added to their mother's warning, it looked as though this may well be the case, she would need to use all of her wits to overcome a possible adversary. She realised their plan must be to gain favour with the Earl and his young son, and by so doing outmanoeuvre Maud de Lusignan; the thought filled her with inward delight. She must tread carefully and guard against trouble but if the need arose then work to undermine the austere Countess without arousing any suspicion. Maybe she would not have to resort to such tactics if the Countess's attitude changed. Maud mused on her mother's words about first impressions being important, the point had been well made in light of this first introduction to the haughty Countess of Hereford.

By the time the Earl announced their move back to Hereford Castle a few weeks later; all their erstwhile fears regarding the Countess had proved correct. However, Maud had already achieved her goal in the de Bohun household. Nell was mesmerised by how cleverly Maud had insinuated herself to the Earl. Maybe, it was Maud's knowledge of military strategy, which had undoubtedly impressed both the Earl and his son, who now frequently included her on their military discussions, much to the chagrin of the Countess. It had been done with such seamless guile that Nell was left in awe of her sister's accomplishments.

'The king must be well pleased by his wife's pregnancy.' Maud smiled up at the Earl as they rode out one summer's day ostensibly to make a final inspection of Huntingdon castle and its lands before their departure back to Hereford.

'Aye! But he is furious at his sister's elopement with that upstart de Montfort.'

'Is it true the couple have fled to Rome to seek a dispensation from the Pope?'

The Earl drew rein as he gazed out across the valley. The scene had become a familiar one to Maud who urged her horse to the Earl's side.

'Of course, I was forgetting, Eleanor was the Dowager Countess of Pembroke, and your late uncle's widow, was she not?'

'Indeed! I believe she took a vow of chastity before the Archbishop of Canterbury after my Uncle William's sudden death.' Maud's words were said quite artlessly; her face expressionless but she had made the Earl aware of the facts. On such a pleasant morning the couple little realised how both of their destinies would become intrinsically entwined with that of Simon de Montfort, Earl of Leicester.

'It is a fine view!' The Earl looked back at his son and Nell who were chatting amicably together. 'Methinks my son is fortunate in his future bride and they appear to have become quite close although I do have to remind him not to tease her so often.'

Maud nodded. 'Nell is quite without guile but she must learn how to deal with her impudent young suitor.'

Humphrey de Bohun chuckled, 'whereas, her sister, if I am not mistaken, is possessed of both wits and guile and would be more than adept at putting a young buck in his place.'

'My lord, I hope that is not a slur upon my name?' Maud looked under her eyelashes at him.

'Indeed it is not! Merely observation my dear, young Mortimer will have his work cut out to hold rein on you I'll warrant!'

'Do you think I will deserve such treatment; to be reined in as you put it?' She looked at him, one eyebrow raised. He chuckled as he urged his horse forward.

'Egad! If I do not envy the lad a little, for you Mistress Maud, will keep any man on his mettle.' With that parting shot he wheeled his horse and the party struck off back to the castle.

'At least for the time being, Llywelyn has failed to capture Huntington.' The Earl's comments appeared to be made more to himself than to his companion but Maud understood his satisfaction that the thick walls of the castle had withstood all the efforts of the Welsh invaders little knowing, it would be attacked within weeks of their departure. The Castle, once again would withstand the onslaught of the Welsh however, much of the surrounding land would be laid waste.

Within days of their departure from Huntington and after an uneventful journey the grey, towering walls of Hereford Castle came into view. The river Wye glittered like rare glass, as they rode along its banks, the reflection of the riders creating a tapestry of rich, moving colour. The voice of the Countess carried over the heads of the riders and could be heard, still full of complaints which had been the case from the onset of the journey. Maud noted how the Earl rode well out of earshot of her moans of dissatisfaction and could not help smiling; the woman was undoubtedly a veritable pain.

As the party rode through the impressive gateway Maud felt a buzz of excitement at the scene before her; grooms and horses, squires and servants, were all bustling about their daily business all eager to please the popular Earl. She caught a glimpse of a livery she remembered from the queen's household and wondered whether the Comte Etienne de Vivonne and his companion, Lord Guy de Longeville, were already there. It would not be unusual for such a visitor; the Earl of Hereford held an important role at court. She had recently learned that it had been the Earl who had brought about the reconciliation between the king and his brother, Richard of Cornwall in the past.

Maud mused at how brothers and sisters, born to the same parents could have such differing characters. It was so with her and her own sisters; Izzy was tall, dark with a quiet, intelligent, and thoughtful disposition. Whereas, Maud had the red-gold colouring inherited from her Irish ancestry with a robust appetite for life, her famous temper had not entirely been quelled over the years. Then there was Eve, who, on the other hand was given more to the de Braose family in looks but her religious and constrained nature had naught to do with the de Braose characteristics. Nell, on the other hand, was a pretty, shy girl with thick dark locks and a pale oval face. Maud liked to think that in creating children, God kept himself amused by such differences.

However, Maud had little time to muse over such matters when she realised that she had been correct about the identities of the visitors who had arrived before them. Later that evening, as the places at the trestle tables began to fill with guests, the French Comte nudged his companion.

'What did I tell you, the de Braose girl has grown into a beauty has she not?'

Guy de Longeville glanced to where Etienne was indicating. It was true, Maud de Braose shone like a beacon; the candlelight caressed her hair and skin. She was talking animatedly to the pretty girl who must be her sister and the Earl of Hereford's future daughter-in-law.

Guy nodded, 'she is certainly a handsome damsel.' He looked hard at Etienne 'I hope you will not pursue the hapless maid; remember, she is already betrothed to a Mortimer and you do *not* want to incur the wrath of that family.'

Etienne merely grinned at Guy's words of warning for what was life if it was not spiced with danger and some pleasures were worth taking risks for, 'now do not spoil my sport mon amie.'

'I do not wish to see you in the role of quarry on this occasion.' Guy's face was filled with concern.

'Pisht! Do you not think a de Vivonne is match for these English nobles?' Etienne's voice held a note of feigned scorn.

'You forget I am an English nobleman!'

'Ah! Yes, but educated in France, therefore you do not count.' Etienne was obviously enjoying baiting his companion.

'Then, if you do not wish to consider your own reputation think how you're flirting may affect the girl's reputation.'

A frown played across the handsome features of the Comte for a moment then vanished with his next words. 'Will it not make her more precious to the Mortimer's?'

Guy could never quite understand Etienne's unquenchable desire to pursue every attractive female he met. He had a wife who was well educated, rich, and fair; she had already given birth to two healthy children and yet Etienne's thirst for romantic adventures remained undimmed.

'Come my lord, how would you feel if a foreigner pursued your own wife in such a blatant manner?'

Etienne laughed, 'you know Guy, sometimes I think you are the incarnation of my father.'

'The reason he wished me to remain with you no doubt.' Guy's voice held a rueful note.

'Does this mean you grow tired of your task and my scintillating company?' Etienne's voice was full of mirth as he looked at the serious expression of his friend.

'You know full well I gave my oath to your father that I would serve you for as long as I thought you needed a steadying influence.' Suddenly his face lit up, 'and I see little evidence that such a time is imminent.' The two chuckled in unison their conversation had fallen into boyish banter.

'However, I still believe to blatantly flirt with the de Braose girl will bring trouble on your head and you know full well what our commission is in England.' The words had the required effect and Etienne's demeanour changed albeit subtlety he slapped de Longeville's shoulder, 'my father knew what he was about when he charged you with my welfare.'

Guy felt, at least for this evening Etienne would not cause further trouble but for how long his warnings would hold he did not wish to dwell. He even found himself studying the girl when he thought no-one was watching and everything the Comte had said was true, she had blossomed into a beauty. He noted more than one man's gaze fell on the lovely form of Maud de Braose, who sat at the top table quite oblivious to the affect she was having on many of the numerous guests, both men and women. To the eyes of the observer, Maud appeared impervious to both admiration and envy.

The following day the exciting news arrived that the queen's lying in was imminent thus delaying the arrival of the Bishop as he would be expected to be on hand for the baptismal ceremony, leaving the Comte and his party free to remain at Hereford for awhile longer as they were to have met up with the august cleric. It was a delay which would prove to have far reaching effects on two young lives.

Maud revelled in the bustling, busy atmosphere of Hereford Castle. The many visitors brought news and gossip from far and wide. It also attracted foreign merchants into the town with their diverse wares. On a warm June morning, the two Braose girls wandered past the brightly decorated stalls inspecting bowls and dishes; ribbons and threads, wools and trinkets, leather boots, shoes and gloves, together with all manner of articles. After purchasing some baubles and threads the two, accompanied by Jane their servant, walked back towards the river.

'Do you think the Queen will have a son?' Nell's question remained unanswered for walking towards them was Comte Etienne de Vivonne and Sir Guy de Longeville. Maud heard Jane's intake of breathe.

'Come Jane; don't let a pretty face beguile you.' Maud's voice held a note of scorn as she turned to look at the moonstruck servant.

'Sorry! My lady! But I do think he must be the most handsome man in the world and when I look at him my legs.......'

Before Maud could say anything further they were confronted by the Comte, his companion, de Longeville and their French squires.

'Ah! You have been busy spending your silver I see!' The Comte waved his hand then made an exaggerated bow. Maud felt somewhat irritated by this man's flamboyant gestures. Her eyes travelled past him to his companion who merely nodded in greeting. How different was the appearance of these two men; one whose dazzling looks were enhanced by his expensive apparel, whereas, Guy de Longeville, wore a plain black leather tunic and a light linen shirt of grey.

'May we escort you back to the Castle?' It was Guy who spoke. Maud liked the rich timbre of his voice.

'Thank you! I have heard cutpurses are rife around the streets of Hereford.' The party headed slowly back towards the safety of the castle walls. Etienne was surprised by the older girl for she had left him to accompany her sister and fell in step with de Longeville. He pondered on how the normally reserved Englishman would deal with this situation, but Guy de Longeville remained his usual reserved self who merely answered Maud's animated questions where necessary and appeared to make no extra effort to engage in any deeper conversation other than one of etiquette.

As the party entered the castle none noticed they were being watched from a window high above; the watcher was the Countess of Hereford, her eyes narrowed at the scene below. The older of the Braose girls had proved to be a thorn in her side and she planned to cause her as much trouble as possible. Turning from the window she beckoned her servant and whispered a command in his ear. Bowing low the man left the chamber and hurried to summon a messenger. Almost directly, a fast riding courier left Hereford and headed for Wigmore.

CHAPTER VIII

Wigmore 1239

Gwladus Ddu, Lady Mortimer, stood before a wooden frame as she worked on a colourful tapestry. She turned a questioning gaze as the messenger entered and bowed respectfully before approaching the dignified figure.

'I have word from the Countess of Hereford who thought it imperative you should be made aware of.......' he cleared his throat and hesitated.

The Lady of Wigmore stiffened then indicated for him to continue. He looked uncomfortable and moved closer as he whispered his message.

Without a flicker of emotion Lady Mortimer nodded and waved her hand in dismissal. Her outward expression betrayed none of the ire she felt within. The Lusignan woman was trying to besmirch the name of her future daughter-in-law, Maud de Braose, the reason was not yet clear, but it was well known that the Lusignan family were viewed as trouble makers; like many others with family connections to the king and his young queen, Eleanor of Provence. If the intent was to drive a wedge betwixt the girl and the Mortimer family then the Countess of Hereford had played a wrong hand.

Years of conflict with unending negotiations between England and Wales had been at the core of Lady Mortimer's life; the valuable lessons she had learned was how easily treaties, friendships, and loyalties could be manipulated to look like a betrayal when no betrayal had in fact been committed. If Maud de Lusignan thought mere words would wreck Maud's reputation she had badly misjudged her future mother-in-law; Lady Mortimer was far more perceptive than the Countess had imagined.

Determined to seek further evidence from a neutral source and wait upon their findings before condemning Maud out of hand; Lady Mortimer put away her needlework and went to sit in her private chapel. It was a place of solace and peace; a place where she could think without being interrupted by any of the household. As she sat in the gloom, she thought long and hard upon the Countess's spiteful words, what purpose could be at the heart of the matter? Maud de Braose would bring great wealth and lands to the Mortimer's so, what would be achieved other than discord between the Mortimer's and the girl's influential family? She was undoubtedly blossoming into a beauty and would naturally attract the attention of many men it was inevitable but, that was something the young noblewoman could have no control over, it was how she dealt with the situation which mattered. Jealousy could have prompted this move against her, and was at the root of the Countess's concern. Gwladus Ddu rose, made the sign of the cross, and returned to her chamber, and called for her faithful confidante, the enigmatic Lord Rhys.

The man who entered was dark and swarthy he moved silently like a cat, his piercing eyes missed nothing in the spacious chamber.

'Ah! My lord, there is a matter of a somewhat delicate nature I wish you to carry out for me. Nothing of what I am about to impart to you must be repeated to anyone else, do you understand?' Her words were soft almost a whisper and in Welsh.

'Indeed my Lady!'

'For some reason, which is at present is unclear to me; the Countess of Hereford is throwing accusations at my son's future wife, Maud de Braose.' She hesitated and watched his closed expression. 'I am inclined to believe it is mischief but need to know exactly the true nature of the situation. As always I know I can rely on you to discover the truth. Your sudden appearance at Hereford should not raise any question at present as there will be many strangers attached to the French nobleman's retinue therefore; it is my guess no-one will question your identity. I would not trust this matter to anyone else.'

The Welshman nodded he heard the note of anxiety in the request.

'My suspicions are the woman is merely out to cause mischief for the Braose girl, and in so doing, could cause trouble for the Mortimer's. Maud is a budding beauty and no doubt has attracted attention. I trust your sound good sense will get to get to the truth of the matter.' She smiled and extended her hand for him to kiss.

'I will be on my way to Hereford within the hour.' He bowed and walked swiftly from the chamber. His feet made no sound on the flagged stone floor. The Lady of Wigmore breathed out a long sigh, if anyone could glean the facts from the fiction it would be Lord Rhys, and upon his return she was confident he would furnish her with the truth.

That evening no-one noticed the dark figure who had attached himself to the Comte's party; Lord Rhys found a discreet position to observe the evening's banquet without drawing any attention to him. It was true, the older de Braose girl attracted many admiring glances but even when the French Comte heaped her with compliments, she merely tossed her head and gave him short shrift to the amusement of those closest to hear her retort.

So, if the fault lay not with the girl, then what was at the heart of the Countess of Hereford's intentions? Rhys turned his gaze towards the top table, he noted the affable manner in which the Earl was chatting to his guests and how often the Countess frowned and bit her lip. Rhys also observed the Countess said little, and was rarely invited to join in the conversation. It was easy to detect from the expressions of the Earl when he looked at his wife, that the relationship between them was not an altogether amicable one, and the watcher guessed the fault lay with the woman for she appeared ill at ease and he judged her sour looks were not merely due to her pregnancy.

Even as the jesters capered around causing outbreaks of mirth her expression did not lighten and when Rhys caught her watching Maud laughing merrily, he saw how her mouth twisted into a snarl. It looked like pure jealousy; the girl had youth, beauty, and vivacity as her assets whereas, the Countess could lay claim to none of those assets. But one evening's observations was not enough to make a sound assessment on the situation. He would seek more information on the relationship between the de Braose girl and the Countess on the morrow and find out exactly where the truth lay; things were invariably not as they appeared on the surface. The Welshman was determined to hold his own council until he had discovered more about the relationship between the two females.

Later that evening as the mood calmed, groups took to playing board games and Maud found herself at the table where the Comte and his companions were sat making wagers with other guests. She watched and moved behind some of the players noting their cards, as she stood behind Guy de Longeville he extended his hand to invite her to play. At first she declined but with the Comte's challenging remarks ringing in her ears, she quickly nodded to the dealer who dealt her a hand of cards.

'I am afraid I have but little coinage to stake but will wager my ring.' Maud slid the heavy gold ring from her finger and placed it on the table.

'Then it is only fair that we all use jewellery for this hand at least.' The Comte smiled as he placed a ruby ring taken from his little finger to add to the growing pile. Guy de Longeville hesitantly removed an ornately wrought gold ring from his forefinger and added it to the rest. For Maud it was a tense rather than enjoyable experience as she could little afford to lose the ring her mother had given her.

As the voices of the players were raised in excitement the outcome was completely unexpected for Maud found herself the winner of a considerable amount of rings, pins and other items of precious jewels. Clapping her hands in glee she leaned forward to gather in her winnings when de Longeville said softly, 'I would consider it a great favour if you would exchange my ring for silver as I set great store by it, for it belonged to my father.'

Maud hesitated for a moment and said with a twinkle, 'It will take a great deal of silver to retrieve it Master Shadow.'

He looked enquiringly at the speaker, 'Master Shadow? My name is ......'

'I know full well what your name is my lord but you follow the Comte so closely I and my sister have dubbed you Master

Shadow.' She blushed at the lie for she had no idea why she had named him thus.

For an instant Maud thought he would think her too pert but instead he smiled and nodded. 'I am merely carrying out the vow I made to his father, to watch over him. He does not always see the danger his pretty compliments to women frequently place him in! Especially here in England.'

'Indeed!' Maud looked into his face; she liked the strong lines of his shaven jaw with the high cheekbones and deep set, dark blue eyes.

'Does the Comte realise how lucky he is to have such a faithful protector?'

De Longeville's face split into a boyish smile making him look very young.

'I doubt Etienne has given it a single thought.'

'Then shame on him for I would ....' Maud stopped realising what she was about to say.

'Thank you my lady!' His voice was low but full of sincerity.

'Come to my chambers on the morrow and I will give you back your ring and ..... you need bring no silver.'

'You are too gracious.'

Maud chuckled. 'Pray do not fall into the same trap as your Comte for shallow words win few favours from me!'

'You think I do not speak the truth? Then Demoiselle, you know me not at all!'

'Oh! It is simply that I receive but few compliments of real worth, so treat the rest with disdain, for they are but hollow and insincere and one thing I abhor, is insincerity.' She put down her collection of winnings and held out her hand, de Longeville took it and raised it to his lips a thrill like no other she had ever experienced coursed through her frame, and she trembled at his touch.

'I am ever at your service, my lady.' With that he rose and left the table, Maud had not seen the mischievous smile of the Comte who had witnessed the scene or, the dark figure in the shadows.

'Sooo! The cool, untouchable Guy has been captivated by a young English noblewoman?' The Comte said teasingly but Maud looked him straight in the eye.

'I will treat your remark with the distain it deserves.' She said giving him a long look of disapproval her green-grey eyes flashed as she spoke.

'No! Lord Guy has merely been negotiating to exchange silver for his father's ring.' Vivonne cleared his throat and pursued the subject no more, for he saw that he had embarrassed the girl and if de Longville learned of it, he would be upset and Etienne de Vivonne knew, that may prove awkward in the circumstances.

When Maud reached her chambers she spread the bright jewels upon her dressing table gazing at the pretty baubles. Her fingers moved the items around until she spotted the ring belonging to de Longeville. As she held it to the rush-light she saw strange symbols and figures engraved on both sides of the heavy ring. They were like nothing she had ever seen before and she knew it must have come from the East possibly, from the Holy Land. She placed it on each of her fingers but the ring was far too big for her slender fingers. But that night when she went to bed, the ring was tucked under her pillow.

The following morning Maud rose with the sense of expectation tingling in her veins; she had Jane dress her hair with extra care. She chose a dark green kirtle – the colour she knew suited her well and jumped when she heard a gentle knock on the heavy oak door. Jane walked over and opened it.

'I believe I am expected?' The rich voice was unmistakably that of Guy de Longeville.

Jane turned but Maud was almost behind her as she invited him in.

'Pray fetch some refreshments would you Jane?'

Jane gave a quizzical look at her mistress but curtseyed and answered meekly, 'as you wish.'

As the door closed behind her Maud indicated to the window seat.

'I can understand why you would not wish to lose your father's ring, apart from the sentiment attached to it. The engravings are unique and like no other I have ever seen. The workmanship is certainly not English or French.'

'No!' De Longeville sat down as he spoke. Maud liked his voice, it was warm and low. 'The story goes that it was given to my father by a Saracen when he saved his daughter from being raped.' He stopped and looked across at her 'It is supposed to keep the wearer safe.'

Before Maud realised it she blurted out, 'did it keep your father safe?' her words trailed off. A wistful smile crossed de Longeville's face: 'no, sadly, he had sent it home upon hearing of my birth. My father died saving the Comte's father.'

Maud blushed. 'You see! My tongue has a way of running away with me at times and although I do try and curb its waywardness I have not completely mastered the fault yet.'

Guy de Longeville took Maud's hand and raised it to his lips his eyes never left her face. 'It is refreshing to hear a truthful response, at court and in society, hypocrisy and subterfuge reigns. I for one would not wish you to change - just be true to yourself without fear - the lesson is to judge the person to whom you speak for yourself.'

Maud smiled ruefully and nodded her heart racing at his nearness. Nothing had prepared her for the emotion which de Longeville aroused within her; no-one had warned her that a heart could be lost in an instant for Maud de Braose had indeed, fallen in love with the tall figure who sat beside her.

Just as she was about to speak the rattle of the door latch warned her of Jane's return. Maud turned so he could not see her face for she felt her emotions were stamped across them for the entire world to read. She was all too aware how these new irrational emotions could be fraught with danger should anyone even suspect her secret. Even a hint of gossip may bode ill for the couple, even though de Longeville was as yet, oblivious to her feelings.

Maud quickly recaptured control of her wayward feelings as she offered her guest refreshments and after some trivial small talk, handed the treasured ring back to its rightful owner.

'I insist you lose nothing by returning the heirloom.' With that he produced a purse filled with silver coins. Shaking her head she took a single coin and handed back the rest.

'I am happy with this coin for I know you can ill afford.......' Her words trailed off as she looked at his expression. 'Oh! I fear my tongue and my head have played me false and I have offended you yet again!'

'I will accept your bounty in the generous spirit it was offered.' But his tone was curt and after slipping the ring back on his finger he bowed and left abruptly.

'Oh Jane I do believe I have given offence to Lord de Longeville.' Jane looked over at her Mistress, 'You tweaked his pride that is all, for if it is true, he has none of the wealth of his patron as he refuses to touch any of his wife's fortune.'

'Nevertheless, I should have spoken less freely - it was insensitive.'

'Maybe, it was - just a little my lady!'

Jane looked questioningly at Maud, why was it so important, could it be this quiet, reserved young knight held more appeal for her mistress than the effusive, handsome, Comte Etienne de Vivonne? Maud sensed she was being scrutinised and began to busy herself in an effort to divert the Jane's attention and shake off her own misgivings - the last thing she wanted was her feelings to fall under suspicion, especially by the intuitive Jane. What did it matter anyway? The French party would be gone by morning and there was no knowing when – or if ever, she would meet with Guy de Longeville again.

She little realised the impression she had made on him, and as he walked down the long passageway Guy de Longeville felt bemused by the affect Maud de Braose had had on him. How had this young girl managed to break through his usual reserve; without apparently trying, this new sensation alarmed him, but try as he might, her image haunted him that night? The scent of her hair, the slanting green-grey eyes, and soft curve of her cheeks, the very thought left him restless and uneasy; lust he could understand but this – this strange, longing was deeper, more disturbing and as he wrestled with the realisation that he had fallen in love, it left him feeling helpless and alone.

Early the following day, just as the grooms and servants were beginning to stir, a heavily cloaked figure rode from the castle heading towards Wigmore. At first, the Welshman let his horse jog unhurriedly away from the high grey walls, but as soon as he reached the bend in the river he urged his mount into a faster gait. He was determined to reach his destination before nightfall; the roads were always hazardous but deadly after dark.

As the sun was beginning to sink behind the trees painting the skies with a vivid pattern of reds, gold's, and yellows, Lord Rhys rode up the steep path which led through the red sandstone arched gateway of Wigmore Castle; horse and rider were weary but they had arrived without incident. A young groom ran forward and took the reins as the rider slipped from the saddle.

'Give him a good rub down and a warm mash we have travelled many leagues today.'

'Aye my lord, I have a clean stable waiting and the manger is already filled with good clean hay.'

Rhys nodded too tired to say more. As he entered the castle he handed his black, dusty cloak to a page and strode on towards the apartments of Lady Mortimer. He knocked with a distinctive tattoo; the door was opened immediately by a young page.

'Pray bring refreshments.' Lady Mortimer spoke to the young woman who had been sitting sewing by the window then, turned from her desk and beckoned Rhys, indicating for her visitor to sit on the cushioned seat opposite her. The maid put down her needlework and hastened from the room to do her mistresses bidding, signalling to the page to accompany her.

'It is good to see you my lord, I have missed you!' Lady Mortimer was not known for familiarity with her retainers but theirs was a tried and trusted relationship forged by many years of service. Lord Rhys ap Ioin had been among the young widow's retinue when she had come to Wigmore after her second marriage to Ralph Mortimer, eight years ago. Gwladus had quickly learned to rely on his loyalty and discretion. His ability to melt into any background had proved an invaluable asset to Lady Mortimer, not least, as a spy. Over the years the Welsh Princess learned that her agent was both accurate, reliable and most of all discreet, the very reasons her father, Prince Llywelyn ap Iowerth had chosen him.

After a few polite pleasantries and the appearance of the refreshments, Lady Mortimer thanked her serving woman then dismissed her.

'I will call for you presently' she said with a half smile. The woman curtsied before she left the couple together. For a few moments he sipped his wine in silence as he ate a morsel or two for it had been many hours since he had eaten.

'Now shall we get down to business? Is there ought to be concerned about our future daughter-in-law?'

Lord Rhys's thin lips curved into a rare smile.

'A lively, vivacious young lady but I witnessed her verbally trounce a French nobleman when he heaped pretty compliments on her head. She merely told him such words made little impression upon her and made fun of his exaggerated overtures.'

'Good! So was there any scandal attached to her name?'

'It is my belief, after speaking with many of the servants and grooms, the Countess is beside herself with jealousy as the Earl frequently seeks the company of the Lady Maud.'

Lady Mortimer's eyebrows arched at this comment.

'Oh! There is nothing untoward or aught of 'that' nature, he merely appears to enjoy the young lady's lively mind and wit, beside his son is invariably in their company so too is her sister, the young Lady Eleanor. The relief on Lady Mortimer's face was evident.

'So! In fact the Countess is merely jealous of the girl and wishes to muddy her future by impugning her reputation and as we know, reputations once sullied are never quite the same again.'

'Indeed my lady! From hearsay, the Countess is constantly pressing for a greater portion of the de Braose lands, which adds an underlying tension to their relationship.' A wry smile flickered across his dark features. 'She takes every opportunity to try and undermine the older girl but invariably falls short, lacking the wit of her younger adversary, if the reports from the servants are to be believed. None have a good word to say for the Countess.'

'Do I detect a note of approval my lord?' The smile which passed between them spoke volumes.

'Well at least that is one matter which has come to satisfactory conclusion. However, I must warn my husband with regard to the issue of the Braose lands, he will need to keep a close eye on the situation which will undoubtedly keep the lawyers busy.

Regarding Maud, I will send a polite note to the Countess to thank her for her concerns. Now to more pressing matters, it looks as though my father is on the rampage again, which means we can look to more fighting along the borders.'

Her companion nodded, this was a more familiar scenario than spying on a maid but it amused him to think that one day the girl in question would rule Wigmore with such a different personality from the dignified lady he served. Young Mortimer would undoubtedly be faced with a challenge on his marriage to the bright haired de Braose girl, of that he would wager all the silver in Christendom.

CHAPTER IX

The Abbey was crowded with nobles, Earls, magnates, and many dignitaries of the realm for the solemn funeral ceremony. Chief mourner was Richard, Earl of Cornwall, in the ornate coffin, were the bodies of his wife Isabel de Clare and her new born son, Nicholas. Maud de Braose stood with her mother and sister Nell, among the grieving congregation. Her gaze was fixed on the stony features of Richard Plantagenet as an overwhelming hatred filled her heart.

Ever since her Aunt Isabel had been coerced into a second marriage her life had changed dramatically. Maud felt certain the reason for her aunt's untimely death lay squarely at the feet of her ruthless husband, the Earl of Cornwall. Even in death he had maintained his dominant hold by overriding Isabel's dying wishes, to be buried with her first husband, Gilbert de Clare. Her wish, overridden by Cornwall, who was insistent that it was his instructions which would be adhered to; the only concession he had allowed was that Isabel's heart should be interred with her first husband at Tewkesbury, just another example of his imperious personality.

After the long ceremony was over, a queue of mourners formed and filed past the coffin, making a sign of the cross as they mouthed prayers for the dead Countess. Maud and her family were among their numbers. As she made the sign of blessing, Maud looked neither to her right or left finding it difficult not to weep, but it was at the banquet which followed that Maud found herself control beginning to slip and she hastily excused her-self. After retrieving her cloak, she made her way slowly into the cold January night pulling the fur lined hood over her hair as she walked. She stopped for a moment realising she was no longer alone.

'Who is there?' Maud's voice sounded bolder than she felt.

'I saw you leave the Hall and merely wished to see you were safe.'

'De Longeville!' she exclaimed her voice, not much more than a whisper.

'At your service, my lady!'

'I had no idea you were even here!' Her voice trembled as she spoke.

'Oh! The Comte is constantly crossing the Channel with messages from the French king. I am sorry to meet under such sad circumstances.'

'Indeed! Did you hear, Cornwall would not even allow ......?.'

'I heard.' De Longeville's voice was low.

Suddenly Maud's control burst and she began to weep, de Longeville pulled her into his arms and let her sob as he gently stroked her back. They stood without speaking for awhile then she looked up at him.

'I am glad you are here!'

He bent his head and kissed her cheek 'So am I!'

Maud gently pulled his face down and kissed him on the lips. He held her more tightly and their kiss was filled with warmth and sensual desire setting their emotions aflame. At the sound of footsteps they drew apart and stepped back into the shadow of the wall.

'Maud! Maud! Are you alright? Mama sent me to find y....... Oh!' Nell faltered as she realised her sister was not alone.

'I just needed some air and to get away from the hypocrisy of Cornwall' Maud's voice was icy but them softened again as she continued, 'and look who I found, a gallant knight to protect me.'

Nell smiled up at the tall, dark figure of Guy de Longeville.

'Thank you for taking care of my sister she does have a tendency to get herself into trouble at times.'

'Have you regained your composure enough to return to the Hall?' de Longeville's question was full of concern and Maud loved him for it.

'Yes, I believe I can mask my true feelings now' she turned to him: 'thank you my lord, you will never know how much in need I was of your .....comfort.' He bowed and together the trio returned to the crowded Hall and back to their former places.

That night Maud lay awake unable to sleep, her thoughts careering around like an unbridled horse. She mourned the death of her aunt and recalled the brief period of happiness she had shared with the de Clare's in her childhood but, her overwhelming thoughts were of Guy de Longeville. The passion he had evoked was an emotion far deeper than any she had ever experienced before; love and romance were for books and poets *not* Maud de Braose. Now she felt vulnerable, and all too aware of not only the dangers such feelings placed her in, but their utter futility. She was unable to still the nagging doubt which now plagued her thoughts - had she imagined his response to her kiss? Or, was it merely a moment of sympathy? And what of the Mortimer's, if they ever discovered her secret, there would be fearsome consequences for both her and de Longeville. The scandal, the shame, she could well imagine how her father's dishonourable death would once again be mooted abroad; sins of the father repeated. She turned her face into the deep feather pillow and wept, but her overriding thoughts were of de Longeville, did he truly feel as she did? There was also another powerful emotion she also wrestled with – one of guilt. Would she also, bring shame to the name of de Braose, and compound her father's reputation by being branded a whore? Maud struggled with her dark fears and slept but little, the evidence of her restless night lay in the heap of dishevelled bedclothes.

The following day Nell, Maud, and her mother Eva, met with their de Clare cousins; they hugged and spoke reverently of their late mother. Maud could not take her eyes off Agnes who, as a child had been so bright and full of life now, now dressed in her nun's habit looked pale, aloof and drained of vitality. Another heinous crime Richard of Cornwall was guilty of - merely because Agnes had refused to marry the man of his choosing, he had placed her within the stark walls of a convent.

As if conjured up by thought the Earl walked into the chamber and greeted Eva Marshal with a perfunctory kiss on her cheek. He gazed round, his dark, piercing eyes, resting on each in turn. Why did Maud get the feeling that he resented her cousins? Was it because they were hail and healthy when so many of his seed had not survived long after birth, the only exception was Henry of Almain. It was no secret, Cornwall had sired many bastards by a variety of mistresses, another fact which Maud knew had caused her aunt a great deal of humiliation and distress.

The Earl turned as if to leave when Eva Marshal stepped forward to stand and face him.

'Why did you choose to ignore my sister's wishes to be buried beside Lord Gilbert?' The words although spoken in low cool tones echoed round the walls of the chamber.

'I did as I saw fit; you forget Isabel was *my* wife, my lady.' His face was set like a granite mask, his retort hissed through clenched teeth.

'Nevertheless my lord Earl, she had suffered much and it would have been the Christian thing to have done.' Eva Marshal did not flinch under his scornful stare, but she held his gaze.

'Is it not enough that I have sent her heart in a silver casket to Tewkesbury? Suffice it to say, what is done is done and let that be an end of the matter.' Without further ado he turned on his heel and stalked out.

A deep sigh came from both Richard and Agnes. Maud rose and went to kiss her mother's cheek.

'Thank you Mama, I am glad you spoke up for Aunt Isabel.'

Eva smiled sadly at her daughter, 'it was the least I could do!' It left the group with little else to say and one by one they made their heartfelt farewells and left.

As Eva kissed her nephew's cheek she whispered: 'have a care, your step-father is not a man to model yourself on! My prayers go with you, and Will, and your sisters.'

As Maud rode away from Beaulieu she felt a deep sense of loss, not only at the death of her aunt but, their hasty departure meant she had not seen de Longeville alone again only catching glimpses of him from a distance. It also left her wondering if they would ever meet again and when she would next see any of her cousins, especially poor, dear Agnes.

The journey through the bitter winter weather was both tiring and slow but at least when they reached their first night's stop Maud slept soundly. It took many days to return to Hereford and it was a more subdued Maud who returned than the one who had ridden away. She realised the day when she would be expected to play an important role in the life at court was fast approaching and resolved to take closer interest in the affairs of the country knowing, she would be expected to support her husband, not only in the March but, also in matters of the state. But it failed to stave off the long hours of yearning she felt for de Longeville, a new and unnerving experience.

Later that year, Maud learned Richard of Cornwall had sailed for France, on his way to the join the French king before they journeyed to fight in the Holy Land. She could not help but wonder if it was to salve his conscience or, to enhance his own reputation, and felt certain it was more likely to be the latter.

On the 29th of September the news arrived that the queen had been safely delivered of her second child, a daughter, who was to be christened Margaret. The people of England were only too eager to find an excuse to celebrate. If Eleanor of Provence was unpopular, at least she was fulfilling her role in producing healthy children for the royal nursery.

Closer to home, a messenger arrived for Maud with a letter from her sister Eve, which included an invitation to her forthcoming wedding, the following year. Eve had lived with the Cantilupe family for some years in preparation for this union as was the custom. Maud hoped the marriage celebrations would re-unite the de Braose sisters at least briefly; childhood seemed so distant nowadays. Izzy had not travelled to Beaulieu for her aunt's funeral, the journey from Wales too hazardous in the bitter winter snows. It would be good to see her beloved sister again.

During the following months, Maud had been diligent in her study of England's political scene. She gleaned information and details from any messenger, and traveller, and sought the company of the Earl of Hereford, whenever he could spare her the time. Many of their conversations occurred whilst travelling between the strongholds held by the Earl which helped to pass the long hours on horseback. She learned from de Bohun of the king's inability to hold his nobles in check and of the growing frustration felt by many of their numbers, that Henry was failing to uphold their rights, as laid down in the Magna Carta.

The king, well known for his piety, had by all accounts allowed his focus to dwell more on religious matters than the urgent business of his parliament. Rumours abounded that vast sums of money were to be used on a great tomb to honour Edward the Confessor, Henry's sainted ancestor. She also learned how the young queen, Eleanor of Provence, was also beginning to anger a number of magnates and barons by sending for more of her kinsmen to fill many of the important places at court and within the church. Her influence over the king did not end there or, so it would seem, she began to arrange marriages where possible between her kinswomen and the wealthy English aristocracy, much to their chagrin, but all helpless to oppose a royal command. This high handed behaviour did little to endear her or her husband, to their subjects. Henry also continued to support his unruly Lusignan half brothers, such actions only managed to compound the couple's growing unpopularity.

One day, as Maud and the Earl of Hereford, rode towards Hay Castle; Humphrey turned in his saddle and smiled at his companion.

'May I enquire why this sudden and inordinate interest in court matters my dear.'

'I am all too conscious that soon, I shall be married to a Mortimer who will one day play a part in the country's governance as well as its defence therefore, wish to be acquainted with all the important issues that will affect our lives. I am well aware the Marcher lords are vital in holding the borders for the crown, without them the Welsh would soon run riot, would they not?' She looked at him out of the corner of her eye which he noted twinkled with mischief.

'Undoubtedly, the Welsh cost me time and money, in fact a great deal of money, as it does for many of the Marcher barons, especially the Mortimer's.'

For awhile the Maud rode on in silence mulling over his words but she was eager to learn more about the young Mortimer who would one day be her husband. He had recently entered the service of the Earl as one of his many squires but as yet she had not come in contact with him.

'Have you had time to make an assessment of Mortimer my lord?' She tried to sound casual but knew she had failed when Humphrey de Bohun checked his horse's gait for an instant and looked across at the speaker. There had been no preamble; the girl was direct with her questions unlike so many women who skirted around a topic before making their point. He urged his horse forward again before answering.

'He is somewhat reckless at times, a little too boastful but I put it down to his youth, his peers will undoubtedly cut him down to size in time but he will, in my estimation, always be in need of a strong bit and sharp spurs to hold him in check. Now does that satisfy your curiosity?' He watched for her reactions but her expression was unreadable.

Maud nodded but his words filled her with dread, a heavy handed husband was not a future to look forward too, especially if your heart already belonged to another. They continued for awhile both deep in thought, and then Humphrey de Bohun edged his horse closer to Maud's.

'One thing you will need to remember when dealing with the lords of the March, take nothing at face value, and look hard at the implications of any suggested actions.' He grinned knowingly and touched the side of his nose with his gauntleted hand, 'We are all self seeking ambitious men. Never show your hand; trust few. That for what it is worth is the only advice I have to offer you.'

Maud rode on without looking either to her left or right for; she did not wish the Earl to know how his words left her with a sense of foreboding. This information only strengthened her resolve to try and understand the political affairs of the nation, especially ones pertaining to the March and Wales, with the emphasis on Welsh issues. Would it be ethical to write to Izzy and see if she could find out from her sister how matters stood within the Welsh court; ethical or not, she was determined to find out all she could. Once Maud had set her mind on a task she would move heaven and earth to accomplish it besides which, her life would be intrinsically bound by issues pertaining to Wales as many of the Mortimer lands and strongholds were dotted throughout that country also, the blood of Llywelyn ap Iowerth, ran through the veins of her future husband.

However, once again it was family matters which presently took priority and occupied Maud and Nell during the early months of 1241, in readiness for the wedding of their sister Eve, to William Cantelupe. New clothes were the immediate concern for the Braose sisters, and even the Countess of Hereford could not dull their excitement, with her withering remarks. Maud had no way of knowing how significant this great occasion would prove to be on her life.

CHAPTER X

Laycock Abbey

The Abbey was filled with the most important dignitaries of the age. Noble men and woman decked in rich velvets, silk, furs and jewels, thronged the holy place of worship for the marriage of Eve de Braose and William Cantelupe. Marriage would bring William the title and the Lordship of Abergavenny, along with lands in the Welsh Marches and from Eve's increasing Marshal Inheritance; due to the fact her Uncle Gilbert, Earl of Pembroke, had been killed during a tournament, only months before in June, the third Marshal Uncle to die without issue, in a hand span of years.

The Braose sisters dressed in their finery looked quite stunning and in truth, outshone the fourteen year old bride who was the plainest of the sisters. Nell wore shades of rich turquoise, highlighting her dark waving tresses and fresh complexion whereas; Maud had chosen a sage green surcote over a darker green kirtle which complemented her amber coloured hair and delicate skin highlighting her slanting, dark green-grey eyes. The bride wore a surcote of deepest red over a dark kirtle edged in silver, which drained what little colour she had from her cheeks. The groom looked nervous and tense throughout the long ceremony.

'Maud, have you seen who is amongst the guests?' Nell's whispered words were almost lost in the loud murmurings of the throng. 'The Comte de Vivonne and the Lord de Longeville are here!'

Maud's heart leapt at her sister's news.

'Are you certain? I wonder why they have been invited.' Maud's voice was a little uneven as she scanned the crowded Abbey until she too spied the tall figure of de Longeville standing next to his patron.

'See, there is Cousin Richard, he looks so grown up now.'

'Hush Nell, it is unseemly to ogle at people.'

'I know but there are so many noteworthy guests and ......' she winced as Maud pinched her arm.

'Enough!'

Nell knew by her sister's expression that she would brook no more interruptions.

When finally the couple exchanged vows at the great altar, all was hushed and only a few shuffling feet could be heard. Maud studied the slight figure of her new brother-in-law; how austere and aloof William appeared, poor Eve, being married to such a seemingly cold man. It left Maud wondering what emotions she would have on the day she married the young Mortimer heir, but she pushed the notion away for that day, was far into the future.

After the formal ceremony the young couple sat at the head of a richly decorated table which groaned with all the finest foods, fruits, and nuts accompanied by delicacies which shone with sugar and honey coatings. Musician played softly in the background as the feast progressed.

Nell's eyes were alight with excitement as she took her place at the top table. Maud on the other hand kept her eyes firmly lowered, fixing her gaze on her trencher, conscious that she was sitting next to the bridegroom's brother, the austere churchman, Thomas Cantelupe.

'I believe your mother and late aunt have made many donations to the church over the past few years.' His voice was clear and too high pitched to be pleasing on the ear.

'Indeed! My mother and late Aunt Isabel are noted for their generosity.' Maud turned to look at the speaker. 'But surely the church already has great wealth of its own and should – in my opinion, be donating much more to the poor from its own coffers.' Thomas Cantelupe's mouth fell open at Maud's words but she continued, her eyes now fixed firmly on his face.

'Fear of hell-fire is a wonderful weapon to use against parishioners who often donate monies they can ill afford. A clever ploy used by many clergy, for no-one is without sin, are they Reverend Father?'

A look of annoyance flicked across the starchy features of the churchman.

'My child, I feel you have maligned the church and need to seek forgiveness for the scurrilous accusations you lay at the feet of the clergy.'

'I merely voice the truth as I see it, is that considered sinful?' She hesitated for a moment before dropping her gaze. 'I have been brought up in the belief that by telling the truth, however difficult, will help defeat the devil in the battle between good and evil. Are you now telling me I shall be damned for speaking my mind?'

The discomfited cleric cleared his throat before answering, aware their conversation was being overheard.

'It is the opinion of the church that women are Eve's daughters; whose sin condemned mankind to a life of suffering and pain here on earth, after her fall from grace we were caste out of Paradise and therefore, women should be guided by the teachings of the bible and be submissive to the will of both the church, and their husband's, without question.'

'But the church is quite happy to accept largesse from women like my mother and aunt, who freely donate so generously to the church out of their *own* convictions and not at the behest of any man.'

Thomas Cantelupe studied the speaker with narrowed eyes his words were seldom contradicted by a woman, especially one so young.

'My lady, I object to this high handed discourse. I will put it down to too much wine and absolve you of your sins on this occasion.'

Maud looked long and hard at the stern faced churchman.

'I did not seek to offend you Father, pray accept my apology if you have taken offence at my personal views.' Maud's expression was artless as she continued. 'My concern stems from seeing towering spires reaching far into the skies to the glory of God which, is both admirable and uplifting but, my spirits are dashed by the abject poverty of many who sleep and beg in the shadows of such buildings, are you saying my opinion is misguided holy Father?'

'Many of those same churches and houses of God offer succour to the starving, following God's teachings, without silver, more would die of hunger and cold.'

Thomas Cantelupe folded his hands and murmured, 'I think we have exhausted the topic for now but, I do concede you have a kindly heart to care so deeply about those less fortunate than yourself and look forward to relying on your generosity in the future.' His words belied the emotions Maud had aroused in him.

'Oh! One day I intend to build Infirmaries to aid monks in the temporal Orders who tend the needy *not*, in order to save my soul but, to salve my conscience and hopefully, by so doing, also serve God.'

Although Maud knew her words had ruffled the churchman's normal composure she little realised just how uncomfortable her outspoken views had made him feel. However, he refused to be drawn further on the subject and throughout the rest of the feasting, remained in virtual silence. Maud was therefore relieved to let Nell chatter to the sombre clergyman, thereby averting what could have been an awkward silence.

After the feasting was over and the remnants of the meal removed by the well trained army of servants, the trestle tables were pushed back to make room for the dancing and revelry. Thomas Cantelupe rose, said a blessing over the newly married couple, and then made the sign of the cross over the rest of the company. Before he left he turned towards Maud and in lowered tones said, 'you are too outspoken for your own good my lady, but I commend your compassion therefore, I will keep you in my prayers.' With that he left.

'Maud you really do stir up a nest of hornets' at times. I hope he does not report your conversation to Mama or Eve, for I am sure it will upset them, he is after all, our new kinsman.' Nell looked earnestly at her sister as she spoke.

Maud tossed her head: 'Like all men they believe women are unworthy creatures and should have no opinions of their own. It makes me so angry, take a look round this gathering, half of the men are dolts, lechers, and worse, but their womenfolk have to obey their half witted notions merely to comply with the teachings of the church. I for one do not, and never shall, believe women to be chattels of men, to use as they see fit. Sorry if my views offend but, that is how I feel!'

'Pray do not lose your temper tonight Maud, let us have fun, you look so pretty in your gown of green and your hair and eyes are all aglow in the candlelight.'

Nell's appeal managed to dispel the tension Maud had felt and as she sipped her cup of wine, allowed herself to be seduced by the music and the merry atmosphere which finally soothed her agitation. She nodded. 'Give me a moment more and I will join you presently.'

Nell smiled. 'But only for a moment.' And with that she rose and went to join in the dancing.

A tall figure moved to sit beside Maud..

'How is it you have been left alone on such a night when you shine like Venus in the night sky?'

'De Longeville!' Maud turned to look into the dark eyes of the man who disturbed her more than she dared admit - even to herself, and in that moment, she knew she would love him for the rest of her life.

'Will you dance with me?' He held out his hand. Hesitantly she placed her hand in his and immediately felt a thrill of utter desire course through her body at his touch.

'Have a care my lord' she whispered, 'I am closely watched by agents of the Countess of Hereford.'

He nodded the expression on his face unchanging at her words. They danced in time to the notes of the rebec, viol, and shawn. Maud's heart was beating so fast, but her feet were as light as air. However, she did not dare to look up into de Longeville's face for, by so doing, would be certain to betray her true emotions. Instead, she focused on his shoulder and moved as sedately as her limbs would allow. When the music ended he bowed and led her back towards her seat as he squeezed her hand imperceptibly, then turned towards Nell and invited her onto the floor.

'You grow so quickly demoiselle I scarce recognised you!'

Nell smiled, 'I am now almost as tall as Maud am I not?'

'Indeed you are!' He turned and looked down into her bright face.

'And like your sister turn the heads of many admirers.'

She smiled as she blushed and bent her head as she twirled away' 'No doubt it will cause my future mother-in-law much chagrin.'

'No doubt it will!' he said chuckling.

'Really, it is no laughing matter, she can be quite .....' then stopped as Nell had spied the dark look of disapproval on the face of young Humphrey de Bohun. Nell wrinkled her nose at him followed by a sweet smile. After the dance ended she returned to her place and dropped a kiss on his forehead before sitting down beside him.

'There, you see, if you refuse to dance with me there are others who are only too willing to oblige, are there not my lord?' She looked artlessly at de Longeville as spoke.

'Be not cozened by your companion, she is out to tease you I dare-swear.' De Longeville patted the youth's shoulder then bowed and excused himself seeing that the Comte was looking at him a frown etched across his handsome face.

'You know, I do believe he is far more handsome, than I previously gave him credit for' Nell whispered as she turned to her sister.

'Is that so? Or, is it because he paid you a compliment and therefore has risen in your esteem?'

Nell giggled. 'Oh! Maud, am I so transparent?'

'In a word – yes!' The sisters laughed but Nell had no idea how hard it was for Maud to remain calm sitting in the same hall with de Longeville when all she really wanted to do was throw herself in his arms and declare her undying love. Nevertheless, she did ponder on what the Comte and de Longeville were doing at the wedding. Her curiosity undimmed by her desires.

The evening seemed to drag on interminably for both Maud and Guy de Longeville. He had been loathed to admit to himself how deeply the de Braose girl affected him and suffered the same urgent desires as the object of his affections for he too longed to sweep Maud into his arms and make love to her. His strong sense of loyalty had been sorely tested over the past months; he was perfectly aware his yearning for this bright haired beauty was doomed, but it had only served to incite his desires even more. He failed to recognise himself or, his wayward emotions, which left him unsettled, restless, and ill at ease; such feelings were alien and disturbed his normally calm equilibrium.

During boyhood, he had learned to accept his station in life which had been determined by both his father, and his father's patron, the late Comte de Vivonne. The only redeeming fact to his plight, he had been saved from entering the church. Now he felt shackled by old vows and resented their tenacious hold. Did he not deserve something out of life for himself? Was he expected to live only to serve the wishes of others? He was young, strong, had constrained the needs of the flesh to a mistress much older than himself, who had been employed by his late benefactor. Until his meeting with Maud, he had believed he was content. Now he knew he had been living an illusion, the old life was no longer enough, he needed to experience true passion; love, a spontaneous relationship with all the rapture and desperation it entailed.

Guy de Longeville faced the stark truth – to travel this path of love, was one he could not escape, his desire, too strong to be ignored. The risks would be great not only for him but also for Maud. Nevertheless, it did not stop him hoping the girl who made his blood run hot, felt the same way about him. Would she be brave enough to let their love fly in the face of convention? His thoughts were heavy and troubled, as he considered the implications of his ungovernable desire.

Whilst de Longeville contemplated his disturbing emotions, he took a deep draught of wine and listened to Etienne de Vivonne's views on the other guests; his condemnation of some of the musicians; the lack of quality in the wines. But a question which had been constantly unanswered was, exactly why they had been invited to this wedding. Were they carrying a missive from the Pope; or the French Queen, sister to Eleanor of Provence, or was there another underlying reason he was not privy too? Determined to discover the truth he faced the speaker.

'If you find only displeasure in your surroundings my dear Etienne, pray tell me why are we here?' De Longeville looked at his companion with an earnest expression etched across his dark, features. The Comte looked across at the speaker and glanced round to see if anyone was close enough to overhear them before he replied.

'Why so suspicious? You must have guessed our frequent visits to England are not merely for pleasure but used as a cover to carry informal messages for France. Sometimes significant matters can be achieved or resolved in this way, besides which, it pay's well.' The last words were accompanied by a wicked smile and who am I to question our saintly king?

'Now are you satisfied my dear de Longeville?'

'Is that the real reason you keep me ignorant of the details?'

'Exactly, should you ever be questioned how could you betray what you do not know? There are times when the information is so 'delicate' it may be deemed treasonable. So, you see my dear Guy, I have your well being at heart. It is not that I do not trust you with such secrets.......' He hesitated before continuing, 'your loyalty is never in doubt; I trust you with my life but sometimes the welfare of our country comes before confidences between friends, don't you agree? Besides which, they are not my secrets to share, but those of France.'

De Longeville nodded. 'I understand, you will suffer no more questions from me for the time being but, I cannot say the matter will not arise again in the future. It is not unreasonable to determine exactly what my role is, and for what cause I am expected to fight?'

'You, my dear Guy, would be fighting for me!' The words were clipped and charged with a warning it was like a physical blow to de Longeville; the sudden change of mood in his companion served as a stark reminder as to his true position, there was no doubting the Comte's authority, he was merely stating his role was that of a bodyguard to the French nobleman. He rose, bowed stiffly and took his leave. Comte Etienne de Vivonne watched de Longeville's departure with a frown furrowing his handsome brow; he realised his words had caused offence and this turn of events would undoubtedly put a strain on the formerly amicable relationship but, he was bound by secrecy in the cause of France and that must be paramount, whatever the personal cost.

The interview with de Vivonne had struck a nerve and that evening after the feasting, Guy de Longeville walked from of the smoky, crowded Hall and into the cool summer night air. He took a long deep breath and went to sit in one of the many flower bedecked arbours in the garden. How long he sat with his head in his hands he was uncertain and only became aware of his surroundings when he realised he was no longer alone.

'Are you sick my lord? I saw you leave the Hall somewhat hurriedly and came to see why.' Her voice was low and filled with concern.

'My sickness is one of circumstance not a malady.' He looked up into her face which was hidden by shadows. She knelt before him 'is there aught I can do to help?'

'No my dearest Lady Maud for I find myself condemned to live without.....' he stopped then said quite simply, *'you* confined to a world of shadows.' Maud drew his hands from his face and slowly reached up to kiss his brow. He pulled her into the darkness of the arbour away from prying eyes and covered her face, hands, and hair with urgent kisses.

'Come away with me, now, tonight, let us seek a life where we can live together as man and wife.'

Maud pulled away but kept hold of his hands. 'There is nothing I could think of that would please more. However, we would never be able to find true happiness knowing that our selfishness was the cause of misery to others.' She watched his expression change from desperation to one of despair.

'You know that to be true my lord. My father was hanged as a felon, his crime - adultery, if I left with you what do you suppose would become of my sisters who would have to suffer further shame. Nell would not marry her beloved Humphrey, Eve's new family would come under a cloud making her life untenable and poor Izzy would be reminded daily of our father's sin. Besides, my mother has already suffered great humiliation I could not bring myself to cause her further pain. Do you really believe I could be happy at their expense?'

He shook his head as he pulled her into his arms.

'So you are happy to condemn me to a life of misery?'

'Yes, where I too, shall suffer a similar sentence.' Her tone was soft but soulful as they clung together lost in the moment.

'Do you love me?' Maud's words broke the silence.

'Do you need to ask the question?'

'Then if we are to be condemned to a sentence of lifelong duty and separation tonight we will make our own, speak our heart's truth to each other so that through the years to come, we can look back and know we have this precious love to share. As yet, I have made no formal vows, my betrothal to Mortimer was by proxy when I was but a little girl therefore, at this moment, I still feel at liberty to act without redress by the church or, my own conscience.'

De Longeville rose and pulled her into his arms where they kissed in a long sensuous kiss; then he took her hand and led her back to his chambers. When they passed some rowdy revellers Maud hid her face in his shoulder and he drew her into the protection of his arm.

Only a rush-light flickered in the darkness. The fire was but glowing embers; a tray with a goblet and flask of wine stood on a bedside table.

'You are risking much and I want you to be cert.......' Her fingers pressed his lips shut so he could not finish the sentence.

'Sometimes we are given a moment in time to recognise its significance. This is our moment. I would live a lifetime of regret if I did not allow myself this one night where I chose to surrender myself and share my desire with the man I love. No hollow words on the altar of ambition or duty but, free to follow the dictates of my own body, heart, and mind.'

De Longeville gathered her up in his arms and took her to his bed where the hours were spent discovering the delights and urgent passions they aroused in each other. Maud trembled under his tender caresses where she learned the language of love, passion and sensuality. As they lay together after their desires had been assuaged de Longeville whispered the words of love which Maud would remember all her life. Words imprinted deep in her heart; words, and ones she would recall as both sublime and heart wrenching. Maud knew her love for Guy de Longeville would last until the day she died. If her love condemned her to the fires of hell, so be it.

The time which, earlier in the evening seemed to drag, now vanished as swiftly as morning mist but the stolen hours of their night of love making, began to wane as they desperately clung to the final moments of intimacy.

'How will you explain your absence?' De Longeville asked as he stroked a tendril of amber coloured locks from her cheek.

'I will think of something have no fear.' She reached up and kissed him tenderly on the lips. 'We must take care not to draw attention to ourselves, or invite speculation on our ......'

'You mean I cannot gaze at you with longing and love.' He teased.

'You must treat this matter with all seriousness for should our secret become common knowledge it would spell our downfall or worse - end in death for us both.'

'Fear not my love, I will be all circumspection as you have urged.'

The couple finally kissed and parted. Maud slipped unseen from de Longeville's chambers. Instead of trying to return unnoticed back into her apartment she had picked up a pitcher of water and with as much noise as possible opened the door.

'Jane! The water jug was empty and I did not wish to rouse you so went and fetched one for myself.'

'Oh! I am sorry my lady.'

'Too much wine tends to make one thirsty, the fault is not yours. Besides, you were so busy yesterday it is quite understandable you slept deeply.' Maud hoped her actions had covered up her absence. Nell would be the one to speak out if she suspected anything and for awhile Maud held herself in readiness to deflect suspicion but thankfully, nothing else was said on the matter.

Later that morning the two sisters were visited by their mother, Eva Marshal. She went and sat on the padded window seat as she studied her two daughters. She was saddened that her eldest daughter, Izzy, had been unable to attend and knew how the news had upset Maud but the current outbreak of hostilities in Wales, had made travelling too hazardous. Eva turned her attention to the girls.

'Considering how nervous Eve was yesterday I think she carried the ceremony off quite well.' She turned her gaze on Maud, 'you look very pale Maud, is aught wrong? I noted you left the Hall early last night.'

Maud dropped her eyes before answering. 'Nothing Mama, I hardly slept that is all.'

'Make sure you take your rest. Are you sure you are not sickening for something?

'No Mama!' Maud said quietly.

The rest of the visit went without any further questions much to Maud's relief. The following days however, found Maud aching for the warmth of her lover's arms and she experienced a fierce physical desire she found somewhat disturbing. The knowledge that she no longer held complete control over her own emotions served to unnerve her.

Throughout the rest of the celebrations Maud and Guy had no further opportunities to spend time alone and only managed brief exchanges of pleasantries, much to their mutual frustration. As the festivities drew to a close it was the Comte de Vivonne's party who were among the first to take their leave and Maud watched the colourful retinue ride away, her heart felt a heavy at her loss.

De Longeville, mounted on a powerful grey stallion, made an imposing figure and she felt both pride, coupled with the deepest pain at his departure. How long would it be before she saw him again? Then as an afterthought, would they in fact, *ever* meet again? But she banished the notion almost immediately; de Vivonne seemed to appear in the most unlikely places therefore he would most certainly be included in the guest list at some function in the future. She mouthed a silent prayer that it would not be too many months before she saw her beloved Guy once more. A sudden fear stabbed at her heart, what if she was pregnant?

CHAPTER XI

'Come Maud there is a matter which I need to speak with you in private.' The Earl of Hereford turned and waved his hand towards his servant, his expression stern, the man obediently bowed, and made his exit. Humphrey pointed towards a seat and continued. 'I will not waste time with any preamble for I know you appreciate plain speaking.'

Maud obeyed his bidding and sat on the seat indicated, which had been placed before a large trestle table. Writing materials were scattered all across the polished surface, some had even spilled onto the flagged floor.

'My wife has brought it to my attention that your behaviour towards her is lacking in respect; in fact, she has described it as verging on insolent.'

Maud's features tightened at his accusations, this irate figure was not the man she had come to look on as a mentor and confidante.

'In fact, you have openly defied her on more than one occasion by all accounts. She feels unable to deal with the matter herself and as a result has turned to me to act on her behalf. These encounters have caused her to become very agitated. Heaven's witness, she is not the easiest of women to live with I know from bitter experience. However, she now claims her health is suffering from these altercations. She even has her physician supporting her complaint and he insists it is affecting her current pregnancy. As she is my wife, I am honour bound to protect her.' He looked hard at Maud. 'I am under no illusion to the failings of the Countess but cannot and *will* not, countenance any disrespect imagined or otherwise - do you understand me my lady?'

'Indeed my lord Earl!' Maud accepted the guilt of defying the Countess at every opportunity but knew the blame was not hers alone. She sat bolt upright whilst waiting to learn of her punishment.

'I have therefore decided to write to the Mortimer's stating it is my belief that the time is right for you to join them at Wigmore.'

The news hit Maud like a physical blow.

'My lord do you really feel Nell is ready to be left with...... with.....' she could not finish the sentence for fear of exacerbating the problem.

'The answer to that is no! Nevertheless one day she will have to learn to become more independent and as I have explained in this instance my hands have been fettered. Do I lose my unborn child and the regard of my wife, suffer a disruptive household, for a few girlish tears?'

Maud bowed her head her mind was whirling with this unexpected turn of events. Then she looked up, 'Would it not be possible for Nell and I to go to another residence for awhile until this...' she rose and began to pace around the large chamber, 'baby is born?'

'You will have to go and live with the Mortimer's one day.'

'I know – but my marriage is some years away my lord and I would rather remain with Nell where I know I am most needed rather than kick my heels waiting to take my place in the Mortimer hierarchy.'

The Earl rubbed his chin then looked at the earnest face as he replied.

'I will sleep on the matter and consider your suggestion most carefully for the truth is, I would sorely miss your company.'

Maud knew his mood had suddenly softened.

'Then I may hope my lord?' Maud smiled at the Earl. She noted his face had relaxed and his blue eyes twinkled with mischief. 'Always live with hope my dear. Now run along and *do* try and keep out of my wife's way.'

'Thank you my lord, you have my word on it!'

With that Maud hurried from the great chamber almost bumping into a servant who was about to enter the door brandishing a rolled up scroll in his hand. Little did Maud realise the scroll was a letter from her mother who had requested her daughters join her at Totnes for the month of September. Upon reading Eva Marshal's words Humphrey de Bohun looked heavenwards and said a silent prayer of gratitude, this was the perfect solution to his problems, a way whereby all parties would be left satisfied leaving him free to turn his attention to matters he knew to be far more important than feminine squabbles within his household.

Within three days the two de Braose girls were riding towards Devonshire on a rare visit to their mother. Maud had told Nell nothing of her interview with the Earl, she was learning to keep her own council on many issues, unaware it was an invaluable lesson for her future. Nell rode close to Maud and whispered.

'Do you think our sister Eve is a wife in the biblical sense yet? She is after all nearly fifteen.'

'It will depend on her new in-laws whether they believe she is old enough to fulfil the role as wife.' Maud tried to keep her words dispassionate and non judgemental.

'He looked such a cold fish.'

'Looks often belie a man's true nature.' Again Maud kept her reply short and to the point.

'Oh, Maud you really can't believe William Cantelupe to be a jolly companion now, can you?'

'Why ever not, he may keep his views from the world but share them with his wife in the privacy of their own chambers and who knows - have a wicked sense of humour to boot.' Maud looked across at her sister disbelief printed all across her pretty face.

'Are you practising diplomacy Maud?'

'Not at all, merely pointing out there are many sides to every-ones character, a fact *you* appear to have forgotten.'

'Oh, you are impossible I can see I shall get no sense out of you today.' Without another word Nell spurred her horse forward and went to chat with Jane who had been happily engaged in conversation with one of the grooms.

The rest of the journey was uneventful and Maud was glad to be left to her own thoughts. Upon their arrival the greeting from their mother was both warm and affection and together they enjoyed a tasty supper. Nell chatted incessantly regaling Eve with the Countess of Hereford's many shortcomings. When the remnants of the meal were cleared away and the little family group went to sit before a crackling fire, Eva Marshal looked across at Maud.

'You are singularly lacking in conversation my dear, pray what ails you?'

Maud stretched her fingers towards the warmth of the flames for the evenings were not only drawing in but after the sun had set, there was a distinct chill in the air, a forewarning of approaching winter.

'To tell the truth Mama, I have nothing further to add to what Nell has already told you. I promise I am not sickening for aught ..... but....' She hesitated 'I must admit I am glad to be quit of the Countess.' She smiled at her mother. 'Besides, it is rare to feel we are truly alone without being spied upon and I mean to enjoy every moment of our stay.'

Eva Marshal smiled, it was true, since her daughters had left for the de Bohun household years ago; they had met only on formal occasions with scant time for family intimacies.

'You are right of cause! No doubt when Nell marries you will be going to the Mortimer's and it will be even more difficult for private family reunions. Let us hope the weather holds so we can ride out and enjoy the surrounding countryside. Autumn is my favourite season and the woods and trees hereabouts, display a wonderful pageant of colours, proof that God has a far richer palette than any artists I have seen. Now, as you are both tired, an early night will serve us all well, methinks. I have had two chambers made ready for you and dressed them in your favourite colours' She moved to kiss each of her daughters as they rose to seek their beds.

'It will be the first time I – or we, have had a place all to ourselves....how thoughtful Mama!' Maud's voice was full of appreciation. Nell looked somewhat abashed: 'could Jane sleep in my chamber?'

Eva Marshal smiled at the sheepish request. 'Of course lambkin, of course!'

The following morning the sun rose in a hazy sky; the early morning mist spiralled and twisted in and out of the branches of the nearby trees and buildings, touching the scene with unearthly magic.

'Come on lazy head!' Maud threw the clothes back off Nell as she splashed icy cold water across her face to waken her to the new day. Nell shrieked in protest but laughed as she tossed a pillow at Maud's head. Jane smiled as the two sisters played like children for awhile but quickly calmed as they began to dress.

'Can you imagine what Lady Misery would say if she had witnessed such a scene.' Jane's smile widened as she helped each girl with their garments.

'Shame on you Jane for even mentioning *that* woman, I forbid you to speak of her again throughout our visit here.'

'Very well my lady.' The smile changed to a roguish grin, 'your wish will be quite easily obeyed.'

They all laughed happily in the knowledge they were free from the watchful eye and constant rebukes of the waspish Countess. It was a bright and carefree start to the day and they went down to break-fast with their mother.

'I hope you are not going to make a habit of missing Mass whilst you are here?' Eva looked at the young fresh faces of her daughters and their maid.

'Just this once Mama, besides we can go to Benediction this evening instead.' Maud looked appealing towards her mother who nodded trying to hide her face so they could not see she was in no way truly annoyed. It had been a long time since Eva had enjoyed a simple meal interspersed only by the light hearted chattering of young voices. A stark reminder of how deeply immersed in matters of law and commerce she had been over the years and it came with the sudden realisation of what she had missed most - the company of her daughters. Her cost however, would be their gain, for she had fought long and hard for lands and properties inherited from her Marshal brother's to ensure the future of the girls, although looking at them now, she could not fail to note their girlhood was fast disappearing.

'Mama, I would like to visit our cousin Amy whilst we are so close.' Nell's voice was filled with anxiety.

'Of course my dearest child' Eva turned to look at Maud, 'will you be accompanying her?'

Maud shook her head. 'I would much prefer to remain here with you Mama, peace and quiet are what I wish for most at the moment.'

'Then you shall both have your way. I will send word directly of your proposed visit and tomorrow Nell; you can ride over and visit Amy.'

The rest of the day was busy as the two sisters chose gifts and clothes for Nell to take to their cousin's. The weather looked settled and after the morning mists had cleared the autumn day was warm and sunny. In the evening the air was filled with songs and stories told to amuse their mother, setting the tone or, so they thought, for the rest of their stay.

By mid morning the following day, Nell had ridden off with a small, well armed party towards Rougemont Castle, waving a cheery farewell to her mother and sister.

'She is gaining in confidence is she not?' Eva's words held a note of sadness.

'Indeed! She will need all her resolve to deal with her future mother-in-law believe me!' Maud reached for her mother's hand. 'Nell has a good heart and young Humphrey dotes on her, although she's not yet totally aware of his affection.'

Eva looked at her daughter, 'And you my dear Maud, how do you view your future?'

Maud hesitated before replying. 'I must admit, the thought of marrying someone who is so much younger does promote some doubts in my mind.' She squeezed her mother's hand, 'but fear not I am your daughter, whose veins are filled with Marshal blood and a mere Mortimer youth will not pose too many sleepless nights I dare-swear.' She grinned for she spoke with far more confidence than she truly felt in order to allay her mother's fears. Eva kissed her daughter's brow. 'Well said my dear, well said,' and they walked back towards the castle keep.

The following morning as Maud and her mother discussed plans for the day a breathless rider galloped into the outer bailey with an urgent request for help. But Maud's heart leapt as she recognised the Vivonne badge on his tunic. Without any preamble, the breathless youth blurted out the nature of his message. One of the Comte de Vivonne's retainers had been involved in an accident when thrown from his horse during an attack on their party. The unfortunate man was so badly injured they feared for his life.

Eva ordered men from the household to accompany the messenger with a wagon filled with soft bedding to help the stricken victim. She sent a maid to the kitchens to warn them of the imminent arrival of an unknown numbers of guests. Then, she asked Maud to ride and fetch Brother Edwin, who acted as physician at the near-bye Infirmary. She sent Margery, her own lady-in-waiting, to arrange accommodation for the influx of visitors. Eva sighed; the outside world had once more intruded on her private life.

It was almost two hours later when the party of riders with the wagon were spied from the battlements. Upon Maud's return, she had run to the vantage point in order to see if de Longeville was among the incoming party; the pain in her chest so tight she could scarcely breathe. Then she glimpsed them through the trees, the sun flashing on their weapons. She hesitated just long enough to watch as they emerged from a clump of trees and sure enough, de Longeville was riding at the knee of the Comte.

'Quick!' She exclaimed to a page as she descended hurriedly from the battlements, 'warn Lady Abergavenny the party is nigh and then go and tell the kitchens.' The boy sped off to do her bidding.

As the party entered the gateway the cries of agony of the unfortunate man could be heard by all. The steward indicated for him to be carried to the castle's Infirmary where Brother Edwin was waiting in readiness for the patient. Eva Marshal, known universally as Lady Abergavenny, stepped forward to greet her guests.

'You are welcome gentlemen I am only saddened that it is under such unfortunate circumstances. Are there any more of your party with injuries?'

Comte Etienne de Vivonne leapt from his saddle, handing the reins of his bright chestnut horse to a waiting groom before bowing to his hostess.

'Some sustained a few cuts and bruises, 'tis all my lady!' He gave his finely tooled gloves to his squire as the rest of the party dismounted. The horses and the injured were taken to be tended by the castle servants. Maud had remained in the shadow of the doorway, noting how de Longeville stood unobtrusively some way back as the Comte bent to kiss her mother's hand.

'I apologise for inflicting my misfortunes on you, my dear Lady.' The French nobleman looked round as he spoke noting the tidiness and orderliness of his surroundings.

'We are only too pleased to be of help be assured, if anyone can save your .....' she stopped uncertain of exactly who it was that had been injured.

'My secretary, we were set upon some miles back and a stray arrow glanced off his horse causing it to bolt.' He smiled ruefully. 'Fabio is not a natural horseman.'

Eva indicated for him to follow her into the castle where the table had been filled with a variety of tasty dishes together with jugs of beers and wine. As they walked, the Comte beckoned de Longeville forward and presented his companion; Guy de Longeville bowed in silent greeting.

'You are welcome my lord.' Eva's voice was full of sincerity. 'My lady-in-waiting will take you to your chamber so you can wash the dust of the roads away before you eat.'

'That would be most welcome my lady'.

As Guy de Longeville entered under the door arch he became aware of the figure standing in the shadows and as Maud stepped forward she heard his soft intake of breathe.

'You are hurt my lord.' Maud's voice was barely above a whisper. A trickle of blood was seeping below the cuff on his right hand. 'Pray let me help you.'

'It is but a scratch.' The look which passed between them spoke a volume of words but as they entered further into the Hall; both had composed their inner feelings and nothing of what they truly felt was betrayed by their expressions.

'Maud, take ......?'

'Guy de Longeville, my lady.'

'Lord de Longeville and tend his wounds.'

Maud needed no further urging as she turned she noted the quizzical look of the Comte but his attention was diverted by further discourse with her mother. Maud walked swiftly towards the Infirmary but as they turned a corner she stopped, listened, and then caught de Longeville's hand.

'Whatever ill fate brought you here this day, I thank God for it.'

Almost before she had finished speaking he had pulled her into his arms and kissed her in a long, passionate kiss, she felt the strength of his powerful body and they clung together for some minutes before approaching footsteps broke the spell.

In silence the couple continued towards Infirmary where, with shaking hands Maud dressed the deep gash on de Longeville's right forearm. They could hear the moaning of the injured man coming from the next room.

'I know my mother has great faith in Brother Edwin's skills, this salve is one of his curatives.'

De Longeville remained silent but kept his eyes locked onto her face. He leaned forward and kissed her again this time very gently. 'I love you Maud de Braose,' his voice, little more than a whisper.

'I know.' She said and smiled as she continued dressing the angry wound.

Brother Edwin entered the room and spoke to de Longeville, his voice serious.

'The man's shoulder is broken but that is not my main concern it is the blow to his head which worries me the most.' He hesitated then continued. 'I have given him a powerful draft which will let him sleep until the morrow. However, what his condition will be upon waking only God has the answer, so our prayers are all we can offer at this time.' He looked at the cleaned wound on de Longeville's arm and nodded towards Maud.

'If you wish to return to your other guests I can finish attending to his lordship.'

Maud shook her head. 'I would like to continue if you please Brother Edwin, if only to test my scanty knowledge of bandaging; I believe it is a necessary skill in times of war, is it not?' She looked innocently at the monk as she spoke.

'Of course,' he stood back and let Maud resume. As she finished he nodded his grey, tonsured head in approval: 'very good for an apprentice.' She noted the amusement in his eyes but as there was no spite or malice in his words, she relaxed and smiled at the compliment.

'My needlecraft is dismal so I should have some hidden talents - maybe I will develop into a good nurse.'

'Practice is the keyword. However, your patient may have other ideas.'

'I have received far less kindly treatment in the past.' De Longeville's said ruefully.

'Then if you are happy to let yourself be practiced upon, I will go and see what other injuries need *my* skills.'

The room remained silent until the sound of the monk's leather sandals on the stone flags grew fainter.

'Some maids faint at the sight of blood.' De Longeville said seriously.

'Not me! Remember I am the daughter of a Marcher baron and was raised with the sight of wounded soldiers being brought home.' Her words said somewhat defiantly but she kissed his cheek then inspected her handiwork. Afterwards, she went and washed her bloody fingers, drying them on a rough, white linen towel.

'I am in your debt my lady.' The words were half serious, half teasingly said.

'Oh believe me; I shall collect that debt with interest.' She chuckled roguishly before she found herself locked in de Longeville's arms, her mouth covered by his urgent kisses.

When he finally released her she whispered 'We must return or suspicions may be aroused and if my mother ever suspects at my true feelings towards you.....' she solemnly made the sign of the cross.

'Do you have another tunic? You will need to change; give the soiled and torn one to a servant and it will be cleaned and repaired before your departure.' As they left the Infirmary Maud directed de Longeville to his chambers and returned to the Hall alone.

After the disruptive events of the day, Eva Marshal arranged a feast for her guests and the excitement and tensions eased as musicians began to strum their harps and sing as the trays of food were brought into the Hall. The candlelight flickered on the rich tapestries and hangings, giving the mythical beasts and ancient warriors, so skilfully worked in vibrant colours, an appearance they were dancing on the walls, almost as though they were part of the entertainment. Conversation, no longer urgent, was enjoyed by the Comte, his hostess, and their retainers, for it was a time of relaxation and relief.

'Ah! Comte, now you have made your plans for an early start tomorrow, I feel I must convey Brother Edwin's anxiety with regard to Lord de Longeville's wound; he has informed me that the cut is very deep and therefore will need a regular change of dressing. I have come to trust Brother Edwin, who is not given to histrionics, so urge you to leave Lord de Longeville here at Totnes, where he can keep an eye on his progress. As we all know, an infected wound can prove fatal. I feel I would be failing in my duty as hostess not to pass on my physician recommendations. Besides, if it aids Lord de Longeville's speedy recovery, it seems foolish not to adhere to the good Brother's advice.'

Maud almost choked at her mother's words. She did not dare raise her eyes but waited with baited breathe to listen to the Comte's response. But it was de Longeville who spoke, his voice low but distinct.

'I thank you for your concern my lady but my duty is to remain at ....' He was interrupted by de Vivonne.

'No, no, of course you are quite right Lady Abergavenny, and your gracious offer is accepted. It is the very least I can do, as Guy saved my life today and it would be remiss of me to fail in my duty of care towards him, would it not?' He brushed aside de Longeville's protests and to the delight of Maud who went to bed that night knowing that for a time at least, she and Guy de Longeville would spend the mellow days of autumn together at Totnes Castle, out of sight of prying eyes. As she mused over the thought she eventually fell asleep in a haze of happiness.

The following morning Maud rose and dressed in her warm kirtle of soft grey wool, and walked swiftly down the passageway and out into the courtyard, the scene was filled with urgent voices, horses' impatient neighs and stamping of hooves, the jingling of harnesses as the Comte's party made ready for their departure.

'Have you come to make sure we leave?' The Comte's eyes twinkled as he came and stood before her.

'No, of course not, my lord, merely to wish you God speed and a safe journey.'

'Take care of de Longeville,' his voice had lost its humour, 'but then I think you will find that an easy request.' The merriment had returned.

'You are a wicked man,' Maud said with a chuckle in her voice. He grinned.

'Don't break the poor man's heart, your flame will mesmerize him and I value him more than he knows.' He gave her a knowing look.

'I do not wish him to return to me a broken hearted man.'

'Rest assured my lord Comte, the last thing I would ever do is hurt my Lord de Longeville.'

The Comte de Vivonne took her hand, kissed it, then mounted his prancing steed and with a wave of his hand signalled the party forward, out through the vaulted gateway where they were quickly swallowed by the curling mist. Maud turned to walk back towards the Castle, and spied de Longeville standing waiting. As she passed she whispered. 'He knows!'

'He will not betray us!'

'Nevertheless, he could hold us to ransom.' Maud's voice was fearful.

'You misjudge him!' Guy de Longeville looked down at Maud.

'I trust no-one with secrets that could bring harm to us both.' Her green-grey eyes flashed, but she reached out to touch his hand and her face relaxed. 'We will not let his words spoil our first morning together. Besides, before we break-fast it is off to the Infirmary where I shall change the dressing on your arm.' She linked her arm through his and together they headed for the cool, limed washed walls of the Infirmary.

The days that ensued were to be the happiest Maud had ever known and the settled September weather only added to their delight. Eva, who was perfectly happy to let the young couple make their own entertainment, little realised that her daughter and the tall, dark knight, were lovers.

For a whole week their days were spent, walking, talking, laughing, and exploring the surrounding countryside. In the evenings, joined by Maud's mother, they played board games, listened to music, and chatted amicably together and in the hours which followed, the couple made love and grew ever closer as they fell deeper under each other's spell.

The idyll was marred somewhat on Nell's return, which proved at times, a stumbling block to their privacy. Nonetheless, they still managed to spend their nights together and even when the weather broke and rain lashed against the walls of Totnes Castle, they were content to stay indoors and read stories, or listen to music, sometimes, they play chess or cards.

Brother Edwin, who visited daily, was pleased with how de Longeville's wound was healing and even gave grudging praise to Maud's improving bandaging skills. His other patient was also beginning to shows signs of recovery and had begun to eat solid foods again. As September drew to a close Maud and de Longeville became ever more aware of the passing of time and their imminent parting. Now their laughter was more muted; their love making more urgent and passionate.

'I shall be bereft when I am forced to return to Hereford.' Maud's voice was filled with pain. 'How can I live without you now after .....after....?'

'Love, is both hell and heaven, and we have known Paradise in these days together.' Guy de Longeville spoke slowly as he stroked Maud's rich, shining tresses.

'Soon we shall come to know hell.' Her words were charged with sorrow.

'We could still run away to Ireland.' He noted the hint of panic.

'Remember, you were the one who said neither of us could live without honour and that sadly, will always be the truth, however painful.'

She hid her face in his shoulder and wept silently as he rocked her gently to and fro, like a father rocks a disconsolate child. But during the daytime the couple tried to retain an air of easy going companionship and Nell's endless chatter helped to cover some difficult moments. Now in the evenings, as Fabio's health continued to improve, he also joined the group, even though his shoulder remained heavily strapped. Surprisingly, they discovered he had a melodic voice and sang the songs of his homeland, which were often laced with longing.

'This has been a unique month.' Eva Marshal said late one evening. 'New friendships, evenings filled with haunting melodies, interspersed with the sound of laughter; it will live long in my memory.' But their happy interlude was soon to end and even with Nell's pleadings to stay awhile longer, Eva knew that October could be a hazardous month to travel and she did not want her daughters to encounter storms and difficult conditions on their long journey back to Herefordshire.

On the last day of the month de Vivonne's party rode back through the gates of Totnes and so the days and nights of love and intimacy enjoyed by Maud and de Longeville, finally came to an end but, both knew their love would last throughout Eternity whatever or, wherever Fate took them in the future.

As the final hours of September slowly made way for October, Eva Marshal viewed her guests. The French Comte was his usual ebullient self taking centre stage, his extravagant gestures now quite familiar. His brother-in-law, the reserved, dark haired knight, whom she had come to like, sat in silence, his expression unreadable, like a mask, and she was unable to gage his true emotions. She sat and watched her daughters'. Sweet Nell, who chattered incessantly to whoever would listen, and Maud, with a faraway look in her eyes, was obviously lost in her own thoughts. Her attention was taken with the sweet voice of Fabio as he sang a lively tune to bring the evening to an end. Eva let out a long sigh; life would return to the mundane again after their departure and the winter months, hang more heavily, for their going.

After the departure of her lover Maud experienced a deep sense of loneliness which kept her awake long into the nights. Her young body had been awakened to the passions of physical love making and now the sense of yearning wracked her waking hours. She was also troubled by the knowledge that she could have conceived de Longeville's child, a fact which could heap shame once more on to the name of de Braose but in her heart, she would love to carry his child.

However, on the homeward journey, at least one of her many worries faded, as she began her monthly flow and uncomfortable as that was, it did alleviate her immediate concerns. The one thing she did fear, was how she could disguise the fact from her future husband, that she was no longer a virgin?

BOOK TWO

VOW OF DUTY

CHAPTER XII

Wigmore Castle

'Do you think this chamber suitable for our future daughter-in-law?' Lady Mortimer looked enquiringly at her husband.

'Well the amount of silver you have spent on the hangings and furnishings should be enough to satisfy a queen.'

'My lord husband, she is entitled to come to surroundings befitting her status, remember, she brings great wealth and lands to the Mortimer's, a detail which should never be overlooked.'

Ralph Mortimer, Lord of Wigmore, nodded thoughtfully before he continued.

'In essence, you are saying she is paying for her own finery, a fact which pleases me greatly, so there is nothing more to add therefore, I leave further arrangements in your capable hands.'

'Good, then that is settled. The girl has received sharp shrift from the Countess of Hereford by all accounts and I do not wish her to feel she is not welcomed at Wigmore. Besides, our son's future is at stake. If she is content, you can be assured she will bring that contentment to their future life together.'

The lord of Wigmore frowned, 'the Braose girls have not had the easiest lives since their father's disgraceful execution, add that to the bitter dispute between the king and her Marshal uncles, I salute the Lady Eva for her dignified handling of a very tricky situation.'

'I agree; Lady Abergavenny brought about reconciliation, between the king and her family but, only after the brutal murder of her brother Richard in Ireland. I believe the whole matter took many months and long periods away from her daughters. I little wonder she never chose to re-marry, given all the trouble brought about by the men-folk of her family.'

The couple took a final look around the warm, bright chamber and both felt satisfied that all had been done to make Maud de Braose feel comfortable upon her arrival.

'Well my dear, we shall know if all the effort has been worthwhile in a few days.'

'Let us hope so!' But Lady Mortimer felt confident that Maud would appreciate her surroundings once she saw the apartments. However, she could not quell the nagging doubt she felt about their eldest son, Roger, who possessed a volatile temperament. A word of warning from his father would not come amiss and she voiced her concerns.

'Have no fear my lady, I will ensure our son is made aware that if he fails to show due respect to his future bride, he will be made to answer to me!'

'Thank you, my lord; your assurances are a welcome relief.' At that the Marcher lord and his wife left to continue with their many duties.

Meantime, at Hay Castle, Maud de Braose gazed out at the distant hills. She was loathed to admit she felt nervous about the coming days. She had been in the de Bohun household for some years; she was familiar with the daily routine, felt at ease with the servants and the Earl, and his son Humphrey, and if she were truthful, enjoyed Nell's incessant chatter. Over time she had even come to accept the acerbic remarks of the Countess without retort. The future now posed a mountain of uncertainties but her main concern was how she would deal with the conflicting emotions of loyalty. Her heart belonged to de Longeville that was a fact, a fact which troubled her greatly but nevertheless, it was an undeniable truth therefore, it would be impossible to ever have such feelings for Roger Mortimer or, for that matter anyone else. She must learn to live and survive, in a life without de Longeville and the knowledge left her bereft for, she knew it condemned her to a lonely existence. Disconsolately she gathered her clothes and belongings and laid them on the bed in readiness for Jane to pack them neatly into trunks and boxes in readiness for her departure.

'Jane!'

'Yes my lady.'

'Promise me you will take care of Nell and let me know if aught is ever amiss with her.'

'You have no need to ask such a promise of me my lady, I would cut off my hand rather than let anyone hurt Lady Eleanor.'

Maud turned from the window and went to hug Jane, a rare demonstration of affection.

'I shall be forever in your debt.'

'No my lady, there are no debts where loyalty and affection are concerned.'

'You have much patience Jane, which must have been sorely tried over the years since the de Braose sisters came to stay.' Maud said wryly.

'Well – there have been times but.....' Jane stopped folding a kirtle as she spoke, 'I would have been the poorer for not having served you both. It has been both an honour and a pleasure.'

A knock at the door interrupted them and Nell entered with an ornately carved box in her hand.

'Humphrey and I want you to have this as a parting gift. It is a writing set which you must use daily with messages to me.' Her pretty face a picture of intensity.

'Come, Nell, daily is a tad too much to ask, surely?' Maud said as she took the gift from her sister's hands. 'But I will write often that I do promise and thank you both for such a thoughtful present.' She went and kissed Nell's crestfallen face.

'Besides, Wigmore is but eight leagues from Hereford is it not?' Nell's face brightened instantly as she nodded her hair moving like a dark, shining waterfall.

Within days of receiving her writing box, Maud sat her spirited palfrey as she prepared for her new life. As the wagonette, flanked by the small armed company of soldiers, gathered at the gateway awaiting Maud's signal, she turned to wave her farewells. Noting the shadowy figure of the Countess of Hereford framed in one of the upstairs windows, she deliberately turned her back to that direction and urged her prancing mare forward. The Earl, and his son, who stood beside Nell holding her hand, was joined by the Castle's chaplain as he made the sign of the cross accompanied by the words, 'Dominus vobiscum' in a blessing over the party of travellers.

Once Maud reached the gateway she spurred her mount into a brisk trot and kept her focus on the road ahead not wanting anyone to see the tears in her eyes. She mouthed a silent prayer, and rode in silence for many miles. The journey was fraught with mishaps. First the wheel of the wagonette came off its axle, causing a delay. Then one of the horses lost a shoe which delayed them further and finally, a rein broke on one of the squire's bridles.

'I swear by All the Saints', we are not meant to complete this journey!' Maud exclaimed to her companion, a wife of one of the soldier's.

'It will be almost dark before we reach Wigmore that's for certain and this incessant wind makes matters more uncomfortable.' Joan Pryce was a thick set, no nonsense woman, who was accompanying her husband to their new posting in Radnor. The squire, who knew of the dangers of travelling in the dark, quickly threaded his belt through the ring on the bit of his bridle, enabling the party to continue with the minimum delay.

The wind had finally dropped by the time the weary party rode through the sandstone archway of Wigmore Castle. Maud looked at Joan and nodded her thanks, too tired to speak. A figure moved from the gathering shadows to take Maud's arm and lead her into the stronghold of the Mortimer family. Lord Rhys, the ever faithfully servant of Lady Mortimer, guided the young woman into the warmth of a chamber whose walls were adorned with vibrant hangings and the chairs and benches, covered by luxurious cushions.

'Lady Mortimer will visit you in an hour after you have washed and changed. There are refreshments on the table.'

'Thank you!' was all Maud managed to say but she noted the man moved round the chamber without a sound. His dark features mask like.

'You have no servant with you?'

'No!'

'Then I shall send one to you!' With that he bowed and upon reaching the door turned and said, 'you are welcome here Lady Maud. However, a word of warning, you will encounter some who do not feel so welcoming, being you are the daughter of Gwilym Ddu.' With that he left her in

the warming glow of a busy fire and the dancing rush-lights.
She discarded her cloak and walked over to the bed; kicked
off her riding boots and sank into the soft covers. She lay for
a moment realising how tired she was; the previous night had
been almost sleepless and the journey with its many delays
and the constant buffeting of the wind, had taken its toll
and she soon fell into a deep slumber.

The gentle knock at the door failed to waken her and she
did not hear the woman enter. Quietly, the figure gathered up
the cloak and the muddy boots, took them to the waiting page
who, sped off to have them cleaned and any tears and snags,
speedily repaired. Returning to her task, Carys went and made
up the fire before going towards the sleeping figure. The bright
amber coloured hair was spread over the pillow and Maud's
face, in sleep, look very young, almost childlike. Another tap
at the door failed to wake the sleeping girl and Carys went and
opened it to the two servants who were carrying a heavy coffer.

'Hush, try not to wake her. Place it over there and close the
door softly as you leave.' Her words were a whispered order,
and the men nodded and obediently did as they were bid.
Carys opened the heavy lid and expertly took out the contents
and filled drawers and cupboards with the clothes, shoes,
and slippers of the new arrival. She left the box and casket
knowing they were of a personal nature. Just as she finished
hanging the last mantle in the closet another knock came
and Carys answered only to find Lady Mortimer standing
in the passageway. The servant dropped a deep curtsey as her
mistress entered. Gwladus Ddu smiled.

'Our young lady is overcome by weariness it would appear?'
'Yes, my Lady.'
'I am glad to see you have let her sleep.' She walked over
to the fire and sat beside the busy flames. As one of the logs
fell and knocked against the fire basket the figure on the bed
stirred, suddenly aware she was not alone.

'Greetings my dear!' Lady Mortimer rose and walked
towards Maud.

'Forgive me! I was so tired I simply fell asleep, the bed
looked so inviting.' Maud smiled shyly at the mother of her
future husband.

'You have had an eventful journey by all accounts and it is perfectly understandable you should feel fatigued. This is Carys by the way, and will be your lady-in-waiting, as I am reliably informed, you do not have one of your own.'

Maud looked at Carys for a moment and saw a woman she judged to be in her mid twenties, she must have been handsome once, but bore an unsightly puckered red scar across her face. Lady Mortimer went and stood beside Carys.

'Carys is a survivor of the siege of Kidwelly; her father was the castellan there. He suffered many losses, including the death of his wife and the wounding of his daughter, but gallantly managed to hold off the marauders until help arrived.' Maud noticed Carys had turned her face away at Lady Mortimer's words. Her reaction had gone unnoticed by the speaker.

Then, without waiting for any comment Lady Mortimer rose, 'If you prefer to have your supper sent up to your room, then I shall inform the serving maid.'

Maud nodded grateful at the suggestion.

'Until the morrow, where I shall introduce you to members of the household.' She walked over stooped and dropped a kiss on Maud's cheek, wished her God night, and left her alone with Carys.

'It is daunting is it not to come among strangers?' Cary's voice was full of sympathy.

'I met Lord and Lady Mortimer some years ago but ......' Maud hesitated, 'yes I must admit I am somewhat apprehensive.'

'You will find a mixture of Welsh, English, Norman, and Gascons here, and a constant flow of soldiers coming and going. It is a busy place, and like everywhere, good and evil live side by side.'

Just then the door opened and a young servant entered carrying a tray of steaming food and a jug of wine.

'Come now enjoy your supper my lady and afterwards, have an early night in readiness for the coming day.' Maud duly obliged and with the knowledge that Carys was to sleep close by, she ate her supper with relish and afterwards gained a good night's sleep.

The following morning the wind had changed and instead of a chilly easterly, it blew from the South, bringing showers. By the time Maud had rubbed the sleep from her eyes, she spied a tub of hot, sweet smelling water, waiting in readiness for her morning bath. Carys had also laid out a kirtle of dark green wool, along with matching slippers and hose.

'I wasn't sure of your headdress my lady so waited for your own choice.'

'Thank you! I usually wear my hair unadorned during the day, I simply have two thin plaits joining in the centre at the back of my head held by a jewelled hairpin to keep them in place, it helps to keep the rest of my hair out of my eyes.'

'Most effective with such glorious coloured hair it would be a pity to hide it!' Carys hummed as she helped wash and dry Maud. The de Braose girl was truly beautiful, with fine skin as clear as the Welsh mountain waterfalls. But Carys made no comment as she finished drying Maud's long, thick tresses.

Once dressed Maud made ready for the forthcoming introductions, glad Lady Mortimer would be at her side as she met the men and women who made up the Mortimer household; no-one present guessed at the apprehension from the new arrival as she walked down the rows of men and women, head held high, pausing only when Lady Mortimer stopped to give more detail of certain more prominent members of staff.

Maud also noted the dark figure of Lord Rhys standing near the doorway; she would soon discover he never moved far from Lady Mortimer's side. The Lady herself turned to the assembled company her voice clear.

'Now you have met the future wife of Lord Roger I expect you all to obey Lady Maud as you do the family, for one day she will be mistress of Wigmore.' She waved her hand in dismissal and as they trooped out of the Great Hall she beckoned the line of waiting squires.

'Ah! This group of young men who are at present learning their knightly duties here at Wigmore and as you well know, part of their education includes their social graces.' She turned to Maud and smiled 'and here in future, I look to you my lady, for your assistance. They are a lively and often unruly bunch, but feel certain you are perfectly capable of keeping them in order.'

Maud was aware of the nudges and grins from some of their numbers as they were presented individually.

'I fear you will have most trouble with the de Grey boys.' Lady Mortimer whispered as she looked sternly toward two of the younger members of the assembly. 'Sadly, encounters with the whip appear to have no effect, so maybe you are in possession of better methods of control.'

Maud nodded, 'I'm sure I know *many* ways of dealing with naughty boys.' The older woman looked at her with a half smile on her face.

'Did you hear that? It would appear your reign of misrule is at an end.'

The culprits smirked at each other but they felt no fear, de Greys' could surely outwit a mere girl and a de Braose one at that! The invisible gauntlet had been thrown down, and it was to be a battle of wits and determination and one, Maud knew she had to win to gain respect in her new position at Wigmore.

As the squires filed passed Maud the tongues of the two de Grey boys both bobbed out at her but as quick as a flash she put her foot out causing the older boy to trip and fall, his brother toppled over him. Maud's expression did not change as she managed to maintain her composure. The incident caused a ripple of mirth which ran through the group and followed and the red faced boys escaped, both swearing silent vengeance on Maud's head.

'I see you are perfectly equipped to deal with those troublesome youths; they are as much a thorn in my side as is their father, are they not my Lord Rhys?'

'True my lady, if I had my way ......' his words trailed off as Lady Mortimer gave him a warning glance.

'If I left them to your punishment I believe they would be returned to their father in pieces big enough to feed to the hawks.'

Maud grinned at Lord Rhys, 'I am in complete agreement with you my lord.' The normally sober expression of Lady Mortimer's chamberlain relaxed into the nearest thing to a smile he was known to have and nodded in Maud's direction.

When Maud recounted the scene to Carys she too showed her approval.

'You little realise what a significant and clever move that was my lady, for Lord Rhys shows little approval towards anyone, for not only has the ear of Lady Mortimer but also holds sway on many of her decisions and his authority throughout Wigmore is unchallenged.'

'Exactly what position does he hold?' Maud looked enquiringly at her lady-in-waiting.

'I know of no exact title but believe chamberlain, bodyguard, and advisor are all appropriate. He accompanied the young Princess on her marriage. It is rumoured her father placed her safety in his hands and that is the extent of my knowledge of the man.' She paused then continued. 'He is a very private person; no-one knows if he has relatives, where he comes from even, he keeps himself very much aloof from the rest of us. His whole life is dedicated to the service of Lady Mortimer and there is no doubt he would die for her without a second thought.'

'Lady Mortimer must trust him completely.'

'Oh! Indeed she does.'

'So, I have made two enemies and a possible one ally today.'

'Watch out for both is my humble advice, the de Grey boys are sly and loathsome, whilst the Lord Rhys, is ever watchful.'

'Thank you Carys does this mean I can count on your loyalty?'

'I merely obey Lady Mortimer who bade me serve you to the best of my ability, which is what I shall do my lady.'

'I respect honesty.'

'As do I my lady, now let me show you around the Castle of Wigmore.'

Maud followed Carys as she guided her through the corridors and passageways of the place which would one day, be her domain. It was impressive in its dimensions but within the grey ashlar walls were many comfortable chambers, denoting a home as well as a fortress. The Great Hall was at the Castle's heart and as they passed through, there were house-carls busily clearing away stale floor rushes and sweeping up the discarded bones. A small boy was laying the fire, as another, stacked huge logs in readiness for when the fire was lit. Two women were scrubbing the long trestle tables whilst a couple of young men polished the great carved armed chairs which stood at either end of the table, these were used by the Mortimer family and honoured guests.

Carys nodded a perfunctory greeting as they passed, ignoring the many curious stares as she directed Maud on towards the kitchens and sculleries.

'To the right is the laundry, on the far side are the stables you will easily find the brew-house; in the castle is the bake-house and kitchens, just follow the smells, and talking of smells, the odour heap is just along the outer walls and wreaks when the weather his hot and over there, out of sight are the dungeons. The soldiers quarters are near the keep, she pointed to a row of low roofed buildings which ran parallel to the curtain wall.

'The gardens are round this corner' and as they turned Maud saw neatly laid beds with flowers and herbs all carefully tended. There were a few arbours set beside weed free pathways, and roses and honeysuckles trailed over a variety of archways.

'This must be lovely in summer.' Maud's voice was full of approval.

'Yes they are delightful, but there is precious little time to enjoy them I fear, as Wigmore is in constant readiness for war.'

'Surely things must be easier since Llewellyn's death? Prince Dafydd signed a Treaty with the king only two years ago and he even made him his heir last October, does that make no difference?'

'Treaties or, whatever piece of parchment is signed, does not change the perspectives of the people of Wales. Only last week two of our men were killed in an ambush as they travelled from one of the outposts. This is a Marcher stronghold where peace is rarely enjoyed, but then you were raised in similar circumstances, were you not?'

Maud merely nodded she was not yet ready to share any of her childhood memories with her servant.

'Pray tell me, what is the hunting like hereabouts?'

Carys looked up and noted the set features of the girl, and understood the change of mood.

'Excellent, as you would expect my lady; the forest is full of game, venison, and boar. Recently, a pack of wolves has been causing the villagers problems and there have been reports of the loss of chickens, geese and even young lambs and goats.'

There tour was interrupted by a heavy shower of rain and they quickly re-traced their steps back to Maud's apartments. Later that day Maud received a summons from Lady Mortimer whom she found sitting at her desk.

'I'm at odds with this menu, maybe you can be of help.'

Maud felt pleased at the request, and went and sat in the seat which had been placed for her by the ever present Lord Rhys.

'May I ask how many people are expected, when is the event to take place, and if it is formal or an informal banquet.'

'You see, Rhys; our young daughter to be, has an instant grasp of the matter.'

'Well, as you are aware my husband and many of the other Marcher lords recently left for France with the king, I thought to take this opportunity to introduce you to the younger members of their families after all, they will be the ones who will make up the majority of your future social circle. I have invited about two score or so, but know, not all will be able to attend. As for the date, a month from today as the daylight hours will be lengthening and weather more clement for travelling. Therefore, the occasion must be viewed as informal.' Lady Mortimer looked up at Maud.

'Is that sufficient information?'

Maud nodded. 'Then how about venison, goose, chicken, and wild boar; I believe your forests have an abundance of both venison and boar. Spiced mutton and beef, and baked carp.'

Lady Mortimer turned to Lord Rhys, 'that sounds a good basis don't you think my lord?'

'Indeed my lady.'

Maud was uncertain whether she was being patronised but held her thoughts in check.

'Then instruct the huntsmen we shall require at least six stags and dozen boars, which we will need immediately, so the meat can hang.'

Silently Lord Rhys left the chamber and Lady Mortimer patted Maud's hand.

'Now we are alone there is a subject I wish to broach without any interruptions.' Maud looked enquiringly at the older woman.

'It concerns my son, Roger.' She hesitated before continuing and Maud realised she was searching for the right words.

'I will be quite blunt; Roger is not possessed with the most equable temperament and I think you should be in possession of this fact. However, I have tried to instil in my children the values of my own people, where women are treated with respect and hold a more honoured position than in England and although they do possess such status this does not extend in law to the matter pertaining to the ownership of land.' She paused and looked earnestly at the listener. 'Sadly, it does fail us where ownership of land is concerned, and leaves us without any redress on that issue, unlike the laws of England.'

Maud noted the sharp edge to Lady Mortimer's voice. 'However, I digress; returning to the matter of my son. I have never witnessed anything but deference and politeness but, I am his mother, and would countenance nothing less.' Before she could expand further on the subject they were interrupted by the click of the door latch which silenced Lady Mortimer and when Lord Rhys re-entered he found the two women leaning over the growing menu. Maud rose, made a curtsey and in a soft voice.

'I hope I have been of some help my Lady.....and.....thank you for your confidence.'

'I can see you will be a great help and know I shall come to count on you in the future. Do not hesitate to come to me with *any* problems you may be uncertain how to deal with.'

'Thank you!' As Maud left the impressive chamber she felt she had gained a valuable ally in the dignified Welsh Princess. She smiled as she walked back to her own apartments, she had grasped the implications of Lady Mortimer's warnings but if Roger Mortimer believed he could easily subdue his future wife, he was in for a very rude awakening. The crux of the matter would be to learn how to handle their relationship with subtly; not easy for one of Maud's disposition. As Maud continued towards her apartment, she felt apprehensive about her forthcoming marriage. Unaware of the conversation between Lady Mortimer and her confidant.

'Well my lord, your suggestion of seeking the help of young Lady Maud appears to have had the desired effect.' Lady Mortimer smiled up at her Welsh chamberlain.

'I believe so, and I am certain it will help her to feel she is gaining a valid position in the family.'

'Indeed! Now let us prepare for the morrow and discover what crisis the two tenants from Leintwardine have seen fit to bring to our attention.'

Over the coming days Maud was kept busy with the forthcoming arrangements, discussing dishes and menus with the cooks, she realised the experience in her own mother's household, now proved invaluable, and quickly earned the respect of the kitchen staff. So, instead of time weighing heavily upon her hands, Maud found the days too short and the preparations quite absorbing and to her surprise, the feeling of satisfaction in her new found authority, was much to her liking.

However, not the entire household was happy with the new arrival and during this time Maud was frequently harassed by Reginald de Grey, the older of the two de Grey brothers, who reigned insults in her direction at every opportunity but one day, he once more found himself the loser, when Maud sent him packing after she had boxed his ears for his impudence.

'Do not waste your energies on trying to outwit a de Braose, for I promise, *you* will come off the worse and gain a dangerous adversary into the bargain. Remember, you are but a mere squire here, whilst I shall be Mistress one day.'

He ran off, carrying not only his wounded pride but also a feeling of embarrassment for the scene had been witnessed by a number of the house-carls who were delighted in witnessing one of the hated brothers get their come-uppance. The news quickly spread throughout the Castle of Wigmore and eventually came to the ears of its Chatelaine, Lady Mortimer.

'Well it continues to appear we have a promising future mistress of Wigmore, does it not my lord?'

Lord Rhys merely nodded but knew an important precedent had been set and that Lady Maud's standard had been raised, albeit an invisible one. Nevertheless, he acknowledged this to be an important move. With the de Grey youths nursing their grievances in resentful silence, the Wigmore servants were left in no doubt that to challenge the young Lady de Braose, would be an unwise move.

The day of the feast drew ever closer and Maud, although outwardly calm and in control, inwardly felt quite the opposite, for in her own mind her reputation rested on the success of the occasion. Her nerves were as taut as a bow string but when she learned that her future husband, the young Roger Mortimer was also expected to attend, it brought a whole new edge to the event. It was during this fraught period, Maud turned to Carys for support and was not left wanting, her many unobtrusive suggestions and sound common sense were invaluable and instead of feeling totally alone, Maud now felt she had gained a useful ally.

Lady Mortimer felt satisfied with her decision to allow Maud to take control and just left Lord Rhys to surreptitiously observe the organisational skills of the young woman who would one day rule the Wigmore household. His daily reports left Lady Mortimer in no doubt her tactical scheme to give her future daughter-in-law a role of importance and standing, would achieve her ultimate aim of gaining Maud's sense of loyalty, and loyalty was the watchword in the tumultuous Marches.

The day before the feast, a fast riding party galloped up the sloping ground and entered the high arched gate of Wigmore Castle. Roger Mortimer dismounted and ran to where his mother stood on the steps before the heavily studded door to the Great Hall. Maud positioned herself well back, watching the affectionate greeting between mother and son. She studied the boy who would, in a few years, become her husband, and noted the thatch of dark unruly hair; his square frame bore little resemblance to that of his tall elegant father. Lady Mortimer turned and beckoned to Maud and she stepped forward and curtseyed but she neither lowered her head or, her gaze. The young couple stood for a moment and studied each other before either spoke.

'Roger, may I present the Lady Maud who has been a Godsend in organising tomorrow's feast.' Lady Mortimer's face hid her true feelings of apprehension at this all crucial meeting. Without any preamble Roger held out his hand and shook Maud's vigorously.

'My dear, you should kiss her hand *not* shake it!' Roger flushed and dropped Maud's hand as if it were a burning ember. Maud smiled, 'I see you have yet to begin your courtly lessons in etiquette.' She noted how the black eyes flashed a warning until he realised Maud was merely teasing him whereby he nodded, a flush of colour spread across his features.

The party moved into the cool interior of the Great Hall, servants were busily laying refreshments onto the trestle tables. Lady Mortimer turned to her son.

'Go and wash the filth of the road from your hands and face and change your riding attire.' As the sturdy youth trotted off he grabbed a cup of small beer and quaffed it down in one, burping loudly as he went.

'Oh! Dear, my son is not known for his delicate manners I am afraid, my years of schooling appear to have been in vain.'

'I think your son is doing it for my benefit. He is trying to shock me!'

'You know, I do believe you could be right.' Lady Mortimer's smile was full of warmth as she patted Maud's arm, 'I can see my son will be no match for his future wife.'

Maud's instinct about the young Mortimer was correct for, he never missed an opportunity to try and alarm her or, those around him. Later that day when Maud found herself and Roger out of earshot of the main party she whispered:

'I see I shall have to hone your tuition in the finer art of courtly behaviour.'

His response was neither subtle, nor discreet, but loud enough for the rest of the company to hear.

'Well – there is something you could take in your hand and it is naught to do with behaviour.' There were sounds of laughter from his attendants, at Mortimer's bawdy words.

'Maybe you have nothing of real size to warrant such a boast!'' Maud's retort was sharp but she raised her eyebrow as she spoke. Again a splutter of mirth at the exchange from the onlookers.

'Pray do not forget, I shall be your Master ere too many months have passed and then you will feel my wrath on your buttocks.' The black eyes glittered with venom as he spoke.

'And you think such '*sweet*' words of courtship will endear me to you? Believe me Master Mortimer, if you *ever* raise a hand in violence against me I give you fair warning, it will be your last.'

There was a hushed silence as the air around the couple crackled in expectation.

'Tell me, how will you excuse such un-chivalrous actions which *could* result in the loss of so much land and wealth to the Mortimer's? Especially if I refuse to marry you? It would undoubtedly heap shame on your family and all because of your uncouth behaviour and undisciplined words?'

She waved her hand around the company. 'There are too many witnesses for you to ever try and deny what you have just said, sirrah!'

The couple now circled each other and Maud knew if she did not win this contest of words her life would be unbearable. She held his gaze unflinchingly and her countenance denoted no fear.

'Come! Let me be a good friend not, your adversary. Remember, one day your life may depend on me.' She hesitated before continuing. 'You have to admit I would be within my rights to walk away from this marriage contract after such churlish behaviour.' She turned and spoke to those closest to her 'you all heard Master Mortimer's threats, did you not?'

There was murmurings, some members of the group turned and walked out not wishing to be drawn into what may prove a difficult situation for their future, especially now as loyalties came in to question.

Then suddenly, Mortimer tipped back his head and laughed out loud.

'Methinks I won that jape.'

'A dangerous jape Master Mortimer, I urge you not to forget *my* words for they were in deadly earnest, abuse me at your peril.' With that Maud turned on her heel and walked out, her heart beating so loudly she thought those close to her would hear it.

No-one noticed the dark figure of Lord Rhys who had been standing at the rear of the group as he slipped silently away to the sound of Mortimer's nervous laughter. This unfortunate incident must be reported to his Mistress immediately; the unseemly conduct of her son was unforgiveable and Roger's threat was one he knew must be dealt with in the most forceful manner, to safeguard the future of the Mortimer's. Should any ill befall the Lady Maud, it would undoubtedly bring down the wrath of her powerful family who, he had no doubt, would wreak certain vengeance, thus bringing the Mortimer name into public disrepute; a situation to avoid at all costs.

Later that evening at the Feast, Maud who was seated beside Lady Mortimer, with Roger on the other side, noted his expression was one of circumspection. Lady Mortimer called for silence before introducing Maud to the assembled guests as they acknowledged her presence in the accepted manner. After grace was said, the delicious feast began and the murmur of voices mingled with the clatter of knives and goblets. The trenchers were filled repeatedly with the tasty fayre and the occasion appeared to be enjoyed by everyone with the exception that is, of the Mortimer heir, who chewed his food as if he were eating a mouthful of maggots. The music and revelry continued far into the night. Maud tried to remain calm as she knew she was the focus for all the curious stares and comments. Although many names of the Marcher families were familiar to her, she was not acquainted with some of those present, due to the fact they were the younger members of their respective houses, but would make it her business to discover the characters and their standing in the Mortimer hierarchy. She had also noted the looks of open admiration from many who attended, which boosted her morale.

During the evening Lady Mortimer introduced Maud to each of the guests individually but there were too many for her to remember them all however, the names which were already familiar to her were Giffard, LeStrange, Clifford, Harley, and de Lacy names she would become acquainted with more closely over the coming years.

On the morning following, both Maud and the young Lord Mortimer were summoned to the private solar of Lady Mortimer. Without any preamble she began, 'It has come to my ears that you have behaved disrespectfully towards Lady Maud, is this true?' She looked expectantly towards her son. Before he could speak Maud stepped forward.

'My Lady, methinks your son has been somewhat maligned it was merely a boyish battle of one up-man-ship, is that no so?' She turned and looked meaningfully at Mortimer who was only too willing to seize the line of excuse Maud had cast him, although he resented the term, 'boyish'.

'I do not believe for one moment there was any real harm intended I, for one certainly did not see it so.' Maud hoped her lie had gone undetected.

Lady Mortimer studied the pair before her, and as if to endorse Maud's words Roger had taken a step closer to her and they stood side by side. Maud reached for his hand; he looked at her, his startled expression quickly turning to one of undisguised gratitude.

'What shall we do with them, my lord?' Lady Mortimer looked uncertainly towards her chamberlain but inwardly felt a rush of relief at Maud's defence of her son. The girl's quick witted response had instantly covered her son's guilt by making little of his appalling behaviour. In that single act, Maud had not only gained Lady Mortimer's respect but, also that of the erring culprit.

'Come, let this unfortunate incident serve to unite the Houses of Mortimer and Braose so they can go forward in harmony; there are too many enemies without to have warring factions within, is there not?'

The sombre words of Lord Rhys brought clarity to the seriousness of the situation and the adverse affect the young heir's foolish behaviour could have upon the whole household. His statement found favour with Lady Mortimer who nodded her agreement.

'I can always count on your sound judgement my lord.' She turned to the couple.

'Do you both see the importance of a united front?' She looked hard into the serious faces of her son and his future wife.

In unison they both answered: 'Yes.'

'Then here and now let me hear you make your apologies and promise from this day forward if you wish to disagree with each other, do it out of earshot of prying ears.'

Then reaching for her well worn bible she said in low tones.

'Do you Roger Mortimer, heir to the barony of Wigmore and son of the Lady Gwladus Mortimer, swear to be loyal and uphold the safety and honour of the Lady Maud de Braose, from this day forward and to the end of your days?'

Roger Mortimer hesitated for a long moment but then took a deep breath and raised Maud's hand to his lips before repeating the oath. The gesture was not a natural one and she noted the flush on his dark cheeks as he spoke. Maud looked straight into his dark hooded eyes and repeated the oath, bowing her head as her words ended.

'There! No more battle of words or gamesmanship do you hear me, it is important to portray a united front to the world however much disagreement there may be between you in private; discuss any differences of opinion without rancour and you may find it can prove beneficial exercise. Disputes are an everyday occurrence but it is how they are perceived by others which counts and how this family is judged, reputation is everything and therefore vital. Mortimer's are renowned for their loyalty to each other and if ever that is threatened, then our very existence here is threatened, never forget my words either of you!' She turned her gaze directly towards her young son.

'You owe your thanks to Lady Maud, who has seen fit to defend you in this instance. However, I think you should be made to pay some form of forfeit but know this, I am disappointed that you did fail to show your future bride the respect she is entitled to especially,' she paused, 'as I have try to instil the values of your Welsh heritage as to the status women hold within the laws of the people. Also, what of the code of knighthood; have your learned *nothing* of chivalry during your years as a squire? You are my first born son and should uphold the values you have been taught. If your father were to hear of this incident, you know full well what your punishment would be, so go now, and let me rest for I am quite wearied by this unlooked for contrariness.'

Lady Mortimer turned her back on the young couple but Roger went and kissed his mother's hand and as he returned, gave Maud a wicked wink. For her part Maud hoped she had managed to win favour from both parties and as she curtsied she cast a glance across at Lord Rhys and saw him nod. Was his nod one of approval, if so, then she had triumphed for, not only had she won the gratitude from both Mortimer's but had also gained respect from the important and trusted advisor to Lady Mortimer, and she instinctively knew this could prove beneficial in the future. Maud felt elated for she knew her reputation within the Mortimer household had risen significantly by her quick thinking. As the couple left the chamber Roger hissed.

'I suppose I must now make you a personal apology?'

'I do not wish to listen to a mouthful of worthless words.' Maud glared back at him as she spoke. They walked on in silence before Mortimer spoke again.

'I know what my mother said was true and that I did dishonour you,' he bowed his head as they continued to walk and Maud knew he was struggling to give voice to his true feelings.

Maud reached out and touched his sleeve.

'If you wish to make amends and prove you are my true knight, would you be willing to carry out a task for me?' His dark eyes narrowed as he looked at her guardedly.

'What sort of *task?*'

'Well, the eldest de Grey has also shown me scant respect, in truth, no respect at all, and although I have sent him off with a flea in his ear on occasions; think he is over prideful and should be made to pay. If *you* were to call him out – and challenge his disrespectful behaviour towards me it would prove not only you were truly sorry but, also demonstrate to the rest of the household you will not allow anyone to treat me in like manner. Thereby proving to disrespect me would bring down the wrath of my future husband. Honour would then be satisfied on all fronts.'

She stopped and faced him, just then a young page ran past, they remained where they stood until he reached the far end of the long passageway, then a door opened and closed with a bang, leaving them alone again.

A slow grin spread over the boy's face.

'I have been looking for an excuse to take issue with either of the de Grey brothers and to do it to serve the honour of a Lady, would give me the greatest pleasure.'

'Does that mean you will?'

'Indeed.'

'And will you let me know so I can bear witness.'

'Of course!'

She clapped her hands, 'splendid! Methinks we could prove a formidable couple if we apply ourselves to the matter.'

The young Mortimer nodded, his thatch of black hair glistening as a shaft of sunlight fell on a lock of hair which had fallen across one eye. Maud felt triumphant that she had found a way to avenge her pride on the de Grey youth and also, bring about a kind of affinity with her future husband. It was the first steps to establishing an unassailable position within the Mortimer hierarchy. The couple took their leave of each other and as she entered her chamber, saw Carys busily picking up her discarded stockings; she stopped and looked up at her young Mistress.

'You looked well pleased with yourself my lady.'

'I am Carys; I believe this has been an important day, for I have found a way to bring the insolent de Grey to heel by invoking the aid of young Lord Mortimer.' Maud gave no details and she knew Carys would not ask any questions on how this had been achieved.

'For what it is worth, I would place scant reliance upon the word of Lord Roger, sadly he has inherited some of the more dubious traits of the family and few of his mother's finer ones, I fear.'

Her words came as a shock to Maud for Carys had never previously spoken a word against any member of the Mortimer family. She didn't look up but continued: 'I learned long ago not to place too much faith in men - even less on the *word* of young Lord Roger.' Maud looked under her lashes at the woman who was still an enigma to her.

'Why so bitter?'

Carys stopped her task and looked directly at the speaker; the sunlight was cruelly highlighting the scarred face which once had undoubtedly been handsome.

'I have witnessed many of his covert acts of spite; he taunts those who are unable to defend themselves and often treats the servants shamefully, but always out of sight of either his parents or tutors, not an honourable boy at all.' She then bent to continue gathering the brightly coloured stockings for the laundry bag.

'I believe his mother is aware of his faults and does everything she can to change them but even she is blind to his real nature, for I am certain the truth would break her heart.'

Maud was quite taken aback by the stark words as Carys had never previously been given to any intimate revelations.

'Why are you telling me this now?'

'Because,' Carys hesitated. 'I have judged you to be strong enough to know the truth and therefore can arm yourself against his wily ways. My loyalty is to his mother and ......also, now to you, for I can foresee it will be you who will ride the whirlwind of his actions once he becomes Lord of Wigmore, if he does not change his ways.'

Maud walked over to where Carys was standing and kissed her scarred cheek. The woman blanched at first then dropped a curtsey.

'Thank you Carys, at last I believe I have found a true ally here at Wigmore.'

'Oh! The Lady Mortimer will also be your friend but where her beloved children are concerned you must realise, like many doting mothers, there is a blind spot. No doubt you will understand that better when you yourself become a mother.'

Maud turned away not wanting her expression to be witnessed by her servant.

'By your comments I feel you have obviously fallen foul of Roger's cruel tongue have you not?'

'Oh! I learned to live with my disfigurement some years ago and have developed a thick skin where abuse is concerned; I am well able to defend myself from such taunts. No! It is not from personal spite or revenge I have spoken thus but, feel you deserve to be in possession of the facts about young Lord Mortimer - to be forewarned is to be forearmed, is that not so my Lady?'

'Indeed it is Carys, indeed it is!'

Maud's former mood of elation had been tempered by her servants warning words. But Maud was not downcast for long for she realised an important step of trust had been reached between herself and Carys and this new found understanding was a great comfort. Now she was primed with valuable information with regards to some members the Mortimer family; common sense told her, in the future such knowledge would be vital. She would endeavour to encourage the best in the young Lord Mortimer whenever the opportunity arose for he was after all, still quite young.

Now she was in possession of some personal facts regarding her Mortimer family she felt it was also imperative to learn more about the Marcher lords she had met last night; which of them would prove reliable and which, were more likely to be self serving. Loyalty was paramount and Maud was quickly learning that treacherous men, who gave hollow oaths of fealty with scant regard to either the king or, country were not unique. There were many, in every rank of society, whose sole purpose was to serve their personal ambitions. As a daughter of Eva Marshal, Maud knew full well that it was her own strength of character which would prove her greatest weapon in times of peril.

Armed with this wealth of knowledge, Maud knew she must apply herself to another matter in hand - her future, not only with regards the Mortimer family members but also, to discover which of the servants, would prove efficient and trustworthy and who were the ones to watch; the ones who would try and undermine her position. She smiled to herself, she felt more confident of her abilities in that direction. Maud judged the day to have been most worthwhile on all fronts and she could go forward laying the foundations for her future role in the knowledge, she had now gained a valuable ally.

However, it was during the hours of night when Maud's confidence began to ebb away and she was beset by doubts. In the darkness, her thoughts strayed to the time she had spent with Guy de Longeville and she longed for the strength of her lover. The very memory of his kiss, his touch, never failed to evoke such powerful emotions within her. She loved everything about him; the timbre of his voice; the sound of his laughter for her Guy, was everything she desired. His honourable reputation as a knight, the unstinting loyalty he showed to his patron; added to which, he also held her undying trust.

But, even as her memories ran free, Maud realised such thoughts could prove dangerous, she must learn to hold such secrets to herself and trust no-one with the truth; she would have to learn to live within the constraints of an arranged marriage, her whole life would depend upon it. She struggled with the facts but knew it was essential to accept the situation now or, forever be imprisoned within the torments of a divided loyalty. The burning question was, did she have the courage to uphold her vows to the Mortimer's, when the time came? The thought tortured her, although she knew this love she felt for de Longeville would last a lifetime and never doubted its honesty but could the passage of time dim his feelings towards her? Was she truly willing to uphold the vows of a marriage she would never honestly feel, in order to restore her family name? Only time and circumstances would reveal the answer.

In her next letter to Nell, she gave details of all the incidents which had occurred since her arrival at Wigmore but omitted to confess she had doubts about the character of her future husband, which left her somewhat ill at ease. She also omitted to say she had received word from Izzy and sensed an underlying warning but as yet, the root cause was unclear. How could she explain to her youngest sister, these sudden feelings of foreboding? The destiny of the Braose sisters lay in the hands of God and Maud prayed fervently, that he would give them the strength to withstand whatever trials they would all face.

CHAPTER XIII

1246

Guy de Longeville knelt in silence as he listened to the voices of the choir. He did not look up as the coffin passed and he remained locked in his own thoughts, until he eventually became aware of the priest loudly clearing his throat. He stood up, a signal for the burial service to begin. He could still scarcely believe that his child like wife was dead; she had simply tripped over whilst playing with her servant and fallen down a flight of stone steps, breaking her neck in the accident. So swiftly, so simply, her tiny flame of life snuffed out, with less effort than it took to snuff a candle flame.

His emotions were in turmoil, being both deeply saddened by her death but also, acknowledging a sense of secret relief. It left him feeling guilty and remorseful in equal measures. Exactly what would this 'freedom' mean to his life now? It changed nothing as far as his vow to his brother-in-law Comte Etienne de Vivonne was concerned. However, it did make him financially independent of his patron, now he would be at liberty to take complete control of the greater part of his late wife's wealth; something he had refused to do whilst she lived, leaving all financial matters to be dealt with by her brother.

But it was not only this new turn of fate which caused him so much mental anguish but also the path his brother-in-law had recently taken becoming ever more embroiled in the political scene not only here in France, but also in England. The many journeys they had undertaken over the past few years either, on behalf of the French king or, the church; even some for the Dukes of France who had paid for his services. Guy knew he was in a dangerous position which would impact on his future and, should the Comte ever fall foul of one of his powerful masters, he would also be implicated, merely by association. The death of his little wife had brought home to him many truths; he had persistently refused to acknowledge but during the long funeral ceremony he reflected on the painful facts of his life.

After the long Requiem Mass, Guy received the condolences of his wife's family and neighbours. He felt as though he was in a trance, nothing seemed real, like some macabre play acted out before an audience of people he hardly knew or, for that matter cared for, with the exception of the Comte and his wife. His sister-in-law drew closer and whispered.

'Maybe you should look on this act of God as a blessed release. Poor Celeste was a dear, sweet child, but in her condition was never a real companion for you my lord. We all pray for her soul but feel sure she is now happy in heaven. The future my dear Guy, is yours.'

Guy smiled sadly and thanked her for her concern.

'At this moment, life is a mystery to me and what God's plans are, hold little comfort. I had not thought losing Celeste as a release.' He felt a pang of regret as he saw her expression change for she had taken his words as a reproof not as he meant them.

The long day finally ended as the last mourners left and Guy retired to his chamber. He flung himself onto the bed beset by memories. He reached for a wine flask and poured himself a drink. Unable to contemplate sleep he wandered out of the castle and towards the house where his erstwhile Mistress lived. He stood outside and looked up at her windows then hunched his shoulders and would have walked away when the door opened.

'I thought it was you my lord. Pray, come in,' for an instant he hesitated but then stepped into the doorway of the house he had known since his youth.

'I have no right to expect ....'

'You own this house – remember? Besides, although we are no longer lovers, surely friendship can serve as a more comfortable relationship?' She led him into the familiar surroundings and poured him a drink and handed it to him, then sat down opposite.

'You look ill my lord. You have taken your wife's accident hard.'

Guy remained silent for a long while:

'I feel my life is at a cross-roads and I am in danger of losing my way.'

'Death frequently has that effect. I felt thus when I learned that my husband had been slain; time is the great physician and heals many wounds. Come! Stay here tonight and after a good night's sleep you will feel more able to cope. There is no immediate necessity to make any decisions, why not give your-self some time to grieve before plunging back into the maelstrom of life.'

'You were ever a comfort ....' She moved to where he sat and folded her arms around him cradling him like a child.

'Do not be too kind .... or, I shall weep like a boy.'

'It will not be the first time my lord.' She whispered. 'Besides, tonight it is better to weep than try to fight your emotions.'

§

As Guy de Longeville's period of mourning began; across the English Channel events were moving inexorably towards the wedding day of Maud de Braose. However, Fate appeared to have other plans when news arrived which was to cause Maud more personal unhappiness as she learned of the sudden death of her mother, Eva Marshal, Lady of Abergavenny. It was such a shock, for Eva had appeared hale and hearty at their last meeting and all her letters were full of plans for various religious houses and improvements to her favourite residences.

The manner of Eva's death however, was quite bizarre. During the previous year Eva's huntsman had found an injured squirrel and had brought it back to the castle. Brother Edwin's healing skills had saved the injured animal whereby, Eva had subsequently taken it upon herself to oversee the tiny creature's recuperation. Over the weeks she had become so fond of it decided to keep it as her personal pet. She had a soft leather harness and silver chain made so she could carry the little animal around with her. One evening, when Eva had gone up to the parapet of Totnes Castle to watch a spectacular sunset, she had turned to hand the squirrel to her lady-in-waiting; the tiny animal had slipped its leash and ran off along the parapet. Eva, so fearful for its safety, had tried to re-capture it herself but as she leaned over the parapet in an attempt to entice it back, somehow, had overbalanced and fallen to her death.

To Maud, the whole incident seemed fantastical for she could not imagine her dignified mother being seduced by a tiny, furry squirrel. The loss hit her hard, even though they spent many months apart, Maud was aware of her mother's tireless efforts to safeguard the future of her daughters' and also, their Marshal and de Braose lands. Eva Marshal's reputation had proved formidable, and had gained the esteem of her male counterparts. Respected by all who knew her, especially by the king, and clergy. It had been mainly due to Eva's personal reputation that the shameful execution of William de Braose was now almost expunged but Maud recognised this was entirely, due to the substantial dowries the girls would take to their various husbands. This undeniable fact, endorsed by the illustrious names to which Eva, and her late brothers, had chosen for the marriages of the four de Braose sisters.

Life would never be quite the same again, for the enemies of the Marshal and de Braose families had long memories where grievances were concerned; not least of their number was Eleanor Plantagenet, widow of the late William Marshal, Earl of Pembroke and sister to the king. Eleanor now married to the ambitious but impoverished Earl of Leicester, Simon de Montfort, was pushing hard to overturn her late brother-in-law's dower settlement, if successful it would undoubtedly affect the inheritance of the four de Braose heiresses.

Maud could envisage the chain of protracted legal battles stretching far into the future but for now, she felt only a sense of deep personal loss. Her maternal uncles had frequently voiced their dissatisfaction with many of the king's decisions, especially the late Richard Marshal, who publicly opposed the king for failing to uphold the terms of the Magna Carta. Silenced only with his terrible death in Ireland, which she instinctively felt held more than a hint of royal treachery.

Although, the actual events had been laid firmly at the feet of the now disgraced and banished, Peter Roche, former Bishop of Winchester. Maud felt the whole incident had been too convenient not to smack of royal complicity. Even though Richard Marshal was long dead, all these facts Maud knew, would have an effect on her life, making her ever more mindful how important her Mortimer marriage now became. Their loyalty to the crown she saw as a buffer to her own vulnerable position. But for now, she must prepare to travel to Abergavenny in readiness to bury her mother.

The long ride enabled Maud to take control of her grief and upon her arrival she greeted her sisters with an outward appearance that belied her inner turmoil.

'Why Nell, you look so grown up and Eve, I can see you are with child and hope the journey was not too arduous.'

Maud turned to the stately Isabella, recently widowed, as her husband Dafydd ap Llywelyn, had died suddenly in February of that year.

'Forgive me for not attending Dafydd's funeral Izzy, but as you well know the weather made travel impossible.'

Isabella nodded. 'It has proved a very difficult time, Dafydd was a good man and I miss him greatly. But we must accept God's will.'

Maud knew those few words hid a depth of feelings.

'But for the moment let us not dwell on life's sadness for certain it seems this year is already marred by too many deaths. We must celebrate our reunion at least.' Maud tried to impart some of her gladness at seeing her sisters after so many months but by their expressions she knew they all felt their mother's death as keenly as she did.

After the Requiem Mass ended and the many condolences accepted and, long after the feasting ended; the four sisters gathered before the dying embers of the fire in the Great Hall. At first they sat unspeaking none wanting to break the silence. A log fell and showered sparks as it crackled into flames. It was Isabella who spoke first.

'The church teaches us that death is but the beginning of a life in Paradise and should be celebrated, not mourned. Why is it I feel 'tis the breaking of the chain and those who are left to mourn can find little solace in such words. First Dafydd, now Mama, do you believe God is punishing us? The words, *sins of the father* haunt my dreams of late.'

'I should not be burdened with such gloomy thoughts, in my condition.' Eve's face was etched with sorrow as she rose, gently rubbing her swollen belly.

'My husband bade me not to over tire myself therefore; I bid you God night sisters.' And without further ado, she left.

'You too look tired Nell.' Maud said looking at her younger sister. 'Maybe you should seek your bed as you do not want to appear on the morrow with dark smudges under your eyes - think of what Humphrey will say.'

'I know, but hate to leave for we see each other so infrequently and who knows when we shall meet again.'

Maud smiled sadly, 'At my wedding that is when!' She looked expectantly at Izzy as she spoke but could read nothing from the closed expression of her eldest sister.

'Then with that happier thought I will also retire for I do feel so weary.' She yawned as she spoke then looked guilty, 'pray forgive me.' She kissed Maud and Isabella and left the two older sisters looking at the glowering embers.

Silence fell again for awhile then Maud spoke in hushed tones.

'What will you do now Izzy?'

After a pause Isabella said softly, 'My fate has already been ordained by the king. I must retire from public life and end the rest of my days in Godstow Abbey. Dafydd's death has brought about a division in Wales. Already his cousins Owain and Gruffyd have taken on the mantle of 'Shield of Wales'.' As she spoke, Maud noted tears in her sister's eyes; she went and knelt before her putting her arms around her waist.

'No-one can ever take Dafydd's place, no-one. I loved him so but, failed in my duty as a wife to give him a son and heir.'

'Did he ever reproach you for that?' Maud gazed up into Izzy's face.

'Never!'

'Then if Dafydd did not hold you to blame so why punish yourself? Isn't his death punishment enough?'

'Yes! Oh yes!' And all the pent up grief and emotion spilled out and Maud held her sister's sobbing frame. The shadows in the Great Hall become darker as even the rush-lights began to flicker and fail; the servants had left the mourning sisters alone to share their sorrows.

When the spasm of grief subsided, Isabella looked at Maud.

'You must be prepared for enemies, especially in the Marches; men will smile but speak false words; trust no-one.' She hesitated before continuing. 'You are clever Maud, you must make yourself indispensable to your husband for Mortimer's are known to have played the treachery card in Wales, and will again, when it suits them. I know of Dafydd's fearful nightmares which he judged a forewarning of things to come.' She paused searching for the words to convey her late husband's premonitions.

'One night, about a year before he died, he woke dripping with sweat, trying to wipe himself and staring at his hands in disbelief. When I tried to comfort him he looked at me as though I were a stranger and just kept murmuring, *'the leopard has devoured the dragon; can't you see its blood? I could not save it!* He just kept repeating the phrase over and over again until eventually he realised where he was; that image remained with him. I know he placed little trust in the king, but do not believe it was of Henry he spoke of as the future enemy of Wales, but his growing son and heir, Edward. The English Earls and magnates are becoming ever more aggrieved with the king's persistent refusal to uphold the provisions of the Magna Carta, and Dafydd feared the Frenchman, who bears the title of Earl of Leicester and has now sided with dissenters. We both know our late uncle paid the ultimate price for his outspoken views.' She paused before continuing:

'This man Leicester is ambitious, ruthless, and single-minded, but an eloquent speaker. His religious fervour has earned him favour within the church, many of his friends are bishops and clergymen, and as we know, Rome holds great sway over men's minds as well as their souls. He has already opposed the king on issues of land and gold, therefore, if he becomes head of the Barons Party in opposing the king, then he could prove the catalyst at some point in the future for civil war. I pray that is not the case; it maybe the conflict between Wales and England will be the tinderbox to set the whole country on the path of outright war again, whichever way there will be a conflict of loyalties to come for many.' Her voice dropped to little more than a whisper.

'Mark my words, Dafydd was not a fanciful man and I have come to believe his premonition that the English Leopard will one day kill the Welsh Dragon.' The room went silent as she paused.

'They must believe those faithful to Dafydd may rally to me as Princess of Wales – hence my impending incarceration into a religious order. I have only been given leave to attend the funeral of our mother out of respect for her past services to the king.'

Maud did not speak immediately silenced by the seriousness of her sister's words.

'What you say is almost too much to comprehend but .... I concede, your sentiments holds more than a vestige of truth and your warning has merit and has struck a chord in my reckoning, especially with regard to de Montfort, who is sorely lacking in funds nevertheless, is successfully building his list of influential friends and among their number is I believe, Eve's husband and brother-in-law, who fall into the category of close allies.'

'Indeed, then be circumspect in what you say in front of Eve, for she appears to be completely under husband's thrall. Our cousin, Richard is also one to be wary of, for he now follows in the footsteps of his step-father, Richard of Cornwall. In that arrogant frame I see a frustrated monarch. Cornwall is all of those things plus, he is brutal, ruthless, and acquisitive and I feel certain that Aunt Isabel would have bewailed the transformation in her beloved son had she lived to see the drastic change in Richard under his step-father's influence.'

When Isabella paused, Maud said softly.

'No doubt Dafydd was privy to far more information than are we, but it is common knowledge that de Montfort falls in and out of the king's favour all too frequently.'

Isabella wiped her eyes. 'Ah! Yes that is true, but Eleanor Plantagenet will be the salve in any quarrel and she apparently, is besotted by her husband so will always seek her brother's absolution on his behalf. Remember, the country is the king and the king is the country; a weak king like Henry, spells disaster for his kingdom. As it stands, he holds neither the respect of his nobles nor for that matter, the French king, a dangerous precedence for our future methinks.'

Maud rose from her kneeling position and walked over to the fireplace she turned and looked thoughtfully at the seated figure of her beloved sister.

'Do you remember when we were children we called life, 'the game of adults'? Now as adults there is no 'game', only cruel reality. Why do I feel so fearful at your words? Is the reason you are sharing all this information on this occasion because, you believe you will not be allowed to attend my wedding? Therefore, it heralds a long period of separation?'

Isabella came and joined Maud before the smouldering ashes and they wept silently together locked in each other's arms.

'Now I must disappear from the Welsh hierarchy for the many reasons I have spoken of but also, for my personal safety, for as Dower Princess of Wales, I still command a substantial amount of power and even though I may not inherit my former dower territories and its income. As you know, Wales is riven by many factions who for awhile had united against the English crown but now they are already beginning to split asunder. Money and lands are always hard fought for and therefore to rid themselves of the late Prince of Wale's widow would smooth the path to power – or at least, that is how they will judge it! For my part, I wish only to retire and will endeavour to build an orphanage for the children whose fathers fought and died for Wales. I believe Dafydd would approve but to achieve this - I must survive to fund such a project, even from the depths of convent life.

There is also another matter upon which I wish you to have knowledge – my personal jewels, Dafydd warned me when he first fell ill and I secreted them away, as yet, I am unable to retrieve them but at some point will see they are forwarded to you.' Her dark eyes flashed as said defiantly: 'I will not see the family heirlooms fall into the hands of either side, they shall remain where they belong, with the de Braose daughters. I know you will distribute them fairly but, have a care what you give Eve.'

Maud remained silent for awhile: 'Will you write?' Concern was etched on her face as she spoke.

'I promise, it may be coded as my every move and letter will be monitored in future but first I must seek the help of the church if I am to achieve my goal of building an orphanage. However, I feel confident someone will assist me in this and find ways and means to allow me to achieve such an undertaking. I can always send my letters via the Franciscan friars who are allowed to travel freely as they spread the Word. Have no fear my dearest sister, I will keep in touch and by the grace of God, we will meet again sometime in the future.'

Maud hugged her sister and whispered.

'Not only have I lost a mother, now I am also faced with losing my beloved sister.'

Isabella drew away and looked deep into Maud's eyes as she said firmly, 'you will never *lose* me Maud, I shall pray constantly for your happiness and well being and as soon as I believe it is safe enough, we will meet again, be assured of that.'

With a parting kiss the sisters retired but Maud lay awake for many hours trying to come to terms with Izzy's words. Her heart was heavy for as she lay alone in the dark, felt far less confident that she would ever see her beloved sister again.

The following day as Maud took a tearful leave of her sisters, she rode many miles in silence, lost in thought. Her life had undoubtedly taken a giant step from the familiar into the unknown and she felt more than ever fearful of the future. If Izzy's predictions were correct, then the Marches could erupt once again into open warfare and the Mortimer family would be plunged into the heart of the conflict therefore, she too would become an integral part of it all, but her immediate fears were of her impending marriage, and how to overcome the inescapable fact she would have to lie with a youth she neither liked overmuch or, held no qualities which she could love. In her heart, it would mean betraying all she felt for de Longeville, this 'game of adults' was proving far more costly than she had ever envisaged.

CHAPTER XIV

Wigmore

Upon Maud's return to Wigmore she was faced by yet more disturbing events. It had been obvious for some time the health of Lord Mortimer was a cause for concern, especially to his wife, Lady Gwladus. Acutely aware of how her husband's indisposition affected the chain of command along the Welsh Marches, as it left the considerable forces under his control, without an experienced commander. She felt it was imperative to demonstrate her son, was now old enough to take his place at the head of the Mortimer troops; marriage would endorse his maturity to the world or, at least, that was how she assessed the situation. By bringing forward her son's wedding, Lady Mortimer felt certain it would give credence to the fact and demonstrate to the world, the heir to their family was no longer a boy but ready to take responsibility when called upon.

It may also be beneficial, under the circumstances, to have a wife who was more mature. It was therefore at the insistence of Lady Gwladus; her son's marriage was to be brought forward with some urgency. The intuitive move proved to be the right one for as feared, Lord Ralph's health deteriorated within days of his son's wedding and he died after suffering a seizure. Guests' who had so recently gathered to celebrate the union of Maud de Braose and Roger Mortimer, only a few short weeks before, now assembled to mourn the passing of a man who had been held in high regard by both by his peers on the Marches, and those who had served with him at court.

It was during this transitional period of mourning the true strength of Ralph Mortimer's widow became apparent, as she took charge with a quiet determination, her loyal chamberlain ever present at her side. Without fuss or confusion, she arranged the funeral of her husband and sent messengers to the king and the Marcher lords who had been unable to attend the wedding ceremony, now informing them of her husband's demise.

In her letter to the king, the widowed Lady Mortimer, urged swift action to confer the lordship of Wigmore on her son and thereby ensuring the continuity of Mortimer authority in the region. She put her own grief secondary in order to secure the future of her son.

Ralph, Lord Mortimer of Wigmore, was buried with all the solemnity his position dictated. Placed upon his coffin was his helm, spurs and gauntlets; his favourite charger had walked behind the slow funeral procession. Attending the service in Wigmore Abbey, were many of the Marcher Earls and barons, whose joint efforts over the past years had kept the warring Welsh at bay. Now they paid their respects to one of their own; any former personal grievances, at least for the period of the interment, were put aside. A number, promised to support Lord Mortimer's widow during her time of mourning but, Lady Gwladus knew how brittle were the words of ambitious men and took steps to ensure it would be her eldest son who retained control of the Mortimer lands and estates, rather than the king's commissioner.

During the meal in the Great Hall at Wigmore, the air was heavy and oppressive, as thunder threatened and flies plagued the many dishes of food. Maud nodded to where the Earl of Hereford sat, for she liked to goodly Earl and was pleased to see him again. He returned her acknowledgement with the merest inclination of his head but his expression denoted his pleasure at seeing her again. Her cousin, Richard de Clare, was also present but he had lost his former youthful innocence and the man who now sat at the Mortimer table that sultry evening, was greatly changed, and Maud gauged not for the better in fact, quite the reverse. His controversial marriage had ended with the death of his first wife, at his side sat his second wife, Maud de Lacy, daughter of John de Lacy, first Earl of Lincoln. As Maud studied the pale, faced young Countess, she became aware of her husband, who reached frequently for his wine cup, she leaned closer and whispered.

'I urge you not to over indulge yourself my lord, remember - a show of drunkenness would dishonour both your mother and your late father and I feel it would prove detrimental to your own reputation.'

Roger Mortimer gave her a glowering glance but did as she bade him, ignoring the filled cup for the remainder of the feast and she noted with relief, he sipped only small beer through the rest of the evening.

The storm finally broke as thunder echoed around the grey walls, flashes of lightening licked the hills and trees, accompanied by lashing rain. Sentries along the Castle walls tried to shrug off the deluge but failed to staunch the heavy rain drops as they trickled uncomfortably down their necks.

'Well his lordship is making a noisy exit that's fer sure.'

'The old bastard always made his presence felt as you can well testify Gil.'

The youth grinned as rain splashed across his broad brow. 'My back certainly bears the scars of a whipping or two.'

'You deserved it no doubt!'

The rest of their words were lost as the thunder roared ever louder echoing around the valley. Eventually the rain slowed to a shower and the storm moved across the skies towards Ludlow, Gil walked along the parapet to where his fellow guard stood.

'Wonder how the young lord will fare.'

'He's one to watch, not afraid to use his fists is he?'

The older man nodded.

'Only to be expected really as he will no doubt, continue the old man's legacy. The Plantagenet's bad blood is in his breeding after all; I can remember my father telling me of the evil deeds done by King John, on his watch!'

'God help us if that be the case!'

'What with that - the Welsh and the de Braose wench, we can look for some lively times ahead, as lively as tonight's storm methinks!' The two sentries chuckled as they continued their patrol.

Within weeks of Ralph Mortimer's death Maud knew she had fallen pregnant. She tried hard not to dwell on her marriage night or, the unwelcome emotions it evoked. Their first encounter in the bed chamber was when Maud had made it quite plain to her youthful spouse; she would not accept being tumbled like some tavern wench. When he tried to ignore her warning she had smacked him hard across the mouth at his vulgar retort. What followed had been a violent tussle which ended in a lustful coupling. Even the thought made her uncomfortable, the experience was one she wished to expunge from her memory. It had been a night of strenuous, physical violence. In truth, there was no love present throughout their first night, just raw, unadulterated lust.

The following morning when young Mortimer left to go hunting with his guests, Maud had remained, refusing to accompany him and when Carys had entered the chamber to bathe her mistress she found her in a state of utter distress. Without fuss Carys had poured some lavender oils into the steaming tub of hot water and encouraged Maud to get into the steamy depths. Gently she had washed the bruised and marked body and when Maud had relaxed a little she whispered:

'You must not allow anyone to see you like this my lady. The young lord will take it as a sign of his dominance.'

Maud had stopped her weeping for a moment and looked at the speaker.

'We both know, when you have recovered your composure you would rail against it but by then it would be too late. You have spirit and courage, now is the time to call on them and turn defeat into success. Tonight, when you sit at the table you must appear calm, assured and hospitable. Whatever it costs you personally to do this, it is a price you must pay or, lose any hope of gaining the upper hand in the bed chamber.'

Maud remained silent for a long time but the tears had ceased and she suddenly dipped her whole body beneath the water and when she emerged she leaned forward and kissed Carys on her cheek.

'You understand, maybe better than anyone, how I feel.'

'I do my lady, and the men who defiled me were brutes, cowards and little better than beasts, but it was the wise words of a nun, who gave me the strength to fight back and gain myself respect; later she contacted Lady Mortimer who took me in.'

Maud realised Carys was right, she must not allow her conscience or this feeling of self loathing to destroy her, even though she felt she had betrayed the memory of her lover, de Longeville but silently vowed to overcome this emotion and endeavour to put aside her feelings of shame.

Desperately she tried to analyse exactly what her marriage vows meant to her. They were the laws of man, church, and tradition, an undisputed fact, which she weighed against the love she had for the man she had dared to step outside convention for; but she felt no shame for the love she held for de Longeville. Besides, there was also another deep seated reason for her tortured thoughts; Maud felt she also carried the sin of her father's adultery and was desperate to prove not only to the world, but to herself, she was her mother's daughter. She must hold fast to the Marshal legacy of honour and not the de Braose one of shame.

Now, with this pregnancy, the conflict between duty and conscience caused bouts of melancholy, leaving Carys, her lady-in-waiting, at a loss as to know how to best deal with such dark moods. It was the invitation to the wedding of her sister Nell, which appeared to break the spell and Maud appeared to enjoy choosing her wardrobe and had an array of kirtles, gloves, mantles, coifs, cauls, jewellery, and shoes displayed, so she could pick her favourites for the occasion. She felt a surge of joy at the thought of seeing Nell again. The child she carried was restless and caused her much discomfort at times. She hated feeling so constrained by her condition but ignored the warnings of her mother-in-law who voiced her concerns about the impending journey which she knew could prove injurious to the unborn child.

'I know you will understand how important it is for me to attend my sister's wedding. It has lifted my spirits already - pray do not cast a shadow over my visit I beg you! Besides, is it not true that a happy mother makes for a happy baby?'

Maud's words caused Lady Mortimer to smile, her daughter-in-law was such a vivacious young woman, and she yielded to the request unable to thwart her appeal.

'Just promise you will make the journey in easy stages and *do* try not to over excite yourself.'

Maud clapped her hands 'You have my promise ...and.... thank you my lady!'

In just a few short days Maud passed through the gates of Wigmore Castle on the first stage of her journey to Hereford. Her spirits rose the further she travelled for she was eager to see her sister once more and catch up with all the news which had not been included in Nell's brief letters.

It had been decided that Roger and his mother would travel to London in order to obtain the king's signature endorsing his inheritance which had been granted in February of that year and if this could be accomplished quickly they would return by way of Hereford and escort Maud back to Wigmore. Maud was perfectly happy to fall in with these plans for it meant she would at least be unfettered from her husband's constant vigilance, a trait she found stifling and one she was determined to break err long.

Upon her arrival Maud felt tired but elated at the reunion and there were screams of delight from Nell as the sisters clung to each other in greeting.

'My, I never thought how pregnancy could change you so!' Nell stepped away from Maud and inspected the once slender figure. 'Even your face is fuller and the circled under your eyes...'

Maud held up her hand. 'Stop! Remember you may be in the state of pregnancy within a few short months by which time *I* shall be the one to make pertinent comments upon your appearance!'

Nell stood perfectly still for a moment, 'I know, and it frightens and excites me in equal measure but there is one big difference - I love Humphrey whereas, I know you do not feel any such love for your husband, is that not so?'

'I refuse to dwell on the matter and intend to enjoy every minute of this visit even though my sister's comments on my appearance are far from flattering.'

The two young women laughed, Maud felt happy for the first time in months and even refused to let her uncomfortable pregnancy ruin it. Nell eagerly ushered her into her chamber where two seamstresses were busily stitching the last adjustment to her magnificent mantle.

'No expense has been spared for the occasion. I intend to wipe out all the years of the late Countess's reign of spite and frugal expenditure.'

'Are you forgetting one small fact?' Maud looked intently towards her sister, 'the Earl will inevitable marry again as we know, both the king and queen are hardly likely to allow him any choice in the matter and will inevitably foist one of their kin upon him.'

'That would be such a pity for he certainly suffered greatly throughout that unhappy marriage and I feel he should have some say in the choice of his next wife.' Nell's bright features clouded at the thought. 'Hope she will be of a more amiable disposition than her predecessor.'

But the two sisters quickly forgot all thoughts of the Earl's future marriage along with their own misgivings on his behalf for there were far more pleasurable issues relating to the forthcoming ceremony to enjoy. When Maud finally entered her chamber she was greeted by the smiling face of Jane, her sister's lady-in-waiting, and without hesitation she hastened towards her and clasped her close.

'It is so good to see you once more. I owe you thanks for taking care of my sister so well since my departure, she has never looked healthier or lovelier, methinks!'

Jane blushed at such praise and hesitantly returned the embrace. 'I can scarce believe you are shortly to become a mother it .....it seems.....' She could not finish her sentence for she was uncertain how to express her feelings towards her former charge who was now a mature, married woman, large with child.

'I see by the dark circles under your eyes this child is not an easy one to bear.'

Maud nodded and moved towards the bed where she sat down heavily.

'It is the most energetic of babes and gives me precious little rest especially throughout the night. Almost from the first, I have felt unwell and although the physician assures me it is not unusual........' she frowned.

'Unusual or not, whilst you are in my care, I will endeavour to make your stay here a comfortable one. I believe I know someone who may be of help and will seek their advice on the matter once you are settled.'

'Oh! Jane, it is so good to be in your capable care once more. I have many servants and one who is especially kind and loyal, but somehow, I never feel *truly* at ease in the Mortimer household.' She looked at the young woman who was busily arranging Maud's clothes which she would be wearing that evening. 'Although, I would never admit the fact to another living soul.'

'And be assured your confidence is as safe with me as if the words had never been spoken.'

'If I ever doubted that I would never have uttered them.' Maud sighed and sank back into the soft pillows, 'I should like to rest now Jane; to tell the truth, I feel such an ungainly lump wobbling about and have yet to be reconciled to this *condition*.'

Jane smiled gently, then came over and removed Maud's shoes and began to rub her feet.

'This will help you to relax.' Maud was asleep within in minutes and Jane left the chamber to seek advice on how to aid the sleeping woman with her uncomfortable pregnancy.

Upon waking Maud found Jane busily finishing off the unpacking.

'Are you feeling refreshed my lady?'

'Indeed!' Maud stretched and was about to rise but Jane shook her head 'Just lie and rest a little longer there is no need for haste the feasting does not begin for another two hours so there will be plenty of time to dress. Besides, I have a tincture made up by the herbalist who swears that two drops of the mixture before bedtime will put the baby to sleep and thereby allowing you to have a restful night.'

'But will it harm the child?'

'No my lady, definitely not - the herbalist assures me he has used it for decades with the great success and no record of any detrimental affects to the unborn infants.'

'Thank you Jane! I appreciate your concern.'

The evening was a noisy, lively affair; the Great Hall was bedecked with fresh greenery and clean rushes; flickering candles arranged around the grey walls cast fanciful shadows which gave the effect that the walls were alive. The delicious smells of roast meats and spiced dishes plus, venison pies, baked carp, and game of every description, which enticed almost all of the guests to taste and indulge their appetites. However, Maud's trencher was hardly touched as she could not be tempted by the exquisite cuisine; instead she nibbled at various fruits which were arranged in colourful mountains on the polished oak trestles. Her eyes moved over the crowded Hall. The Earl looked at ease and was talking and laughing with Nell who looked a picture of happiness. The candlelight played over her dark, shining tresses and glowing cheeks, her eyes sparkled and Maud could see by her countenance how much she was enjoying the whole occasion. The change to the once shy little girl, whom she had accompanied all those years ago, was quite remarkable.

Happy to sit and watch the colourful throng, Maud relaxed as she laughed at the antics of the jesters and tumblers. She felt somewhat removed from the activities, almost as though the scene was part of a play, and she was merely a spectator.

A voice interrupted her thoughts.

'I hope your lack of appetite is not a comment on the chef's efforts.'

Maud looked up at the speaker and was taken aback when she realised who had spoken.

'No my lord Bishop, just my condition.'

The pair studied each other candidly in the flickering candlelight.

'The approach of motherhood has I hope, turned your thoughts to matters more befitting a wife and mother as it has for your sister Eve.' Thomas Cantelupe, Bishop of Hereford's clipped tones carried a note of undisguised triumph.

'Oh! I am certain Eve is far more pliable than this de Braose.' She hesitated as she watched the expression on the pale, sharp featured face. 'Even though I have married a Mortimer and am shortly to become a mother, it has not curtailed my freedom of thought, my lord Bishop, which has remained unfettered by any marital restraints.'

The Bishops' face tightened; what was it about this young woman who always managed to penetrate his mantle of self assurance.

'Remember, sinful thoughts can often precedes, sinful deeds.'

'And you have cast me in the role of having such thoughts?' She studied his expression for she instinctively knew she unnerved him.

'Does it count as a sin if it is merely a fleeting thought?' He looked down at the seated woman with an expression which could only be described as contemptuous.

'Unguarded thoughts are a playground of the devil, I fear. You would do well to commit such wayward reveries to the past and seek the guidance of your husband who, let us say, is possessed of the higher intellect.'

Maud could not suppress a smile. 'Oh! My lord Bishop, I marvel at your un-worldliness, locked as you are within the confines of Holy Scriptures and surrounded by the security of the church. Answer me this, who runs the households of the nation prey? Who over sees their husbands estates, the education of the children, whilst they are overseas or fighting for king and country? I believe even in the kitchens of many churchmen's houses there lurks women who performs many *duties* which do not fall within the teachings of the church. Is that not so?" The inflection in her voice made it clear she was referring to many priests who kept common law wives, under the guise of housekeepers. She continued in a more conciliatory vein.

'Besides, even the king seeks the advice of his wife on occasions therefore, how can you so denigrate the role of womankind? I am well aware that we have been condemned forever for being cast out of Paradise but, maybe if Adam had not been so weak and refused temptation.....'

The bishop was aware that their conversation was drawing attention. He cleared his throat and murmured.

'My lady I would end this conversation and bid you a safe confinement.' He raised his hand in benediction and moved to where the Earl and his son and future daughter-in-law were sitting. His face, stern and set, resenting the fact the de Braose woman still had the power to ruffle his normal icy composure.

'It never hurts to give these churchmen a slice of truth pie.' The buxom woman leaned over and patted Maud's hand smiling broadly as she did so, 'if men bore the babes the world would quickly come to an end, for they have no concept of what suffering they cause us. Bess Turbeville is my name, I rarely attend such grand functions but felt it my duty to accompany my husband to save him from making a fool of him-self. I swear if he didn't have a body servant he would not even find his own boots or, remember what he had to do each day.'

Maud nodded. 'Pray excuse me I am feeling somewhat faint.' And without further ado Maud rose and left the Great Hall to seek the sanctuary of her own chamber. She failed to witness the piercing gaze of the bishop of Hereford as she left the Great Hall.

As she reached the door of her chamber a young page stepped forward and opened it allowing her to enter. Once inside, she was greeted by the warm and comforting atmosphere and felt cheered to find a fire burned in the hearth. Jane's friendly smile of greeting, as she moved forward and took her hand, Maud immediately let out a long sigh of relief.

'Come I have prepared your bed. Prey do not forget to take the tincture before you retire it will help you gain a good night's sleep.'

'Oh Jane I do enjoy being pampered and cosseted, as my own waiting woman is not here, as she rarely leaves the confines of Wigmore.' Maud hesitated then continued. 'I suppose it stems from the wounds she received and the fear of cruel comments on her scarred face.'

Thankfully Jane made no further comment as she could see the weariness etched on Maud's pale features.

As Maud was helped out of her finery she smiled: 'My meeting with the Bishop has once again ended on a somewhat icy note. Why he feels the need to repeatedly point out what he sees as my shortcomings, is beyond me!'

'Maybe he fears your independent spirit and sees it as his God given duty to try and *change* your ways.'

'Mmm! Nonetheless, these bejewelled churchmen often leave me cold. When I compare their lives with those of the Franciscan friars who preach the word of God and take their Faith into the most impoverished hovels in the land, sharing whatever little food or wealth they have, often in threadbare habits and sandals held together by ......'

Jane interrupted 'Now my lady, do not distress yourself and take your tincture which will help you sleep.'

For once Maud was quite happy to allow Jane to administer the heady mixture and almost immediately the babe lay still and within minutes she too fell into a deep, restful slumber. The following morning began with a heavy shower of rain which was accompanied by watery grey skies but as the morning progressed the weather lightened and the rain ceased. The castle was abuzz with excitement and anticipation as in every quarter the occupants made ready for the great day and none more so, than in the apartments of the bride to be.

Eleanor de Braose stood before a long reflector and gazed at her image. The rich folds of her wedding gown displaying the full magnificence of the embroidery which sparkled and glinted with the coats of arms of the de Bohun's and de Braose families. The kirtle of deep gold offset by the dark red mantle complimented the young woman's dark colouring. Her thick, waving tresses were bedecked with jewels from the palest pearls, to the fieriest rubies and dazzling sapphires.

When Maud entered, she stopped and gasped, for never in her wildest dreams had she thought Nell could look so stunning. The scene caught her heart and she felt an overwhelming sadness that their mother had not lived to witness her youngest daughter at the zenith of her youth and beauty. Not normally sentimental, Maud could only put her fey mood down to her condition. She shrugged off the notion, and smiled her approval, as she offered up a silent prayer for her sister's future happiness.

When the page finally arrived to summon the bride to her wedding Nell glanced at Maud who squeezed her hand.

'You look so beautiful; Humphrey is a truly lucky groom. Now walk tall and proud remember, you are granddaughter to the great, William Marshal.'

Nell could not speak her heart was too full; so she meekly followed the page as he escorted her to the great doorway towards her future which would begin, with her journey down the aisle of the great cathedral of Hereford. She heard the heralded notes of the fanfare, as all eyes turned towards her; she trembled, but Eleanor de Braose did not falter, and made her way unerringly towards her waiting bridegroom. Maud was heartened and noted that Nell held her head high and walked to the altar with slow, measured steps, and in that instance she knew her little sister had come of age, if not in years, then in her awareness of her new status.

Once again Maud felt a pang of sadness for she would have liked Izzy to have been a part of the day instead of mewed up in some remote convent. However, the receipt of the jewel box some weeks ago, assured Maud there were still those whom Izzy could trust. The struggle in Wales was not only between the Welsh and the crown but now, also amongst Dafydd's cousins, and at least Izzy was no longer amid the volatile situation.

Without an heir, it left Izzy in an unenviable position; in England she would have been protected by law however, in Wales, women were not allowed to own lands; exactly how this situation left her dower lands, Maud was unsure. Obviously King Henry, had taken measures to remove Izzy from having any further influence either, in Wales or England but, would he be able to take possession of her estates in the Marches and Wales?

After the colourful ceremony, the rest of the day was filled with feasting and merrymaking and although too heavily pregnant to participate nevertheless, Maud's foot tapped in time with the music and she even nibbled on some sweetmeats. But before the evenings dancing began she made her excuses and slipped almost unnoticed from the merrymaking.

As soon as she reached the chamber, she kicked off her embroidered slippers and went to lie down on the large bed. Almost immediately there came a light tap on the door which swung open.

'Oh! Jane pray go and enjoy in the fun I shall be alright, there is a page outside who will fetch me anything I may require.'

'I am simply making sure you are well and settled my lady. Besides, there is someone I am trying to avoid.'

'Tell me more!' Maud sat up slowly, intrigued by Jane's words.

'I appear to have gained an unwanted suitor.'

Maud looked enquiringly at the speaker.

'He is a widower, and old enough to be my father.' She hesitated and then continued. 'I made the fateful mistake of showing kindness to his children after their mother died last year. Unfortunately, Sir Percy Treanor, now believes I would make a good mother to his children.' She looked up at Maud. 'The children are quite charming however, their father is not to my ....taste.'

'Mmm! And therefore he feels in your position, you should be flattered by his attentions and is suffering from the misguided belief, that you will accept his proposal and count yourself lucky to boot?'

Jane nodded. 'Exactly! I appreciate that as mere lady-in-waiting and of no real status, to refuse his offer would be seen as an insult. But ..... even so........'

'Well then, maybe in this instance I may find a solution so fear not dearest Jane as you have cared for me and Nell over the years so now, I shall show my appreciation and find a way of removing your Sir Percy from the scene, without you losing face.'

Jane's expression said it all; her relief was unmistakable.

'I can never thank you enough my lady.'

'Now run along and enjoy the rest of the evening's diversions.'

'Oh! And may I ask if the widower finds no favour in your eyes do you have someone else in mind?'

'No, but I promise when I do spy a likely contender for matrimony - you my lady Maud, will be the first to know.'

With that Jane bobbed a curtsey and left Maud to rest.

The following morning saw the arrival of Roger Mortimer and his mother. Maud could scarce believe her eyes for the young man who walked towards her bore little resemblance to the one she had bade farewell to. In the days prior to his journey to London, Maud had engaged a quiet youth, from a decent local family to serve as Mortimer's body servant. His instructions, to *cure* her husband's former careless regard towards his appearance, which given his new status, would no longer be acceptable. Towards this end his duties were to ensure the lord of Wigmore should never appear in public with marks and stains on his apparel. He was also to ensure that his linen would always be clean; so too his boots, at least whilst indoors, must be free from mud and marks. Her instructions had obviously been carried out to the letter.

Maud was full of admiration at Mortimer's transformation which was truly remarkable. Gone was the dishevelled youth transformed into a stylish courtier, bedecked in fine apparel, not overstated but nonetheless, denoting his important standing as lord of Wigmore. His dark, thick hair, which had always reminded Maud of a derelict thatch, now looked well styled and shone in the morning sun. His boots, of fine Italian tooled leather, finished off the overall effect and she noted he had also lost his ungainly slouch and now held himself erect. His expression had also changed, no longer his normal glowering expression of resentment, replaced with a much more amiable air. The change was nothing short of a miracle and Maud glanced past her husband to nod her approval to young Rufus, who simply bowed and left.

'Well, my lord, your sojourn at court appears to have been a great success judging by your air of well being.'

Roger stepped forward, took her hand, and kissed it – something he was not previously accustomed to doing. She smiled at Lady Mortimer, 'Pray what magic has brought about this transformation?' She smiled as she fell in step beside him and they walked together along the lavender paths until they reached an arbour where Maud sank onto the rustic seat with a sigh of relief.

'I will take my leave and let Roger give you all the news from court.' With that, Lady Mortimer turned and walked back towards the castle, attended by her lady-in-waiting.

'You would have enjoyed London –life at court is a busy procession of lords and their entourages promenading along the endless passageways. The king denies himself nothing of the refinements of life. The tapestries, statues, stained glass, silver and gold objects are a sight to behold.'

'And the Queen?'

'Haughty, cold, aloof, and full of her own importance. No-one I spoke to actually likes her. She has surrounded herself with her Savoyard kinsmen and women just as the king with his Poitevin relatives, leaving the English born nobles and magnates feeling aggrieved. The king is spending a vast amount on a tomb for his favourite Saint and forebear, Edward the Confessor. There are workmen from all over Europe busy embellishing the monument in Westminster Abbey. I have also learned, there is word that Louis is recruiting men for a Crusade to the Holy Land. The king's brother-in-law, the Earl of Leicester has voiced his intentions of going.'

Roger turned and looked at Maud, 'The man has a great opinion of himself considering a few short years ago he merely inherited a title. No lands, no fortune, nothing, and now - he is - the king's favourite, although I did hear whisper their relationship can be somewhat volatile at times.'

'And how were you received by the king?'

'To my surprise he expressed a deep sadness at losing my father and told me how proud my father was of me! He went on to say that if I served him half as faithfully as my sire he would be well pleased as the Mortimers' hold the key to the Welsh Marches and were vital to the safety of the nation. He made it clear, he entrusts the Marchers to withstand any assault the Welsh may launch against us.' His voice dropped as he added thoughtfully. 'You know, I never once heard my father praise me. He never appeared satisfied with my efforts however hard I tried to please him, only to learn, he told the king he was proud of me! '

Maud reached over and took his hand. 'Your father knew he had to be a hard task master to ensure you always strove to be the best, to do the best, to aim for the best, for he was aware just how difficult the life of a Marcher lord actually is!'

'You know, I have always felt unworthy of being his first born son but now ....'

'Now, you know he thought you worthy and said so to the highest power in the land.'

Mortimer grinned; his face still had a boyish look about it. 'You know, my visit to London gave me the chance to evaluate my life. To look at it almost as a stranger and like a puzzle that has always eluded me, now it has become clearer. I have always been fighting myself, have never been at ease, but have come to realise my fate lies in my hands and I must carry on in the name of my father, and fight for all the things he valued. Loyalty to the crown, his family, and his honour. My fight is out there not within, is that not so my lady?'

'Indeed, as you so rightly say, the fight is against the king's enemies. I pray you will continue to learn from this experience for I believe you went to London as a boy and returned, a man.'

He bent down and kissed her hand.

'There is one thing I noted that even with all the French fashions and fancy styles at court there was not one of the ladies I met could hold a candle to your beauty.'

'Mortimer! I do believe they have made a gallant of you!' Maud exclaimed.

The couple laughed and Maud would often remember it was the first time they had actually had a conversation as a couple, rather than as adversaries in the war of words and wills.

The rest of the wedding festivities continued with a grand joust, where Mortimer distinguished himself, much to Maud's satisfaction but she was becoming ever more aware that she needed to return to Wigmore to await the imminent arrival of her baby.

Some days later on their journey homeward Maud had chance to speak more intimately with her mother-in-law, Lady Gwladus.

'The visit to court has had an extraordinary affect on Lord Roger it would seem!'

'My son has finally discovered his true status and responsibilities; thankfully he appears to have accepted them in the spirit of a Mortimer. His father would have been relieved to have witnessed his new maturity which, I might truthfully admit, I doubted would come about on occasions. I am also glad that his attitude towards you has improved dramatically, which bodes well for the future, as I have always had confidence in your abilities, my dear.'

'Let us pray that his new found wisdom continues to grow and that he comes to value those who will serve him best.'

The two women continued their journey in silence both lost in their own thoughts of the future.

CHAPTER XV

1251

The unrelenting winter had held the country in an icy grip for months and even with the lengthening days of spring, the east wind continued to batter the land mercilessly. Its constant howls echoed around the walls of Wigmore Castle like some angry traveller desperately seeking entry. Within, the stench of death hung in the air like an invisible curtain; for Lady Mortimer, Gwladus Ddu, lay on her deathbed. There was nothing more the physician could do but wait for the inevitable outcome; only her shallow breathing could be heard in the darkened chamber.

Maud rose and stretched her arms she had been sitting for many hours trying to comfort the dying woman. It was only her iron will, which refused to loosen the last strands of life before her son returned from Wales. Even death could be kept waiting by the Royal Welsh Princess. Lord Rhys sat silently in the corner of the room, his face a study of utter misery.

'My Lord, you must go and eat or at least drink something, or you too will become ill.' Maud placed her hands lightly on his bowed shoulders.

'We will need your experience and wisdom through the coming months my lord.' Her words were hushed.

'My duty dies with my lady!'

'Duty *never* dies my lord. Do you really believe Lady Mortimer would wish you to forsake your duty with her death?'

His sleep starved eyes tried to focus on the speaker.

'Have I not given enough of my life to the Mortimer's? It is only for my Princess I have served this family, my loyalty is not to a Mortimer, nor, to the English king, but in obedience to

Llywelyn ap Iowerth's wishes and now, with my lady's death, I shall be absolved from my service to this family.'

'And do you think she would be happy to hear of your intentions to desert her beloved son?'

The intensity of raw emotion was etched on both faces as the couple stared deep into each other's eyes.

'I would beg you to reconsider – at least for a year, my lord. I urge you to stay with us, for not only will we have lost our anchor but also, our wise councillor? I foresee the rising storms which will assuredly beset us over the coming months and not all will be from without. This Mortimer's steel has yet to be tested and without his mother's guiding hand my concerns are he may stray from the path of moderation. Your experience will be sorely needed to help curb any rash decisions he may make. As we both know, mistakes are easily made but not always easily mended!'

Only the low, gasping breathing of the dying woman could be heard and for many minutes Lord Rhys searched his heart and his conscience for his answer. His expression left Maud in no doubt his decision was one of reluctance.

'A year, that is all!'

'I thank you my lord, you will never know how much I appreciate your generosity of spirit.'

Two days later Lady Mortimer, daughter of Llywelyn ap Iowerth and Joan Plantagenet, died. Her son, daughter-in-law, and trusted chamberlain were at her side and for at least two of those present, knew with her passing, a chapter in the history of the Marches had closed. If the young Lord of Wigmore was ignorant of the fact, his wife and Lord Rhys, were not. How the next generation of Mortimers' would be judged – now lay squarely in the hands of the heir, his wife, and their children.

Maud indicated to the waiting priest who, only hours before had administered the sacrament of *extreme unction*, his voice rose as his prayers became audible and with great reverence he made the sign of the cross over the recumbent figure. Although the three mourners made no outward sounds of grief, Maud knew without doubt, both her husband and Lord Rhys were lost in the valley of sorrows. She had admired and respected the dignified matriarch whose position as a Marcher wife must have torn her loyalties asunder on more than one occasion. A woman, who had learned to hide any personal loyalties from the world, a Welsh princess who had staunchly supported her Marcher husband, but at what personal cost, Maud wondered how she had reconciled her Welsh ancestry during the wars in the Marches. It was odd to think that Gwladus had once born the name of de Braose when little more than a girl. After the death of her first husband, Reginald de Braose, she had subsequently married Ralph Mortimer. A life filled with so many changes, so many emotions, all now laid to rest, freed from earthly ties. Maud knew she must now take control, at least for the time being, and allow the two men their period of grief.

Without delay, Maud summoned messengers and ordered them to carry the news to all the neighbouring Marcher lords, to the Earls of Hereford, Gloucester and Warwick but first and foremost, to the king. The abbot of Wigmore Abbey was summoned to make arrangements for the forthcoming funeral. Maud felt relieved to be kept so busy as it helped to stave off her feelings of doubts; would her husband be capable of fulfilling his role as one of the most important Marcher lords or, would he flounder now he was left without his trusted mother's support? This question was at the foremost of her mind and she felt it was imperative to ensure her husband turned to her and Lord Rhys in the future. Towards these ends Maud was determined to do everything within her power to bring about the change of authority aware, that subtlety was the key word in her scheme, knowing this may prove difficult, given her quick fire anger. Although she battled constantly with her wayward temper and had done so since childhood, to keep it in chained had proved difficult over the years, now it was even more important not lose control.

The young Lord of Wigmore's period of inactivity lasted just a few short weeks; then it was like an eruption as he realised there was no longer anyone to gainsay his actions. He strutted around meting out orders shouting at anyone whom he thought tardy in their duties. But when Maud heard he had dismissed Lord Rhys, her rage knew no bounds. She entered Mortimer's chamber without being announced and stood facing the seated figure.

'How dare you dismiss Lord Rhys without a word to me? I have watched you parade around like some prize game cock these past few weeks, upsetting all and sundry. Can you not see what you are doing?'

A sly smile crept across Mortimer's narrow lips giving the effect of a sneer.

'I see it is about time everyone understood who is in command here!'

Maud began to pace around the chamber like a caged animal. She was grappling with her rising rage.

'Oh believe me everyone knows exactly who *is* in command, a fool! Do you hear me - a damned fool?'

Mortimer rose to his feet his face flushed scarlet at his wife's outburst.

'Have a care Madam for I shall..........'

'Exactly what will you do my lord? If you lay one finger on me....'

'And who will come to the rescue of a de Braose brat, pray?'

'You forget I have kinsmen in high places who will not stand by and see you ...'

'And how will they learn....'

'Do you really believe I do not have in place a means of summoning help?'

'If I shut the gates then your messenger will be .....'

It was Maud's turn to sneer. 'Oh! Come my lord, I do not rely on anyone within these walls.' He could not be sure she was bluffing. Now she came and stood directly in front of him her dark, green-grey eyes, blazing.

'Are you not aware on how your actions affect your reputation? Remember, what your position is here on the March, unlike your father, you are not the senior commander, that position is currently, Lord Deveraux's. Consider carefully what president you set, in times of war the men you now harangue and taunt, will be at your back, it will be their valour and bravery you will depend upon to defend you and your lands. Answer me this, would you lay down your life for a man who shows little respect towards you. Who constantly finds fault; that beats and abuses you on a regular basis. Which is what you have been doing these past weeks?' She paused to let her words find their mark.

Then continued in lowered tones.

'The treaty with Wales will not last forever and precisely what happens if you are away and I am left to face your enemy with demoralised servants and soldiers?' The brief silence was only broken by Maud's heavy breathing. 'If you undermine men's pride, and their self confidence, what you have left is but a husk, unwilling to act without a direct order. Surely I do not have to spell it out? War is not like that - it is often immediate, urgent, and instinctive action can often save the day; take away their self reliance and what you are left with - is an army of worthless warriors. Respect is gained my lord, not ordered, or demanded, and if you cannot see that then we are lost.' Her voice dropped even lower and the rage ebbed from her face replaced by a look of stubborn determination.

'If you care naught for yourself think of our children and what state you will leave for them to inherit.

'Your apology to Lord Rhys and retraction of his dismissal will suffice for now; otherwise, you will be dining alone and denied my bed.' With that Maud turned and walked briskly from the chamber leaving her bemused husband to ponder over the scene. When Maud reached her solar she called for hot water and a cup of the finest wine.

Two hours later a note was handed to her from Lord Rhys which simply read:

'I have received both an apology and a request to remain in your service by his lordship.'

Maud let out a long sigh of relief. 'Thank heavens; let us hope Lord Rhys shows more generosity of spirit than does my husband.' Maud had spoken to herself but Carys had caught the relief in her words. She had pitched her will against that of her husband and knew on this occasion she had been successful; she offered up a prayer of thanks. What the outcome of future confrontations would be lay in the lap of the gods.

From the outset the relationship between Maud and her husband had vied between a grudging harmony and direct contradiction. Their childhood vows had long since been discarded regarding keeping their differences private and since the death of the Dowager Lady Mortimer, had frequently spilled over into their daily lives.

But one relationship had flourished the one between Maud and Lord Rhys. As the days passed into summer, it took another step forward as they found they worked in accord with each other it made the transition period at least bearable. To have Carys and her chamberlain as dependable allies in her administration, gave Maud a sense of security and confidence.

It was during such periods she found scant time to play the role of doting mother to her growing brood. Isabella had been born just a few weeks after returning from Nell's wedding. The baby had been named after her beloved elder sister. A year later, Maud had been brought to bed with their son Ralph, named in honour of her late father-in-law. He had been quickly followed by another daughter, Margaret. If Mortimer was no tender lover, he had proved his virility –fathering three healthy children and he had not yet reached his majority.

Motherhood had not been easy for Maud, as she discovered she was not naturally possessed of the maternal trait of many mothers. However, she was fiercely protective of her children and devoted all her efforts to ensure they had a bright future and prayed they would survive the vagaries of childhood.

It amused her to note, Ralph's dependency on Carys who would only sleep if she crooned a Welsh lullaby to him each night. Carys had been present at his birth and Maud was quite adamant that she had only survived the difficult birth through the prompt actions of her lady-in-waiting.

Maud recalled the scene as Carys dismissed the midwife when she saw how totally incapable she was of fulfilling her duty and took charge, even though it called for drastic measures. When it became obvious the baby had not turned, she had deftly managed to succeed where the panicky midwife had failed. Maud was ever conscious that Carys had saved both her life, and the life of her son. From that time the invisible bond of trust had deepened between them.

It had been due to Ralph's dependency on Carys, and their mutual love, which made it an easy decision for her to change roles and take charge of the nursery. So whenever Maud found her busy life left scant time to visit her children, she felt secure in the knowledge that Carys would make sure all was well with them.

The night of Ralph's birth had also brought about a profound change in the young Lord of Wigmore. Whenever he recalled that night, he remembered learning of Maud's plight, and how he had defied convention, and rushed into the birthing chamber to find her screaming in agony. Bloody sheets were strewn across the floor. Candles had guttered and died as he entered, to the cries of horror from the womenfolk. It was a scene he would never forget, one which few men ever witnessed. The writhing, figure of Maud, whose face, contorted by the agony of childbirth was altered out of all recognition; her copper coloured hair, black with sweat as she strained to bring forth their child; the darkened chamber reeked of gore and perspiration, a scene as brutal as any battlefield; he had been shocked by this scene from hell.

Carys had tried to usher him out of the chamber.

'My lord this is no place for you, I will call you when the time is right.'

'Will she live?' His eyes had been filled with fear.

'If determination is ought to do with it, my lady will survive, all you can do now is pray my lord, and pray well.' Her last words were softly spoken.

With that Carys had ushered him out and returned to the task in hand. Six hours later she had carried his son and placed him in his arms.

'Is my wife....?'

'Exhausted but well, it seems your prayers were heard this time my Lord Mortimer.'

Roger had looked into the scarred face and for the first time failed to notice the disfigurement and saw only the look of genuine relief and happiness in her deep blue eyes. That moment of pure joy was a memory they would share for the rest of their lives. Upon learning it was Carys who had saved both his wife and son, Mortimer never again showed anything but respect towards her.

For Roger, the birth of his first born son had wrought an emotion in him like none he had every experienced before. He often questioned how a tiny bundle of humanity could capture his heart so entirely. He had only ever felt true affection towards his mother and this sudden bout of tenderness was unnerving. Maud's difficult labour had opened his eyes to the fact he had nearly lost his wife and child, a fact he did not wish to contemplate. Maud may be all shades of contrariness but his mother had championed her daughter-in-law on more than one occasion and he had witnessed her strength of purpose and ability on many occasions. She was a true daughter of the March and over time; he had slowly come to accept her not as he had once done – as his chattel but as a woman of worth – and mother to his healthy children.

Soon after the heated exchange between husband and wife, Maud found a situation closer to home was about to take precedence over her marital woes. When a messenger, wearing the de Bohun livery, raced through the gateway at Wigmore on a lathered horse. She could tell by the expression on his face the news her carried was urgent and she gave orders for him to be brought to her private chamber immediately. As he entered he dropped to one knee and she saw he was weeping.

'Come. Come, pray tell me what is so.......' Before she could continue he sobbed

'Tis the Lady Eleanor, she .....she is....dead my lady.'

Maud sank into a chair her face ashen.

'Nell, dead!'

'Aye my lady, she took a fever and with her so close to her time she had no strength to fight off the infection.'

'Dear God! Why was I not sent for?'

'It happened so rapidly my lady - all within two days.'

'And the child?'

'Died with her my lady.'

Maud waved her hand unable to speak and the messenger left the bereft woman with tears running unchecked down her pale cheeks.

'They fall like leaves in autumn.' Her words barely audible but Carys heard, and after placing the child she was nursing in the arms of a nursemaid went and without fear, gathered the weeping woman in her arms. The two stood for some minutes until Maud's sobbing subsided then Carys moved away and took the sleeping baby from the trembling arms of the girl.

'Poor Humphrey will be inconsolable I must go to him at once.'

Within hours Maud and a small party rode swiftly through the arched gates of Wigmore. She was glad to be on the move and not left to wander aimlessly around Wigmore. Her urgency for even greater speed, gave her groom so much concern he voiced his fears even though he knew he courted rebuke.

'My lady if you insist on continuing at this pace our mounts will founder before they reach Hereford'. She heard the note of caution in his voice, and saw the worried look across the face of Hal, her young groom. As the realisation of his words began to penetrate she became aware of the peril she had placed the horses in by her overwrought need for haste and ease her mount back to a steadier gait, patting its neck by way of an apology.

On their arrival, the atmosphere throughout the castle of Hereford was bleak; all mourned the passing of their beloved young Lady Eleanor, whose sudden death left them sorrowing, most noticeably, amongst those who had been her personal servants. Maud was shown to her old chamber and there she met the abject figure of Nell's beloved lady-in-waiting, Jane. Without speaking the two just fell into each other's arms and wept. When Maud at last found her voice she spoke in husky tones,

'Did she suffer?'

'The fever left her delirious towards the end, so I do not believe she knew much about her condition. At the onset, she was so hot and thirsty but after she fainted it was obvious she was seriously ill.' She looked at Maud her face full of anguish.

'I did everything within my power to ..... to save her my lady.'

'At least you were with her at the end and that brings me great comfort. How is Lord Humphrey?'

'When he saw her draw that last rattling breath he called her name, ran from the chamber, and has spoken to no-one since.'

'I must go to him.' Maud kissed Jane's wet cheek then without discarding her travelling cloak walked swiftly to Humphrey de Bohun's apartments. As she knocked the studded door she squared her shoulders to brace herself for what she knew would be a difficult interview. As she entered she caught the strong smell of stale wine. A pale faced page hovered in the shadows; at a table was the slumped figure of the heir to the Earldom of

Hereford. Maud indicated to the page to leave as she stepped forward and placed her hands on the slouched figure.

'Come my lord, this will not do! All our tears will not bring Nell back to us, neither will our prayers but, I do know she would not have wished either of us to feel this pain of grief. After all, if we believe the churchmen have spoken the truth about Paradise, our beloved Nell is in a far better place than are we!'

'Get out and leave me alone.' His voice was thick and full of anger.

'No! My lord I will do no such thing we have a duty to those around us but also a greater one to my sister; you must begin to make arrangements for her burial.'

'Get out! Get out! Get out!' His voice growing louder with each word.

'I refuse to leave, and will only do so once I have your sworn oath to rouse yourself from this state of selfish grief. It is at such times we are judged and I will not allow you to be found wanting, if not for your own sake, then for Nell's.'

As he raised his tousled head she could see his abject misery, and went and knelt before him.

'Humphrey, my sister loved you so, and I understand the depths of your distress. I know you two were blessed with a deep love for each other which even death cannot subdue. Nell is past all earthly cares, the bare truth is, we mourn for ourselves, for we are left to carry on – remember, your children will need you now more than ever. Your father will need you – pull yourself together and be the man my sister loved, not wallow in this pit of self pity.'

He raised his mottled, tear stained face. 'I would have struck anyone other than you if they had spoken to me as you have just done!'

'If it makes you feel better I would understand.' Instead Humphrey reached for Maud and clasped her close to his chest. She could smell the strong odour of wine and sweat, but she embraced him, and rocked him for a moment before pulling away.

'Now call for hot water, a change of clothes, and take control my lord.'

Without another word Maud turned on her heels and swept out of the chamber holding tightly onto her own self control as she did so. By the time she reached her chamber she felt a sense of relief and prayed her words had breached the barrier her brother-in-law had hidden behind.

Shortly afterwards, it appeared that Lord Humphrey had responded to Maud's urgings and arrangements for Nell's funeral began almost immediately. The following day Roger Mortimer rode into the courtyard of Hereford Castle and was presented to the grieving widower, then shown to his wife's chamber.

'De Bohun looks a broken man.'

Maud nodded. 'Let us pray that time will be his physician. I know his father will keep him occupied, upon his return, busy enough that he will have scant hours in the day to dwell on his loss. It will be during the hours of darkness he will encounter his greatest struggle.'

Mortimer threw off his cloak as Rufus quickly removed it from the chair back and left.

'The quicker he re-marries ....' He suddenly realised his error as he saw the look of complete horror on Maud's face.

'Forgive ......'

'Leave – please leave, if you are so lacking in sympathy and understanding I dread to think what mischief your lack of perception could cause in the future. Such thoughts should remain unspoken as they are totally out of order during this period of mourning.'

She hesitated before continuing. 'It will take me some time to forgive such remarks whether intended or not!' She had caught his sleeve and had ushered him to the door for once he made no move to resist knowing his thoughtlessness had caused his wife great pain.

After Nell's funeral Maud had slowly accepted the bonds of her childhood were broken, like links in a worn chain. The realisation struck her like a physical blow. All she had to comfort her were her memories. Until now she had been too busy to realise she was no longer a girl but a wife and mother. She mourned not only the loss of her sisters but also, the loss of childhood and the bonds of kinship.

It had begun with Izzy, whose death at Godstow Abbey in 1248 had been almost imperceptible to those outside of the family; she had seen so few people since she had been taken, at the behest of Henry III, into the Order of Benedictine nuns. Now Nell had joined her in the afterlife which only left Eve, and although Maud was bound to her by blood, she despised her submissive nature. She mused over the fact she had never really felt any empathy with Eve. Maybe it was the difference in their ages or, simply being parted at a very young age, which had brought about the coolness between them. There was also the incontrovertible fact they were also worlds apart in their individual personalities, which was undoubtedly the true reason, for Maud quite simply, had never really liked her youngest sister over much.

When Maud felt confident that Humphrey would not sink back into his mood of melancholy she announced instead of returning to Wigmore she would visit Tetbury for awhile to mourn in private. Mortimer knew it was useless to argue with her and as he was still out of favour, meekly accepted her decision. Since the death of his mother he had quickly come to rely on Maud and her strength of character. Besides, it had been some months since anyone had inspected the castle and Maud would undoubtedly ensure any repairs would be attended to, so he comforted himself with his conclusions and made ready to ride back to Wigmore alone, he was never over burdened by compassion.

Maud felt relieved Mortimer had offered no objections to her proposed visit to Tetbury, it was her undisputed property inherited from her father's family and never included in her marriage portion; instinctively she felt it was the right place to seek solace during this dark time in her life. The death of her sister was a personal wound, one she must accept as the will of God. Nevertheless, it left Maud acutely aware her loyalties must now be to the living and the most important, were her children.

It was during this visit to Tetbury, Maud took advantage of her solitude to stare un-blinkingly at both, her past and present. A time, to reconcile herself to her previous life, to acknowledge mistakes and seek absolution of the mind and soul, and be determined to strive not to repeat previous errors. Although she never felt guilt about her secret love for Guy de Longeville, she did accept she had to put her true feelings aside, to rail against her fate was useless, if she did not adopt this philosophy, her life would be eaten away by regrets, and undoubtedly, destroy her future. Maud prayed she would not languish in this reflective mood for long but felt grateful for this personal period of solitude and reflection. There was also a secondary benefit to being apart from Mortimer; it would allow her body to recover from her recent pregnancy.

Eventually, in the days that followed, Maud put aside her negative thoughts of the past for they were beyond changing, her focus must be on the path ahead and not the path already trodden; to these ends she began to take careful stock of her life with all its implications and come to terms with her lot. She was thankful she was unhindered by her normal duties at Wigmore for the time being at least and the pressures of her abrasive relationship with her husband.

Marriage she found challenging. Mortimer was in many ways still a boy, yet in others, both stubborn and ruthless, who frequently lacked perception. His skills as a commander however, were growing under the guidance of William Devereux, who had been appointed by the king to take seniority in the March after the death of her father-in-law. If her husband was fearless in the field of conflict, he was sadly lacking in matters of diplomacy, therefore she must continue to steer him through this delicate but vital area without his knowledge. Her invaluable ally in this matter was Lord Rhys, whose subtle suggestions had guided her through many tricky situations. One thing she could never deny was, even if she lived to be a century, Mortimer would never win her heart, that was forever, Guy de Longeville's.

Once she felt she had regained her equilibrium Maud focused her attention once more on the present. Although she had locked herself away for a few days Maud had not been totally alone at Tetbury as Jane had been allowed to accompany her during her time of grief and once she emerged from her private contemplations, began to share her precious recollections of their childhood. Sometimes, they laughed at the happy memories, other times they wept at sad ones but talked, not as a noble lady to her servant but as two young women who, through their mutual grief, found solace sharing in their sorrow for a lost loved one. This personal time to speak openly and freely about the past, helped Maud immeasurably, and knew she would cherish it for the rest of her life.

Two weeks later, Maud reluctantly made the decision to resume her duties at Wigmore, and suggested Jane should return with her, to join the Mortimer household. Jane was acutely conscious Maud had given her the freedom of choice which, she knew to be a great honour. It was an offer she accepted with alacrity for life with the de Bohun's would never be the same without her beloved Mistress.

However, Jane was totally unprepared for the reality of her new life which came as something of a shock. It was not the hustle and bustle of a busy castle; she was quite used to squires, grooms, men-at-arms, and servants all hurrying about their duties. It wasn't the clamorous, noise, and smells of daily life; it was the general atmosphere at Wigmore. There was an under currant of tension within the castle which affected every man, woman and child within its walls. The most alarming change was in Maud as she assumed her role of authority. There was also a subtle change in their former intimacy replaced by an imposing persona Jane had not previously witnessed. She discovered Maud ran Wigmore Castle with a rod of iron and no-one was immune from her sharp reproofs. As a newcomer, Jane understood without rigid discipline chaos could quite easily prevail and that would be a disastrous state of affairs for a Marcher stronghold. However, understanding the reasons did not make matters any easier to accept for the bemused waiting woman.

Another fact which became obvious to Jane was Maud's total lack of maternal instincts, although she did ensure the welfare of her offspring's was second to none. She was perfectly content to leave the day to day lives of Isabella, Ralph, Edmund and Margaret, in the capable hands of the disfigured woman named Carys. Jane was struck by Ralph's undisguised affection for his nursemaid, which was surprising since he was a precocious little boy at the best of times. Oddly enough the stresses of the main household in no way pervaded the nursery apartments and it was good to listen to the giggles of the two older children at play as they remained oblivious to the rest of the castle.

Jane also noticed the lack of courtly manners at Wigmore; so unlike the de Bohun household. Here, life was raw, and little given to the niceties she had been used to, she felt more, and more isolated unable to reconcile the situation she found herself caught up in. The change in Maud was quite obviously brought about by her husband, Roger Mortimer.

Mortimer was an imposing figure; powerfully built, with a swaggering walk, and a sneering expression. His eyes were as black as coals, and Jane likened him to a bird of prey, as he appeared to watch everything and everyone around him apparently missing nothing. Jane felt nervous in his presence and could understand why many feared him. Although well dressed, this young Marcher lord possessed few of the refined manners of most noblemen she had formerly known but she felt this could be a deliberate ploy he used to unnerve people. If it unnerved some, it positively irritated Maud, and Jane judged this to be just another symptom of their often discordant relationship.

At first Jane tried to console herself and put such thoughts aside and concentrate on trying to assist Maud in her position of responsibility, but Jane had many sleepless nights over the coming months pondering over whether this move to Wigmore may have been a grave mistake.

After some time had passed, Jane learned to cope with her situation; she noted how the tension eased whenever Mortimer was away. Maud reverted back to the woman Jane knew and loved. Therefore, it was something of a relief to hear that the Lord of Wigmore was about to depart for London without Maud. The reason for such a decision had been made due to the recently signed treaty of peace with Wales. Nothing could guarantee how long the peace would hold, as the Welsh Marches were notoriously unstable and any excuse would result in the continuation of hostilities.

Only one single light brightened Jane's days, she had been re-acquainted with someone who had brought a glimmer of hope into her life, Master Rufus, Lord Mortimer's body servant. In

Rufus she discovered all the qualities that appealed to her; kindness, thoughtfulness, courtesy and a gentle humour. Jane quickly realised Rufus had stolen her heart and was overjoyed to learn her feelings were reciprocated. Even this new found relationship came with its own problems for, almost as soon as they had declared their feelings for each other they had to face the fact that Rufus would be accompanying his master to court and even though it was expected to be a short separation, Jane felt fearful he may meet someone younger, and prettier, and she suffered pangs of insecurity and jealousy.

Upon the arrival at court Roger Mortimer found himself plunged into the sea of growing discontent which had long festered amongst many of the nobles and magnates. The age old grievances had once again erupted. Rumours abounded, and Mortimer was quickly caught up in some heated debates. It was no secret how the king's appointments of his Poitevin relatives to high office over the years, had enraged many of the hereditary nobles, but it was their overbearing arrogance and total disregard for the laws of the country, which they so flagrantly flouted, which fuelled much of the unrest; especially as the king continually refused to rebuke them.

It was obvious that Henry had not only ignored the accusations but also, the murmurings against the enormous expenditure on the memorial to his favourite saint and predecessor, Edward the Confessor, in Westminster Abbey. Artisans from all over the Continent had been employed to build and embellish the impressive structure. The beleaguered king's total disregard for the opinions of his advisors meant England was ruled by a sovereign dangerously out of touch with his subjects.

Faced by this precarious situation, Mortimer soon became embroiled in the arguments which raged, for he was also bent on rising up the ladder of ambition, but it was Maud's words of caution before his departure, which now served to hold him in check. Whatever their personal relationship was, he knew Maud's loyalty was unquestionable. She had emphasised how their future success lay in the hands of the king, albeit he was an inept one. Whatever the opinions of his nobles and magnates, power remained in the hands of their anointed king.

The fact was indisputable, and Maud had made this point plain on more than one occasion. But Mortimer sometimes felt compelled to add his voice to the complainants wishing to show his independence, thus ignoring the constraints of his wife's advice.

Upon his return to Wigmore, Maud listened to his worrying report on the deteriorating situation. She guessed her husband had ignored her words of caution. It was a difficult time for Mortimer's wife, as she now found herself ranged against her own husband on this issue. But it was events in Gascony which served to divert their personal differences as both acknowledged the circumstances sounded so serious it must take precedence, and whatever the quarrels at court were, for now at least, it must take a back seat.

Gascony was the last English province in France, and therefore a significant foothold in Europe. By accounts arriving from the Continent, Gascony had risen up against the harsh rule of Simon de Montfort, Earl of Leicester, the king's brother-in-law. As word filtered through from the court, it became apparent that the situation in Gascony could not be ignored, as it was confirmed the Gascon's had openly rebelled.

In light of this turn of events, the young Lord Mortimer, acted quickly to set in motion the wheels of war. Wigmore teemed with men and horses, and the clash of steel could be heard constantly from morning until night, as knights and squires practiced their military prowess. Men from around the county arrived daily to join the swelling numbers of fighting men. Armour was mended, polished; chain mail was checked for hidden damage; blades were honed; arrows fletched; horses shod and schooled; everything in readiness for when the summons arrived. The Mortimers' would not be found wanting in the forthcoming conflict in Gascony

Maud ensured that Mortimer had clothing for all occasions and supplied Rufus with a new cloak, boots and tunic for her husband's imminent departure.

'Are you sure everything is clean and ready to pack?' Maud looked enquiringly at Rufus.

'Yes my lady I have sent for new hose which should be here any day.'

'Good! Good! And you Rufus, what are your thoughts on this adventure to Gascony?'

'I go wherever my lord needs my services.'

Maud nodded. 'As we all do Rufus, and what about you and Mistress Jane?'

Rufus looked embarrassed and dropped his eyes at the question.

'You do not have to answer Rufus just nod, will you really miss her?'

He nodded then turned away so she could not read his expression.

'Well have no fear; I will see no harm comes to your lady whilst you are away.'

'I know Jane will be well cared for in my absence, my lady.'

'Look to yourself Rufus, and see no treachery befalls my husband.'

Rufus looked enquiringly at her words.

Maud lowered her voice: 'Some of my family members have been ill served by acts of treachery in the past. I hold doubts on the unexplained deaths of at least two of my uncles. I can accuse no-one directly but, note the Lusignan, who now bears the title of Earl of Pembroke, and from whom he received that honour. Be circumspect on who you speak with whilst you are away, a careless word can bring a mountain of trouble on you and those you serve – do you understand Rufus? There are those bent on mischief, especially those closest to the king.'

'Be assured I will keep my eyes and ears open and serve my master to the best of my abilities.'

Maud patted his sleeve, 'in you, I have every confidence Rufus, for we live in troublesome times when a friend can become an enemy overnight.'

There was a knock at the door which put an end to their conversation.

That night Maud repeated her fears to her husband but she could see by his expression her advice was in danger of a rebuttal until, she blankly refused his amorous attentions, whereby he gave her his oath to heed her words.

§

The king sat in silence as he listened to the sickening complaints listed by the Count Béarn at the hands of his brother-in-law, Leicester. His long fingers clutched the arms of his chair as he heard all the details of the intolerable cruelty which had been meted out in Gascony. Details, which had until recently, been viewed as hearsay. Now, as the list of atrocities grew ever longer, they served to confirm all the previous rumours, and the longer Henry listened, the more enraged he became.

During the years King John, Henry's father, had ruled, the English had lost most of its French lands. Now Gascony looked in danger of being lost through de Montfort's mishandling of his position as its governor. Although the king had hated being faced with such offences, there was no denying the truth in the claims laid before him. It placed him in an intolerable dilemma, for he did not wish to be the king that was responsible for losing the last English region in France.

The problem stemmed from when Henry had originally replaced the former Governor of Gascony, Richard de Grey, with Leicester, a ploy to stop the latter from going on Crusade with the French King Louis. However, this decision now proved to have been a grave error of judgement. The accusations by Count Béarn himself, on his arrival at court, had brought condemnation of Leicester's harsh rule and his uncompromising stance on Gascony's old traditions and the facts stated, were irrefutable. Angered and frustrated by the position his arrogant brother-in-law had placed him in, Henry summoned de Montfort to return and answer his accusers.

Upon his return to England Leicester found the allegations brought against him had been upheld by Henry and had resulted in his arraignment which was to be answered before the court in what would prove to be a controversial trial. Henry, a man of great piety was nevertheless a Plantagenet, and faced with the allegations and grievances ranged against the Earl of Leicester, now felt his own reputation had been maligned and had acted accordingly.

Leicester, was quick to offset his actions, and laid blame firmly back at the feet of the Henry himself. The fault, he insisted, lay with the king's persistent refusal to refund him costs incurred in quelling the original uprising in Gascony. He vociferously reproached the king for not only the lack of funds, but railed against the number of troops, which he claimed had been woefully inadequate; these accusations only inflamed an already volatile situation.

The relationship between the two men had never been a stable one and the widening rift between them boded ill, not only for them personally, but for England's future, as it now looked like war would be the inevitable outcome to the affair. Henry had been so incensed, he was determined to bring the recalcitrant Earl of Leicester to heel, and when he had ordered the trial, it was only partly to placate the enraged Gascon's, the main reason was in order to make a show of his authority.

Although the trial had begun in England, it was set to continue in Gascony regardless of the difficulties it posed; de Montfort needed to be reminded it was Henry's hand that held the sceptre of state. Besides, he had to demonstrate his power to the Gascon people in an effort to keep them on side and what better way than a public trial.

Simon de Montfort had never been a popular figure; he was viewed by many as a foreign upstart and viewed with suspicion, due to his close ties with France. He was also condemned for his grand life style and his arrogant attitude towards his peers, especially given his personal lack of funds. His scandalous marriage to Henry's sister, Eleanor, had merely compounded their opinions. Even his title of Earl of Leicester was not through a direct line of inheritance; de Montfort was after all a younger son, and had until his marriage, been virtually landless.

However, not all the voices were raised against him in fact, he had over the years, made a number of powerful friends both at court, and in the ecclesiastical circles, who were now ready to uphold his views. Amongst those whose considerable authority lay in the church and therefore, ultimately with Rome, was Robert Grosseteste, Bishop of Lincoln and Thomas Cantelupe, Bishop of Hereford. Also, ranged against Henry on this matter were, the Earls of Hereford, and Gloucester, and even his own brother, Richard, Earl of Cornwall, who had all spoken in Leicester's defence on this single issue of funding which, once again placed the king at odds with some of the most powerful men in the land. A fact which had not escaped the Queen.

Knowing the importance of retaining the hold on Gascony, Eleanor of Provence, was determined it should be defended at all costs for her son, the young Lord Edward. Eleanor had never been popular with her subjects, resented for appointing her powerful Savoyard kinsmen, whom she had installed in positions of influence since her arrival in England. The royal couple were both guilty of nepotism, and had between them sown the seeds of disaffection amongst the Anglo-Norman Earls, magnates, and landowners throughout the kingdom. Men who would now be called upon to finance Henry's forthcoming war in Europe.

Although Henry believed he was vindicated for his decision to take a stand against de Montfort, nevertheless, it did not alter the fact that the exchequer could scarcely afford the cost of a tournament let alone a war, which left, him vulnerable, particularly as he must now turn to his disgruntled nobles for help as they would have to bear the immediate cost of the forthcoming campaign, causing yet more aggravation for the king to deal with. Inwardly, Henry fumed at this situation, blaming de Montfort for placing him in this untenable position.

The king had insisted de Montfort's commandership was now a hollow title, another bone of contention between the two men, as the Earl saw this as a slur on his abilities not only as a soldier but also a governor, and to a prideful man, it was a serious blow to his reputation. Time would tell if his eloquence would restore him to his former position of trust.

Meantime, as the bitter war of words raged between the king and Leicester; heralds and messengers were sent throughout the land with a call to arms. There were few who had not been prepared for the summons, so within weeks, the roads, lanes and highways were soon filled with the tramping feet of men, horses, and carts, all heading towards the coast. As the Marcher contingency began to converge on their journey to rendezvous with the armies from the north and south; all were fully aware that the pending conflict had been brought about by the haughty Earl of Leicester.

The morning Roger Mortimer rode out of the gates of Wigmore Castle at the head of his contingent of troops, Maud and Lord Rhys looked on, hoping that not only the armour he carried would protect him in battle but that he would not become embroiled in the even deadlier verbal battles.

Soon after his departure, Maud received word that Mortimer had been knighted by the king at Winchester that Whitsuntide; the news filled her with a sense of satisfaction. Mortimer wrote of his pride at accompanying the king. Maud was certain that as a newly dubbed knight, he would be eager to make his name and emerge from the shadow of his father's prestigious reputation, and prove his own worth. Maud conveyed the momentous news to her chamberlain.

'A shrewd move by the king to bind his youngest knights to him, they have not been over exposed to the personal wranglings with Leicester. Besides, he coats the bitter pill of extra taxes by conferring such honours; they will be less likely to add their voices to the dissenters.'

Maud frowned. 'Well, whatever the reasoning behind this move, I hope it will act as a curb to any indiscreet outburst Mortimer may make in the coming months.'

In his subsequent letters, Mortimer began to recount the numerous complaints of the older peers. Maud understood that many of the Marchers were loathed to source troops from their own coffers. This war would affect everyone in the land in some measure or other. In reply, she urged him yet again to be circumspect in voicing any personal opinions and wait to see how events infolded.

If her husband did not see the dangers, then Maud did; whatever faults Henry's possessed, and whatever poor decisions he made, he was still the anointed king and figurehead of the nation and as such, must never be underestimated or, openly defied. For all his piety this move to head his army proved that as king, he would not stand by and meekly allow de Montfort and the dissenters to override his authority. It was an outward show to the world that Henry of England would, when necessary, bear arms to uphold his crown.

Over the coming weeks Mortimer's letters began to give details regarding the relationship between the king and Leicester and she felt vindicated by sharing her feelings of mistrust towards the haughty Frenchman. Since his scandalous marriage to Eleanor Plantagenet, widow of her late uncle, William Marshal, Earl of Pembroke, she had from the start, instinctively disliked him. After all, in her eyes, he was merely an impoverished upstart, who had gained a position of wealth and status from his propitious marriage into the royal family; a move she had viewed with distain from the onset.

Maud had not been alone in her feelings of outrage at the union of the Earl; it had also infuriated the king. It was no secret, that by breaking her sacred vow of chastity, made after the death of her first husband, Eleanor had also fallen foul of the teachings of the church. So much for the couples so called piety! Their subsequent visit to Rome to seek absolution, had gained a pardon from the Pope, and some time later, a resumption of close ties with the king, which had caused Maud to feel even more resentful. The current situation however, only underlined how fragile the family ties actually were, and Henry had not hesitated to bring his haughty brother-in-law to book.

As the king and his army prepared to set sail for France, at Wigmore, Maud felt grateful the year had been marked by a lack of any serious fighting in Wales, but she knew, like everyone in the Marches who lived under the constant threat of attack, never to become too complacent or place any trust in the written agreement of peace. Maud could not quell the uneasy feeling she had; would the Welsh seize this opportunity to strike now that many of the Marcher lords were away and heading for Gascony. She shared her fears with her chamberlain.

'What do you know of this young Llywelyn ap Gruffydd?' Maud posed her question one morning as they were working on a set of claims sent in by a tenant. Lord Rhys looked up and leaned back in his chair. 'Nephew to the late Prince Llywelyn ap Iowerth and therefore, cousin to Sir Roger. He has emerged as the Welsh leader and over the past few years; has quickly gained power. By all accounts he is establishing himself as a capable leader as well as a charismatic one and is currently trying to re-unite Wales. However, the news filtering through from Wales is that Llywelyn is, for the time being at least, also content to uphold the truce, but for how long no-one is certain given the long standing enmity between England and Wales. In my opinion, he is using this time to recruit and train more men and is looking for support in Europe.'

Maud nodded. 'Your views echo the doubts I have with regards to this peace; it is but a temporary lull methinks!'

'Then we must also take advantage of it and see that we continue to engage the best men, horses, and armourers, and encourage our young squires to train even harder.'

'You are right.'

Maud smiled, relieved that she had unburdened her fears and have been given such positive advice from her ever loyal chamberlain.

As Maud prepared to galvanise Wigmore into action, across the Channel the English king was weighing up the cost of this campaign in Gascony, which would inevitably mean more taxation a move he could foresee would mean more vociferous opposition and make him even more unpopular with his subjects.

If Henry was at odds with his nobles, he was not without support in Gascony, his wife, Queen Eleanor of Provence, had accompanied him as she still retained strong family ties in France. Eleanor was determined to do everything within her power, to safe guard the future of her son. Whatever Eleanor's reputation was, she had demonstrated her devotion to her son during his infancy, by leaving the king's side to personally nurse Edward through a childhood illness, a rare demonstration of motherly love.

Over the months Maud received sporadic letters of the unfolding events in Gascony and she was left in no doubt that her husband was becoming ever more involved in the disputes; it was apparent that his loyalty to the king was being severely tested; rekindling her fears that he may commit to a cause she was certain would lead to disaster.

Her subsequent replies urged her husband to be cautious, and underlined her warnings by pointing out the fate suffered by her own uncle, Richard Marshal, after the Battle of the Curragh in Ireland in 1234. Albeit the king had denied any knowledge of the murderous actions of Peter de Roches, the former Bishop of Winchester. Nevertheless, Maud knew her family believed his hands had also been stained with the blood of her uncle. Plantagenet's were renowned for a perfidious streak in their nature, another reason to step with the utmost care during these unsettled times.

Maud felt it was an unceasing struggle to restrain Mortimer from his own unbridled actions which was proving difficult even for his resourceful wife, but it was a struggle Maud would never relinquish in an effort to steer him through the maze of men's over riding ambitions. To such ends, the Lady of Wigmore spent many hours discussing these issues with Lord Rhys, whose opinions she valued, and was heartened by the fact he also held similar views with regard to the dangerous precedent her husband was currently exposed to.

At first she knew her warnings were viewed with contempt by the young Mortimer but, undaunted, over time; she began to see her persistence bear fruit; until finally, she felt she had achieved at least some measure of success and that her misgivings were finally been accepted. All she could do was pray that Mortimer would not fall under the spell of de Montfort's eloquent tongue and be gulled into openly opposing the king.

The next letter she received was full of excitement and details of his preparations for battle, which he felt was imminent. Within days, Sir Roger Mortimer rode out with the king's army of knights, barons and their retinues, with banners, standards, and gonfalons, all fluttering in the breeze, as they made ready to confront the enemy

CHAPTER XVI

1253

Soon after the departure of Roger Mortimer and his retinue; there was a distinct easing of tension amongst all those who remained at Wigmore, and the change was most apparent in Lady Mortimer. Jane was heartened to see the strained look slowly slip from Maud's face although personally, she would know no peace until the safe return of her beloved Rufus. She had learned long ago the reason for Maud's aloof attitude, when in company, and noted her effort to show no particular favouritism towards any of the household, especially her personal staff, thus avoiding any of the servants being singled out for possible spiteful reprisals by her husband a trait abhorred by his wife.

Mortimer possessed a streak of malice which, on occasions could be aimed towards Maud or her staff. Jane had once witnessed Maud's defence of a young page who had accidentally spilled wine on Mortimer's sleeve and would have been viciously beaten but for her intervention. It was such fearlessness which gained the unstinting loyalty of those who served her; but it did not detract from her high standards which were expected to be upheld at all times. Besides, the Lady also had a temper, but it was curbed for the most part, only a withering look from those dark green-grey eyes betrayed her inner rage.

One morning, Maud and Jane stood and watched Carys play with the Mortimer children on the wide verdant sward below their casement. As they listened to the childish chuckles and shouts of joy and excitement, it caused them both to smile, in a moment of mutual amusement. It was obvious to Jane in that instant, what a strain Maud lived under, enduring as she did this marriage of convenience. It was Jane who broke the spell when she picked up the hair brush in readiness to dress her mistress thick, rich, coppery tresses.

'It is good to see you so relaxed my lady.' Jane continued the steady rhythmic brushing as she spoke.

Maud smiled. 'Is it so noticeable? Mortimer always seems to have that effect on me when he is here. As you have witnessed there is frequently a battle of wills and he never fails to find opportunities to thwart many of my decisions.' She smiled wryly: 'that is until he finds himself at a loss and then seeks my support which, as his wife, it is my duty to give, unstintingly. He knows full well I am perfectly capable of running, not only his household, but can deal quite competently with all of his affairs but, for some reason known only to himself, he refuses to admit the fact and delights in displaying his role of authority, trying to give the impression I am subservient to him in all things.'

Jane chuckled.

'Why pray, do you allow him live with his illusions my lady?'

'It serves me well to do so, at times Jane! Over the years I have come to understand something of his perverse nature, Mortimer often acts far too rashly and does not always consider his words wisely. I believe it is a sign of immaturity, therefore I sometimes play the role of subservient wife, in public at least.' She paused then continued. 'Through the years I have learned to '*handle*' my husband at least, for the most part, as he still has much to learn. I live in the hope, with age will come wisdom. Now, enough of prettifying methinks, we will take ourselves off to Ludlow, I believe it is a market day.'

It was during this period Jane had begun to appreciate her surroundings. She had eventually been accepted by the other members of the household and had even become friends with Carys. She also enjoyed days of riding and hawking with Lady Maud, and she often accompanied her on visits to the neighbouring churches and friends. But the leisure times were scarce as Maud was frequently engaged in local or legal matters and one morning she found her sat poring over a set of scrolls which Lord Rhys had brought to her attention.

'I swear this woman is the bane of my life!' Maud exclaimed as she rose and paced around the chamber like a caged animal.

'I thought you needed to see for yourself the Countess of Leicester's claim.'

The documents were a legal application against the will of Eleanor Plantagenet's first husband, William Marshal, who had been the Earl of Pembroke, Maud's late uncle.

Maud had never forgiven Eleanor for abandoning her vow of chastity, made after she had been widowed and had blatantly chosen to disregard on her subsequent marriage to de Montfort. Now Eleanor was suing for what she viewed as unpaid dower from the Marshal estates. Lawyers from both parties had been busily trying to unravel the shrewd measures her brother-in-law, Richard Marshal had put in place after his brother's untimely death.

Sadly, he too was now long dead, and the manner of his betrayal at the hands of, the former king's favourite, Peter de Roches, still angered Maud beyond words. Even though de Roches had been banished, his hatred had reached across the Irish Sea and through his agents had ensured Richard was so mistreated after being wounded at the Battle of the Curragh, he had died from his injuries. So much for the charity of churchmen!

One single account of Richard Marshal's death which, if true, was genuinely shocking. He and a fifteen of his knights had been lured into a trap and the informant claimed, although they had been greatly outnumbered, gave a valiant account of themselves before being overwhelmed. The legs of Richard's horse had been sliced off bringing him and the dying animal crashing down, before he had been stabbed in the back but it was the treatment he had received which had in fact killed him not the original wound, and for that act of treachery, Maud burned with justifiable anger.

Richard Marshal had inherited his father's unquenchable courage and had attained the respect of his peers, both in battle, and in the lists. Maud and her family had always felt deeply proud of their Marshal ancestry and she was not going to stand meekly by and allow the lands of her forefathers to be filched away by that upstart, de Montfort and his wife.

Maud calculated that if the law upheld Eleanor's claim it would mean a vast repayment would be awarded from the considerable Marshal Inheritance. The very thought infuriated Maud as she felt such findings would be totally unacceptable. Land equated to wealth and power and Maud had become ever more conscious of the fact during the years of her marriage. She understood the Mortimer policy on land acquisition during the time of her mother-in-law but since her death, she had learned much from Lord Rhys, especially on pending law suits and had taken over some of the outstanding cases. Now, she bore the title of Lady Mortimer, enjoyed the cut and thrust of each case, and with every passing day, appreciated exactly how much expertise in such matters lay in the scope of her trusted chamberlain.

Although Maud was a great heiress who owned many estates and properties inherited from both her paternal and maternal families of de Braose and Marshal, nevertheless, to yield even an acre to the de Montfort Countess, she deemed would be viewed as a failure. It was her duty to withstand such claims for the future of her Mortimer offspring's and ensure not an inch or, a single coin would be forthcoming through any legal wrangle, for that would be a very unpleasant pill to swallow. There was no doubt in her mind this pursuit of Eleanor's dower had been instigated by the haughty Earl of Leicester who was forever lacking in the funds to sustain his lavish lifestyle.

In an uncertain age, wealth and land was the only unchanging surety and therefore most important fact when it came to power and position. Even though Maud lacked any mawkish feelings towards her growing brood, not uncommon in an age when so many infants died within months of their birth. She was nevertheless, attentive to their needs and deemed it part of her duty to invest her time and energies in securing the maximum for those who survived childhood to inherit.

Over the years Maud was fast gaining a reputation for being shrewd and hard headed, but was also known to be fair in her judgement in disputes brought before her– that is, unless it touched on matters where she had a personal interest, then she showed a tenacious ruthlessness which equalled any lawyers. However, her fearsome reputation stood her in good stead when Mortimer was away. A grievance brought before Lady Mortimer, was certain to be dealt with in a no nonsense manner. Some, who had presented false claims, were sent packing when their duplicity had been discovered, and some had even suffered a spell in the stocks or prison for their pains.

It was during such times, she leant on the wisdom and knowledge of her chamberlain Lord Rhys, and the quietly spoken advisor never failed in his duty towards her. Their relationship was founded on mutual respect and confidence in each other's abilities. Maud was conscious without him she would have found life at Wigmore, very difficult. Although his title of Lord was not valid in England, *Arglwydd*, Rhys ap Ioin, had been held in high regard by the late Lady Mortimer, and therefore Maud saw no reason to make any changes and insisted all in the household should honour his Welsh title by addressing him as Lord Rhys.

Maud never forgot that originally, their agreement had been for him to remain in her service for a year after Lady Gwladus had died, but when the date expired there had been no further reference to his leaving and he continued as both confidante, and right hand, to the young Lady Mortimer. Even though his presence was often resented by her young husband.

The resentment dated back from his boyhood days when he felt jealous of his mother's dependence on Lord Rhys. Now, although he grudgingly admitted that his wife's chamberlain was an important member of the household, nevertheless his feelings remained unchanged, even though he knew his presence was invaluable, in particular during the periods of absence, in assisting his wife to maintain law and order in his demesne.

There had been a brief period soon after Mortimer had become Lord Mortimer; he had tried to take complete control over the affairs at Wigmore; even demanding the removal of Lord Rhys. However, Maud had deftly diverted his wishes and the matter had eventually resolved itself with Lord Rhys remaining in his position as her chamberlain.

On such occasions, the Lord of Wigmore, felt somewhat at odds in his feelings towards his wife. He could not deny she had proved a fertile, and a successful mother of healthy children; had brought great wealth to this marriage; was kin to some of the greatest nobles in the land, besides, he enjoyed their energetic marriage bed; Maud was a beautiful woman and he knew he was envied by many of his peers and of course – she had given him the most precious gift of all Ralph, on whom he doted. His birth had brought about a significant change in his attitude towards his wife. He never forgot how fearful he had been when he thought she would die. However irked he felt at times with Maud, he had realised in that moment, he would be bereft without her and thus she had gained her place in his esteem.

Gascony was proving another significant milestone in his life, and it had given Mortimer time to take a long, hard look at his own emotions. Faced by the maelstrom of war in a foreign land, he had realised war was proving, not only a feat of arms but also, one of words and loyalty. Initially, Maud's letters of warning had virtually been ignored but as the weeks wore on, Mortimer began to understand her concerns were well founded.

Upon their arrival in Gascony, Henry had discovered the treachery of Gaston de Béarn and the methods he had used to condemn de Montfort in Westminster. Enraged at discovering the Gascon's duplicity, Henry began to adopt the same strategy and turned his army against the perfidious Gascons.

The relationship between de Montfort and the king had once again been restored. In fact, when Henry learned that de Montfort had refused the offer of stewardship of France after the death of Queen Blanche in the previous year, he was eager to restore their former friendship.

This about face by Henry, underlined for the young Lord of Wigmore, exactly what Maud was always trying to demonstrate, to take sides in a personal argument between these two men was not only foolhardy but also, dangerous. Nevertheless, he could not deny many of the older nobles were still unhappy at the king's persistent refusal to address their long standing arguments and Henry's persistent failure to uphold the terms of the Magna Carta, and felt sympathy for their cause. However, in his letter's, failed to share such sentiments with his wife.

What he did write, was that the king had now agreed to pay a significant sum to de Montfort if he agreed to take command of his troops, once again in Gascony. The twists and turns of this whole situation was confusing for the men that fought but not so surprising to Mortimer's wife and her chamberlain back in England.

'De Montfort is like a cat; always lands on his feet. Whilst the rest of his nobles lose money and men to support him - de Montfort gains more income.' Maud stormed as she read the letter to Lord Rhys. 'It seems that they are heading for a place called, Benauges. Heaven knows when we shall hear from him again as the weather is deteriorating and the roads will soon become impassable.' She looked across at her chamberlain: 'how long do you think this war will last?'

'That all depends on the manpower of the Gascon's. If they put up little resistance, then our troops should return quite soon. However, if there is a siege, who can say how long they will be able to hold out!'

'So we shall be celebrating Christmastide without his lordship?'

'That, my Lady, looks ever likely.'

CHAPTER XVII

Off the coast of France

The salty wind blew across the foaming waves filling the canvas sails; seagulls dipped and swooped overhead, their rasping cries could be heard above all the other noises of the ship. Two figures stood gazing over the bows to the shadowy outline of the distant shore.

'How much longer before we reach land, my lord?' The young squire, his face tanned to a dark nut brown, looked up at the man at his side.

'The captain assures me we will reach port before nightfall.'

'Thank God.' There was no mistaking the relief in his voice. 'I fear the horses have suffered much and I will be glad when we can get them on dry land.'

'Aye, they have had much to endure over the past months under burning skies, trekking over blistering sands, only to be confined in the bowels of a leaky tub which threatens to succumb to the waves.' Guy de Longeville, spoke softly to his squire not wishing to be overheard by the master of the ship.

'Do you think they will ever truly recover my lord?'

'There is no knowing; time, good food, rich pastures and rest, may do the trick but there are no guarantees, like humans who have reached the bottom of their stamina, we can only hope and pray for their recovery, especially after their gallant service, we can only try to reward their courage.'

The youth nodded, 'I will go and check on them again and give them what comfort I can.' He hurried off leaving his master to watch the coastline draw ever closer. To port, sailed the ships of the larger fleet, one carried the Comte de Vivonne, returning to France after delivering the huge ransom for the French king's release from their heathen enemy. An enemy, who had paid the ultimate cost of his magnanimity, with his own death by the hand of an assassin.

Even though he had gained his freedom, Louis had chosen to go to Acre but de Longeville failed to see what would be achieved especially, as they had already lost Damietta and so many of their men in this Crusade. The Battle of Fariskar had been a blood bath, and Louis had lost his own brother, Robert of Artois, at the Battle of Al Mansurah, along with many brave Templar knights.

He sighed, they had fought for months locked in a deadly, bloody campaign in the name of God, but he wondered if God of any religion would really find such atrocities acceptable inflicted in their name. He had encountered such fanaticism, where men, would use women and children as shields or worse, as sacrificial decoys. He had witnessed terrible punishments meted out to prisoners and those deemed unworthy to serve Allah. He had seen knights lay down their lives needlessly, in vain attempts to hold un-defendable positions and all for what? A beleaguered Crusade in the misguided belief that God would reward those that fought in his name, the kingdom of heaven.

Right now the only thing he felt was an engulfing tiredness, so deep, that even if he slept for a thousand years he would not wake refreshed. So much blood spilt, so much pain endured but that was in the past finally, he was returning home to a motherless son, and an empty chateau. He comforted himself with the fact that at least he and his squire, Lucien, were still alive; the wounds of the flesh they had both received were partly healed. Thankfully his squire had suffered only a few minor injuries but de Longeville knew it was the unseen wounds of the mind and spirit which could actually prove the more damaging, these would reveal themselves in the months to come; only then they would learn if it was true that time was the healer it was deemed to be.

The '*Bon Homie*' landed just as the sun began to dip in the sky. Lucien quickly took charge of unloading the horses as a matter of urgency. Within the hour the weary men and animals were housed at a nearby Inn.

'So, twenty more leagues and we should be home on the morrow.'

'Aye my lord but methinks the journey will seem much longer given the condition of the horses.'

Guy de Longeville smiled 'if we can survive the carnage of Egypt surely we can survive the lanes and roads of France? Besides, we can hire horses and lead our own mounts.'

Lucien nodded and although not yet fully grown, he was in his fourteenth year; the young squire had fought as bravely as any knight in the army of the French king.

'And what do you wish for now that we are home?'

'A bath, some new clothes and sleep, lots of sleep.'

'Will you return to your birthplace?'

Lucien shook his head, 'I no longer have any reason to return to Picardy. My mother is dead; my father refused to give me his name, although did make some small provision for my future. I would like to continue in your service, if you will have me!'

'I will be proud to have you remain in my service Lucien, you have proved your worth a thousand fold, I only hope my son grows up to possess even a few of your qualities.'

The weather beaten face broke into a broad smile, 'then I am content, for all I wish to do, is to serve you faithfully, and well, my lord.'

'Then that is settled you shall come and make your home with me. Now let us retire in readiness for our journey *home.*'

As Guy de Longeville and his squire made ready for the final step of their journey home; across the Channel, Maud de Braose sat trying to decipher a letter from her husband.

'I swear there are more blots than words!' she exclaimed as Lord Rhys pause from writing up his ledgers.

She looked up to see if her chamberlain was listening, then continued. 'They are about to lay siege to a place named La Reole.'

Lord Rhys leaned back and tapped his fingers on his desk as he considered the news.

Maud dropped the letter onto the table, 'so it all rests on when the siege ends, when we see Lord Mortimer again.'

He nodded.

'I will enquire if Jane has had word from Rufus,' and with that she made her way to the solar where she knew her lady-in-waiting would be busy with her needlecraft.

As she entered Jane looked up and smiled.

Without any preamble Maud put her question.

'Have you heard from Rufus recently?'

Jane put down her needlework and looked up at the speaker.

'He assures me that Lord Mortimer is well and is fast gaining the respect of his superiors for his ability as a commander.' She looked at Maud to see her reaction. 'You must be pleased to hear this, no mean feat given his lack of years, my Lady.'

Maud nodded. 'Let us hope he keeps that respect!' Her words were said almost to herself.

'And does Rufus say he misses you?'

Jane's smile deepened.' He says he wishes to marry me upon his return - with your approval of course.'

'As long as you are sure that is what you want Jane, you will not only have my blessings but a house and land to safeguard your future.'

Jane rose, and came and caught Maud's hand and kissed it, 'how can we ever thank you?'

But Maud, who was not normally given to shows of outward affection, touched her cheek and looked deep into her eyes.

'Your loyalty and love is enough Jane, we will speak no more on the matter. I will instruct Lord Rhys to draw up the necessary documents so that your claim will stand in the eyes of the law should aught befall me!'

Months later they received word the king, with most of his army, would soon be returning to England. Although they had received no further word from Gascony, assumed the siege must have ended successfully. Maud therefore presumed Mortimer would be among their numbers; the news brought mixed emotions for his wife. If Maud was completely honest with herself, the thought of his imminent return filled her with some apprehension. Questions ran round her head like children playing hide-and-go-seek. Would his time in Gascony prove to have been beneficial, or detrimental to his overall character? His letters had been intermittent and vague on his personal welfare, so the only clue to what had really happened were those from Rufus to Jane.

Maud also faced the prospect of their more intimate relationship resuming and the inevitability that she would soon be pregnant again. The months of Mortimer's absence had given her body time to recover from the traumas of childbirth. Inwardly she battled with her own misgivings, outwardly; she began to arrange for a welcoming, homecoming feast.

All her efforts for Mortimer's homecoming proved to be a great success, Wigmore had resounded with the sounds of merriment and singing. As the couple sat at the head of the table, Maud noted the difference in her husband; gone was every vestige of boyhood nowadays, he appeared far more self confidant, which to her mind, bordered on arrogance and she felt a sense of misgiving.

His appearance had also altered; he had gained weight, together with a beard and moustache. The result did not meet with Maud's approval as she felt he looked more like a Frenchman than an English knight of the realm. Throughout the feast he regaled the company with his exploits and boasted of many personal victories on the field of battle. Maud noted he kept his wine cup filled and the more he drank, the louder his voice became. It would appear all her former efforts of teaching him restraint with regard to the consumption of wine had apparently, been lost in the fields of Gascony.

As she sat watching the company of young knights and squires enjoying the evening, she mused on her own future, which she did no doubt would prove difficult; where she had once been confident in guiding the boy, the man may prove far more of a challenge. However, it was the hours ahead which Maud braced herself for - the encounter she had been dreading most, the one of the marriage bed. By the time Mortimer mounted the stairs to her bedchamber he was drunk, very drunk. He reeked of stale wine, sweat, and spicy food. He swayed in the door-well leering at her.

'Time for shum sheed showing.' His words were slurred and husky.

'Your drunk and I will not tolerate you in my bed in such a debased condition.'

'You Madam, will shpread your legs....'

He got no further Maud picked up a pitcher of water and before Mortimer could move she had hit him as hard as she could over the head with it. The impact felled him like an ox and he lay at her feet bleeding from the wound on his head. She called out to a servant instructing him to remove her husband to his own chamber, simply stating he had tripped and fallen and to fetch a physician as quickly as possible. If Mortimer thought he could come home and treat her like some tavern bawd, he must quickly learn the error of his ways.

The following day the Lord of Wigmore did not appear until well after noon. Rufus had told him of his *mishap* and that the physician had assured him he would only suffer a headache and the wound would soon heal. No-one dared to question Lady Mortimer's account of the *'accident'* not even her husband. The incident however, was not lost on Jane, and she watched the couple very carefully noting how Maud's attitude had once again reverted to a more aloof nature when they were in company.

However, just a few weeks after Mortimer's return to Wigmore, Maud realised she was once more with child. She was not really surprised as her husband had been a constant visitor to her bed since he had recovered. Their coupling had been fierce and sometimes brutal but, Maud had established terms by which she would not allow him access to either her chamber or, her body. One of which was if he was drunk and secondly, if he had not bathed. Oddly enough, he agreed and adhered to these terms even taking more care of his personal appearance without any prompting from his servant, Rufus. But it was not always to please Maud, whilst in Gascony he had noted some of the fastidious habits of the more elegant of his contemporaries and was simply adopting their practices. It amused him to think he had gained a small victory over his wife albeit; she was ignorant of the truth.

Almost immediately Maud began to feel really sickly and had to retire to her own apartments during periods in the first few months of her pregnancy. Trying times as she hated being inactive and her temper suffered due to her frustrations. But as the summer reached its zenith, she regained much of her health. The niggling doubts that Mortimer may have contracted the 'French' disease, whilst in Gascony had passed.

As September drew to a close, a messenger wearing the livery of the Cantilupe family, brought the tidings of the death of Maud's brother-in-law, William Cantilupe. His health had suffered during the campaign in Gascony and within weeks of his return to England, he had died. Maud could imagine how devastated her sister, Eve would be. She had doted on her husband's every word and obeyed his every wish. But although Maud wrote a long letter of condolence she knew the journey to Warwickshire would be detrimental to her own condition and begged Mortimer to attend the funeral alone.

Upon his return from Warwickshire, Mortimer described the eloquent eulogy made by Simon de Montfort, the Earl of Leicester, during the service at Studley Priory. He acknowledged their friendship and how heavily he had leant on William for support in his arguments with the king. He and Humphrey de Bohun, heir to the Earldom of Hereford, had both expressed deep sadness at the loss of such an important figure who had played a vital role, both at court, and on the field of battle. The king also acknowledged the loss, on a personal level and as a valued advisor, for he counted William de Cantilupe, Lord of Abergavenny, to be a man of honour.

Maud listened and nodded as Mortimer quoted de Montfort's words spoken of his friend saying: *'he had been cut down in the prime of his youth'*.

'He will undoubtedly miss the backing of such a revered man of that there is no doubt! But was William ever young? He always reminded me of a severe tutor. But how was my sister throughout the ceremony?'

'As pale as death; she leant heavily upon de Montfort during the service and wept copiously afterwards.'

'She will be like a ship without a rudder but now she has to think for herself. No doubt, her saintly brother-in-law, Thomas, will steer her into his control, under guise of brotherly love.'

Mortimer looked hard at his wife, his dark eyes narrowing as she spoke. 'That sounds very close to blasphemy as the Bishop is considered a saintly man of God.'

Maud cocked a knowing eyebrow at him. 'I do not trust many of these churchmen, they know how to wave the religious whip at us and often try and shame us into donating silver and land for the sake of our souls but, which conveniently profits the church.'

Mortimer blew out his cheeks. 'I should keep such thoughts very much to yourself, my lady. You will be condemned as a heretic.'

'Oh! Have no fear husband I would plead my belly besides, I speak such words for your ears alone!' Love would never be part of their marriage but loyalty was and even when they argued and played the battle of wills, both understood how important it was to present a united front to the outside world on important matters and in this, they invariably acted as one.

But even as the king mourned the untimely death of the Lord of Abergavenny, it did not halt the marriage arrangements for his son and heir and within the month, a royal messenger arrived bringing an invitation in celebration of the marriage of Lord Edward and the young Spanish princess, Eleanor of Castile. The wedding was part of a treaty between Henry and Alfonso X, King of Castile.

Once again Maud's pregnancy precluded her from attending, much to her chagrin. When she stood at the casement and watched her husband's colourful retinue ride through the gates of Wigmore she was filled with a mixture of frustration and relief. Nothing forewarned her of events which were about to follow.

Two days after Mortimer's departure, as dusk was falling, two black cloaked riders trotted into the outer bailey of the castle. A breathless servant rushed in to announce their arrival adding somewhat uncertainly, the visitors had refused to give their names. Intrigued Maud ordered the servant to show her mysterious guests up to her solar. As they entered, and with only the slightest intake of breath, she dismissed all the servants as soon as she recognised the tall stranger. Once she was certain that they were alone, she rose slowly and walked forward, her hands out in greeting.

'My Lord de Longeville! What brings you to Wigmore?' Her voice not much more than a whisper.

'My Lady Maud,' he hesitated. 'You look so pale and wan.'

She smiled thinly, 'I am with child and my pregnancy is a debilitating one I fear.'

He stepped forward, dropped to his knee, took her hand, and kissed it. The chamber was silent for a moment; only the light from the flickering candles cast shadows on the walls and tapestries giving them a strange, unearthly imagery. As he rose, de Longeville turned towards the youth who had not uttered a sound since entering the chamber.

'Let me introduce you to my squire, Lucien de Lisle.'

'You are most welcome, Lucien.' Maud's voice was still little more than a whisper. Inwardly her heart was racing. It had been so long since she had seen or even heard of de Longeville, and was still wrestling with her emotions at his unexpected appearance.

'Let me call for refreshments.' But de Longeville shook his head.

'First I need to speak with you in private.' He looked at Lucien. 'Take our cloaks if you will, and see they are dried and cleaned.'

'Yes my lord.' Without another word the squire moved noiselessly to the door and disappeared.

'This sounds mysterious!' Maud moved to her chair and sat down.

'Forgive this unexpected intrusion but when I was so close, could not deny myself, at least a glimpse of you,'

The couple looked into each others' eyes but neither moved. She noted the change in him; there was a marked difference from the young knight she had once known, before her was a hardened, weather beaten Crusader.

'I will be brief, my patron, the Comte, is carrying letters from France and also Rome, to the Queen and the Earl of Leicester. Exactly what the letters contain I am not privy to, but they are both to be handed to them personally, which leads me to believe their contents could prove controversial or, even compromising if they fell into the wrong hands. Although I have striven to disassociate myself from the intrigues of France, as you know, have been drawn in, simply by my association to the Comte. My role in this venture is to avert suspicions away from him and act as the decoy. But fear not, we have given our pursuers the slip, at least for the time being.'

Maud gasped audibly. 'De Montfort, his name always provokes apprehension within me. I am constantly warning Mortimer not to be drawn into his circle of friends but I know he is not convinced especially after the events in Gascony, he feels the Earl had cause for legitimate complaint. I have no real proof on what my fears are based, other than his obvious arrogance and continual need for money; therefore my arguments are treated as merely the misguided intuitions of a woman.'

'Your instincts are not at fault my lady. I am unable to betray my patron but feel that I must at least put you on your guard of what ..... I am, as yet, uncertain.'

Maud looked up at him. 'Thank you for your concern, at least I am not alone in my misgivings, your warning will make me ever more wary and I will certainly look for any untoward signs of intrigue' She hesitated. 'My deepest fear is treason.' Her words were hushed, and her tone, full of fear. 'The man is so full of arrogance and pride but, due to his devout beliefs, appear to blinker the churchmen to such sins.'

'All that can be done for the present is to wait and watch. All you can do my lady, is continue with your efforts to divert your husband away from becoming too close to Leicester, which may bring him into mortal danger.'

There was a tap at the door which interrupted their conversation. De Longeville went and sat down stretching his long legs before the fire. Steam rose from his sodden boots and clothing.

'You must change my lord or you will catch your death.'

He grinned and suddenly the years fell away and he was the young man she had known and loved all those years ago.

'We have no change of clothes we left them back at the Inn to divert suspicion for this journey which was a ....sudden decision.'

Maud rang and ordered food for her unexpected visitors.

'James will provide you and your squire with a change of clothes whilst yours dry out.'

'I am obliged my Lady.'

'I have also ordered hot water so you can bathe before supper.'

'Again my thanks!' He rose and left the chamber bowing before he turned to close the door.

An hour later refreshed, clean, and sporting some ill fitting robes, de Longeville and his squire sat once more in the comfortable chamber. They had ridden hard to reach Wigmore before nightfall and as the warmth of the fire and the effects of the hot bath began to take hold; both visibly relaxed and ate the tasty meal with relish.

'I was saddened to learn of the deaths of your sisters, although it was Eleanor's untimely end which was the cruellest, she was the sweetest young demoiselle that ever walked God's earth.'

Maud nodded. 'I miss her every day! Her death had a profound effect on Humphrey; he is quite a changed man.' She looked thoughtful, 'even his second marriage has done nothing to soften him.'

'True love can never be forgotten.' De Longeville tried to keep his voice on an even note as he spoke. At Lucien's return, Maud remained silent but she had heard the sincerity in de Longeville's words and during the meal glanced surreptitiously across at the seated knight who focused his gaze on the plate of food, his expression unfathomable. After they had eaten their fill and James had removed the empty platters and trenchers, Lucien yawned behind his hand.

'Pray seek your bed I will also retire presently as we have to be away before dawn.'

Lucien left bowing to his hostess and uttering a muted God night. Once alone, de Longeville looked across at Maud.

'And you my lady? Is Mortimer kind to you?'

Maud screwed her face. 'Mortimer could never be described as *kind* my lord but, he has long since learned to treat me with a measure of respect.' She hesitated, 'that is until his recent return from Gascony where he appears to have gained some overbearing habits. I must admit my relationship with Mortimer is not the easiest, partly due to our age difference and partly his own mercurial character. Apparently, his father was quite hard on him during his time as his squire and never praised him in any way, thus he grew up with a grudge against the world. Sad really, because he learned after his father's death that he was forever singing his praises to all and sundry but not within his son's hearing. I believe it left its mark on him! He possesses some complicated characteristics which I fear, make life difficult at times.' The last sentence was hardly audible but de Longeville had noted the wistfulness.

'And you my lord? The last I heard of your whereabouts you and the Comte were about to embark on a Crusade.'

As the fire dwindled and died he related some of his experiences in Egypt and touched briefly on the death of his second wife soon after the birth of their son.

'And the name of your son?'

'Alain. He is a bright little boy but we are complete strangers to each other as I am rarely at home and I cannot see that situation changing any time soon.'

'So much has happened to both of us and yet........!'

De Longeville looked into her eyes. 'For me at least, nothing has changed in my love for you.' They gazed at each other for a long hushed moment.

Maud took a deep breath, 'My marriage was arranged by my mother and uncle, my duty is to obey, not only out of respect but, also expediency.' She paused. 'My father's execution besmirched the name of de Braose and I vowed to myself to do everything within my power to expunge that shame.' Her voice had taken on a sharp edge as she spoke.

'The feeling of shame I carry for his sins are only outweighed by the pride I feel in my Marshal ancestry.' She hesitated. 'A twisted legacy, is it not my lord?' She looked earnestly at de Longeville as she spoke.

'How could I have known my heart would refuse to obey commands of honour and duty? Upon meeting you I experienced emotions which filled me with such feelings, too powerful to control.' She hesitated before continuing.

'My love was given freely and honestly so, whatever befalls me in life, know that you are my one and only love. I love you more than my own life, beyond duty even but.........I will not betray the honour of my family. Can you understand?'

De Longeville came and knelt at her feet taking her hand and covered it with kisses. She reached and caressed his hair. They remained so close, neither daring to move, both bound by their own codes of honour. She bent down and kissed his hair then, gently raised his face and kissed him on his mouth and the world of love, tenderness, and heartbreak, was encompassed in that one moment. Afterwards he rose and returned to his seat and they sat in silence whilst they regained control of their emotions.

Eventually Maud spoke. 'You are always in my thoughts and I will treasure this brief visit forever. The bonds of duty are cruel and we both suffer constantly from their consequences. Such a moment as this may never occur again in this life but, I pray that will not always be the case. I never realised until now, how much I missed you. I have suppressed my true self for so long, but pray one day, I shall be released and come to you unfettered by duty and honour with only my feelings of love. The very thought of being free fills me with such overwhelming joy.' She paused: 'that sounds shameful, as it would mean Mortimer was dead and much as he irritates me at times, I never wish for his death.'

De Longeville nodded. 'So we must continue to walk the road of life alone and yet, not alone, for the sake of honour and duty.' He smiled sadly as he spoke. 'It is also my constant prayer one day somehow; we *will* find a way of being together but for now at least, must leave our fate in the hands of God.'

Maud looked thoughtful. 'I have come to believe that it is my destiny to guide a rash and stubborn young man to fulfil his role as a leader, not only in the Marches but, at the English court. Why I feel thus, I cannot explain, but it is a notion that has grown within me over the years and to those ends I must strive in order for the family of Mortimer to continue along a path to success, my legacy to my children, and one they can be proud of.'

He smiled. 'Knowing you my Lady as I do, leaves me in no doubt whatever you aim to do, you will achieve and if I can ever be of service, in whatever capacity, know I am your servant.'

Maud turned her face away so he could not see her tears.

'Now, I must seek my bed for I must leave before you rise on the morrow but I feel easier in my heart now I have seen you once more. Whatever befalls us in the future, I know I hold your heart as you hold mine and that for now, that knowledge must give us the strength to survive. However, I will never forsake the hope, one day, this weight of duty will be lifted, and we can find a way of being together. All we can do is hold fast to that dream, and that our paths will cross again when we are no longer bound to serve the wishes of others.' His voice had sunk low but she heard the deep emotion in his words.

Without further ado he rose and left the chamber. Maud remained motionless, silent tears ran unchecked down her cheeks. How long she remained there she never knew. Eventually she regained her composure, wiped her eyes before she too rose, and sought the sanctuary of her bed. The following morning before the cock crew, de Longville and his squire were heading towards Chester, resuming their cat and mouse game with their pursuers.

Their departure had not gone unnoticed by the ever watchful gaze of Lord Rhys. Later that day he approached the subject with Maud.

'They were messengers being pursued, who merely sought sanctuary for the night.'

His dark eyes narrowed at her words. 'I understand if the nature of their visit is one of secrecy, my lady and will speak of it no more.'

'Thank you! Sometimes we are unwilling pawns in the game of kings.'

Weeks later, upon Mortimer's returned from London, he brought some disturbing news concerning Wales. Llywelyn was once again stirring up trouble and the English agents had sent word to alert a number of the Marches barons. Maud was aware of the importance of his announcement, which would undoubtedly impact on their future, but for her it must play a secondary role to the needs of her own body. Oddly enough, the visit of the two strangers was never mentioned by Mortimer, therefore Maud concluded that no-one had seen fit to inform him of the matter, maybe it was in the light of this new development they deemed there was nothing untoward in the situation.

As Maud retreated to await the birth of her baby, she had time to mull over how the recent death of William de Cantelupe, would impact on the growing unrest in Wales. If trouble was erupting once more, then as Lord of Abergavenny, his voice of moderation would now be sorely missed, not only in Parliament and at court but, here on the March.

Whatever her personal views were regarding her late brother-in-law, it had not blinded her to the value of his worth, and now his loss would impact, not only on the king and the Marches, but also the haughty Earl of Leicester who, undoubtedly would feature at some point in the country's ills. The king had undoubtedly lost an invaluable advisor in William. What the future held was out of her hands and all she could do now was await the birth of her baby.

CHAPTER XVIII

1255

The news of Maud's safe delivery was carried far and wide. The child, a boy, was named after his father. As she looked down at the puling infant she felt a rush of incredulity. She had born five children, three sons, and two daughters. Like Maud's previous off-springs, the baby was duly delivered into the care of Carys and her growing band of nursery maids and wet nurses. Due to outbreak of hostilities in Wales, it meant the celebrations for the child's safe delivery, were short lived. Wales must take centre stage. Once Maud had been churched and the child baptised, she was free to focus her attention on the imminent threats in the Marches.

Llywelyn ap Gruffydd, and his younger brother Dafydd, were locked in a struggle for supremacy, which had finally brought them into open warfare. It had challenged the loyalties of many of the leading Welsh leaders including, some of the Marcher lords, who had inextricable been drawn into the conflict.

When a messenger arrived with word of Llywelyn's outright victory at the Battle of Bryn Derwin, the news sent ripples of apprehension through the barons, not only of the Welsh Marches but, as far away as the court of the English king. It meant that Llywelyn ap Gruffydd was now undisputed leader in a large part of Wales; this would inevitably pose a threat to the fragile peace treaty between Llywelyn and the English. At the head of a united army, Llywelyn would undoubtedly renew hostilities with the English at some point, leaving Henry in grave danger. Everyone was acutely aware it would take little to ignite hostilities again; so the Marches braced itself for the inevitable onset of war.

But once again, it was family matters which took precedence in Maud's life, as she learned that her sole surviving sister, Eve, had sickened and died. It was no real surprise, in fact she had almost expected such an outcome, and the *sickness* was due to a broken heart, and no other illness. Whatever the truth, Maud once more found herself donning the apparel of mourning and rode towards Abergavenny to the funeral of her last remaining sister. She did not believe Llywelyn would dare to attack the funeral party but nevertheless; scouts and armed guards accompanied them on their journey.

Even though Maud held no strong personal bonds with Eve, it did not dilute their blood ties and she could not quell the pang of real pain of this latest family loss. As she sat through the long service she could not suppress the memories which flooded through her mind. It opened the wounds of grief she had suffered at the loss of Izzy and Nell, and her mother, whom she had respected and loved.

But Maud was not one to dwell on negative thoughts and as she made her homeward journey her pragmatic nature quickly returned and she focused her thoughts on the lands and estates Eve had left, especially in the light of her widowhood. There would be the couple's children who would inherit but Maud was determined to make it her business to explore any possibility that the Marshal and de Braose lands, not included in Eve's dowry, may now revert to the sole surviving de Braose sister. She consoled herself with these plans as she neared her favourite castle of Radnor. Mortimer had remained behind for discussions with other Marcher barons on strategies in readiness for the inevitable outbreak of war with Wales.

On her arrival at Radnor, Maud revelled in her surroundings which brought happier memories flooding back of her childhood, the unpleasant ones she had cast from her consciousness. She watched the drovers and their flocks moving along the well worn highway, on their way south. Voices of travellers and the lowing of cattle and bleating of sheep rose and fell in an age old rhythm of life; occasionally, notes of a song or, the sound of pipes would filter through the windows of her chamber. Radnor was a fortress, rather than a home nonetheless, Maud loved this castle more than any other place on earth. She trusted it stout walls and loved its defiant stance at the gateway of the March. Whenever she got a chance, she would take a walk beside the fast flowing river, which danced and babbled as it hurried on towards the sea. Water, the life blood of men, crops, and animals. She knew the river had run with blood in the past and did not doubt it would do so again but Maud offered up a silent prayer this was a long time in the future. Her short sojourn was interrupted one day when she spied Mortimer and his company of retainers, riding towards them on the road from Wales.

The mood of the company was already sombre, but as news from around Wales, which arrived almost daily, served to endorse what each man feared; the growing threat from their long standing enemy was imminent.

After Llywelyn's victory over his youngest brother, Dafydd had been taken prisoner, but by all accounts, was not only free, but the errant brother had been forgiven and was re-united with his older sibling. Now, acting together, they were ready to take back lands which had been lost since their grandsires death, more than a dozen years ago. Urgency was the key word, as drovers and shepherds hurriedly moved large flocks of sheep and cattle towards the markets in Shropshire and further south knowing, they were vulnerable to armies, from either side, who would take livestock to feed the men regardless of who suffered the loss. Families had often been left to starve after raids by marauding forces.

Llywelyn did not leave the English long to wait wondering where he would strike first and when it came it was swift, savage, and effective. Castles from the coast to the Marches were attacked and left in ruins; many of them were Mortimer strongholds. Maud knew this was not only a deliberate act to undermine her young husband's position, but an open challenge from his cousin. She watched Mortimer fume and rage as he prepared to return to Wales at the head of his army.

Maud made ready to return to Wigmore but sent urgent word ahead, that the children should be taken to Tetbury immediately. The fast riding messengers, who arrived daily, brought news of more and more Welsh victories. The Marcher lords sent pressing missives and pleas for more men and aid from the king, but their pleas were ignored, leaving them to face Llywelyn's army undermanned and underfunded. In an effort to swell his troops, Mortimer ordered the regular guards at Wigmore to join him in Wales.

Upon her return Maud had organised food, horses, and weapons to be sent to Radnor but the orders to deplete Wigmore of its men-at-arms, caused Maud and her chamberlain, much consternation, as it left Wigmore vulnerable to attack. Only days after the departure of the men and wagons of supplies, the fears of the castle's occupants were proved to be sound.

One of Llywelyn's swift riding raiding parties descended on Wigmore with such speed, men, women, and children, died on the streets, and in their homes and fields. Few headed for the safety within the walls of Wigmore Castle, but some had found the gates had been closed and they were cut down; death met them at every corner; as arrows and bolts found their targets, and swords slew the unarmed peasants indiscriminately.

As the noise of the screams, mingled with the curdling yells of triumph and echoed around the outer bailey, Lord Rhys ushered Maud and three young squires to one of the towers, urging them to follow him. He grabbed a few crossbows and quarrels he had placed in readiness some days beforehand. On reaching the tower, he indicated for Maud to hurry to the small chamber at the head of the winding stairwell. Gasping for air, he hurried after her. Hastily he took a sword from the trembling hands of one of the youths and pushed the crossbow at him.

'If you stand here at the top of the stairwell you can pick off anyone on their way up before they reach us.'

To the other two, he asked for their belts and as they watched, he quickly buckled the two belts together.

'Once they are on the stairs, you will position yourselves either side of the door, kneeling and keeping low so anyone who reaches here will be tripped up before they strike a blow. Once they are down you can finish them off with your swords.'

He turned to Maud, 'my lady, hide behind the coffer over there in the corner.'

Her green-grey eyes flashed with fury as she hissed.

'If I am to die this day it will not be cowering in a corner be assured of that. Pray do not fear for my safety, I will be worth more to them as a hostage.'

Lord Rhys could tell by the expression on her face to argue would be fruitless. So he turned his attention back to the squires.

'Your names?' He looked to the tallest of the trio who held the crossbow.

'My name is Edwin de Saye' he nodded towards the smallest of the threesome, 'that is Richard of Clun and over there is Arthur de Peshale.'

As they looked at each other the sounds and shrieks from outside continued to echo around the shadowy walls of the tower. 'All I ask is that you each give a good account of yourselves today. How you defend your mistress will be recorded in Wigmore history. Let us pray the Saints are with us and that we hold our nerve, our courage, and honour, and may God give us strength to face our enemy without fear.'

Maud looked at the unlikely band. An aging Welshman and three squires all under the age of fourteen. But she also noted the affect Lord Rhys's words had had on the boys. Honour was the code they understood, knighthood was the goal they all aimed for and their actions here, could make or break their reputations and each knew it would be how they were judged in the future, that is - if they survived. To die bravely in battle, was all any knight wished for and this was about to be their testing ground.

Maud stood before each one in turn and took their hands in turn then she moved to Lord Rhys;

'Give me a blade, they will not take me lightly on that you have my word. To each of you I give my thanks, and offer up a prayer for our salvation.'

Just as she finished speaking they heard a loud thundering crash as the battering ram struck the mighty oak door at the base of the tower. Lord Rhys handed Maud his deadly looking dagger and made the sign of the cross. The tension as they listened to the resounding noise as the door withstood the onslaught. Maud heard the smallest boy, Arthur take a shuddering breath and moved to touch his shoulder.

'You were named after a warrior King of England, he will give you strength.' Then she turned to the boy named Richard. 'You too were named after a king known as 'Lionheart', she smiled towards the oldest squire. 'You bear the ancient name of many of the Anglo-Saxon warriors, who proved they were fearless in their fight for freedom.' She felt she was babbling but wished only to give comfort to boys who may never grow to be men.

After what seemed like eternity the mighty door finally splintered and with a triumphant whoop there was suddenly a hoard of Welshmen trying to mount the twisting stairs. Edwin looked across at Lord Rhys who nodded. As the first attacker reached the killing zone, a quarrel hissed through the air and hit him full in the chest, he fell back gurgling on his last breath, as his dying body fell onto the man following, there was a momentary confusion, as the attackers climbed over the corpse of their dead companion.

Swiftly, young Edwin picked up the second crossbow and fired a second lethal bolt into the approaching enemy. His moment of truth had arrived but he was determined not to be found wanting. His face was full of resolve, so too were those of the two younger squires who pulled out their blades as they knelt in readiness to strike at the legs and thighs of their attackers. They pulled the belts taught with their other hands. Their young faces were full of fear but they nodded to each other as they made ready to defend their patroness.

Maud heard a barked order in Welsh and Lord Rhys whispered, 'they have sent for a spear.' He looked at Edwin 'be ready, do not give them an easy target'. Behind them an arrow whistled through the window falling short of its mark but startling Maud. Then as another Welsh attacker charged for the door, Edwin swiftly drew his sword and swung it at the yelling Welshman; they heard him shriek as the blade found its target. The man collapsed backwards, hampering the man following, as the lack of space once again caused mayhem. Edwin quickly snatched his dagger from his belt and thrust it into the body of the second attacker, as it struck into his body; he felt the impact as it jarred his shoulder. Edwin had shown a cool head under pressure but knew he did not possess the strength to keep a seasoned warrior at bay for long, already his muscles screamed with pain at the intense exertion of the last few minutes.

As Edwin's victim moaned and fell to the floor, Lord Rhys struck at another advancing enemy who he thrust back down the stairwell.

Then someone shouted. Lord Rhys turned back to his companions his face, filled with concern. 'Fire, they have sent for firebrands.'

Maud breathed the words. 'God help us!'

Somewhere in the distance they heard the sound of a horn.

'Sweet Jesus!' Young Arthur gasped, 'are we saved or, are more of them coming?'

A look of horror spread over the boys' faces as the adults held their breaths. The commotion below and on the stairs suddenly ceased as urgent calls could be heard. Lord Rhys said softly, 'they are ordering a retreat.'

Maud let out a long sigh, turned her eyes skyward, and said a silent prayer. She looked to her chamberlain but the retreating Welsh had set a fire at the foot of the tower and already plumes of thick, black smoke, curled up and began to fill the air.

Lord Rhys moved to one of the arrow slits and took a deep breath; he beckoned for the others to do likewise. Then he called out, 'A Mortimer, a Mortimer.'

Somewhere below them, figures looked up and saw the billowing smoke, quickly running to fetch buckets of water to douse the flames. One enterprising young servant had caught and mounted a horse, hooking the fireball and galloped off pulling it away from the building. Once out of harm's way, he had dismounted and ran back to help the others to douse the remaining flames with water.

Eventually, the quintet made their way down the stone stairs, littered with dead Welshmen, taking care not slip on the blood of their enemies. They finally emerged from the blackened building where they were met with a scene of utter carnage. Some of the remaining walls of Wigmore Castle stood with gaping holes; fires blazed from many of the buildings, billowing smoke belched from the hay stores; animals, some injured careered around the courtyard. There were bodies covered in blood and gore, lying at macabre angles. Death had paid a deadly visit, one which would live long in the memory of those who survived that day. Maud was thankful she had sent Jane and Carys away with her children, knowing her lady-in-waiting was expecting her first child.

Once Maud had caught her breath she turned to the little group and in a voice not much more than a whisper.

'Today I have witnessed your true courage and thank you all for your valiant efforts.' Her next words were spoken to the three young squires. 'In my heart, I know you have earned your knights spurs this day.' She went and took each of their hands in turn as they bowed somewhat awkwardly. 'But our work is not yet done!' Maud then turned to her chamberlain, 'come, and let us see what is left of the Infirmary. Edwin, gather all those that are unhurt and organise them into working parties to put out the fires as quickly as possible. Richard, you gather all the water buckets, and try and save the hay. Arthur, you stay by me and serve as my messenger.' At that moment a band of armed men rode through the scene of devastation. The leader dismounted and hurriedly came to meet Lady Mortimer.

'My Lord Devereuax, you are a most welcome sight.' The thickset knight bowed and kissed her hand. She looked at the youth holding his horse and recognised her own groom, Hal.

'I am only sorry I could not get here any sooner. Your messenger......'

'I sent no word, it happened all too quickly.'

They both looked enquiringly at the red faced groom and in stilted tones he began to relate the events which had led him to seek help.

'I had taken one of the young charger's away from Castle to school somewhere quiet when he bolted into the forest, by the time I got him quieted and was returning, saw a band of fast riding soldiers. I knew by their apparel they were not from these parts, guessing where they were heading and with my mount all but spent, knew I could not outrun them so I headed towards Ludlow and by chance met his lordship, who was returning from Wales.' Maud looked at her groom.

'Thank heaven for the wayward steed and your quick thinking. You undoubtedly saved our lives.' Her warm smile said everything.

'As you can see my Lord Devereaux, we have much to do!'

'I will send help of course, and rally more assistance. God's Blood Lady, you had a lucky escape. Mortimer will be incensed when he learns of this outrageous attack. I must ride to Brampton and see if they have suffered a similar fate.' Without further ado he bowed and rode off at a gallop through the charred gates.

'Hal, see what you can do to help, and round up the horses.' She patted his shoulder. 'I give my heartfelt thanks to you and God for our salvation.'

As Maud walked round assessing the worst of the damage her mood changed from relief to rage, and the focus of her rage was her husband. By depleting the troops at Wigmore, it had left them with too few men to offer any real resistance against hardened raiders? In the days that followed her anger simmered beneath the outward appearance of calm. Thankfully she was kept busy, relying on her chamberlain to translate the needs of the villagers as he spoke their language, as well as Welsh and Norman French. True, she did understand some words and phrases but with such complicated details to deal with was glad she was not at a disadvantage. It left her determined to learn the local dialect in the future.

When Lord Mortimer finally arrived at Wigmore he could not contain his fury when he saw the scorched and damaged walls and ruined buildings.

'I swear by all the Saints my accursed cousin will be brought to book for this. I will see him at the end of my sword where he will find no mercy. How dare he attack my home and .... my wife?' His words echoed round the Great Hall.

Maud looked at her husband with unveiled scorn. 'Maybe some of your rage should be directed at yourself for leaving Wigmore without proper protection. It was folly to leave us with so few troops so you must bear at least some of the blame!'

There had been no personal greetings between them and the retainers present felt the raw resentment in Lady Mortimer's statement.

'Your words are no more than a bag of wind, my lord. The actions of my chamberlain and three gallant squires hold far more worth for me than your hot air.' She turned on her heels and walked swiftly towards the Infirmary leaving the Lord of Wigmore looking after her retreating back with a look of pure bewilderment spread across his face.

During the months which followed, Maud was kept busier than she had ever been. The urgent work to repair Wigmore and the village was paramount; there were men and horses constantly coming and going. Workmen's voices joined in the cacophony of noise as they set about re-building the walls and roofs of the Castle and the cottages and houses in the village. Carts filled with all types of masonry and timbers, trundles daily through the gates of Wigmore. Most of the authority for the work fell at Maud's feet due to the fact her husband, was constantly riding off to either attack or defend the castles still under threat along the borders or, to attend countless meetings of war.

The king had finally been roused into action by his son, Lord Edward, whose own lands and castles had been attacked by Llewellyn's forces. He in turn vented his ire on Mortimer for failing to stem the invaders and during the months which followed, the disgruntled Marcher found himself rarely out of the saddle. It was no secret, Mortimer felt he had been let down by the king especially, when Llywelyn had overrun Gwrtheyrnion, mainly due to Mortimer's lack of men and equipment.

However, at home the Mortimer couple had eventually made their peace and it was during this period Maud needed all her persuasive skills to keep a tight control on her husband's volatile temper. The irony of the situation was not lost to her but; she knew it would take little for him to become so disenchanted with the situation; it may well prompt him to act rashly. Maud was trying to emulate her grandsire, the legendary William Marshal, who had displayed not only outstanding bravery, but staunch loyalty to the five kings he had served but had also demonstrated circumspection when necessary. She truly believed that the fortunes of the Mortimer family lay with the king, however unpalatable that was to bear at times.

By January of 1257, Maud's persistence finally appeared to have reaped its rewards. Henry had sent letters of protection, as long as Mortimer served the crown. Later that year he also promised a sum of 200 marks in gold to aid with the defence of the Marches. Maud felt vindicated by her support for the king and relieved that she had played her part in averting what may have proved a dangerous split from crown. The role of subtlety and guile had at times been quite difficult and she sometimes marvelled how much she had changed from the tempestuous child. Maud also acknowledged. her current strategy and tactics were due mainly to the example set by Lord Rhys.

There was a visible easing of tensions when finally, the long requested funds for the Welsh campaigns arrived from the treasury. However, the sense of euphoria at this small success, had quickly evaporated when only half of the promised gold had actually materialised, leaving Mortimer to pay the mounting costs, much to his chagrin.

At court, the political situation was almost as uncertain as those in the Marches. Maud understood the financial pressures imposed on her husband but, she also recognised the position the king now found himself faced with and could foresee the pitfalls her husband's feelings of dissatisfaction could once again lead him into, especially in these difficult times.

It had been the losses of the cantrefs of Gwrtheyrnion, and Maelienydd, which had left Mortimer utterly frustrated but he had had scant time to dwell on the matter, as the struggle for supremacy in areas throughout the region became paramount. However, when news arrived that Llywelyn had been declared Prince of Wales by Henry, Mortimer's rage was awesome.

Fury was also an emotion experienced by Henry Plantagenet, who now felt besieged on all sides. The current wars in Wales and Llywelyn's successes, made him feel it was like a personal slight to his authority. But there was also growing discord within his own court, which stemmed, from his mishandling of the agreement with Rome on Sicily, which had been instigated by the Pope. An arrangement, much opposed by many of his senior advisors at the onset, as the exorbitant payments the agreement entailed, now promised to push England to the brink of financial ruin.

The growing feeling of unrest had also been fuelled by Henry's persistent refusal to listen to the grievances of his nobles. Even his beloved son Edward's voice had joined those of his accusers, a fact which hurt both Henry, and his wife, Queen Eleanor.

Eventually under extreme pressure, Henry finally agreed to a meeting and listen to the voices of his subjects who hailed from every level of society, from the high born nobles, to merchants, artisans, farmers, scribes, burgesses and yeomen. It had been agreed that a dozen men from each county would be elected to represent the Shires of his kingdom. The place arranged for this momentous occasion, was to be Oxford.

CHAPTER XIX

By June 1258, the streets, lanes, and market squares of Oxford, bustled with the influx of men from all counties and every walk of life anxious to voice their complaints. The king was consumed with indignation at the situation he now found himself in. Strife surrounded him like an angry sea of unrest; de Montfort, as usual, was at the forefront of any confrontation, backed by some of the most powerful magnates in the land. The Earls of Gloucester, Hereford, and the respected Justiciar, Hugh Bigod, now joined by men from the Shires.

Over the years the heavy burden of taxation had fallen on everyone in the realm and the sheriffs, whose task it was to see that these revenues were collected, had become the focus of resentment as many abused their positions of authority and became rich on their nefarious activities.

Originally the summons had been to recruit men for the Welsh wars but now Henry was about to face subjects who were echoing many of the complaints of his barons. One of the core issues in the ever growing list of complaints was the king's half brothers, the Lusignans'.

Since their arrival in England, they had been awarded lands, high offices, and lucrative marriages in preference to the native born nobles. This had fuelled a growing resentment by the deposed landowners whose properties had been stripped and the anger was for both the hated Lusignans, and Henry who persistently refused to acknowledge the crimes committed by his half brothers. Even after one of them murdered a servant, it had failed to move Henry from his intransigent position.

Matters looked as though a long standing personal quarrel between William de Valance, Earl of Pembroke, and the Earl of Leicester, Simon de Montfort, which had recently re-ignited, would overshadow the forthcoming parliament. William de Valance, eldest of the four siblings, had attracted personal hostility from the first. Now, Henry's, brother-in-law, Simon de Montfort's voice grew ever louder in accusations against his rival, a deadly ingredient to the mounting feeling of unrest. Once again Henry and his brother-in-law found themselves on opposing sides of an argument.

It was into this maelstrom Sir Roger Mortimer now found himself as he had been elected to attend parliament as one of the twelve representatives for the Marcher barons. His election was at the insistence of some of the most powerful of his contemporaries, who had forced Henry's hand months earlier, to call this parliament. It was in part, a controversial idea put forward that governance of the country should not lie solely with the king and his few advisors but, be debated amongst representatives from every shire in the land. Reluctantly Henry had agreed to this move and that in future, parliament would be made up of twelve elected nobles and twelve men from every rank of society, in an effort to represent the will of the people.

Everywhere Mortimer visited in Oxford he felt the atmosphere bristling with nervous tension; men walked around with hands never far from their swords hilts and vehement language could be heard on street corners and taverns. But in other quarters, there was also a sense of muted optimism; could this be the beginning of a new era where the mismanagement of Henry and his close advisors, would finally be addressed and the power of the Lusignans and Savoyards be curbed.

Maud had watched her husband ride away at the head of a company of his retainers. She felt apprehensive, Mortimer had become a hardened soldier especially after his service in Gascony; ruthless in his approach to war. She feared however, he may find he was ill equipped to grasp the nuances this new position he had been elected to, and would require from him. There was no doubt, he often lacked perception in diplomacy, and this, coupled with his inability to read peoples character; a necessary requisite in delicate matters of negotiations, could prove a stumbling block. All she could do was pray he would rise to the occasion and prove all her doubts unfounded. She recalled her words to him in the privacy of their bedchamber where she had used terms she hoped had not prompted any violent aversion

'Do you believe this new idea of Parliament will bring about any real change of heart by the king?' She had kept her tone light and conversational rather than probing.

'He will have to recognise the complaints they have been on the table for years now and the patience of the barons grows ever shorter.' Mortimer's tone had been somewhat dismissive.

'But we know the king's decisions are like quicksilver, and de Montfort and his cohorts are un-bendable, so where does that leave you, my lord?'

Mortimer glanced across to where she stood at the window, the sunlight illuminating her dark green kirtle, and the gold filigree caul holding her hair, and he was for a moment, taken off guard by her beauty. Childbirth had done little to dim her physical charms and there were only faint lines at the corner of her green-grey eyes, to denote the passing of the years. Maud's words interrupted his train of thoughts.

'I still distrust de Montfort; this latest quarrel with de Valence is all to do with land. You can guarantee his ambitions and greed, lie at the heart of any altruistic actions.'

'I think you are mistaken Madam.'

She walked towards him and looked him directly in the eye. 'In the matter of wealth and power, I trust no-one, my lord. Maybe it would be politic to listen to all the arguments before jumping in with any confrontational comments which may be construed by the king as treasonable!' The words were spoken without rancour. She continued.

'This feud between de Montfort and de Valence is bound to add fuel to the discord. Do you forget that when de Valence married Joan de Munchesni, a Marshal co-heiress, he was given the title held by my late Uncle Anselm, Earl of Pembroke? The quarrel is all about money.' She paused and went and looked deep into his dark eyes

'Pray consider this, a cornered Plantagenet may prove a treacherous adversary, and I do not believe Henry will meekly accede to de Montfort demands, or for that matter any this Parliament may put to him, do you?.' She hesitated before continuing, 'should the throne be threatened, remember Queen Eleanor will fight for her son's inheritance, so too will Edward himself, and you have already fallen foul of that Plantagenet's ire, pray do not do so again.'

'But the Lord Edward upholds our complaints and sides with de Montfort on this matter.' Mortimer's voice was thick with resentment he hated being reminded of his shortcomings.

Maud rounded on him her voice filled with misgiving.

'I am in agreement with the cause, any right minded person would uphold the demands – but, if all fails and it came to open conflict where do you think the Lord Edward would stand then? With de Montfort, I think not! He, like his mother, would defend the throne at all cost, for one day he will rule. Do you believe he would put his succession in jeopardy?'

Maud circled the room before continuing.

'There are other ways to bring about the changes required and one which does not involve open opposition.' She stopped in front of him. 'Often it is the softly spoken word which holds the most worth. Sow a seed of doubt here, and grain of suspicion there, and very soon, you have former friends at each other's throats. It is an age old art used throughout history. Power and silver are a prize not many men or, king's are willing to forego, even the pious and seemingly ineffectual ones. Eleanor of Provence, and her Savoyard uncles will never let the balances of power tip towards de Montfort, they will guard Edward's Plantagenet throne, whatever the cost.'

'My God Madam, you are a formidable woman. So you would employ intrigue as opposed to open argument?'

Maud had patted her husband's shoulder; 'I would indeed my lord but' she hesitated, 'choose your allies with care, and watch your enemies with even greater care.' With that, she had bade him God night, left the chamber, not waiting to see her husband's reaction but as she walked away, hoped her words had found their target.

Maud felt certain that Henry would never easily submit to the demands of his subjects, especially under duress; there was much at stake in the coming months and her express aim was the furtherance of the Mortimer cause. All she could hope for now was that her husband did not become enmeshed in the outright opposition to the royal family.

Whilst the Lord of Wigmore rode off to attend to his parliamentary duties, Maud was left with more personal matters to address; her chamberlain, Lord Rhys, had suffered a debilitating sickness during the winter which had left him weakened and unsteady. It was obvious that he could no longer continue carrying the burden of responsibility of his day to day duties. So, it was with a heavy heart Maud had to acknowledge her faithful advisor needed to retire but her chamberlain was not the only one who would be leaving her services, as Jane was carrying her second child and would soon be relieved of her duties. It was a situation that would not easily be resolved; to find a competent chamberlain and a trustworthy waiting woman within a short space of time would be no easy task.

The answer to one of the vacancies came from within her small circle of trusted servants in the guise of young Arthur de Peshale. Since the raid on Wigmore Arthur, Richard, and Edwin, had been attached to Maud's personal household. Against all odds, Arthur had formed a close relationship with her chancellor and had plied Lord Rhys with a mountain of questions on the correct ways of administration. At first, the aging chamberlain had found it a source of irritation but quickly came to realise the young squire's potential and realised his wit, combined with the ability to retain information, could be a great asset to Lady Mortimer. He had given him piles of books and manuscripts to read and been impressed at how rapidly Arthur had absorbed the knowledge.

When Lord Rhys suggested Arthur become his natural successor the matter appeared to have been successfully resolved. But Maud was not about to endorse Arthur's position to chamberlain, the title would remain with Lord Rhys who would continue to act as her advisor, but with Arthur as his pro-active assistant. Maud was pleased the situation had been so amicably addressed. In due course, this arrangement would prove to be a valuable partnership.

With one position filled it left Maud free to concentrate on her search for a new lady-in-waiting however; her growing concern of late was the situation in the Marches. Wigmore had not been alone in being sacked by Llywelyn who, if reports were to be believed, had reached the very walls of Chester in his audacious raids. The Welsh gauntlet had been well and truly laid down to the English. Wales was once more led by a warrior prince who was accepted by the majority of its peoples in both, the north and south of the country. The ranks of Llywelyn's army swelled in numbers with each successful raid. His guerrilla tactics of warfare were proving the most affective, much to the chagrin of his English adversaries.

To recruit proficient men-at-arms, archers, knights, and soldiers was still of paramount importance. Maud knew that if Llywelyn's challenge was to be met the Marches must have sufficient troops to fill any requests for fighting men. This would cost money and the coffers of the nation were known to be perilously lacking in gold and silver. Maud's practical mind could not comprehend how a nation's king could have sanctioned the enormous expenditure on adorning the tombs of a long dead king, before the needs of his people. Surely, it did not matter one jot, that Edward the Confessor needed such an elaborate tomb to honour him as a Saint? Then of course, there had been another disastrous decision by Henry, to have his second son, Edmund, named as King of Sicily, a decision encouraged by the Pope. The cost of this folly had proved unsustainable, and negotiations with Rome were ever ongoing. If the health of Lord Rhys was failing, his strength of mind remained as sharp as ever and Maud frequently discussed these pertinent matters of the day with him.

When Mortimer returned from Oxford he was filled with optimism, the king had agreed too many of the terms laid down in the treaty dubbed, '*The Provisions of Oxford*' and had surprisingly, dismissed the Lusignans from the kingdom. He sat in the solar and recounted the details of the talks and the views of many of those who had attended. Maud listened quietly mulling over his words then said:

'You mark my words my lord, Henry will find a way of side stepping these agreements,' she hesitated

'The idea of representation of all classes has no doubt found favour with many but it does not directly affect the majority;

the power therefore remains with the nobility. Henry, may be a pious man but he has only conceded to these demands because he is in dire need of funds which will be raised through taxation and who will he need to support such requests?' Maud looked knowingly at her husband.

'I applaud many of the proposed changes but it does not blind me to Henry's true nature. Look how his father treated those that served him. My family's history bears testament to exactly how dangerous it is to cross the descendants of King John. Pray, who holds the title of Earl of Pembroke today, Valence?' She paused, 'it matters not, that they have been banished, they will be recalled ere long, I'll wager. This situation is but temporary; an effort to quell the protestors. Henry is convinced, as king, he answers only to God, not to those he deems to be his subjects! The word should give you the clue, *subjects,* which means obedience to his, will.' The look which passed between the couple spoke volumes and it halted further discourse.

In late July Mortimer had cause to remember his wife's words of caution as news reached them that both Richard and William de Clare had been poisoned. William had died a horrible death and Richard, although he had survived, had lost his hair, eyebrows, and teeth. The murderer, Walter de Soutenay, who had served as steward to the de Clare family for many years, but as to the reason for his wicked act, it was as yet uncertain. Maud, however, was sceptical at Mortimer's conclusions it had been a personal grudge. Although Maud did not openly contradict her husband's views, she did discuss the matter at length with Lord Rhys.

'Do *you* really believe it to be a grudge killing my Lord?'

Lord Rhys sat steepling his fingers as he leaned back in the tall backed chair.

'I could try and discover the truth my Lady, if you so wish!'

'Without questions being asked or, fingers pointed?'

He smiled. 'I have chosen my agents over the years, with great care. Those that have served me in the past will continue to do so for as long as I call on their services.' The tone of his voice assured her if there was an unknown truth to be gained behind such a foul deed, it would discovered by her aging chamberlain.

When Maud attended the funeral service of her late cousin William, she was truly shocked at the macabre appearance of the once handsome, Richard de Clare, Earl of Gloucester. His skin was yellowish and tightly drawn over his cheeks, he had been given permission to wear a hat in church to cover his sore and hairless scalp; and when he spoke it was little more than a whisper. During the service he had to be supported by his squire. For once, Maud found her normal iron resolve was unresponsive and she shed tears of grief, not only for William, but also for Richard, so cruelly disfigured.

In the autumn of the year Maud's well founded fears regarding Henry's failure to uphold the treaty of Oxford, were proved correct. He sailed to France for a meeting with Louis and sources stated, it was in an effort to gain a dispensation from the Pope to absolve him from upholding the terms of the treaty and also to negotiate the repayment to Rome, for Sicily. The pledge, made some years ago, was now proving too heavy a burden financially for England and the hollow title of King of Sicily, held by the king's second son, Edmund, came at a price too great for the nation.

The French king had offered Henry his support, the price, to cede Normandy, Anjou, and Poitou and swear fealty for Gascony. Louis felt triumphant; he had gained this victory without a blow being struck. What Henry had agreed to would have a profound effect, not least for his son, the young Lord Edward, who it was reported, to have raged like a wild beast at the news. These were desperate measures by Henry, who continued to be harried by his barons, and their spokesman and leader – Simon de Montfort.

Upon learning of this momentous news, Maud recalled the words of her mother's old chaplain, when he had preached against the sin of pride, which he believed to be the greatest of the seven deadly sins. It would appear that even the most devout of king's had fallen victim. There was also another whose pride she believed would be his downfall, the haughty Simon de Montfort, Earl of Leicester. However, for the moment, he too was in France, leaving the English Marcher lords to face Llywelyn and his Welsh hordes, unaided in the continuing struggle for supremacy.

Over the following years Maud witnessed the ever changing fortunes of war in Wales and the mounting opposition to Henry's rule. All she could do was support her husband, her children and the people of Wigmore. The deteriorating relationship between the king and his nobles left everyone in a state of anxiety as the dialogue had now in certain areas, turned to violent actions.

Nothing could quell Maud's growing apprehension. It was like waiting for a storm to break; everyone knew it was coming but no-one knew when. Personally, Maud was becoming ever more fearful that her husband was being drawn into the party of dissenters. All she could do was to reiterate her own fears and hope common sense would eventually triumph. She never forgot the warnings of Guy de Longeville; maybe the letters from France had been the forerunner of what had subsequently transpired between Henry and Louis. It looked as though if violence did break out wholesale in England, Henry would turn to Louis for aid – the consequences of such an act would be catastrophic.

BOOK THREE

ERA OF THE SWORD

CHAPTER XX

1262 Wigmore

After Henry's visit to the French court, where he had successfully gained the Papal Bull, which absolved him from the terms of both, *'The Provisions of Oxford'*, which had subsequently been replaced in 1259, with *'The Provisions of Winchester'*. The ruling made it obvious to the disgruntled magnates, that England's king had no intentions of ever relinquishing any of his powers or, upholding their Rights, originally laid down in the Magna Carta and a clash between sovereign and nobles looked inevitable.

During the intervening years, as Maud had so rightly predicted, the Lusignans had returned, which only added to the simmering resentment against those seen as avaricious 'aliens'. Attacks had spread throughout the kingdom against men viewed as 'foreigners', which included the Jewish money lenders. It was common knowledge the Queen hated the Jews.

As the north wind whipped across the valley and along the streets and lanes of Wigmore, the mood in the castle was tense. News arrived that Lord Edward had landed in England accompanied by a contingent of Flemish mercenaries, their apparent aim, to defeat the Welsh. But there had been no call to arms and this omission appeared to show that Edward was intent on fighting Llywelyn without assistance from the Marcher barons.

Word quickly spread, and the Marches fizzed with bitterness and anger at this royal action. By ignoring the hereditary defenders of the Marches in this way, the heir to the throne had, single handed, united many of the most powerful barons to the de Montfort faction as they perceived this to be a personal affront by the young Lord Edward.

If the loyalty of the Marchers was in question, there had been voices raised against his own actions during the past two years. After falling out with his father, Edward had left England with his friend, Robert Burnell and a few retainers, and had toured around Europe attending numerous tournaments rather than stay to try to resolve the ever growing list of complaints from the English magnates. Now, with the relationship between father and son restored; mainly due to the tireless efforts of Edward's uncle, Richard Plantagenet, Earl of Cornwall. Edward had turned his attentions to the conflict in Wales. But the Marchers felt somewhat vindicated, when Edward and his mercenaries, had been soundly beaten by Llywelyn and his doughty Welshmen.

News of his ignominious defeat had obviously preceded him, for when he and his foreign army arrived in London during the first days of July, there had been no welcoming party to greet them by the citizens; instead, Edward had been embarrassed by the request of the official party, to leave, as residents did not wish foreign knights, and soldiers, staying within their city.

Their reason – Londoners had sided with the Barons Party and were concerned by the current discord between the king and his native born barons, which originally stemmed from the influx of the 'aliens'. These foreigners now held some of the most senior offices in the land; therefore this mercenary army was viewed with suspicion and alarm, and would not be tolerated.

It would seem the fears of the Londoners had been upheld, for by the month's end the troops had moved to Windsor where they set up a garrison, devastating the countryside around the area as they did so. The final humiliation came in the form of a writ delivered to Edward, bearing the king's own seal, ordering the immediate removal from the country of the mercenaries. In effect, it appeared the king was challenging the authority of his son and heir.

The truth of the matter was that Simon de Montfort, had confiscated Henry's seal, on behalf of the Barons Party, and had used it to remove the foreign forces, who had subsequently been escorted back to the coast by some of the dissenters.

This piece of information had been just one of many messages to reach Wigmore. Messengers arrived from all quarters of the kingdom, bearing details of the growing unrest, and bloody disputes, and everywhere, the mood was one of anger. Everyone knew at the heart of it all was the king's continued intransigence and his refusal to listen to the age old list of complaints and comply to the terms of '*The Provisions of Oxford*' and '*Winchester*'. This coupled with his unstinting support for both the kinsmen of his wife, the Savoyards, and his own half brothers, the hated Lusignans, added fuel to a volatile situation.

Maud looked out across the valley to the wooded hills of the Mortimer Forest, but she saw nothing of the rich green of the trees or, the apron of ripening crops, her thoughts were filled with a mixture of hatred and sadness. The recent family news had affected her deeply, more deeply than she wished to admit to. Rich, her dearest cousin, was dead; he had never recovered from the terrible crime committed against him by his onetime steward. Nevertheless, his sudden death came as a great shock.

By the details in the letter, he had died after dining with Peter of Savoy, uncle to Queen Eleanor. Maud could not dismiss the terrible thought, that his death could be murder. Whatever the true cause, it was distressing for his family, especially as Richard de Clare, had already survived one poisoning attempted only a few years ago. Once again Maud trod the well worn path to the door of her old chamberlain, Lord Rhys.

'No doubt you have already heard of my cousin's death?' She did not wait for his answer. 'Am I being too cynical to hold the notion that this could be a deed of ....murder?

'There is no doubt Lord Richard had his enemies, as do most in any position of authority. The question has to be why?'

'I know it is a scurrilous accusation and whether it is just my personal suspicions or, whether there is any truth, at this juncture I can't really say. But Richard did have the ear of some powerful people and maybe this may have some bearing on his awful death. I believe he was close to his half brother, Henry of Almain?' He paused. 'Almain is known to be a supporter of the Barons Party maybe he had swayed your cousin to join them.'

Maud felt a cold ache in her heart, and her doubts ran riot through her head. Was Savoy guilty of murder? Had he acted on his own or, at the behest of his niece, the Queen of England? There was no denying the fact, there were intrigues afoot she had no privy to. Then of course, control of the vast wealth and estates of the Earldoms of Hertford and Gloucester, would come under the control of the crown as Gilbert, Richard's eldest son, was under age and it was no secret, Henry was always looking for ways to bolster the exchequer. Was an act of murder committed merely for gold?

'Do you have any intelligence of Savoy?' Maud looked at her trusted advisor.

'First, you have to discover where the loyalties of your kinsman lay at the time of his demise. We both know that in these precarious times, the pendulum of argument swings to and fro. Do you wish me to try and discover the facts?'

Maud nodded. 'But pray do not place anyone in danger or...........draw attention to this family. Maybe Rich has been killed, due to a change in his allegiance from the crown to the dissenters or maybe there is another explanation.'

§

Whilst Maud prepared to attend yet another funeral of a family member, Eleanor of Provence, was considering her eldest son's current conduct. When he had left England, Eleanor had been deeply upset, and had rejoiced when he and his father had been reconciled. Since then however, she had noted the change wrought in him and was determined to put matters to rights. In her usual decisive way she took matters into her own hands and began by dismissing many of Edward's former friends. She blamed them for her son's more outrageous behaviour. Eleanor still retained a strong hold over her son which was demonstrated, as he did not openly defy her on the matter. Leyburne, Clifford, LeStrange and the others, were ordered to leave court and banned from attending tournaments, as it was thought they may continue to cause mischief.

Upon learning of Eleanor's move to distance her son from possible troublemakers, Maud felt justified in her persistent advice to Mortimer to ally himself to the king. Whatever her personal views on the shortcomings of the Plantagenet characteristics, her enduring belief that power would be retained by the royal family at whatever cost, and in this belief she had never wavered.

If there were divisions in loyalties at court, the news from Wales was not much better; the list of castles and lands laid waste by Llywelyn grew ever longer, leaving the disunited Marchers with bloody noses and battered pride after they had resumed their usual role of guardians of the March. Mortimer's reputation struggled to survive his continual defeats, as did many of his contemporaries. She sighed, it was no use worrying about what had happened, too late to change anything, the key was to try and bring success out of all of this mess.

The woes of the age had not remained outside the ashlar walls of Wigmore, for within her own household, Maud had suffered a tragic loss when Jane, her beloved lady-in-waiting, had drowned in the river at Leintwardine, earlier in the year. The result of an accident, whilst she was out looking for her son. It appeared that she had apparently slipped on the thin ice, and been pitched into the water. Later, the little boy had subsequently been found, fast asleep in the manger of their neighbour's barn.

Maud however, had other ideas about the circumstances of her servant's death. Since the birth of her second child, Jane's mind had been much troubled. She had never been well enough to return to her old position; and had lost her former good health. Her mind appeared to have travelled into a dark world of doubts and fears. On a personal level, Maud felt the death of her former lady-in-waiting very deeply; it was another link to her past life lost. The affection she had for Jane, and her tragic death, was one shared with Rufus, Jane's husband.

The two children of Jane and Rufus had joined the youngest members of Maud's growing family at Wigmore to be raised by the tender ministrations of Carys. This arrangement had helped Rufus through his time of mourning as it enabled him to visit his children daily. Also during this period the position of lady's maid had been filled by Arthur's half sister, Beth. Although a quiet girl, Beth had fitted into the household with ease, being both diligent and affable.

One gloomy morning, Maud went and sat at her desk to try and complete the letter she had been penning to Rich's eldest son, Gilbert, known as 'Gilbert the Red' or, 'Red Gilbert', due to his thick, bright red hair. He had inherited, not only the distinctive Irish colouring but, also a volatile temper to match. Maud knew better than most, what an impediment this would be in future dealings with his peers. She smiled ruefully, and could well imagine exactly where her missive would end up but, nonetheless; she had to try for she above all could empathise with his hot-headed nature. She still battled daily against her own wayward temper, and knew it was a battle she could never forego. Little did she know just how important this link with Gilbert would be in the future, not only for her own family but, also, in the fate of the king, and the country?

As the storm clouds of dissent grew darker over England and Wales, the plight of many who had fallen back into dispute and disruption, became ever more desperate. With the return of the Lusignans, their rule of greed had continued with a vengeance. As Henry feared for his safety he had retired to the Tower of London, uncertain of the loyalty of his subjects. He had been alarmed upon hearing that some of the disgruntled nobles had urged the return of a man they knew would be more than a match for a king without a moral conscience, Simon de Montfort, Earl of Leicester.

The mood of the people grew daily more hostile, which was aptly demonstrated when the Queen journeyed to join her husband down the Thames, and the royal barge was pelted with muck and rotten waste. Little did the Londoners know the dangerous enemy they made that day, for Eleanor had a long memory, coupled with a vindictive nature?

During the autumn and winter of 1262, rumours surrounding the royal family flew about the countryside like birds on migration. Truth and conjecture mixed with lies and mischief, but one fact came to light, that Edward's former companions, Roger Clifford, Roger Leyburne and Hamo LeStrange, had all been re-instated with generous gifts of money and lands.

'It is like watching the ebb and flow of a fickle tide - the vagaries of men's loyalties.' Maud passed a cup of wine to her husband as she spoke. 'Sadly, silver can salve most men's conscience it would seem. Methinks, this change of heart by the Queen, is to keep her son, the Lord Edward and his friends on side, and bolster the ranks of the royalists.' She continued: 'now that De Montfort has returned, he uses his gift with words to colours his arguments and lures men to his cause.'

Mortimer nodded before he spoke, his tone, thoughtful.

'But he argues for the Provisions and we both know that although it is a just cause, albeit a dangerous one!' Maud studied her husband's face for some clue to how he was thinking.

'There is no denying the man has powerful friends both in the church, in France, and Rome.'

'So to, the Queen!' Maud chose a small pear from a bowl of fruit and began to peel it.

She paused. 'If Henry continues in his refusal to listen to these renewed arguments, which we know once had the backing of his son, what do you believe will be the outcome - civil strife?'

Mortimer slammed his cup onto the dark trestle top, 'by all the Saints in heaven I hope not, the Welsh are enough trouble without drawing swords on our own people.'

Maud continued peeling her pear, 'Let us pray such calamities do not arise and the storm clouds pass.' The couple continued their meal in silence lost in their own thoughts.

However, next morning Maud went to visit Lord Rhys with her fears and his words left her with a cold chill in her heart.

'My agents tell me that de Montfort has had meetings with Llywelyn and that can only bode ill for the English.'

'God have mercy on us!' Maud crossed herself as she spoke. 'Do you believe that de Montfort's aims are totally unselfish? Or, are your views as sceptical as mine that he is driven by ambition for himself and his ever growing brood?' She looked intently at the man she had relied on for his wisdom throughout the years. His expression spoke more eloquently than any words and the couple remained silent in the moment.

'I fear for this coming generation; ideals are so urgent when one is young and the desire to change the world into a better place burns brightly. Sadly, age brings wisdom, and the inevitable truth that the pursuit of wealth and power invariably overrides good intentions.' Maud's words hung in the air like incense. 'My concern is how will this all affect my children's future and how will they deal with all the machinations of the realm? Ralph maybe handsome, but already shows an arrogant and selfish streak - like his father was when young, too rash in many of his judgements. Unlike Edmund, who even at this age shows he has steady head on young shoulders, therefore they disagree on almost everything.'

Lord Rhys waved his hand, 'as they grow older their differences may evaporate. As you say, young Edmund has a keen mind and thirsts for knowledge. Already he shows an aptitude for studying, which will prove be a great asset if he goes into the church.'

Maud nodded. 'Although the church is the usual route for younger sons, I cannot bring myself to wholeheartedly support Mortimer's decision in this instance. And as for young Roger......' her hands flew up in the air 'that child bears all the traits of the Braose family, even now he is full of spite and mischief and no amount of beatings alters him one jot.'

'May I suggest you try changing tactics and instead of force, use guile?'

'Carys has said as much, but he does worry me more than any of my other children. I have lived in dread that my father's bad blood would one day emerge; it would seem my fears have come to fruition.'

'You are perfectly capable of keeping your son's wayward traits under control my lady; a tight rein on his upbringing is perfectly feasible is it not?'

'Mmm! Let us hope you are right, but no-one had much influence over my father, did they?'

'Sadly not, but he paid the ultimate price for his indiscretions, as we both know?'

'At least you are blessed with daughters who are both handsome and tractable.'

'Indeed; Bella and Meg have many characteristics of my mother and sisters and as for William and Geoffrey, as yet they are but infants but thankfully both appear of an amiable disposition.'

Not many days after her conversation with Lord Rhys a black cloaked messenger arrived bearing a letter that would have a profound effect, not only on the people of the Welsh Marches, but the entire nation. Maud could tell that Mortimer was agitated as soon as he stepped out of his chamber, the scroll still gripped in his hand.

'Is aught amiss?' She could read her husband's moods.

'You were right about the Plantagenet's.' He moved closer so that only she heard his next statement. 'It has been cleverly worded but stripping out the facts, the king has made it known that should I attack de Montfort's lands in Dilwyn, Lugwardine and Marden, I would be serving not only the interests of the king but, also my own.'

Maud let out a long sigh, 'were these not the lands given to de Montfort by Henry as part of the repayment for his previous services?'

'Aye! He believes the action would divert de Montfort's attention from a meeting with Louis in France.'

'The king fears de Montfort's standing in France. Well we all know that in a war of words de Montfort would win every time but .....' she hesitated 'in the war of prevarication and cunning, the prize may be Henry's. Never forget, his sister-in-law Marguerite, is Louis wife and Queen of France.'

The couple looked at each other. 'I will need your support in this for the Marches are divided in this damnable argument and I am uncertain nowadays who is to be trusted. Damn Henry for his stubbornness! Damn de Montfort for his ambitions!'

Maud reached out and touched his arm, 'surely you have no need to ask, for you have had my unswerving loyalty and have done since the day we married.'

In a rare moment of tenderness Roger Mortimer leaned forward to kiss the cheek of his wife.

'You are my greatest ally and I beg your forgiveness for being so tardy in taking such a long time to realise it. If I carry out this action there is no doubt de Montfort would retaliate and Wigmore and the Mortimer strongholds will be his target.'

Maud could hear her husband's frustrations and knew he was filled with misgivings but even though it may cost them dearly, she did not waver from her beliefs that there only real option for future advancement, lay in the service of the crown.

She took a deep breath, and in unwavering tones said, 'We will not shirk this opportunity to serve the king for it will place you high in his favour and who knows where that may lead!'

'On the road to hell I dare-swear!' Mortimer exclaimed.

'There is another matter which is directly related to this situation and one as yet you are unaware of.'

'Oh! How so?'

Mortimer began to pace up and down the chamber pulling at his beard.

'The matter obviously disturbs you my lord is it not better you share this with me?'

He cleared his throat before he began. 'Last year one of my scouts came across a body. It turned out to be the body of a messenger who had been carrying letters written by Henry of Pembrugge.'

The tension in his body and the tone of his voice signalled that what he was about to divulge was of some importance.

'It appears that our former friend and ally, Pembrugge was consorting with both the Welsh and de Montfort.'

'Are you certain?' The incredulity in her voice was noted by Mortimer.

'Dammit, the man's seal was plain enough!'

'And have you confronted him with your discovery?'

Mortimer looked uncomfortable. 'I had him brought to Wigmore to question him further.'

'Wigmore!' Maud echoed the word. 'When? I did not hear of this!'

Looking ever more uncomfortable Mortimer continued.

'It was whilst you were visiting the church at Leintwardine.'

Maud shook her head in amazement. 'And you did not think to apprise me of this *visit?*'

Mortimer cleared his throat, now thoroughly agitated.

'I knew it would upset you!'

She looked at him with an unflinching stare.

'So what was the man's defence?'

'That it was not his seal and the letters were never written by him.'

'So – did you believe him?'

'No!'

'Pray do tell me what you did next!' He noted the irony in her voice.

Again Mortimer cleared his throat. 'He is here, in the dungeons.'

'Are you mad? You have kept Henry of Pembrugge prisoner here at Wigmore without breathing a word to me? Exactly how long has he been here? I visit Leintwardine frequently to visit Jane's grave.'

Mortimer looked decidedly uncomfortable under his wife's angry gaze.

'And pray what do you propose to do with him?'

Mortimer shrugged his shoulders. 'That I have yet to determine.'

'Bring him before me immediately!'

Mortimer could see by his wife's expression she would brook no refusal and to argue, he knew to be pointless. Within a short space of time the very thin, pale figure of Henry of Pembrugge, stood before them in the chamber. Maud could smell the stale body odours and noted how ill he looked.

'This is a sorry state I find you in my lord.'

Henry's bloodshot eyes blinked against the light but he remained silent.

'I have just discovered your plight and ask you are these perfidious claims true?'

For what seemed like an age Henry of Pembrugge remained silent then, dropped to one knee his body shaking.

'I swear, by all that I hold dear, this accusation against me is totally false. I damaged my seal which had been taken to be repaired at the time I am supposed to have written these letters.'

Maud turned to her husband. 'Do you have the letters in your possession?'

He nodded.

'Then pray bring them forth and let us study them.'

Without any argument Mortimer sent for the incriminating documents.

Maud took charge and laid them on the table and read the letters.

'Well it cannot be denied what is written here is damming my lord.' She looked across at the pathetic figure. He walked unsteadily towards the table and peered down.

'But this is not my hand or, signature on that you have my word.'

'That can easily be verified.' Without further ado she called for writing materials to be brought immediately. In the matter of minutes Henry of Pembrugge had proved the hand that had written the letters and the signature were certainly not his.'

Mortimer was undoubtedly embarrassed but remained unmoved. 'It merely demonstrates you did not personally write them but your scribe could have!'

'This is not the hand of my scribe; I will swear that on the Blessed Blood of Christ.'

'Enough!' Maud's words were unmistakably sharp. Without further preamble she turned to Henry, 'My lord Pembrugge, do you swear on the life of Christ you did not write, or have any true knowledge of these letters?'

His voice not much more than a whisper Henry whispered. 'I swear to you, I am innocent Lady Mortimer.'

'I believe you my lord but can see that my husband still has his doubts. Maybe we can resolve this matter to everyone's satisfaction.' She turned to Henry, 'you must see that my husband needs to know he does not harbour enemies of the king within his jurisdiction. Pembrugge Castle is a strategic site and could, in times of war, be used by our enemies therefore I suggest you surrender the Castle to my husband thus avoiding further fears of treachery.'

The chamber fell into a hushed silence. Mortimer looked across at his wife in admiration but what Maud did next completely took his breath away.

'My lord, simply sign over the castle today and all your troubles will be at an end.'

'If I agree to this move will I be free to return to my parents in Tong?'

'You have my word my lord. By this act you have demonstrated beyond doubt that you are no traitor to the king and it also puts you out of harm's way.'

Maud had been silently applauded by her husband for such an astute move, but in private she felt far from happy and left him in no doubt of her feelings. There were also questions to be answered by members of the household who had kept such a dark secret from her. One of those was Lord Rhys, who was normally in possession of such facts but it transpired, he had been laid low with a fever at the time of the unfortunate incident.

Still angry, Maud was determined to discover the truth of this strange matter and felt sure that Lord Rhys would aid her quest to unearth the truth. As soon as she entered his chamber he could see by her expression that this was no social visit. Without any preamble Maud related the events which had just taken place. All the time she was speaking the old man watched her as she recounted in detail all that had transpired.

'My Lord, the burning question which Lord Mortimer appears to have overlooked is, if Henry de Pembrugge is innocent, then who actually wrote those letters.'

For a moment he stroked his beard.

'My first guess would be Lord Devereaux.'

Maud looked stunned.

'William Devereaux!'

He nodded.

'Remember, his father-in-law is John Giffard and Giffard has recently been linked with the Barons Party.'

'Of course, and Giffard's brothers are high ranking churchmen and supporters of de Montfort. We are surrounded by dissenters; young Humphrey de Bohun; my kinsman Gilbert, Giffard, and now Devereaux! God have mercy on us, which means we will, in all likelihood, have to draw swords against our former allies and friends and kinsmen.'

'The implications are unthinkable'. Maud continued. 'But there is no proof at this moment, we are just guessing, therefore we cannot openly lay blame on anyone, merely stay alert and watch closely the reactions of those around us.'

A week later Henry de Pembrugge rode out of Wigmore Castle gates and headed towards his family home of Tong. Although still frail, his clothes and servants had all been restored, so too all of his furniture which was already on the road to Shropshire

. In the first few days of December of 1263, Mortimer gathered a small army of well armed, well mounted men, and rode briskly through the archway of Wigmore towards Dilwyn. Maud hated the thought of the Marches being so divided by their loyalties but if by striking at de Montfort's strongholds it restored Mortimer to the king's favour, she would happily placate her conscience; besides, de Montfort needed to be brought to heel.

Christmastide at Wigmore that year was one of muted celebration. Although Lord Mortimer's attacks had gained easy success on the three sites in Herefordshire it was inevitable there would be reprisals. As most of the Mortimer household toasted each other, Maud felt a strong sense of apprehension which was further exacerbated by the news that Henry Plantagenet was about to sail for France. The long standing dispute between the king and the Barons was going to be brought before the French king for a ruling. There was no doubt he was determined to silence any further opposition in his bid to finally have the terms of the *Provisions* overturned. Surprisingly, de Montfort had been persuaded to accept these conditions also, and the judgement of Louis of France on the matter.

When Henry arrived in France he was re-united with his Queen who had remained in France since his previous visit in September. Eleanor had not been idle through that time; she had argued eloquently on her husband's behalf and through her sister, Marguerite, Louis' wife, now felt confident that although Louis had previously supported the *Provisions,* he appeared to have accepted the arguments, his change of heart obviously influenced by the two women.

However, there was one fact which worried both Henry and Eleanor, de Montfort's power of persuasion especially, as he was held in high esteem in France. There was no doubt he would bring all of his skills to bear in the cause he had taken upon himself to champion, and both knew he would prove a formidable adversary not only in the field of battle but also, as an advocate.

Unfortunately for de Montfort, Fate appeared to have taken sides, for on his way to catch the boat for France, his horse had stumbled, and he had been thrown, breaking his leg in the accident. Now, Thomas de Cantelupe, Bishop of Hereford, would be the spokesman for the barons and although he was undoubtedly an able and learned man, would not bring to bear the forcefulness of de Montfort. The royal couple felt more confident of success than they had for some time.

It was not therefore not surprising, that within days of the French king's judgement, news arrived from France that Louis had upheld Henry's arguments and ruled, that as King of England, should be allowed to reign unfettered. This verdict would become known as the '*Mise of Amiens*'.

Reactions to this outcome reverberated around the kingdom; in Kenilworth, the pent up venom of Simon de Montfort who, upon learning of the failure of his envoys, had turned against the king's supporters, especially those who had recently attacked his lands in the Marches. It was Sir Roger Mortimer of Wigmore, who now became the focus of his fury.

But for those who supported the king the news came as vindication of their decision to remain loyal. One thing was certain, the thwarted Earl, and his followers would never accept this defeat, and left him feeling betrayed by Louis, his former friend.

CHAPTER XXI

'There are soldiers moving towards us my Lady, we spotted the reflection of their weaponry glinting in the sunlight.' The breathless sentry's words sent a shiver down Maud's spine. It was the time to set the well rehearsed manoeuvres into action. Carys had instructions to take the children, the page boys, and younger members of staff to the sanctuary of the church. Maud felt certain de Montfort's troops would never violate a church. The bell, which had been attached to the gatehouse, would ring its message of warning to villagers of Wigmore and the surrounding district. Fires were doused, weapons handed out to all those able bodied men and women who could use them. Archers quickly assembled and hurried to vantage position on the towers and walls of the castle.

Maud felt a quiver of fear run through her body, as she spied the standard of de Montfort fluttering in the chilly wind. The pale wintery sun bathed the scene in an eerie silvery grey light, which seemed to drain away all colour. She said a prayer under her breathe for their safe deliverance. Why was Mortimer never here when she needed him? Turning to the group that now surrounded her, she said with far more conviction than she felt: 'let us hope the de Montfort army honours the code of sanctuary. Should they invade the church we will not allow ourselves to be taken without a fight? We can look for no mercy, therefore, give none, hesitation will spell death! I commend our souls to God, our courage to each other and pray that we find strength to deny our enemies victory.'

The blood curdling yells could be heard long before the attackers reached the village. Maud had done everything within her powers to defend Wigmore but soon realised they were vastly outnumbered and the screams and shrieks of the frightened men and women as they fell before the swords and maces of their enemy, terrified voices mingled with that of the horses, and the deafening noise filled the air.

At first, the accuracy of the roof top archers proved most effective, as their arrows and bolts found their mark and many of de Montfort's forces fell in bloody heaps, but all too quickly the arrows ran out and with no way of replenishing the stocks the onslaught ceased. A group of seasoned troops had formed into a wedge, with their shields outward facing and stood, drawing the attack of the de Montfort army away from the gates.

All day the battle raged until the walls of Wigmore began to crumble as fires raged; reaching many of the chambers and kitchens. Heavy black smoke curled skyward, darkening the late afternoon skies. But somehow, the tight knit band of Wigmore squires, knights, and troops manage to withstand the repeated attacks of the de Montfort army. Then, as darkness fell, all went quiet as the invaders melted away into the deepening gloom leaving a scene of utter devastation. Once more Wigmore Castle had suffered severe damage and its village lay in smouldering ruins.

Maud stood pale faced and trembling. 'Unbolt the doors Arthur, after we have given thanks to God for our safe deliverance.' En mass they all made the sign of the cross and knelt in prayer for a few moments. Then Maud emerged from her position of safety, deep in the vaults of the church, to be faced with the scenes of death and carnage. She looked back to see if Lord Rhys was being helped through the rubble before she continued.

A few hours later, the Lord of Wigmore and his eldest son, Ralph, galloped into the midst of the devastated castle, their horses almost collapsing after their frantic exertions. A short while later, the heir to the English throne, Edward Plantagenet followed. He quickly dismounted, and went and took Maud's icy hands.

'I fear we have come too late to save your home and many of your household, Lady Mortimer but, I swear this act of destruction will be avenged, on that you have the word of Edward of England.'

Maud nodded, 'I look to you to keep that vow my Lord Edward.' Then she turned to look around before murmuring: 'strange thing is, we have only just completed the restoration from Llywelyn's attack. Ironic is it not? Besides,' she looked back directly into the piercing blue eyes of the young Edward, 'the bible states and 'eye for an eye' and - Mortimer did make the first strike.' She dropped a perfunctory curtsy then said, 'I must see to my people and what can be done for them.'

Edward bowed releasing her hands and let her walk away knowing that tears were not far from her lovely eyes. He turned to Mortimer, 'we will do all that we can tonight, tomorrow I shall leave some of my men to assist, but we must move swiftly to seize Hay and Huntingdon, before de Bohun can unite with de Montfort.' Without further ado he turned on his heel and strode away, his tall figure unmistakable in the confusion.

Mortimer went to seek out his wife and learn the details of the day's events from her and those who survived. He moved to put his arms around her but she move away.

'Have your men gather the corpses and dig graves so that we can bury them as quickly as possible, only then can we begin to repair the damage. Make sure they take their direction for the burial plots from the priest, I would not incur the displeasure of the church.' Maud's voice sounded cold and impersonal, veiling the true depth of her emotions.

Mortimer nodded his grizzled head. Then looked hard at his wife, 'are you alright?'

Maud suddenly snapped, her eyes blazing, 'of course I am not alright; this mess will take months and much silver to repair again. But have no fear, it will all be in hand whilst you are away wrecking someone else's home but' she lowered her tone as she continued: 'be certain what you destroy belongs to de Montfort for, I curse every last drop of blood in his veins along with that entire brood of his.' The venom of her words filled the air around her. With that, she turned and walked swiftly into the gloom. Mortimer was satisfied that Maud, in this mood, would be equal to taking on the devil himself.' He went to find his captain to give the order to collect the fallen. As luck would have it, the number of those slain, were not as numerous as first thought, many had been away at the market in Ludlow when the attackers had struck. However, the blacksmith, head groom, as well as a number of men-at-arms, plus four archers and three of the young squires had been killed. Maud was thankful that Richard of Clun and Edwin de Saye, had not been amongst the fallen. The villagers were yet to be counted. Wounded were taken to the Great Hall where makeshift pallets were arranged in rows beneath the scorched timbers.

'At least the roof is sound in here. It is only smoke stained.' Maud looked relieved at Arthur's observations.

'Have you sent word to Brampton, Lyonshall, and Pembridge, to see if they escaped?'

He smiled wryly, 'Aye my lady.' She patted his shoulder, 'you will be kept busy for the coming months, I fear.'

She moved among the rows of wounded and tried to aid those in most need. Their moans echoed eerily in the flickering shadows of the fire, which had been lit, and fed with the broken trestles and benches. Two young pot boys carried a huge cauldron, as two more began to erect a makeshift spit to heat the nourishing contents. Maud nodded, 'well done! Hot food will put new life into us all.' She did not question where the contents had been gathered from.

Outside, men-at-arms were also busily making camp fires whilst others collected discarded weaponry. The hunt for food was now the main aim for no army could function without it. Later, the three Mortimers' sat in a state of silent exhaustion. It was Maud who broke the silence.

'I did not know you were with Lord Edward.'

'No, we met up with him as he was returning from a Welsh raid; it was Ralph who saw the smoke on the skyline.' He patted his son's shoulder as he spoke.

'Has Edward resorted to hiring mercenaries again?' Mortimer nodded.

'So, most of the men camped outside are foreigners?' Maud's voice was hard and toneless.

'Yes.' Mortimer replied gruffly.

'Once de Montfort realised Henry had the backing of the French king he knew his only alternative was to take up arms; a move which will test men's true beliefs.'

'Do you think Henry really understands how deeply this situation between himself and de Montfort is affecting the whole country?'

'I fear it has gone far beyond either party acting logically.' Maud noted the rueful tones of her husband's statement.

'But are both sides now so entrenched in their beliefs they are blind to where this deadly argument is leading us all? Civil war!'

'It is no longer about their private differences it is a matter of pride? The Earl has taken this whole matter of the Barons Rights and made it a battle of wills between him and the king.'

Maud, Ralph and the Lord of Wigmore sat for some moments in silence.

'And what of this current situation and Edward's foreign troops; are you happy to take mercenaries to attack de Bohun?' She looked hard at her husband.

'What choice, do we have Madam? You were the one who urged loyalty to the king.'

'It is one thing to fight the enemy of the king but........' her words trailed off for a moment, 'I never thought we would raise our standard against a friend.'

'The Earl of Hereford's position has been somewhat compromised by his son's support for de Montfort.'

Maud sighed. 'Poor man, to have to choose between one's king and one's son is nothing short of hell.'

She looked at the two figures before her, the war hardened knight and his squire, his beloved son, and heir. At nearly fourteen, Ralph was almost as tall as his father and had already proved his talent with sword and mace. She felt a shudder run through her still slender frame. She did not shy away from the thought she may lose them both in the forthcoming confrontation, which now appeared to be inevitable.

Again the group fell into silence, and then Maud rose: 'sleep is what we are all in desperately in need of. Tonight is one we will look back on as the beginning of a civil war, sadly, a war which many will not live through. I pray that our fortunes survive the vagaries of men, whose pride means more to them than the people they purport to serve.'

Ralph spoke for the first time, his words stopped Maud in her tracks, 'but they have to defend what they believe in - surely? Honour is worth dying for is it not?'

Maud looked at her son her voice scathing, 'pray tell me where the honour is in slaying your own people? Compromise should have wrought a resolution to this dispute not bloodshed.'

'Surely to take up arms for a principle; for change; to defend the king is right?'

'De Montfort's pride and Henry's stubbornness is not worth spilling a drop of English blood for; when will you all not realise that whilst Henry Plantagenet sits on the throne of England, he will fight the *'Treaty of Oxford'* and the *Provisions*, or whatever title you wish to put on it, with every last breath in his body. But sadly it will *not* be his blood or, his body that will suffer, but the men, women, and children he rules. What of their well being? No doubt one will be victorious but it will never solve the underlying cause, only a sensible compromise will achieve that and neither of the protagonists appears to be – sensible men!'

'You better not utter such sentiments outside of this chamber my lady, our enemies grow like weeds, and we do not wish to attract royal enmity especially now we have taken royal favours.'

'I know, I merely voice my own fears, for myself I grow weary of it all; sadly it is the women who have to pick up the pieces left by king's, Earls and whoever else sets themselves up as a higher authority. We bury the dead, nurse the wounded, and re-build the broken lives and buildings left in the wake of what...' she waved her hand in frustration and left the two men to ponder on her words.

'Your mother is a fearsome woman at times, but I have learned, over the years to trust her strength and wisdom so can forgive her occasional outbursts.'

'I swear, I will never be led by a woman.' Ralph's voice was thick with emotion.

'You are too young to understand the unique relationship between a man and his wife. One day, when you too have a wife, you will take a different stance. Now let us find somewhere to rest.'

The following day dawned with the wind blowing from the east as the makeshift tents flapped and strained at their guy ropes. Horses stamped and sidled round trying to free themselves from the lines they were tethered to. The sound of hammering began at first light. The Blacksmith's son had taken charge of the forge and was coaxing up the flames with the well worn bellows. Armourers tapped at buckled harnesses and dented shields. Fletchers were sat, with bundles of arrows and geese wings. Grooms fed and watered the lines of horses before grooming and brushing their charges, and cleaning the saddles and bridles. Servants hurried, as they carried trays of food and jugs of ale to the hungry soldiers.

By mid morning, funeral services were well under way and many of those who had died the previous day were being buried. Just before noon, Lord Edward, accompanied by Roger and Ralph Mortimer, rode away from the scene of devastation, with a heavily armed force of foreign and local men. Maud stood and watched, then raised her hand, returning her husband's salute. She sighed and wondered if she would ever see her son and husband again. Her heart felt heavy; for she knew the coming days would be filled with news of death and carnage but such thoughts accomplished naught, so quickly put aside her misgivings to face the pressing issues of the day.

Throughout the following weeks, a flurry of messengers arrived and left Wigmore, bearing news of the constantly changing fortunes of events which now affected, not only the Middle lands of England, but stretched as far as London and Dover. Londoners had risen up against the king and there were accounts of fierce fighting in the streets. Richard of Cornwall's castle at Isleworth had been wrecked along with many other properties of those loyal to the king.

News arrived that John Giffard, had taken Warwick Castle for de Montfort after being beaten by royalist forces at Worcester. Where, by all accounts, Edward had wreaked his brutal revenge on its citizens for their defiance. Then word came that Henry's forces had won a significant battle against the town of Nottingham, thus signalling, England was now in the throes of all out civil war.

Although Maud was not surprised, nonetheless she felt a deep sense of sadness that issues could not have been resolved in a more civilised manner. It was one thing fighting their perennial enemy the Welsh, a completely different matter when bearing arms against family and friends who merely held differing views.

But closer to home, she was satisfied with the progress of the re-building and recruiting that was now a daily part of life at Wigmore. Horses and men came and went and amongst the banging and knocking of the workmen, the sound of steel upon steel could also be heard, as men practiced the art of warfare.

One evening as the temperature dropped, heralding the promise of a frost, two mud stained horsemen rode into Wigmore. Neither removed their black cloaks or hoods, even when they entered the castle. The shorter of the two spoke.

'My master wishes an urgent audience with Lady Mortimer.'

'I do not think she is receiving any more visitors today.'

'We have important news which is for her ears alone.'

The servant hesitated for a moment; in the gathering gloom neither men had removed their hooded cloaks, which made him feel uneasy. But there was something in the taller man's bearing which denoted he was not any ordinary messenger but a man of importance and so he went and did their bidding, summoning the Lady of Wigmore. As soon as Maud entered the chamber she recognised her visitors and waved the servant away before summing her page to fetch food and wine. Before speaking, both threw back their hoods, and went and kissed the hand of their hostess. Although her heart was racing, Maud had long since learned to hide her emotions, but as the taller man rose, they looked long and hard into each other's eyes.

'You are welcome my Lord de Longeville.' She turned to the younger man 'as are you Master Lucien. Pray what brings you to Wigmore?'

Guy de Longeville unfastened his cloak but remained silent as the young page entered with a steaming bowl of rabbit stew, accompanied by a flagon of wine.

'Thank you Errol, you may go, I shall ring if I need you.' The boy bowed and grinned, then left. 'The fare is humble but nourishing.'

The two men fell on the food and ate with relish. It gave Maud time to observe the couple in more detail. De Longeville looked sun burned and threads of grey peppered his dark hair; lines of fatigue were etched plainly on his face. His squire had lost his boyish looks and now, bore the appearance of a seasoned traveller. She could only guess at their lives since last they met; no doubt de Longeville and his squire, still served the Comte de Vivonne, so she was curious to learn what were they doing in the depths of the Welsh Marches?

Maud sat quietly until they had finished their meal and de Longeville sat back in his chair.

'Pray forgive our tardiness in making the reason for our visit known, but we have not eaten since yesterday in our haste to outrun our enemies.'

Although Maud felt alarmed at his words but she remained silent.

'Hopefully, we have outwitted them for the time being at least.'

'And why are you being pursued this time my lord? Surely you have the king's licence to travel freely!'

'But not if he thought I now bore messages for his enemies. It is no secret that all parties have their agents scattered throughout the land and I now bear messages which, if they fell into the wrong hands, could cause much mischief and mayhem. Our diversionary route to Wigmore was an effort to confuse and confound them.' The look that passed between the speaker and the listener said much more than the spoken word.

'You have succeeded in arousing my curiosity my lord?' Maud tried to keep her voice under control, and betray nothing of the turmoil she felt at seeing the man she had loved for so many years.

'As usual nothing is straight forward on our mission here. We originally carried messages from the French Queen to her sister, your Queen Eleanor, and of course, King Louis also added messages of his own to Henry. However, there were other letters addressed, to de Montfort. Now I bear messages to Llywelyn, from both de Montfort, and the English king.'

Maud sucked in her breath at his words. 'A dangerous game, delivering messages between all the enemies of the nation it would seem!'

'Indeed!'

'So at what stage are you presently at?'

'Those messages have been delivered and we are now carrying missives from Llywelyn to both men.'

'Then you are returning from Wales?'

'Yes!'

'And the agents who pursue you are....?'

De Longeville looked across at his squire 'We are uncertain which side they are allied to; maybe neither; or maybe they are Welsh, French or even English.'

Maud said softly, 'or maybe they are the Pope's spies.'

'You see Lucien, not only is Lady Mortimer beauteous but, also has a wit that is sharper than a barber's blade. All we ask is a few hours sleep and fresh mounts.'

She nodded 'I will make certain the horses are the fastest in our stables and without distinguishing markings.' As she spoke she noticed that Lucien's head had fallen forward and his eyes were fast shut.

'Methinks your squire should seek his bed or he will sleep where he sits.' Maud summoned her page and had him lead the weary squire to one of the undamaged chambers which was currently being used by her eldest son, when he was at home.

The couple sat unspeaking for a moment before de Longville broke the silence.

' You are right in your assessment that Rome may be involved, for Henry, de Montfort, and Llywelyn, are all seeking support from France and Rome. It is certain that this English dispute has reached the point of no return as neither the king or de Montfort, will negotiate with each other in any meaningful talks. All out war therefore, is inevitable, and my latest information, the two sides are heading south.'

'So how do you propose to deliver your message to de Montfort without discovery?'

'Although there are people on both sides who may recognise my face, I have kept Lucien's identity a secret, in fact, he never accompanies me on the final few miles of any of the journeys. A strategy adopted which would save his life in an emergency. Also, he could always return to France to inform the Comte who would, I hope, negotiate my freedom. If on this occasion, these agents do catch up with us, maybe they mean to kill us therefore my plan is that we separate, so that at least one of us has a chance of success.'

He came and knelt before her taking her hands in his, 'I would ask, should Lucien find himself alone in England would you give him shelter and assist his escape? I appreciate this is a great favour I am asking of you but I would feel easier in my mind if I knew I could count on you to aid the youth, if I am caught or slain.'

Maud reached out and gently stroked his cheek. 'You do not need to ask but pray do not speak of death; my heart would surely break if I learned you had met such a fate.'

She dropped down onto her knees and the couple held each other in a long embrace. Then Maud lifted her face and looked lovingly into his eyes before she reached up and kissed him in a long, ardent kiss. Eventually they drew apart and he helped her to her feet but she moved back into his arms.

'To live my life without knowing where or, how you are, is at times almost too hard to bear.' She hesitated before continuing, 'I still hold fast to the vain hope that one day somehow, somewhere, we will find a place we can live in peace together, unencumbered by duty or, war.'

He felt a sob shake her body and held her closer to his chest. Both knew their hopes were but wishful dreams; neither wanted to speak of the fear of never meeting again..

Wiping the tears from her eyes Maud reluctantly moved out of his embrace, 'I also have a favour I would ask of you; to deliver a message to my kinsman, Gilbert de Clare, he is one of de Montfort's supporters but, feel he will live to regret his present misguided loyalty. He is too young to realise the true nature of his royal adversary.' She looked up into de Longeville face.

'But now, you must sleep, or you will never have the strength to stay in the saddle long enough to reach your destination. Although I abhor this age of treachery, it has at least brought us together for a short while and therefore take some comfort from a bad situation.' She walked to the darkened casement and without looking at him, rang for Errol, who beckoned for de Longeville to follow.

That night Maud lay awake for hours but eventually fell asleep and did not hear de Longeville and his squire depart. The following day she plunged into all the urgent duties in an effort to blot out her burning fears, not only for de Longeville but, the future and the fate of her family and the people of England.

CHAPTER XXII

Lewes Castle
May 1264

Edward Plantagenet paced to and fro in the well lit chamber of his host, John de Warenne, Earl of Surrey.

'Do we have any intelligence of Leicester's whereabouts yet?'

'No my lord but many men have been sighted by our scouts and if reports are correct, only a few are well mounted, the rest of the numbers are mostly London peasantry.'

The striking features of Edward Plantagenet were marred by a scowl.

'Cursed Londoners, I will make them pay for their insults to my mother 'ere long.'

John de Warenne smiled. 'We will avenge your mother's honour my Lord and make them pay with their lives.'

Humphrey de Bohun, Earl of Hereford stepped forward, 'I hope vengeance will not cloud your judgement, Lord Edward. The lie of the land favours those holding the higher ground and that should be......'

'I am all too aware of battle strategy my lord Earl.' Edward's words were spat out and no-one in the chamber doubted that their future king was not about to listen to anyone's advice. A telling glance passed between de Bohun and the lord of Wigmore, Roger Mortimer.

'Has my father sent word yet?' The question was almost a bark.

'No my Lord.' His squire answered hesitantly not wishing to enrage his master further.

'Then let us presume my uncle Cornwall will command the centre with the Scottish Earls. Surrey, you together, with my uncles, Pembroke and de Lusignan and my Lord Hugh Bigod, will take the right flank. Leaving me, with my lords de Bohun and Mortimer, to strike at their left.'

Humphrey de Bohun cleared his throat before speaking, 'Should we not await the king's decision on the order of the field, my Lord?'

For a moment there was complete silence then the royal heir slammed his fist onto the heavy table in his frustration.

'Of course we will await the king's orders but believe we will be of one mind in this decision.' He glared round the chamber at each in turn just to see if there was to be any further comments. No-one else uttered a word, they were all beginning to realise when Edward Plantagenet spoke it was a brave man to gainsay his decisions.

Meanwhile, at the Priory dedicated to St. Pancras, Henry of England mused over the prospects of the forthcoming battle which would impact on his future as king, whatever the outcome. He blamed the whole situation on his brother-in-law, Simon de Montfort, Earl of Leicester. How dare he oppose the will of the anointed king, now he would be made to pay for his years of dogged resistance?

'We will show this recalcitrant Earl that his reputation as a soldier and Crusader stand for naught against the army of the king. Can he not see we are in the ascendancy? Surely after being soundly beaten at Northampton, Nottingham, and Leicester, and with Winchelsea and Tonbridge added to the list ......' Before he could continue a breathless messenger entered and dropped to one knee.

'Sire, Leicester is at Fletching to the north.'

'Distance?'

'Some three leagues, Sire,'

Richard, Earl of Cornwall leaned forward: 'our troops need rest; they have scarce been out of the saddle for days. My guess, de Montfort will wish to parlée before he gives the order to take to the field.'

'Dam him to all eternity, he has brought naught but trouble since the day he married our sister.' Henry looked at his brother as he spoke. Cornwall nodded his shaggy head in assent.

'If he believes I will countenance some sort of compromise the man is more delusional than I thought.'

'There is still time for him to withdraw his troops.' Richard of Cornwall's words echoed in the vaulted chamber.

'And you believe he will bend that proud neck in submission?' The king's words held nothing but incredulity.

'We can always hope there could be a better outcome than the one that is staring us in the face.'

'I know, I know, but matters have gone too far and he must be taught the lesson that to take up arms against ones king is tantamount to treason.'

As predicted, there was an attempt by de Montfort and the barons to try and bring about negotiated terms but the herald knew the missive he carried had only infuriated the king even further and upon his return, reported as much to his superiors.

On the morning of the 14th of May, Simon de Montfort and his followers realised the time for talks were at an end and openly offered the challenge of battle. There were tensions in both camps, but the harsh words of Edward Plantagenet left no-one in any doubt on the royalists' side, what the fate of the Londoners should be.

Roger Mortimer watched the tall figure of the England's heir pace to and fro like a caged bear. There was no doubting the battle lust which shone from the Lord Edward's bright, blue eyes, even Mortimer's own son had caught the mood, for although Ralph had taken part in fierce skirmishes and battles with the Welsh since he was very young, this would be his first taste of a full scale war.

The rhetoric bandied around left Mortimer with a sense of unease. He had learned over the years how rash judgements were often fatally flawed. With some trepidation, Roger and one or two older members of Edward's retinue, tried to bring the tone down, but they were quickly left in no doubt what Edward thought of such advice.

The moment Edward mounted his prancing charger, it was clear his sole aim was to spill the blood of his enemy. He turned and signalled for the mounted band of knights to follow as he waved at his standard bearer and without waiting for his father's orders, rode from the gates of the Castle and was soon surging forward at a full gallop. The yells of the riders echoed and reverberated as the thundering hooves of the royal cavalry charged at the ill equipped infantry of de Montfort.

Mortimer shouted at his young son to stay close and as the rampaging royalists put the terrified enemy to flight he quickly came to realise that Edward was so intent on avenging his mother's honour, that only the total decimation of his adversaries would appease his blood lust.

The momentum of the charge had quickly taken the cavalry out of the field of battle and what ensued was a disorganised pursuit of the fleeing hoards; many having dropped their billhooks, sickle, and pikes, in their effort to escape the slashing, flashing swords and lances of the royalists.

Mortimer shouted at Edward to try and gain his attention but Edward was not for heeding anyone and he failed to realise that in galloping so far from the field of battle, he was leaving his father effectively without any supporting cavalry. It was soon clear that the headlong charge, had left the knights and squires, mounted on exhausted chargers. By the time some had managed to turn their horses, they were miles from Lewes.

Meantime, Henry was informed of his son's rash action and with a heavy heart, ordered his army to take their positions, knowing the lack of cavalry would leave his troops exposed. As de Montfort sat and waited on the brow of the hill, he watched the scene unfold below him and felt his confidence grow; even though he had fewer men, when he saw the royal cavalry charge away from the main field of battle, he knew his position was virtually unassailable. De Montfort had chosen his ground well, and quickly realised the advantage now lay with him.

The battle which ensued was fierce and bloody but even though Henry fought like a true king, losing two of his horses in the process, it was with bitter regret he came to accept that the day was lost and that de Montfort was the victor. Many of his men had fled back into the town of Lewes, pursued by de Montfort's men who burned, butchered, and left the town in ruins; bodies were strewn in bloody confusion where they died.

As Edward and his cavalry reached the scene of decimation, the realisation that all was lost, left them feeling totally demoralised. He began to search the burning town for his father, Mortimer grabbed his son's bridle: 'we can do no more here, the day is de Montfort's; go and make good your escape I will remain but your mother will be in need of support.'

Ralph Mortimer looked at his father with undisguised astonishment on his face.

'Are you saying I should leave the king and Lord Edward to their enemies?'

'I am saying, de Montfort will come to realise he does not have enough men to contain most of his prisoners and will need the Marcher lords to hold some semblance of order, fear not I can negotiate terms. Besides he will treat the royals with due consideration for he needs the king's seal, to give credence to his authority.'

Without further ado Ralph Mortimer spurred his horse away from the screams and groans of the dying and yelled for their supporters to follow his lead away from Lewes and the scenes of defeat. After a few miles he drew rein, not only to give their exhausted mount a breather, but also to discard his armour before continuing on his way back to Wigmore.

Almost a week later Maud witnessed the return of her son and the straggling band of men who had managed to escape. There was no sign of the proud banners and gonfalons which had preceded them on their outward journey; now the blue and or of the Mortimer standard, was nowhere to be seen. Shining armour, exchanged for muddy, torn cloaks and tunics. She knew of the royalist defeat, but as Ralph entered the gates of Wigmore, he appeared to have brought another visitor with him, and his name was – despair.

The days that followed were full of subdued men going about their daily routines with more who had escaped from the battlefield returning in small groups. Some wounded, some so exhausted they could not speak. They learned the fate of the king and his followers, who were currently either, being held in close confinement, or prison.

Maud stamped her foot as she looked across at her son's dejected figure.

'This will not do my lord, if de Montfort sent men to attack us today he would most assuredly be the victor.'

Mortimer glared at her words. But she continued with her remonstrance.

'The air of defeat permeates throughout this castle, in the tilt yard, in the stables, even in the kitchens. You must stem this feeling of futility and find a way to engage the men's sense of honour. Force is not always the best way, sometimes, against all the odds, it is the will, if strong enough, can prove the finest weapon of all.'

'And how Mama, do you propose I should bring this miraculous change about?'

Maud hesitated as though she had been caught her off guard, but Ralph little realised his mother knew full well what she had planned to say, all along.

'Well, why not have archery competitions and prizes each week for the fastest and most accurate archer? In the tiltyard, prizes for the most hits at the quintain. The best groomed horse, the best set of armour, the speediest ....'

Ralph raised his hand and for a moment Maud thought her son would dismiss her ideas out of hand but instead, he looked across and for the first time in weeks, a smile crept across his handsome features.

'By all the saints in heaven, I do believe you may have hit on a good notion.'

Maud turned away so he could not read her expression, when she turned back to face him again she said: 'we can throw a feast each week and have storytellers recite tales of valour and glory, musicians playing rousing songs.'

Within days her suggestions were put into practice and the mood in the castle slowly began to lift. Stable boys started to whistle in the yards once more; the voices of the men were more cheery and laughing challenges replaced the former words of regret.

As Maud looked down from her window she was well pleased with the changes, if nothing else de Montfort would find men ready to take on his armies with fire in their bellies instead of the bitter bile of shame. However, when de Montfort sent a messenger demanding she submit her youngest son, William, as hostage for her husband's release, her mood changed to white hot fury. Nevertheless, there was little she could do and gave her youngest son her blessing and warned him to behave and to keep his eyes and ears open and his mouth firmly closed.

As the days shortened, Mortimer had returned to Wigmore; then word came that de Montfort had moved the Lord Edward from Dover to Wallingford and by spring of the following year, Edward accompanied his captor to Hereford, but not to the castle, instead to Blackfriars Priory, which lay just outside the city boundary.

This news set Maud's mind racing, with Edward so close, she felt certain, there must be a way of freeing him from his captors. This notion nagged at her remorselessly and she sat and spoke of her feelings to the one man she knew would not make light of her thoughts, Lord Rhys.

The firelight flickered and danced in the hearth as the couple sat one evening and talked long into the night. Although age had curtailed the Welshman's mobility, his wits had not failed and remained as sharp as ever, a fact Maud thank God for daily. His unswerving loyalty was deeply comforting. As he looked across at the woman he had come to revere, he pondered over her many suggestions, his mind assessing the details they would need before an effective plan could be devised.

'The first thing we will need to know is how many guards there are; and the exact location he is being held.' He paused then continued. 'I have contacts in Hereford who could easily find out the Lord Edward's daily routine; once we know the exact number of guards; maybe then we can formulate an effective plan of escape.'

Maud nodded, 'of course, it would be reckless risking someone's life on a foolhardy mission.' She smiled across at the face of the man she had come to trust above all others in the Mortimer household. 'I knew you would not fail me.'

Less than a week later Lord Rhys sent word to Maud that he was now in possession of the information which would help them in the next step of their scheme. It always amazed Maud how her chamberlain managed to obtain such information without apparently leaving the castle, she never considered the silent messengers used by the Lord Rhys - pigeons. The unnamed agent had already begun to gather intelligence, certain his master would need to know at some point, all about the royal hostage; his sharp eyes and ears had watched and listened, gleaning anything that he thought may prove beneficial.

Although de Montfort held the king and his nephew prisoner, his former relationship with the Lord Edward gave the Earl an insight into the personality of the heir to the throne, and extended him far more privileges than to any other of his captives. Edward had been allowed to ride out each day upon his arrival from Wallingford. Blackfriars Priory, which lay close to Widemarsh Common, had proved a more comfortable prison, one where he was even allowed to go hawking on occasions but, always under heavy guard. He also had access to books and writing materials, although any messages he sent, were strictly censored. Such details fired Maud's imagination and she and Lord Rhys began to mull over many ideas which ebbed and flowed like the waves on a winter shore.

Another piece of information Maud received with joy, was that her young kinsman, Gilbert de Clare, had fallen out with de Montfort and was now seeking to change his allegiance; with his considerable army of men and weapons the news was received with a sense of relief, it not only put a spring in her step but bolstered the confidence of her son and husband. The letter she had trusted to be delivered by De Longeville must have held some weight.

'I feel the tide is turning my Lord Rhys, and that de Montfort's days are numbered.'

'I believe you could be right my Lady, indeed the wheel of Fate never stays still, that I have learned through my long life.'

However, although the pair had turned over a dozen ideas for effecting Edward's escape none seemed feasible enough to pursue. It was one day when young Arthur, who had been practising his equestrian skills, returned extolling the praises of the Mortimer horses which finally cracked the puzzle.

'My Lady, I swear I have never sat a better mount and am glad my recommendation to change your horse dealer, proved correct. I have won each and every race this morning and the road is still full of .....'

'A race! Of course!' Maud looked at Lord Rhys and in an unusual display of emotions she went and kissed Arthur's brow before sitting down before her aging chancellor.

'We know the Lord Edward rides out daily could he not race his guards; tire their mounts keeping his own mount fresh. We can arrange to have the fastest of our horses at the edge of the trees........'

'Disguise a number of riders to set off in all directions ....'

'But how do we get word to the Lord Edward?' Maud's face had clouded as she realised the plan had to be conveyed to the young royal.

'You forget my lady; my agent already works at the Priory and will devise a way to get a message past the guards.'

'He risks his life.'

'That goes without saying my lady – as we all do!'

In the days that followed over a dozen of the best horses were selected to be fed and exercised to bring them to peak fitness. The tallest squires were given extra lessons in horsemanship as well as sword practice as yet, none being told they had been chosen for one of the most daring escape plans in decades.

When news arrived from the agent to say the Lord Edward was to be allowed two visitors in the coming days and they were his former friends, Roger Clifford and Roger de Leyburne, it seemed like the perfect opportunity to put the escape plan into action. A fast riding messenger was sent to locate and inform the duo of the proposed tactics to free the Lord Edward from de Montfort's clutches.

By Early May, 1265, the Lord and Lady of Wigmore summoned all those who were to be involved in the daring adventure to map out the details. Afterwards a buzz of excitement ran round the chamber. The tallest of the squires would play the main, decoy whilst the others would be ready to ride on diverse escape routes, but with relays of fresh mounts for the royal escapee. After swearing a vow of secrecy the young men all went away to hone their skills further in preparation for the forthcoming event.

Maud was on tender hooks and could not relax, but had to accept she must now let matters run their course as the exact date of the escape was finally chosen. All she prayed for was the young royal would not let his impatient nature thwart their daring ruse.

Before the sun rose on the 27th May, what looked like a hunting party left Wigmore Castle; the young squires, who were decked in huntsman's clothes, rode out at a steady pace, although their mounts pranced and tossed their silky manes in their impatience. At various points along their route some would peel off and disappear taking with them a rider-less mount. Finally, the remainder of the party arrived on the outskirts of Hereford and concealed themselves in the woods which fringed the common. There they remained hidden for the rest of the day, some fed their mounts and then took turns to sleep, eat, and play silent games of dice, to fill the hours until nightfall.

The following morning, as the dark cloak of night began to fade into the silvery rays of dawn; the entire company saddled their mounts, then they all made the sign of the cross and offered up their prayers. All the members of the party knew how important their roles were as they took silent leave of each other, acutely aware, some may never survive to see that day's sunset. They all knew exactly what was required of them and moved in readiness for the events of the day to unfold. The horses caught the tense mood as they stamped their hooves, and jostled nervously as the sidled around eager to be off.

Three of the party made their way to the edge of the tree line. They heard the shouts and laughter of the guards and heard the thundering hooves which only made their own mounts more fractious and restless. Hal, Maud's head groom, was in one of the waiting groups, chosen as he was unequalled in his horsemanship. He sat the powerful dark bay stallion with effortless ease stroking its sleek neck with a soft, light, touch.

It was when the tones of the voices changed to alarm that Hal urged his mount forward and saw Edward Plantagenet galloped his steed towards them at full speed. He raised his hand and quickly leapt from his sweating horse and into the saddle of the waiting stallion; without a word, Hal jumped onto the steaming mount and headed off deep into the woods where he knew a fresh horse would be waiting about a mile away.

Meantime, the four squires chosen as decoys all spurred their horses off in various directions, the blood surging through their veins in excitement; capture was not an option, for they knew death would await them if they failed.

As the parties all made good their escape, at the first relay change, Edward clapped the nearest member of the rescue party on the back, 'God Bless you all - England will never forget your courage!' He grinned at his two companions; 'de Montfort will live to rue this day, on that you have my oath!'

In record time the royal party reached the gates of Wigmore and clattered through the archway, watched by the waiting figure of Lady Mortimer. Edward learned that it was his hostess who had conceived the clever plan and as he ate and drank he smiled and congratulated her.

'I always knew you were a remarkable woman my Lady Mortimer, whose beauty is matched only by your wit. You have played your part now, it is up to me and those that have remained loyal to the crown, to prove worthy and recover the Great Seal of England and show de Montfort, that kinship will not save his head.'

'My Lord, I have a boon to ask.'

'Nothing shall be denied to you this day my Lady.'

Maud smiled and continued. 'The Earl of Gloucester, who as you know is my kinsman, has recently broken away from the de Montfort camp and awaits you at Ludlow in a state of apprehension. He seeks your forgiveness for his former actions, and he assures me, it was entirely due to your father's refusal in granting him his Earldom. In his frustration he turned to de Montfort but has regretted his error of judgment.' She smiled as she continued. 'Not only has he inherited the Irish red hair but, also a hasty nature which brought him into the rebel camp. Something I am assured, he now deeply regrets.'

Edward looked into the depths of her green-grey eyes.

'How can I refuse you ought my Lady, I know all too well how one hasty decision can alter ones whole life and if it is a sin, I also stand guilty of.' He smiled up at her 'have no fear; I shall not take my vengeance out on young Gloucester. Besides, how can I ignore the value of an ally with his considerable influence, especially with his well armed troops?' He winked at his hostess.

'Now pray excuse me whilst I make ready to continue my journey, for haste is of the essence. As I have no desire to return to my prison, however comfortable it was!'

Within the hour Edward Plantagenet, accompanied by Lord Mortimer and his son, together with a number of other Marcher lords, who had rallied to greet the royal visitor, moved off at a smart pace towards Ludlow. That night Maud slept but fitfully, she feared de Montfort's men may arrive at Wigmore full of vengeance, to wreak havoc and death once more. She would never forget the trail of mayhem left by his sons, at Radnor and Pembrugge. Mercifully, the only visitor was the old barn owl who hunted the fields and hedgerows close to the castle, but during the night, he went about his task without interruption.

Thankfully all the squires and grooms had returned safely from their dangerous escapade, and were full of anecdotes, which they would recount throughout the coming months. But life quickly returned to its usual pattern at Wigmore, the emphasis being on the renewed urgency of knightly combat practice, which for all the young squires, was of the utmost importance, as they were eager to reach a level of competence which would ensure their call to arms.

Maud had hoped for a breathing space but such hopes were quickly dashed when she saw her desk had filled with ever more complaints and requests. The whole of England had become almost lawless after the king's capture. She sighed, but instead of beginning her task, she closed the door and went up to the chamber occupied by her youngest children.

Carys sat sewing as she rocked gently on an old bow legged chair; at her feet sat the youngest Mortimer daughter, Margaret. The girl looked up at her mother as she entered.

'See what I have fashioned.' She handed a neat piece of tapestry for her mother's inspection. Maud looked at the colourful needlework.

'You have skills I could never master; I think Carys has taught you well.'

Maud smiled, 'soon I shall be able to draw a much larger pattern for you to work.'

'Indeed, very soon you will go to live in the house of your future husband.'

'But no yet, Carys says the unrest in the land will affect everyone and I would not wish to leave home just yet.' The words were said more in hope than conviction.

'Have no fear child, I would never send you away until we have more stability in the land, I have no intention of putting you at risk.' Her words appeared to placate the girl who looked up and smiled shyly at her mother's reassuring words.

Carys had not risen and continued with her task.

'Is there any news?'

Maud clasped her hands together and Carys knew this to be a sign of anxiety: 'news pours through the gates like rain down a broken drain. What I fear most is Llywelyn, will he make mischief during this period of turmoil.'

Carys looked up at her, her needlework dropped in her lap. 'I thought he was already in league with Leicester?'

'Indeed, hence my fears. The Lord Edward has wasted no time in ravaging the lands of de Montfort's allies therefore; we can look for more reprisals.'

'The gossip is that Sir Roger is now one of the Lord Edward's most trusted adherents.'

Maud nodded, she looked at Carys, 'it would seem that months in captivity gave the Lord Edward time to come to terms with his own recklessness. Let us pray, he will never forget the part the Mortimer's played in attaining his freedom.'

'Which could mean it may help in the advancement, not only of his lordship, but also your children.'

'Just so! Now I must return to my own duties. No doubt your life has become less fraught since young Roger has begun his training as a squire?'

Carys smiled ruefully. 'If ever the devil had a possible recruit I would swear, it is with that one.'

Maud's brow furrowed at the words.

'He is the replica of my father I fear; even in his appearance. I have lived in dread of such a truth, but Gwilym Ddu has marked this son as his own, and all we can do is pray the strict training will in some way, curtail his more overt failings.'

Without waiting for any response Maud turned on her heel and walked out.

'Roger makes Mama sad does he not?'

'Yes child, I think your brother makes your mother very sad.'

'Why is Roger so naughty? And why....'

'Hush Meg!' Isabella Mortimer, the oldest of the seven Mortimer children, wagged her finger at her young sibling. At sixteen, she remained at the family home due to the uncertainties of the times. Unlike her brothers, Edmund, who had recently left for York Minster to study, in readiness for a role in the church and Roger, who had gone to train as a squire? Leaving Geoffrey, to continue with his studies alone, until William's return, before they too would be sent to serve as pages and later as squires; eventually becoming knights

When news arrived that the Earl of Pembroke, William de Valance, and John de Warenne, Earl of Surrey, had landed in Pembroke, Edward sent word that he, with many of his army, would return to Wigmore. The two Earls had made their escape to the Continent after the debacle of Lewes. The intention now was to meet up with the returning nobles and plan their future strategy. Wigmore was once again host to the future King of England.

It was during this time they learned of de Montfort's move to have the Lord Edward replaced as the heir to the English crown. A measure which would make it easy to have his own son Henry elevated as future ruler. The revelation only managed to infuriate the Lord Edward even more and this act alone had in fact, sealed the fate of the de Montfort family.

Maud looked across at the powerful figure of her second cousin, Gilbert de Clare.

'The hand de Montfort, so cleverly concealed, is now revealed, his treachery hidden beneath the voice of self righteous indignation at the failure of the king to uphold the *'Provisions of Oxford'*. I am only thankful you eventually took note of my letter of warning. It is plain his true aim is to attain the throne of England.' Maud lean across and patted her kinsman's arm as she spoke.

'He is eloquent in his speech and has obviously convinced the clergy, who remain his staunch allies but I am glad at least, you saw the truth before it was too late and the number of his followers appear to be waning, if we are to believe recent news.'

Maud looked up at the fire haired, young Earl of Gloucester, as she spoke.

'Thankfully my brother was far more astute and has served the crown well in this matter.' De Clare's words were somewhat rueful.

'Thomas always did have a canny head on his shoulders and you would do well to listen to him more in the future.'

Gilbert's face clouded for an instance but since his father's death Maud was the one blood relative he trusted and he reached out and took her hand.

'My father always said you were never afraid to speak the truth, even against his step-father, the Earl of Cornwall, although you were still very young.'

Gilbert lifted his head as the rays of the summer sun, which slanted through the window, made it look as though he had hair of flames. Maud squeezed Gilbert's hand, 'I know how hard it is for you, but at least try and be a little less impetuous in future.'

'Where de Montfort and his murdering brood are concerned, I will never stay my hand and should I meet any one of them, I vow they will feel my steel in their craven flesh, on that you have my word, Lady Maud.'

'Go with God, and know you are always in my prayers.'

The young Earl rose, and bent to kiss Maud's cheek.

'That means a great deal to me my Lady.'

In the following days they learned that James de Audley had taken Beeston Castle, in Cheshire for the royalists, and soon after, news arrived that Chester Castle was presently under siege. The towns of Shrewsbury, Bridgnorth along the River Severn, together with Ludlow, on the Teme, were also taken. Bridges were smashed and the cunning plan of deepening fords and pulling boats onto the eastern banks, thereby denying access to de Montfort's army, was also undertaken. Gloucester and its bridge were soon captured. However, the castle withstood the onslaught, its garrison vigorously defended its position but, by the end of June, that too fell leaving the strategic lands and towns lining the River Severn, firmly in the hands of the young Lord Edward and his followers.

De Montfort's response was to have Richard, Earl of Cornwall, and Edmund, his son by his second wife Sanchia, put in chains at Kenilworth. The Earl of Leicester was not about to give these valuable hostages any chance of escape. He also made a formal alliance with Llywelyn, which was signed by his royal prisoner, Henry. The terms of the agreement thus acknowledged Llywelyn as rightful leader of an independent Wales for the princely sum of 30,000 marks, to be paid in instalments. The money was sorely needed by de Montfort to pay his many mercenaries, which also included landless knights.

The treaty was deemed shameful by his rivals. Many castles were subsequently destroyed on Llywelyn's orders and under this premise one of the number was Paincastle, which had been built at Henry's expense, in 1231-2. Another strategic site was the de Clare's castle at Usk, which was also taken by de Montfort, but Gilbert and Edward moved swiftly in response and retook the castle within days. Their fast riding army also regained Hay, Brecon, and Huntingdon and burned and plundered de Montfort's ships, leaving him only one choice, to retreat back to Hereford.

Meanwhile, de Montfort's eldest son, Simon, looted Winchester before moving on to Oxford, he continued to Northampton, before finally reaching the family stronghold of Kenilworth. Only to be faced by Edward and Gilbert de Clare, who had marched from Worcester to confront the de Montfort heir. Where, they found their enemy sleeping after celebrating their successes; most of the troops, heavy in drink, had slept outside the castle and were easily taken. However, Simon and some of his best forces had managed to gain the castle and refuge, thus avoiding being captured.

Roger Mortimer was elated when he took the powerful baron, Richard de Grey prisoner, whom he saw as a treacherous adversary, especially as he also hailed from the Marches; their boyhood rivalry had been re-ignited . There were other important figures amongst the captives, Baldwin Wake, and Adam of Newmarket. When Gilbert de Clare discovered the clerk who had been at the heart of the de Montfort's dispute of de Clare's lands, he beheaded the hapless scribe in a personal act of vengeance.

As the two armies moved inexorably towards a confrontation, Mortimer wrote to his wife apprising her of the situation but the news was received with mixed emotions. Experience had taught her that even victory in battle did not immediately quell all opposition and the subsequent consequences could often prove disastrous. Revenge, retribution, and treachery would undoubtedly abound, no matter how many of the enemy were slain or captured on the day. Resentment would fester for years after, and such enmities were never easily laid to rest.

However, Maud did not dwell long on her sombre thoughts as she made ready for all eventualities with food, bedding, and dressings, whatever the outcome there were always many wounded who would need treatment. She also ordered the doubling of the patrols as a matter of expediency. Conflict always affected the poor whose livelihoods were inevitably wrecked by marauding armies in the quest for food, both for the men, and their horses. For the victims, their losses were without redress, as foraging parties fired buildings, barns, slaughtered all the livestock leaving nothing for their enemy in an effort to cause as much hardship, as they could. But the results of such tactics, also left the hapless peasants and farmers homeless and without means of existence.

Daily, similar events were happening throughout the country and inevitably by the onset of winter, many families were faced with starvation. This knowledge left Maud even more determined that de Montfort's rebellion would not plunge the Mortimer villeins into this situation.

Whilst Lady Mortimer busied herself ensuring the defences of both Wigmore and the surrounding districts were addressed, Sir Roger and his son Ralph rode beside the king's son, Edward Plantagenet. Day by day, he was proving his mastery of arms and as a tactician was earning respect even from his more experience commanders. Following a skirmish, one of his sergeant's had picked up a de Montfort's standard and gonfalon and Edward nodded his approval.

'That could prove most useful,' he grinned. 'The wolf and his cubs will soon be brought to earth eh! Sergeant?'

'Aye Sire! The Old Earl may not have heard of his son's debacle at Kenilworth. I know at least one of the messengers met with ....' he cleared his throat, 'a sudden exit from this earth.'

Edward clapped the man on the back.

'Then let us pray our quarry meets with a similar end.' The young royal and the battle hardened soldier shared the thought before making ready to move off towards a day that would mark a turning point in the history of England.

CHAPTER XXIII

August 1265
Evesham

Gilbert de Clare stood fidgeting as his squire buckled on his armour.

'For Mercy's sake Lionel, hurry up!'

'I am trying my Lord but my fingers are all thumbs this morning.'

Standing close by was another of Gilbert's squires holding his brightly burnished war helmet

'God's wounds, I swear we shall still be standing here long after everyone has departed if you do not make haste.'

The flustered squire finally managed to buckle the last fastening and stood up only to receive a cuff round his ears from his impatient master. A Mortimer servant arrived at the flap of the marquee.

'My Lord, Lord Edward is calling for his Commanders to meet in his tent immediately.'

When Gilbert arrived he nodded greetings to men, who until recently, he had opposed, but who were now ready to unite and fight together for the royalist cause. One of the Marcher baron's, who had also recently joined Edward's army, was John Giffard. Giffard was a respected soldier and as they stood waiting for everyone to assemble, Roger Mortimer went and stood beside his one time ally.

'Seen sense at last Giffard?' The expression on Giffard's craggy face was wary but Mortimer continued without hesitation, 'tis good to have you fighting at my side again.' The pair looked at each other and Giffard's face relaxed into a knowing grin.

'My ideals have not diminished but came to realise, Leicester was somewhat less than honest in his aims than he led us to believe.'

'He always did have an eloquent turn of phrase; it took my Lady Maud's shrewd judgement to make me see sense a long time since.'

Giffard chuckled, 'the lovely Maud is worth a dozen men.'

Mortimer nodded. 'Aye! Indeed.' Their conversation was brought to an abrupt end as Edward raised his hand for silence.

'It appears we have finally caught up with Leicester, at last, and although he has sent messengers to negotiate terms, I have refused. Today, he and those misguided men who have chosen to support his cause, will learn that Edward Plantagenet has no truck with those that bear arms against the crown.'

A murmur ran round the group.

'Today, with God's good blessings and your skill of arms, we will bring down this treacherous cur or, die on the field.'

A roar resounded amongst the party of Earls and barons.

Edward held up his hand again for silence.

'We will split into three columns. The left flank will be led by Gloucester, I will lead the centre, and Mortimer and his Marchers will be on the right flank, cutting off any attempt of escape in that direction. To give us the element of surprise we will fly Leicester's own colours making him believe his son is at hand to swell their ranks. Therefore, none of our standards shall be shown at first but, as soon as we have reached our goal, then mark well your Commanders device. Are there any questions?' The keen blue eyes raked the faces of his audience. 'I make just one proviso - there will be no quarter given this day. Then gentlemen, I wish you God's blessings and pray we meet shortly to celebrate the fall of our enemies.'

The words left those present stunned for a moment but soon the silence changed to cheers before everyone departed to take up their positions in readiness for the day's action. The two Mortimer's, together with many of the Marcher barons walked back towards Mortimer's tent.

Roger was the first to speak. 'There are many who face friends and family and to be given the order of 'no quarter', is an unexpected shock.'

'Aye! I can only wonder at poor de Bohun whose first born son is one of their numbers.'

'As is our former friend, Sir Peter de Montfort, together with many good men. However, we must obey our future king's orders or be judged as weak kneed.'

When they reached the tent Mortimer waited for everyone who would fight under his standard to arrive before he spoke.

'Watch for my signals, as we know, Leicester is no fool in any conflict be it words or weapons and the tide of battle can change in an instant therefore, we must be ready to change and counter any tactics the Earl or his men may use. Remember, our orders, even though some of those we fight today are former friends, and kinsmen. God have mercy on their souls and His everlasting forgiveness on ours.'

Mass and had already been heard and communion taken before dawn. Now, under low, heavy, skies, the might of the royalist army made ready to mount and take up their positions. Just as the first slanting rain drops began to fall; in the distance, thunder could be heard as it rolled ominously, moving ever closer towards Evesham.

When Edward handed Leicester's colours to his standard bearer he saw the look of pain and relented.

'Call for the sergeant who captured them, he shall have the dubious *honour* of carrying Leicester's colours. Once we have engaged the enemy, I give you leave to raise my standard.'

'Thank you Sire.'

Edward mounted his magnificent war charger, and then made the sign of the cross, followed by the signal for his troops to move forward. The de Montfort colours hung almost lifeless in the heavy, humid air, as the column marched steadily forward. To his right Edward could see the young Earl of Gloucester take up his position; to his left Mortimer's columns moved to cover the route across the Avon.

Evesham lay in the loop of the great river and de Montfort, believing his son Simon was riding to join his men, had taken up position there. One of his look-outs shouted, but the tones were not of jubilation but horror.

'Go and see what the fool is quaking at!' Simon de Montfort sent his barber, who was noted for his sharp eyes and knowledge of heraldry. Racing to the Abbey tower, he ran up the winding stairs to the roof where he scanned the horizon and although the approaching army was flying the de Montfort standard, the watcher knew the leading knight was no de Montfort. Quickly he descended and recounted his discovery in breathless tones to his master.

De Montfort turned to his companions. 'Gentlemen, it looks as though we have been gulled by the Lord Edward and his men. We are in a virtual trap and there is but one way we shall win free by forming a tight, fast riding column to push through their ranks in order to gain better ground.'

They clasped hands in turn knowing this could be their final day on earth.

'Trust in God, trust in your sword arm and stay close, they will not win an easy victory this day I swear that by all I hold dear.' But when his loyal companions had departed the words he uttered to his faithful barber were prophetic.

'God have mercy on our souls for they have our bodies.'

As a shout rang out, the royalist sergeant dropped the captured colours and moved back allowing the Lord Edward's own standard bearer to ride in his place now flying the proud leopards of England. As the mighty chargers thundered across the ground the earth shook just as the storm broke, the battle was conjoined.

The shrieks of pain and fury pierced through the growling rumbles of thunder and for those who survived that terrible day, swore that it appeared that every element in heaven and on earth, were at war.

True to his plan de Montfort's men charged full tilt towards Edward's troops. Quickly the fighting became furious and bloody. Chargers screamed in panic and pain as they slid and slithered on the ground, slippery from rain and blood. The initial impetus of de Montfort's men had at first threatened to rout Edward's ranks but then begun to founder as many fell dead or, dying, blocking their path. Gloucester had sent in his light cavalry to relieve the faltering royalists. The manœurvre proved successful as the few rebels who had managed to win through were now faced with Mortimer's Marcher barons, who stood in their way.

Roger Mortimer spurred his charger forward as he saw the muddied colours of Hugh Despencer, he raised his lance a little higher as he thrust the cruel spike at his enemy's head where the force of the impact drove it through the visor, Despencer screamed as blood flew from his dying lips. The contact had hardly checked Mortimer's steed and as he continued he heard Ralph shout above the melee.

'Its Leicester, he is unhorsed,' he pointed and dropping his lance Mortimer drew his martel de fer and raised it high above his head swung the blade of the heavy axe down into the body of the Earl who had been left on foot after his charger had been killed. Mortimer felt the muscles in his arm and shoulder scream in pain but knew he had dealt a blow his enemy would never rise from. As soon as the Earl had dropped to his knees Mortimer adherents continued to reign blows until his body was dismembered like some sacrificial beast.

After two of the bloodiest hours of fighting, a shout rose and although some sporadic fighting continued the main parties drew rein and gathered to cheer their Commander–in-Chief, Edward Plantagenet.

'Find the king.' Edward's words were gruff and urgent. He urged his weary charger towards Mortimer and his son who held the spear sporting the head of his enemy, Simon de Montfort.

'Well done my lords we have vanquished our enemy but there will be no more mutilation of any of the bodies on pain of death. I will have a list of the dead. Find my cousin, Henry's body and have the monks tend it. Also, allow the knights who fought and died this day, honourable burial.'

Edward dismounted and went and clapped the young Earl of Gloucester on the shoulder,

'Quick thinking on your part my lord; the old warrior almost succeeded in his bold charge.'

Gloucester grinned, his face streaked with sweat and smudged with grime and blood.

'He fought like a lion.'

'As did those with him. Do we know the name of his standard bearer; I swear he was wounded to death but still held on to his standard?'

'A Scot Sire, Guy Baliol, I believe.'

'Have his body treated with the utmost honour. By the way, what happened to the Welsh contingents?'

'They fled the field my Lord.'

'Then deal with them accordingly when you have captured them.'

'Aye my Lord.'

The aftermath of the Battle of Evesham would have repercussions that were to last, for many decades to come. As for the Lord Edward, he attended the funeral of his childhood play mate, Henry de Montfort, and it was said, he wept openly during the service.

The head of his enemy, the Earl of Leicester, Simon de Montfort, he sent to Lady Mortimer at Wigmore as a token of his gratitude; with a message, stating that he and his father would return to London in an effort to restore law and order as quickly as possible.

Mortimer, and his son, accompanied by many of the Marchers were ordered to carry the macabre mascot of the battle, to Wigmore. On learning of the victory, Maud had heard Mass at Wigmore Abbey in thanks for the safe delivery of her husband and son. She was acutely aware that the name of Mortimer would now be synonymous with loyalty and thus hold a place of respect in royal circles. She arranged a great feast for the return of her men-folk and their Marcher allies. As *'guest of honour'* she had the lance with de Montfort's head placed at the head of the table, where he was toasted with copious amounts of wine, all celebrated his demise.

Although the guests enjoyed the sumptuous fare, and danced and sang through the long evening, for Maud, who nodded and smiled at one and all, it was difficult hiding her true emotions from the assembly. The feeling of pride in the achievements her husband and son were real, as was the sense of triumph over the defeat of a long standing enemy but, it did not entirely quell the niggling sense of unease which accompanied her mixed emotions.

De Montfort had not died alone and numerous men of integrity had fought and died for an ideal which, in her heart, she felt to be a just one. Pride had been the ultimate enemy, and had ridden with both parties that day. The king and de Montfort were guilty of ignoring each other's voices. Instead of choosing to seek another approach, they had put their own pride and arrogance before the well being of the country. But then she remembered, England was not de Montfort's country, he was a Frenchman, and through all the years he had supposedly served England, his ties with France had always been as close as those to his wife's family. The thought went some way in placating her conscience; as she had much to be thankful for, her son and husband had returned with only a few minor wounds and bruises, unlike so many others who would live with the terrible consequences of that fateful day.

In the aftermath of the feast the clearing up lasted for days. The head of the '*guest*' had been sent on to London where it would be displayed on London Bridge. It was also, a period when many of the wounded returned to Wigmore, and were treated for a diverse range of minor injuries, in the Infirmary. Later they would be joined by the more seriously wounded who arrived on wagons and carts. Maud visited the patients regularly and helped in many ways to ease their suffering. She also had masses said for those who had died and sent aid to the families who would suffer at the loss of their breadwinner, conscious they had given their lives not only in the service of the king but also, to the Mortimer family.

As Maud predicted, the Battle at Evesham fought on that hot, stormy August day, had not ended the fighting, which subsequently broke out intermittently in all parts of the country. De Montfort's son, Simon, had fled back to Kenilworth where he was holed up under siege. It appeared that he was wracked with remorse, as it had undoubtedly been his tardiness in failing to ride to his father's aid, which was the cause of his father's humiliating defeat.

News had leaked out that he had refused to eat for many days after learning of the deaths of his brother and father. There was no way of knowing if such rumours held any truth. So much had happened in such a short space of time, countless noble families mourned the loss of loved ones and there was a sense that nothing would ever be quite the same again. Some murmured the age of Chivalry had died on the field at Evesham, with the order of 'no quarter' being issued by Edward. Maud however, realised that as the future King of England, he had sent a message not only to his own subjects but, also to the world that once he was king, anyone who dared to draw a sword against him would receive no mercy.

It did not help her own feelings of regret in the passing of an age where brave enemies were treated with honour but, being a pragmatic woman she knew she, like everyone else, would have to learn to live with this new code of conduct and a strong ruler would undoubtedly bring stability to the country once more.

September proved a busy month for the Mortimer family; Roger and his son, Ralph, left for London as they had been summoned by the king to attend Parliament. For Maud and the household of Wigmore, life continued in the rhythm of the seasons. The harvest or what there was, had to be gathered; the beasts and flocks, who had survived, were brought to lower pastures, some to be selected to fill the larders and stores. Nuts and fruits were gathered, and logs and fuel were stacked in readiness for the onset of winter. Some of the wounded healed and returned to their duties, others to their families but, for those who had succumbed to their wounds, they were buried and services held for the repose of their souls.

News which arrived from Wales was not unexpected; Llywelyn had once again begun a series of raids. Also, the king had allowed his sister, de Montfort's widow, and her daughter, safe passage to France. Richard, Earl of Cornwall and his son Edmund had been released from their chains where they had been held since the Lord Edward's escape in May of the previous year.

Maud received an invitation from her eldest daughter, Isabella, better known to the close family as Bella, who had been sent some months ago into the household of the FitzAlan family, upon her marriage to the young heir to the Arundel earldom. Bella was presently at Clun Castle and wished her mother to visit on a matter of some urgency. Intrigued, Maud was delighted for an excuse to meet with her daughter as it was some months since they had been in each other's company.

On a bright, chilly morning Maud and a small party left Wigmore at a steady trot. It dawned on Maud as she journeyed to Clun; it had been some considerable time since she had visited. As they approached, she noted the meandering river, fringed by clumps of willows whose elegant branches trailed into the water, leaving rippling shadows and patterns which dazzled in the early winter sun and as the Castle walls came into view, admired the packhorse bridge which spanned the swift flowing waters. A familiar figure stood on the steps of the castle keep as the group clattered into the inner bailey.

'Welcome to Clun.' Bella moved down the steps to greet her mother, kissing her on both cheeks as she did so.

'My, you have blossomed from a girl into a young woman in just a few short months.'

Bella smiled ruefully, 'I wish you would tell my husband and his parents as much, they still treat me as though I am a little maid!'

Maud could tell by her daughter's words that the situation rankled but made no comment within earshot of the servants.

'This is indeed a most pleasant spot Bella, why have you not stayed here before?'

'We have, but this is the first time we have been allowed to stay alone.'

Maud looked speculatively at her daughter, 'I see!'

The couple moved into the castle and Maud removed her travelling cloak handing it to the waiting servant. Bella led the way to a pleasant solar where a merry fire crackled in the hearth. The table was laden with meat pies, fruit, nuts, and dishes of delicacies, both sweet and savoury. Bella indicated for the servant to pour the wine and then dismissed him.

'By your tone I gather married life is not as you imagined it?' Maud looked across at her daughter.

'No! I have scant to do as John's mother controls the Arundel households.'

'Well, she is not here now is she?' Maud looked intently at her daughter as she spoke, 'so let everyone know that you are the heir's wife and it is you they should now look to for instructions whilst you are here.'

Bella looked askance at her mother's words.

'I do not wish to upset my husband even before he *is* my husband.'

'You mean you are still a virgin?' Maud look truly amazed at her daughter's revelation.

'I told you, John continues to treat me like a child – under his mother's instructions of course!'

'And you; do you want to become a wife with all its responsibilities and share your bed with Arundel?'

'Yes – I think so!'

'Bella, you must be certain, this is what you truly wish for because once the step has been taken, it cannot be reversed. Your husband will demand he shares your bed at times it may not be what you want but denial will no longer be an option - remember. Besides, childbearing is no easy condition, in fact far from it, and your body will never be the same again.'

'You have retained your youthful figure Mama, after bearing seven children.' Bella's words sounded almost accusatory.

'Believe me, I have unseen scars and internal wounds that frequently plague me, sometimes affecting my health. Although we are bound by the vows of marriage to fulfil our duty to bring forth life, I freely admit I am ever thankful that I was past my majority when I became a mother for the first time. Just because your body is capable of bearing a child it does not always walk hand in hand with maturity, are you certain you feel ready for all the emotion and pain motherhood entails?'

'The simple truth is, I resent being considered too young, and I cannot stay a child forever now can I? Besides,' she hesitated, 'I want to become more important to John than his mother.'

Maud smiled. 'And how does John feel about that?'

'Oh! Mama, I have never discussed it with him in as many words, but do try and hint I wish to become his wife in every sense.' She blushed feeling suddenly shy at revealing her thoughts to her mother.

Maud looked at her daughter, 'Well, most men would not need a second invitation for you are a comely young woman, even though I say it myself.'

'Am I?' Bella's face lit up at her mother's compliment.

'Surely your reflector makes that fact obvious, even to you?'

'You see, in just a few short months I have become so inured in my position as a minor I have almost lost my own self confidence.'

Maud's expression clouded for an instant. 'As a Mortimer, with the blood of the great Marshal family coursing through your veins, you must never allow *anyone* to overlook your status, do you understand Bella?'

'Yes Mama!' The young woman almost regretted telling her mother of her private thoughts but what Maud said next changed her opinion.

'Well if you are sure you are ready to take on all the duties of a wife and mother, I may have a notion which should bring you at least one step closer to your goal. Upon the return of your father and brother I will throw a feast for a number of neighbouring friends including you and Arundel, where you will have to share a bedchamber. What could be more natural, and if your father and mother believe you are old enough to be considered truly wed, why then should there be any opposition from your husband?'

'Oh Mama I knew I could rely on you to help me. Thank you!'

'My dear, my whole life is focused on my children and their future wellbeing.' Then she added mischievously, 'as well as to advance of the Mortimer fortunes. Just because I never lingered overlong in the nursery, does not mean I do not love you. Besides, Carys fulfilled that role much better than I ever could, as you must have realised by now, I am *not* overly maternal by nature.

Also, do not condemn John's mother for being too protective towards you, she may have had a bad experience when still little more than a girl herself and did not wish a similar situation for you. The anguish of childbirth before you are ready can have a devastating effect upon any young woman.'

Bella nodded thoughtfully. 'I never considered that to be her motive but, it is quite feasible I suppose.'

'Take charge of your household, become a wife, make sure your husband begins to see you as his support and by so doing you are then in a position to quietly relegate your mother-in-law to a place in the shadows. It will follow the natural order and therefore make it easier for her to accept you as capable of fulfilling the role she once held.'

'I have been pondering this for some weeks, and feel so glad I turned to you for help.'

Maud patted her daughter's hand.

'You are my beloved daughter and where else would you turn?'

The rest of the two day visit was spent in riding, talking about fashions and family, in a manner which made it clear to Bella that her mother, if no-one else, was treating her as an adult and she revelled in her new status. Until this moment she had always viewed her mother as somewhat remote, but suddenly realised the fact, Maud had always been kept busy with affairs of the Marches. Now she understood that motherhood did not necessarily mean being tied to the nursery. She was filled by a feeling of excitement at the thought, her mother was about to give her, the key to her future. Bella knew it would be how she chose to use this opportunity which would determine the rest of her life.

On Maud's return to Wigmore she began to make arrangements for the forthcoming feast. Days later, when her husband and son returned from London, she learned that the lands and estates of Robert de Vere, Earl of Oxford, and father-in-law to her second daughter, Meg, had been awarded to Mortimer for his services to the crown. A just cause for celebrations.

November saw a cavalcade of guests arriving at Wigmore, among their numbers was John FitzAlan, heir to the earldom of Arundel, and his young wife, Isabella Mortimer. It would be a night many would have cause to remember for years to come. Wine flowed, the trestle tables groaned with savoury dishes, which filled the Hall with delightful smells of spices and herbs, all accompanied by delicious mouth watering roasts, which ranged from roast boar, ox, sucking pigs, mutton, swans, geese, and chickens. The finest musicians had been hired from far and wide and their music filled the Great Hall. Laughter rang out at the antics of the jesters and when the trestles were pushed back couples took the floor and danced to the rhythms of tunes new and old.

Maud sat beside her husband and played her part of hostess to perfection but from time to time, her eyes strayed to where her daughter and son-in-law sat. John FitzAlan was not overly tall but he was well set, with regular features and dark eyes, fringed with long lashes. He was no vain popinjay but it was quite obvious, Bella was undoubtedly smitten, although she was trying not to make her feelings too obvious. The young FitzAlan however, showed nothing but courtesy towards his wife and Maud was uncertain to his true feelings towards her daughter. The morrow may give a clue to how the couple would spend their first night in their marriage bed.

The behaviour of her eldest son also did not go unnoticed by Maud, as she watched him flirting with almost every young woman in the Hall, causing much chagrin to some of their husbands. Her frown, warned him of her displeasure at such antics and he soon joined a group of knights and squires who were drinking and laughing on the other side of the Hall. Ralph's vanity was a trait Maud disliked intensely and since Evesham, it had grown considerably, fuelled by his father's constant praises.

As the hours passed, voices became more slurred and many slumped into their seats obviously overcome by the effects of their overindulgence of both wine and food. Slowly the Hall became less crowded as many sought their beds. Maud saw Bella signal her husband that she too wished to retire. She noted his hesitation at first but then he duly followed his wife to their bedchamber. Maud knew she had played her part and what happened in the coming hours was entirely up to her daughter. At the sound of raucous laughter her attention strayed to where her son, who was obviously drunk, lay sprawled holding a tearful young servant, she rose and walked over to where he was trying to pull open the bodice of the unfortunate girl.

'Go to bed Ralph, you are making a spectacle of yourself, as usual.' Maud's tones were low but full of warning. His hair was tousled; his apparel spattered with wine and his face was red and blotchy.

'I swear at this rate you will drink yourself to death long before you reach your majority. You are a disgrace to the name of Mortimer. Now go!' The servant leapt up and ran off sobbing as Maud beckoned to a servant to come and help her son to his chamber. She heard his oath which was undoubtedly aimed at her, without hesitation she walked back and struck him hard across his face. Blood spurted from his mouth. 'If I ever hear you swear at me again sirrah, I promise they will be the last words you will ever utter. Do you understand me?' The Hall suddenly fell hushed at the scene and Roger Mortimer hurried somewhat unsteadily to where his wife stood over the prone figure of their eldest son.

'Pray, what's amiss?'

Maud turned to face him. 'Your son has just dishonoured me and has received a warning if ever it happens again he will die at my hands.' Without further ado, she brushed passed her open mouthed husband and out of the Hall. Upon reaching her chamber she picked up a water jug and threw it across the room, as the contents spilled across the fur rugs, which were scattered across the stone flagged floor.

Sometime later when Mortimer entered, he found Maud was sitting up in bed.

'You really must do something about Ralph's behaviour.' She said as she punched the pillow she had been nursing. 'I had hoped after Lewes and Evesham, he would have matured and discarded such behaviour but judging by tonight's ......'

'He's young; he is still revelling in the glow of success on the battlefield and also his trip to London. You have shamed him....'

'*I* have shamed *him*! I will not be cursed at by my own son, in my own home, and if you believe you can find an excuse which will exonerate him I would like to hear it!'

'Maud, you have threatened to kill your own son.'

'Believe me my lord, it is no idle threat, my womb gave him life and by all the Saints in Heaven....'

'Please, say no more or, you will be guilty of the sin of blasphemy. I will punish him tomorrow on that you have my word. Now, can we put this distasteful incident behind us?'

'As you will my lord.' Maud lay down with a thud and turned her face into the pillow.

In another part of the Castle of Wigmore, a far different scene was being played out by Bella Mortimer, and her husband John FitzAlan.

'I am glad you agreed to this visit to Wigmore. I have always wanted you to see where I grew up and to become closer to my family.' She poured a cup of wine and handed it to him; she could see how uncomfortable he was being alone with her. She smiled shyly up at him. 'Tomorrow we will go hunting in the Forest and I know you will enjoy it as there is such a variety of game.' She moved closer to where he stood. He was about to move away when she caught hold of his hand. 'My lord, do you not desire me? Is it not time we consummated our marriage?'

'You are too young.'

She guided his hand under her shift and let it rest on her breast.

'Are these the breasts of a child?'

Bella could see his face redden. She stood on her toes and kissed his mouth; she felt him tremble at her touch. Her own heart began to race; for she was aware what happened in the next few hours would determine their relationship for all time.

'Hold me John, hold me, and never let me go!' Her words were little more than a whisper.

For what seemed like eternity he remained motionless. She could feel her feet grow cold on the flag-stones. Suddenly, he pulled her to him and returned her kiss at first, gently, but the emotion quickly changed to passion. He gathered her up and carried her to the bed. All his former reserves fell away as he made love to his wife, and fulfilled all her passionate desires.

On the following morning Bella entered the Hall in readiness for the hunt with a secret smile on her face. Maud however, was still quietly seething and even the apology she had received from her son had done nothing to quell her disquieted spirit but nothing of her inner feelings were revealed in her expression.

'Ah Bella I see you at least spent a satisfactory night.'

Bella smiled. 'Oh yes! Today I feel truly a woman and it feels so .... So'

'Grown up?' Maud's face had softened at her daughter's words.

'Mmm! Quite, quite grown up. Thanks to you, Mama.'

'In months to come I wonder whether you will still be thanking me!'

Bella pulled on her leather gloves in readiness to join the hunting party.

'Are you not coming Mama?'

'No, not today, I have matters to attend to here.'

Bella knew better than to argue with her mother's decisions and walked towards the door, a page quickly opened it but as she was about to leave, she turned and blew a kiss to her mother, then left to join the chattering group. For a moment Maud stood, her expression unchanged but the seething anger, which still raged within her remained undimmed, but she did feel a sense of satisfaction that at least her daughter's marriage status appeared to have been settled.

Presently, she too left the chamber and went and sought the council of her aging advisor, Lord Rhys.

'Do you think Ralph will ever control his excesses?' She looked intently towards the frail figure, sat wrapped in furs.

'He must be in control on the field of battle, as he obeys the orders of his commanders therefore; he should be able to bring such discipline to his private life.'

'His total disregard for his own reputation as well as that of the families will be the ruin of him I fear and I do not wish to see him suffer the same fate as my father.' Maud's words had faded to little more than a whisper.

'In truth, I lay blame at the feet of his father who allowed him too much rein when he was a boy and now, he will find, like an unruly young stallion, the whip, and the spur far more painful.'

'Is there nothing that can be done to bring him to his senses?'

'Is there no-one he truly respects?'

'Let us pray he will listen to his father but' she hesitated, 'when he is in drink I have my doubts. for he appears to lose all what few inhibitions he has.'

'Then let us use the church and see if they can bring about some kind of warning which will at least make him aware that his lifestyle is causing concern to the clergy.'

'I know Edmund can always cut him down to size verbally, at least.'

'Well why not write to him and invite him for the Christmas festivities?'

Maud's faced lightened. 'That is an excellent idea and at least it will be good to see Edmund once again.' She rose, walked over, and stooped to kiss the brow of her aging confidante.

'You never fail me with your wise council my Lord Rhys, my indebtedness to you grows ever higher.'

The old man nodded a rare smile flickered around his lips. 'I believe you are the one who will bring your son to heel one way or another. However, I pray your actions will not cause a rift which can only weaken the Mortimer family.'

'That is not a route I wish to travel but I must and will find a solution, on that you have my word.' With that she left to deal with more immediate household matters but the thought of seeing Edmund again had raised her own mood and upon the return of the hunters they found their hostess waiting with a welcoming smile.

The following morning Maud wrote to her favourite son inviting him to seek leave from his studies and join the family for the Christmastide celebrations. Without penning the exact words or, the urgency of her invitation, Maud knew Edmund would understand and she did not doubt he would find some way of travelling back to Wigmore for the festivities.

Just days later a messenger from Beeston Castle in Chester, brought tidings which caused Maud to reflect how drastically life could changed in a short span of time. Humphrey de Bohun, heir to the Earl of Hereford, and her former brother-in-law, had succumbed to his wounds received at the Battle of Evesham. She offered up a fervent prayer that he had finally found the peace which had eluded him ever since Nell's death. Mayhap, they would be re-united in the afterlife. Calling for Arthur, she dictated a letter of condolence to the Earl. It was a difficult missive as there had been some conflict of interests with regard to the ownership of various Marshal lands recently, and the former close relationship she and the Earl had once enjoyed, had become tainted by the legal wrangling.

However, some weeks later, she received happier news, it was the reply she had hoped for – Edmund would be home for Christmastide and during the second week of Advent, he rode through the arched gates of his family home. Elated at his arrival Maud greeted him with open arms.

'You will never know how much I have longed to see your dear face again.' She stood back and looked up at him.

'You are too thin, and I swear you have grown inches since last we met.'

Edmund embraced his beloved mother and laughed at her comments.

'Well – the food is not exactly abundant and I do try and keep up with the knightly exercise but in secret, I have to admit, as the Prior does not approve of his churchmen bearing arms.

'But you are not yet ordained so surely that absolves you!'

'Whether it does or not, he is a hard taskmaster, and to defy his orders only brings down his wrath and severe punishment.'

She nodded. 'Being a Giffard, I understand your circumspection. I place the death of poor William Devereaux at the door of the Giffards'.

Edmund looked enquiringly at his mother.

'Devereaux was always a king's man but, under the pressure from his Giffard wife and her churchmen uncles, what chance did he have?'

'Too many good men died that day, take Peter de Montfort, a more genuine soul never drew breathe and look at poor Humphrey's death, it has caused much heartache for his father.'

'All we can do is pray for their souls and look to a brighter future, but I cannot believe your letter of invitation was to apprise me of the deaths of former allies.'

Maud went and sat down indicating for him to follow suit.

'You know me too well my dearest son.' She paused before continuing.

'The truth is - I fear Ralph is becoming......' she opened her hands as she spoke, 'more wayward and although your father admonishes him one day, the next he is condoning his unacceptable behaviour, making umpteen excuses for him. As you know, Ralph and I have never been close, being his father's favourite, but when he swore at me in front of a room full of guests I'm afraid my temper got the better of me and I threatened to kill him if he ever showed me such disrespect again.'

She looked deep into Edmund's eyes. 'Of all the people on earth I trust to understand my frustrations, it is you!'

'No-one would believe you really meant what you said.'

Maud paused; her hands gripped the arm of her chair so tightly they turned white. 'But I am ashamed to admit that I meant every word.'

'And you believe I can bring Ralph to heel?'

'Yes, I do! You have always been able to outwit him and somehow I feel it is imperative that he is stopped in this headlong race to destruction.'

Edmund passed a hand over his eyes.

'Not an easy quest I grant you, but I will think long and hard on the matter and am sure we can resolve this between us.'

Maud walked over and kissed the top of his head.

'Now you are aware of the situation we can look for some celebrations to lighten the mood. Your brothers, William and Geoffrey will be pleased to see you; Roger is away and won't be joining us!'

How is Will? His time in captivity cannot have been easy for him.'

'Will is quiet, unflappable and resilient but I grant you, there is a subtle change.' She smiled sadly. 'I hope it is just growing pains and that there will be no long term effects.'

'What of Roger?'

'He is unable to join us this year.'

'Then at least there is one less troublesome son to take care of!'

Mother and son laughed together and Maud felt happier than she had done for some time.

The festive season at Wigmore was a time of merriment and to the greater part; fun. There was much frivolity and singing and general high jinks. Edmund, without drawing attention to him-self, observed his brother's preponderance for wenching and drinking, and could well understand his mother's concerns. How to bring about a change would be a very difficult matter, knowing the stubbornness of Ralph's nature.

On a crisp chilly morning, as the host and his guests mounted for a day's hunting, the courtyard was filled by the banter and ribaldry of the riders as they rode off, watched by Maud and some of the ladies. With the men-folk gone, the women relaxed and spent the day chatting about their families or playing board games. Some sat sewing as they talked. A minstrel played softly in the background, adding to the atmosphere of ease and well being.

Some hours later, all the calm was shattered by the sudden return of the Mortimer's and their huntsmen. It was obvious by their stern expressions that all was not well. Maud hurried towards her husband and sons as they dismounted. Her face full of concern. As her husband walked towards her she could see his face was ashen but his expression was one of relief rather than anguish.

'Pray, what has happened, my lord?'

'Ralph has had a very narrow escape but, thanks to Edmund and Simon, their swift action saved the day, and all is well.'

Maud beckoned the party into Great Hall where refreshments were served as Maud listened to the detailed account of the dramatic events of the morning.

The party had quickly picked up the scent of their prey, and the hounds and huntsmen had managed to turn the boar towards the hunting party, but none had noticed there had in fact, been two young boars. Sensing their danger, the pair had split and taken two separate routes of escape. However, a couple of the older hounds had scented the second boar and Simon; their handler had followed, together with Edmund and a young squire. The first beast, upon hearing his pursuers, who were quickly gaining on him, suddenly broke through a thorny thicket and plunged along a path which circled back to the rear of the main party. Ralph's horse, sensing the imminent danger, had reared, twisted, bucked, and unseated his rider, who hit the ground directly in the path of the second boar. The impact had winded him, leaving him totally vulnerable. Edmund had yelled as loud as he could to attract the charging animal's attention giving Simon just enough time to raise his spear and plunge it into the rampaging quarry. As he did so, Edmund spurred his horse forward bending low over the side of his saddle and as he reached Ralph, held his arm for his brother to grasp, snatching him from the thrashing, screaming moments of the dying boar.

Upon hearing the screams of his companion, the first boar, then turned round to face his pursuers and roaring its fury, had made straight for the centre of the pack. The two oldest hounds had acted in unison, and had leapt onto its back only to be thrown and gored before the enraged beast had been killed by Selwyn, the head huntsman.

One of the hounds died as it hit the ground, a tusk had pierced its heart, the other, survived but its cries and groans were pitiful. However, Selwyn assures me, although the wound is deep, it is not life threatening so we carried the hound home on a hastily constructed litter, back to where he can be treated.'

One of the squires interrupted excitedly. 'I witnessed the whole incident with my own eyes my lady. It all happened so fast.'

Maud's eyes had grown wide with horror as she listened to her husband's account of the morning's events.

However, Simon did not recount the scene which had *not* been witnessed by anyone in the main party; which was the hug of relief and gratitude between Ralph and Edmund. Only Simon, who had been bent over his wounded hound, Gwayne, heard the words which passed between them.

'You could have left me to die and become the heir of Wigmore, brother.'

'Ralph, you really are an ass, do you truly believe I want to inherit the weight of responsibilities such a position entails? If you think that then you are a bigger fool than I thought you to be.'

Ralph had reddened at the rebuff.

'Whatever notions whirled around in that miniscule brain of yours that is the most idiotic one to date.' Edmund would have re-mounted his horse but suddenly Ralph grasped his shoulder.

'Today could quite easily have been my final day on earth but thanks to you...'

'Not only to me Ralph but to Simon and the two hounds. We acted as a team, instinctively, protecting the heir of Wigmore, who just happens to be my brother. Now, maybe you will consider your future position and act like an heir, not like some wine soaked, whoring sot.'

Edmund had swung back into his saddle his face stern but he nodded at Simon as he did so.

'Well done, and I will ensure my mother learns of your courage and that of your hounds' He looked at the bloody bodies of the boar, and the dead hound. You will undoubtedly receive her gratitude in an appropriate way. A lifetime of good food for Gwayne, and a purse full of silver for you.'

Just then a panting groom came back to where Ralph stood, leading his sweating mount. Whilst the rest of the party headed back towards Wigmore the two boars had been gutted and slung on poles to be carried back for the butcher to finish the job.

Maud went over to Edmund and kissed his cheek as she whispered.

'Thank you, my dearest son.'

Before he could respond she walked on to where Ralph stood the shock of the accident still evident on his face. Maud took his hand as she spoke.

'It seems you were nearly lost to us today?'

He nodded. 'It would have saved you doing the deed.'

'Oh Ralph, even now you are trying to provoke me. When I see you abuse yourself especially in front of guests, what do you expect me to do - applaud! Come, you know how my temper rules at times. We should forgive each other and then forget; God has given us both a sign so let us give thanks and celebrate together throughout the rest of Christmastide, for although you may not believe me - you would have been deeply mourned by both your father *and* your mother.'

Ralph looked deep into his mother's fascinating eyes and saw for himself the intensity of her expression.

'I thought you would have been glad to be rid of me it would leave your favourite to inherit!'

Maud looked visibly shocked at his words; the former look of relief had vanished.

'I sometimes despair of you Ralph, and if you truly believe that then you are more foolish than I had thought - for all your faults, and there are too many to count at times; your wellbeing is always close to my heart. Why do you think your disgraceful behaviour pains me so and why do you think I am always trying to change your shameful ways? Simply because I am aware how it detracts from both you as a man, and a knight of the realm but, also the name of Mortimer and if you have ever doubted that then the mistake is yours and I am aggrieved that you judge me thus! But' she added wryly, 'such thoughts demean you and wound me and the rest of your family.'

As she turned away there were tears in her eyes.

Ralph suddenly reached and pulled his mother back and into his arm, his eyes filled with tears. The couple stood unmoving for some time then Sir Roger came and joined them his arms encircling both his wife and eldest son.

Later, Maud sent for Simon, and thanked him personally then enquired after his injured hound.

'He's been stitched up and is resting now. It will take some time for his wounds to heal and for him to recover but, sadly, not to hunt again I fear. Don't know how he will take to losing his brother, Merlin.'

'When he has recovered bring him to the castle and he will live a more pampered life here with me.' She reached and took his hands in hers. 'We shall never be able to repay what you and your hounds did for us today. I am saddened at the loss of one of our best hounds but had it not been for their bravery we would have lost our dear son. I have instructed the kitchen to roast a goose for you and your family and will send for you presently to reward you with something more substantial. Be assured you and your family will always be cared for by the Mortimer family for the service you have given today.'

Shyly the tow haired youth said softly, 'it was lord Edmund who.........'

'As I understand, you both re-acted together, as did your hounds. May God go with you, as does my undying gratitude?'

He bowed and left, his heart full of pride for, Lady Mortimer rarely paid compliments. The rest of the Christmastide festivities continued with more heartfelt joy than had been experienced for many seasons and when the time came for Edmund to leave there was genuine sadness, not only from his mother, but also from his brother, Ralph.

'Your dusty libraries will seem somewhat dull after Wigmore.' Ralph grinned as Edmund swung into the saddle.

'Well a few hours a week reading would not go amiss with your education brother.'

'Back to your hair shirt, and mind, you may be sporting a tonsure err we meet again.'

'One day you will grow up Ralph, but I just wonder whether anyone will live that long!'

With that parting shot Edmund spurred his mount forward raising his arm in salutation to his mother who stood at the window of her solar. She voiced a silent prayer for his safe journey, and then turned back to begin to answer the pile of letters placed neatly on her desk. Arthur would have filed them in order of importance.

As the days lengthened into spring Sir Roger was kept busy with both visits to court and into Wales as Llywelyn's campaign of harassment had begun again in earnest. The income from de Vere's estates, were quickly swallowed up in the continuing fight with Wales which invariable ended in much re-building of castles, barns, houses, and boundary walls, and there was also the re-stocking of livestock, and clearing mountains of rubble and the like.

By the autumn it was obvious the long siege at Kenilworth was nearing its conclusion, but not before the young de Montfort had long since made his escape; whether the rumours of his naked midnight swim were true, no-one could either confirm or deny, as the actual date and details of his departure were unknown.

The death was also announced of Bishop Thomas Cantelupe, erstwhile friend of the late Earl of Leicester, his health had deteriorated soon after Evesham, and many said he died a broken man. Closer to home news arrived from Bella that she was pregnant and would have her baby early the following year. Maud studied the letter for awhile smiling at the thought of the forthcoming birth until, she realised it would make her a grandmother and that thought did not lie too well, for it prompted the realisation of Ralph's unmarried status. Thus she resolved to discuss the matter of finding a suitable wife for Ralph with her husband at the next convenient moment.

A month later, as Sir Roger Mortimer stretched his legs before a roaring log fire, his eyes half closed, his mind wandering over recent events as he enjoyed the comforts of home. Maud cleared her throat, a sign she wished to speak with him.

'Whatever it is my dear, can it not wait until the morrow?'

'You may well be called away and what I have to say is paramount to Ralph's future.'

Her words had had the required effect as the Lord of Wigmore sat up his eyes wide open.

'Due to all the confusion and uncertainty over the past years the subject of Ralph's marriage has forever been left in abeyance. Now, I believe it should be a matter of urgency.' She waited for Mortimer's response.

'Well at least this year he has shown a little more maturity and he has undoubtedly proved his worth in battle so, maybe it is time to cast our gaze upon prospective brides for our son.' He looked across at his wife, 'have you anyone in mind?'

'No-one as yet but, there are a few to take into consideration. I believe it is important, if possible, she should come from the Marches, ideally with lands adjoining those of the Mortimer's.'

'Indeed there is merit in that notion.' He smiled. 'The wench will have to be as strong minded as her mother-on-law to survive some of Ralph's shortcomings.'

Maud snorted her derision. 'A strong constitution and good child bearing hips will also be invaluable.'

The couple paused in their conversation as the door opened and as if by some unseen summons Ralph Mortimer walked in and casually dropped into a chair before the fire.

'The nights are drawing in fast now and the chill of the oncoming winter begins to bite.'

'Indeed, maybe you need a wife to fill your bed.'

Ralph sat bolt upright at his father's words.

'Surely there is no hurry I.....I....'

'What ails you? I was betrothed before I could walk why does the suggestion alarm you so?'

There was a long hesitation before Ralph spoke again.

'I can think of no easy way to tell you merely to say, I can never marry any woman of your choice' he hesitated before continuing, 'as I am already married.'

The words hit the air like a war hammer, stunning both husband and wife, as they sat open mouthed at their son's revelation. Ralph added in a flat, toneless voice 'the ceremony took place before the Battle of Lewes.'

It Was Maud who gathered her wits first.

'Considering you were still only a boy, who deigned to marry you? And pray who is this mysterious wife? And why have you not chosen to disclose the fact of this marriage before now?'

The only sound in the gathering gloom was the sound of a log dropping, causing sparks to rise, as it sizzled in the hearth, illuminating the chamber for an instant as Gwayne moved away from his favourite spot. At the intensity of her words, the hound came and put his head on Maud's knee. She stroked the rough head as she waited for her son's response.

'Quite simply, she is the daughter of a rebel.'

'The name of this rebel family?'

'A name you will not like to hear but it is Despencer.'

'God's Wounds Ralph, whatever possessed you to enter into ....'

'She was carrying my child.'

Maud and her husband exchanged a look of disbelief.

'Well! May we know if we have a grandson or daughter?' Maud's was struggling not to lose control of her emotions her voice was husky in the effort.

'My son is named Geoffrey, and my wife is perfectly content to remain anonymous to the world.'

'Is she indeed!' It was Roger, who now spoke, 'and how long do you think she will be happy to remain in the shadows? '

'As long as *I* deem it necessary.' Ralph looked defiantly at his parents. 'She is an obedient wife and a doting mother.'

'Does she know your father killed a Despencer at Evesham?' Ralph shook his head.

'Pray do not press me on this matter, I will not betray any confidences my wife has told me, regarding her father's whereabouts.'

'You are stepping on dangerous ground and could at some point be accused of treachery towards the crown.' Roger Mortimer's voice was low and troubled.

'I swear, I will never be found to be false to any oath I have given either to you, the king or, my wife.' With that Ralph rose and walked swiftly from the chamber.

The Lord and Lady of Wigmore sat for some minutes in complete silence.

They sat both knowing this union with a rebel family could prove more than a little difficult.

'Well at least it solves the problem of finding a wife for our son. I have just realised, we never asked the wench's name.'

If Ralph Mortimer believed his mother was satisfied with his confession he was gravely mistaken. As soon as Maud heard his footsteps fade she turned to her husband.

'We must make certain that his marriage is a legal one and try and discover more about this so called 'wife'. If possible, obtain an annulment'

Sir Roger Mortimer nodded with a wry smile on his lips. 'As you say the matter requires delicate handling and I will leave it in your capable hands.'

Satisfied her husband was in agreement with her, Maud settled down and poured two cups of wine handing one to the seated figure.

'You must take care not to mention this matter to anyone at least, for the time being.'

'Well if Ralph has managed to keep the secret for almost two years I am certain we can do likewise or, until we have discovered the truth.'

The couple sat before the fire for a long time before either spoke again. It would take time for either to reconcile themselves to the reckless actions of their eldest son but both knew it could have a profound effect on the future of the Mortimer family.

CHAPTER XXIV

*Wigmore Christmastide
1266*

Although the weather was frosty visitors found the roads to
the castle were quite passable. Wagons full of food and wine
trundled through the arched gateway to fill the pantries and
stores with produce in readiness for the Christmas feasting.
The air echoed with voices and shouts, even laughter could be
heard as a juggler entertained the younger Mortimer children
in the courtyard.

Maud watched proceedings from her window, the castle
would soon be full of family and guests, and she was glad that
at least the skies did not look as though they threatened snow.
She had received word that Edmund would arrive sometime
today and this year, young Roger would also be joining them
for the celebrations. Bella would not be amongst the guests
as she was in the final months of her first pregnancy. Ralph
would soon return from visiting his wife for Christmas Day,
it had been far easier than expected to keep his marriage
secret as Lord Mortimer had given him more official duties
which gave him the freedom to come and go without causing
undue curiosity.

Whilst preparations were nearing the final stages for the
forthcoming celebrations, and with the servants, kitchen maids,
and house-carls, all hurrying about their duties. Maud was
occupied with examining her new wardrobe.

'Is my blue kirtle nearly finished Martha?'

'Yes my lady I just need your opinion on the trimmings.'

Maud looked down at the dark blue garment. 'Finding you
has been a Godsend.'

The girl blushed. 'I thought the gold thread which we purchased at Ludlow, could be worked in the Mortimer crest down the front.'

Maud nodded. 'As long as it is not too garish, as the slender line may make me look like a walking standard – not a look I would wish for.'

Martha chuckled. 'Maybe a leaf motif would look more delicate.'

'Mm, I like that suggestion better and not in gold but silver; save the gold for the next visit to court.'

Martha was a new arrival to Maud's ladies in waiting and had quickly proved her skill with the needle. She was a pleasant, unassuming girl, who was quite happy to turn her hand to any task Maud asked of her and was swiftly gaining her trust. A knock at the door interrupted their labours and a tall figure strode in, dropped to one knee, taking Maud's hand to kiss it in greeting.

'Edmund! I have been watching for you. My, how tall you have grown in this past year.'

'As you grow lovelier.' Edmund beamed up at his beloved mother.

'Edmund, this is Martha who has joined us since you were last here and as you can see she works wonders with her needle.'

Edmund nodded a greeting towards the servant who blushed with embarrassment as she bent to gather the garment and silks, politely excusing herself, before leaving mother and son alone.

'Come and tell me all your news and I will tell you a family secret.' Maud said.

Later, after they had talked for awhile, Maud told Edmund of Ralph's marriage and that he was now an uncle and explained the reasons for keeping such a secret.

'Trust Ralph to go against all the conventions. Have you any idea who she is?'

Maud nodded. 'Although I have kept the truth to myself for fear of alienating your father.'

Edmund looked expectantly at his mother. 'Don't keep me in suspense!'

Maud glanced towards the door then leaned forward and

whispered, 'She is a Despencer by blow! Although Ralph does not know I have learned her true identity.'

Edmund looked askance at her words. 'What in heaven's name possessed Ralph to make such a match?'

'Does the girl know it was a Mortimer that killed her father?'

Maud shook her head.

Edmund let out a long, low whistle.

'So, you are telling me that the future heir to the House of Mortimer will have our enemy's blood flowing through his veins!'

Maud nodded, 'you can see my dilemma and why I have kept this information to myself. I believe such knowledge may damage any relationship between your father and your brother's wife. It could cause an irreconcilable rift, the last thing we need right now. Such a revelation would devastate your father of that I am certain, and I will not allow that if I can help it.'

'I am surprised my father has not discovered this for himself.'

'My dear Edmund, your father has been kept very busy with fighting in Wales plus, his frequent visits to court, and the sitting in Parliament.'

'A blessing in this case. So what happens when the time comes for her to step from anonymity and take her place here a Wigmore? You can guarantee someone will know her history even if she is genuinely ignorant of her true parentage.'

'Time may bring about its own solutions, so for now, I am prepared to play the waiting game precarious as it may be.'

'A heavy burden for you to bear nevertheless!' Edmund reached across and gently gripped his mother's arm. She smiled at him, 'at least it is a burden shared, and feels lighter already. Now, go and seek out your father and brothers; and see if you can take young Roger down a notch or two, his time away from home does not seem to have tamed his waywardness overmuch.'

Edmund grinned. 'Is that little knave still causing trouble, I thought a year and half as a page would have calmed him down somewhat?'

'I fear your brother has inherited the de Braose traits, and if I thought it would prove a cure, I would gladly beat them out of him myself.'

'Your children are proving somewhat problematic, are they not?'

Maud smiled wanly. 'Not all of my children thank God. Bella will soon become a mother and you have already gained respect both at York and Oxford and, for one so young, have made both your father and I very proud. Young Geoffrey and William are showing promise, and Meg has found her feet at last, so I have much to give thanks for!'

As Edmund moved to leave, she mused on the changing relationships she had with her children as they grew up. Edmund had always been determined he would never be overlooked by her; as a baby he would scrawl to her feet whenever she entered the nursery. The bond had deepened throughout his infancy and although she hated to admit it even to herself, Edmund and Bella were her favourites.

After the merrymaking of Christmastide, when most of the visitors had left, the wind swung round bringing with it heavy snow and Wigmore was held fast by the vagaries of the weather for many weeks. During a break, and a rapid thaw in February, a messenger arrived with news that Bella had given birth to a son and both were well. Maud gave up a silent prayer of thanks and later that week a service was held to celebrate. However, the health of the old Earl of Arundel was causing alarm, and when word arrived in March, that he had died, Lord and Lady Mortimer sent their condolences. However, although Bella's husband was heir to the Earldom, he would not inherit the title at this time meaning, Bella would not become a Countess. Nonetheless, Maud felt a sense of satisfaction that she had played a hand in bringing about their marital union and she consoled herself that titles were not always of the utmost importance.

Although the winter was hard, and cold, it had given the Lord of Wigmore and his eldest son, a chance to rest from the physical demands of constantly being in the saddle or, waging war on their eternal enemy, Llywelyn ap Gruffydd. Spring would bring about a resumption of hostilities and the familiar cycle would resume. Llywelyn was proving a canny adversary and had inflicted much mayhem in the Marches and Wales. Sometimes, admitting to defeat, for Sir Roger Mortimer, was a humiliating fact as to date, it was Llywelyn who was proving a better tactician using the rugged countryside as an effective shield in these battles.

However, in England, there was news that the protracted siege at Kenilworth was finally drawing to an end although, the final outcome was as yet, uncertain. But it was news of events closer to home, which would have an impact on the life of Maud at Wigmore, when she learned of the death of Ralph's young wife, who had died giving birth to a daughter. Without waiting for word from her son, Maud sent Carys and some nursemaids to collect his children and bring them back to Wigmore. Sadly, it was only one child that returned, as the baby had died with its mother. Once again the Mortimer nursery became home to the newest member of the family.

For whatever reason, Maud, in the confusion, decided to announce the arrival of the little boy quite simply as Ralph's son, without giving any further details; it was the cause of some raised eyebrows but no-one dared to question this announcement or, ask the name of the ill fated mother.

Ralph was lost in a world which many judged as grief but in truth, it was shame which haunted him. He admitted as much to his mother one day and she sat and listened to his outpourings of regret and remorse without uttering a word.

'I can see now that my act of selfish lust caused so much anguish, not only to you and Papa but, also to Alys.' He had looked so young and vulnerable as he sat voicing his innermost feelings.

'I thought marrying her would absolve my sin but ....' he paused; 'it only made things worse. I think we both knew that one day ....'

'Hush, these recriminations show you at least have a conscience, but nothing can alter what has passed. You must ask God for forgiveness and learn from this bitter experience.' She took his hands in hers as she spoke. 'If you are truly sorry, then you must try and live a better life, not only for yourself but also, for your son.'

Ralph raised her hands and kissed them.

'It would ease my conscience if I knew I had your forgiveness.'

'It is yours, if I have your promise to strive to live a less selfish life. Being the heir to an important family often means self denial and self sacrifice, for the well being of the family. Always remember that! I have given instructions for prayers to be said for the souls of your wife and daughter. Where will she be buried?'

'Leominster Priory. I have already made the arrangements. I think it best if I alone attend the funeral after all......' His words trailed off.

Maud was relieved and merely nodded. Inwardly she felt that the death of the unfortunate Alys had resolved a very awkward situation, Maud knew that time would prove an effective healer for her son.

After the siege at Kenilworth had ended in 1266, there had been a treaty drawn up entitled, the *Dictum of Kenilworth,* and much to the surprise of Maud, her husband, and many of the Marcher barons, no executions were ordered. Maybe Henry had realised alienating his nobility again was not the way to govern the country. The lawless bands which had been roaming the counties were also slowly being brought to book and England was settling down to a more ordered existence.

This however, did not apply to the Marches, since Llywelyn was proving the stronger in the Welsh conflict. Eventually, even Sir Roger Mortimer had bowed to the superiority of his adversary, and realised he had no alternative but to sign the '*Treaty of Monmouth,*' which at least had restored some of his sacked castles and homesteads, back into his hands. Being escorted back to Wigmore by his Welsh cousin was, for the Lord of Wigmore, a bitter experience and one he did not wish to dwell on.

When the Mortimer's next visited London their reception had been far cooler than it had been on previous visits. Mortimer's reputation had slipped due to his unsuccessful exploits in Wales. The king, who had already agreed that Llywelyn, now widely acknowledged as Prince of Wales, much to the disgust of his son Edward, had proved more than an effective adversary over the years.

During her visit to court, Maud heard whispers that the king was planning to go on a Crusade as a penance for Evesham, and emissaries were already preparing to travel to Rome to seek the Pope's consent. So when Maud saw a familiar face at court, she was not totally surprised.

'My Lord de Longeville, it has been and age since last we met.' She looked deep into his eyes as she spoke but nothing in his expression denoted how deeply he had been affected by the sight of the elegant and confidant woman who stood before him.

'Indeed Lady Mortimer, time treats you far more favourably than it does the rest of us poor mortals.'

'Flattery as I recall, my lord, must be a recent addition, for flowery speeches were not normally in your vocabulary.'

'Surprise is always a good defence, don't you think?' He gave a wry smile.

'Why do you feel you need to defend yourself from me my lord?'

'Recent events have taught me to treat everyone with caution, yesterdays friends sometimes become today's enemies.'

'Surely that no longer applies de Longeville?' Sir Roger Mortimer had joined his wife.

'Ah my Lord Mortimer, England's civil strife may be over, but intrigue is never far away and there are many ties with France which may not be immediately apparent.' With that he bowed and moved to the group that surrounded the Lord Edward.

'Never trusted that one!' Mortimer muttered as he took his wife's arm and led her to another part of the Great Hall. Maud remained silent, but glanced at de Longeville from time to time, for if her husband had stated he did not trust him it would be difficult to speak to him without arousing suspicion.

However, an opportunity arose late in the evening, after the consumption of much wine and as the countless guests were busily amusing themselves, Maud caught sight of de Longeville leaving through a side door. After noting where her son and husband were seated, and confident they were too far in drink to note her whereabouts; she followed.

The darkness enveloped her like a huge cloak as she hurried after the disappearing figure. De Longeville must have realised he was being pursued and stepped into the shadows, his hand on his dagger.

'Who follows me like a thief in the night?'

But before she could answer she felt herself being pulled into his arms his mouth on hers. Time stood still in that moment as the couple kissed locked in a long, hungry embrace. Eventually as they drew apart she whispered.

'My lord you never cease to amaze me! How did you know it was me behind you? Your words earlier left me wondering and I felt they were a warning.'

'We were being watched.'

'At court, everyone spies on each other; it is a legacy from de Montfort era I fear.'

'Nowadays, it is agents of the Queen and her son.'

'But surely they have no cause to ....'

De Longeville kissed her brow before stopping her mouth with another kiss.

'The Queen is a woman who holds fast to her French roots and in France; Louis is already making ready to go on Crusade. I have carried messages, not only from his wife to the Queen but, also to her uncle.'

'Peter of Savoy?' Maud's voice was hardly a whisper. 'What mischief is he brewing up this time I wonder?'

'You must go back or you will be missed, much as I am loathed to let you go.'

And with a thousand questions left unanswered Maud moved back towards the doorway patting her gown and straightened her headdress before re-entering the noisy throng. De Longeville was not one for exaggerations and she knew from his tone he was concerned about his visit. Maud remembered how Eleanor of Provence had rallied mercenaries to her husband's cause before Evesham, whilst he was still imprisoned by de Montfort. Maybe there was more to this Crusade than a holy war, money was always available from Rome to fund any move against the barbarians but, was there a deeper motive? If the Savoyards were involved it was highly likely. The thoughts bubbled through her head like a busy cauldron but she knew only time held the key and for now, she must wait however impatiently, for the next move to be made in the game of power.

The following day de Longeville left the English court but not before he had spoken briefly to Maud.

'My numerous visits to this country have aroused many interested parties, so now I often have to adopt a variety of disguises.' He wrinkled is nose as he spoke. 'Not a method I find sits easily with me *but*, when you are in the service of others you are obliged to use whatever methods are necessary. Be assured if I ever discover anything which may be of help to you, I will find a way of letting you know. Trust any bearer of my father's ring.'

Maud looked down at the heavily embossed ring as she recalled how she had won it in a wager, so many years ago. Too full of emotion she could not bring herself to speak but squeezed his hand as he bowed and walked swiftly to where his horse stood waiting, circling around the long suffering groom in its impatience to be off. With a heavy heart, Maud made her own way back to her chamber to make ready for the coming day.

Martha had laid out a warm woollen kirtle and cloak of dark green velvet.

'It may be chilly on the river my lady.'

'If the Queen truly believes a day on that smelly river is a pleasurable diversion, I fear she is much mistaken.'

'But the royal barge is so luxurious my lady and I have heard there will be minstrels to serenade your journey.'

'Unless they are sick!'

'Oh! My lady, they must be used to travelling thus and would not be chosen for the duty if that were the case.'

'Mayhap you are right Martha! I am just put about by sitting all day on a rocking barge when I would much prefer to be riding to hounds, like the men-folk.'

Martha smiled, if nothing else, Lady Mortimer was not one for sitting around for long periods unless it was at her desk, this sojourn at court was not a pleasurable experience for her mistress, she was well aware but, one of strict duty.

As expected, Maud found the day one of abject tedium. She listened to the idle prattle of the ladies and judged it dull and uninteresting, so too, the journey along the dark, dirty waters of the Thames; in her view the whole experience was a complete waste of time. Eleanor of Provence was at her most imperious and hardly deigned to speak but, Maud noted the dark eyes of the queen, were ever watchful of all the passengers aboard the sumptuous barge. She had felt a moment of triumph when the royal gaze had fallen on her and noted the hardly disguised reaction of surprise on the Queen's face. Maud had merely smiled and nodded but, the smile had not reached further than the corners of her mouth. The message had been unmistakable, the watcher, watched!

The evening's events did nothing to divert Maud either, as she felt the deep emptiness of loss at de Longville's departure, coupled with a sense of inner unease. She tried to lose herself in the spectacle of the jesters and the music of the royal minstrels, but her mood remained sombre for the rest of her stay at court.

CHAPTER XXV

Wigmore

The journey from court had been a very difficult one and Maud was relieved when they finally arrived back at Wigmore. One evening, just days after their return, Maud headed towards the chamber of Lord Rhys to talk over her latest concerns. She found her aging Chancellor sitting before a glowing fire; across his knees was a large board and on it a map and some letters.

'Forgive me for disturbing you my lord.'

The old man moved the board and its paperwork and indicated to the seat on the opposite side of the hearth,

'I am ever at your service my lady.'

Maud sat down and remained silent for a moment trying to frame her thoughts.

'Do you think Louis' Crusade has any underlying motive?' She looked hard at the Welshman.

'Louis is renowned for his piety and his faith, over the years it has brought about a close link with Rome.'

She was aware of his keen gaze. 'So you do not have any suspicions that the expedition may be a cover for other more covert ambitions?'

Her words hung in the air between them for some minutes.

'Is it Louis you are worried about or – Henry?'

Maud looked up and their eyes met. 'You know me so well my lord.' She said softly.

He continued. 'Remember, Henry made a promise to go on a Crusade some years ago but events put an end to his plans. Now, his health, which has undoubtedly been affected by recent events, precludes him from going but his vow will be fulfilled by his two sons, Edward and Edmund, thereby keeping faith with Rome, thus keeping them on side.'

Maud nodded. 'But I cannot quell my misgivings and we both know, the Savoyards and the Pointevins are inveterate schemers, and fear one or the other faction will make mischief in furtherance of their ambitions.'

'Their mischief, as you describe it, stems from the insatiable desire for wealth and lands which may coincide with their loyalties to France.'

'There you have the nub of it – France! Could the Queen and her relatives be planning something detrimental to England?'

There was a long pause as the old man considered her words.

'I do not believe Eleanor would compromise her son's path to the throne or, that she has any ulterior motives against her husband. She has time on her side whereas I fear, Henry may not!'

'So what in essence you are saying, my fears are unfounded?'

'My dear Lady Mortimer, it is always good to be wary of the opposition but with regard to the Crusade, I do not believe you have ought to fear. However, the aftermath of de Montfort's death is another matter, and the resentment felt by many noble families, still lingers and will do so for a long time hence, which could prove both difficult and costly. However, the king for once has shown some acumen with the '*Dictum of Kenilworth*,' and his promise to restore many to their former estates, without rancour.'

'But not without heavy fines.'

'Better to pay a fine that pay with one's life!'

'You are right of course, and at least de Vere will regain the Earldom of Oxford, which must make Meg's future more secure.'

'And his fine will be to your husband.'

'Mmm! I am glad Mortimer remained on civil terms with de Vere even though it was a somewhat chilly one. I feared for Meg for awhile after the signing of the Dictum, but at least that situation has been resolved satisfactorily. But now it seems there has been a falling out between Gilbert and his lordship.'

Lord Rhys nodded slowly.

'That could prove a trickier situation to resolve as it concerns a matter of principals and we both know, neither men are going to surrender their ideals.'

'Let us hope they will see sense and bury their differences for the greater good, and that all the disruption and hatred will be brought to an end in the coming months.'

'Hatred has a long memory in my experience, my lord. Besides, it has given Llywelyn time to build his army and he will be anxious to harry his English enemy wherever and whenever possible, much to the chagrin of the Marcher lords.'

'But do not forget, my Lord Llywelyn has an Achilles heel, his brother, Dafydd.'

Maud smiled. 'And I am certain the Lord Edward will exploit that vain poppinjay's ambitions to the detriment of Wales, at every opportunity.'

Maud rose and went and placed her hands on the shoulders of Lord Rhys.

'Your support and wisdom are most valued my lord.'

He smiled ruefully. 'My frame may be failing but thank God, my wits are still at your service.'

'I often wonder what your own feelings are in this never ending conflict with Wales. You serve a family loyal to the English crown which must go against your own conscience.'

'I merely continue to honour my vow made to my Welsh Prince; there is no conflict my Lady Mortimer.'

Maud bent forward, and in a rare demonstration of affection, she kissed his snowy white hair.

'I will send Hugh in to make up the fire and bring you your supper.' Then she turned and left.

As she walked towards her own chamber thoughts whirled in her head for Maud knew the future was fraught with dangers both, for her family and for England; a piece of signed or sealed parchment had all too frequently failed to bring about any lasting solutions, the past was littered by broken and dishonoured treaties.

Throughout the rest of that year Sir Roger Mortimer and his family, were busy with both matters at court and in Wales. Maud often found the comparison of his roles as courtier and soldier, an interesting contradiction. Rufus saw that his court robes were immaculate, whilst the squires kept his armour

and harness mended and cleaned. But Mortimer did not go
unscathed in his many battles with his cousin, and she often
saw the marks of war on his body, marks and wounds which
were ever increasing as the years passed.

'We are wearing thin in the service of this king.' Maud said
one evening as she sponged off a bloody wound with oil of
lavender. 'You should get this stitched or it may fester.'

'Don't fuss woman, just put a clean pad on it and come to
bed.'

'Blood marks the sheets.'

'Never mind the sheets, come and give me ease of this!' He
waved his erect penis at her as he spoke.

'Only if you promise to visit the surgeon on the morrow.'

He snorted but would have promised anything to gain his
prize.

She walked over to their great bed and raised her nightdress
as she climbed on top of him; he grinned up at her.

'Service me wench!' He chortled as she lowered herself
on to his manhood. The coupling was quick, fierce and for
Mortimer, satisfying. As Maud rolled off her panting spouse,
her expression was lost in the shadows of the bed hangings.

The following morning Mortimer visited the surgeon but
only after Maud had threatened him with refusing to fulfil
any further matrimonial duties if he did not. Their bedroom
battles were an experience he enjoyed although; he would
never admit it to his wife. He took his pleasure with many
women but Maud was the one who kept his lusty appetites
satiated. He considered himself lucky on that score, for many
of his contemporaries complained of a cold marital bed. But
Mortimer had scant time to dwell overlong on his marriage
as he was constantly riding between Wales and the court of
the English king.

Weeks later, young Roger had been sent home in disgrace
and would, in future, serve in close attendance on his father.
Maud would ensure this move would keep him too busy to
have any excess energy to make further mischief. Whereas
in contrast, Ralph acted as his father's deputy commander in
Wales, whilst Edmund continued to gain considerable respect
from his tutors in Oxford.

In the late Spring Maud received a complimentary letter from Alice, the Countess of Oxford, regarding Meg's studies and excellent demeanour. So with just one blot on the family's honour, Maud had reason to feel proud of all but one of her children. The younger boys were still taking lessons from a tutor although Geoffrey appeared to have already made up his mind on his own future as he had expressed a wish to enter the church; this eased a decision, which in some instances, brought about a conflict within families. The perfect example was of Robert Burnell, the Lord Edward's friend and confidant. Although ordained, Burnell persistently defied the laws of the church on celibacy; family life for him was far more important. Maybe the result of being sent away into an austere life in a monastery whilst still a little boy. But for Maud it made the man more human, more approachable.

As the months passed into years life remained in a constant state of flux. The pressure to recruit men, and purchase good horses flesh, together with finding enough forage and food, was a never ending process. The sound of hammering was like the beating heart of the community, constant, rhythmical, lapsing only on the Lord's Day, Sundays, and Saints days. Archery, jousting and sword practice coupled with the sound of shouts and jeers were the daily anthem at Wigmore.

Maud was ever busy sending fresh supplies to the outposts and men and horses to Kingsland, Pembrugge and Radnor and the outlying forts which had been rebuilt after the attacks by the de Montfort faction a few years earlier. Her infrequent visits to court, the only punctuation to her normal routine. But Maud was a Marcher through and through and knew no other life. She shared good times and bad with the people around her; resilience and her directness had given her a unique standing in the community. Like many of the populace, she too had experienced the devastation of war but had ensured those who fared less well were never left without support. Lady Mortimer was both respected and feared but everyone was in no doubt, if crossed, she would deal out severe punishments without hesitation. The law of the Marches had to be upheld in an unstable world, or chaos would reign

Early in 1268, Pope Clemens IV had died and closer to home in May, Peter of Savoy, Archbishop of Canterbury, had also passed into the afterlife; whilst in France, Louis's grandson, Philip was born. In England, Lord Edward pursued money to fund his Crusade but even the churches promise of one twentieth in levies, would still leave a gaping hole in his finances and the debate on imposing a property tax did not sit well with his advisors.

By late 1269 the Lord Edward and his brother were putting the final touches to their plans for the journey to the Holy Land. But with the king's health giving cause for concern it had been decided that Robert Burnell should remain in England to help with the administration of the realm. He, along with Philip Basset, Roger Mortimer, Walter Giffard, Archbishop of York, and Richard of Cornwall, the king's brother, would act as Regents in Edward's absence.

In late October, Maud rode alongside her husband towards the residence of Robert Burnell in London. The weather had been wet and blustery and the roads had proved hazardous, slowing their progress. In fact they had left some of the wagons back at the last Inn as the horses were exhausted after days of struggling through roads sticky with mud.

'I shall be glad to discard this sodden cloak and dry my aching limbs before a fire.' Maud's words almost lost in the deafening throngs of people.

'I hate this noisy, smelly city, it turns my stomach with its obnoxious smells and as for the people – do they ever sleep?'

The Lord of Wigmore's answer did nothing to appease her.

'It is called progress, Madam!'

Maud did not answer she was too busy negotiating her way through the throngs trying to keep her horse from shying from the many distractions that were either hanging from the windows or from being soaked by sudden ejection of waste being tipped out by some of the residents.

Finally, she saw two smartly liveried servants beckoning to the riders to enter a heavily gated property. She let out a deep sigh of relief; the horrendous journey had finally reached its end. What awaited them quickly salved the day's ills and Maud soon found herself relaxing in a tub of warm, scented water, in an apartment which left its occupants in awe. The Flemish wall hangings were lavish masterpieces of needlecraft. Highly polished furniture adorned the large chamber and the bed was the biggest Maud had ever seen. Robert Burnell had spent extravagantly, but with taste and in a style second to none, even the Palaces of the royal family would struggle to match such luxury.

After resting and changing their clothes Maud and her husband were shown to a large, warm dining hall. The table was filled with tasty dishes of roast joints of meat, pies, fruit nuts and bowls of steaming vegetables.

'Welcome, I thought it fitting that we should get to know one another better seeing that in the months to come, the responsibility of England will lie in our hands.'

Robert Burnell offered his guests silver goblets filled with the finest French wine.

'As I understand it, my position will be Commander of the King's forces here at home.' Sir Roger Mortimer cleared his throat before he continued.

'And the matter of governance will be yours!'

'Oh! My dear Lord Mortimer, if only life were that simple.' Robert Burnell stared down into his silver goblet.

'Let us speak honestly here tonight. I am more than happy to leave any decisions regarding war or, any outbreaks of hostility in your capable hands. However, as we know, joint Regency may prove far more difficult than it would first appear.' He hesitated.

'There are two named I can see will give trouble: Cornwall and Giffard,'

Burnell looked at Maud and smiled.

'I see you have grasped the situation in an instant my Lady.'

'The Earl of Cornwall is incensed that you have been given command of the army. And as for me – Giffard despises my appointment as he is forever reminding all who would listen; I am no true churchman having a mistress.'

Maud sipped her wine; the intoxicating liquid brought an extra sparkle to her green-grey eyes.

'Cornwall is renowned for his arrogance and being superseded by a mere Marcher knight must have caused him to choke on his pride.'

Robert Burnell chuckled. 'I forget you have known the Earl almost all of your life.'

'Sadly, that is true, and watched him wear down my Aunt Isabel's spirit.'

'Indeed, and it is common knowledge he has spoiled many a young maiden over the years. However, what I need from you is an assurance I have your unstinted support in any future arguments regarding the running of this country?'

Mortimer nodded his head.

'It is well known that you and the Lord Edward are of a mind on all matters to do with the country's well being therefore, I can see no reason why I should ever oppose you.' He added. 'And can I look for your support in matters military my Lord Robert?'

Robert Burnell noted the Marcher lord had not used his title as a churchman.

'As you say, Lord Edward trusts your loyalty and knows you have proved your ability as a Commander in the field. Besides........' he looked at Maud, 'you have an excellent wife who I know holds Lord Edward's admiration. Now let us enjoy the excellent food before us; tomorrow Lord Edward will join us.' He clapped his hands and a musician entered and played a medley of popular tunes.

Some hours later when they were alone in their apartment Maud sighed contentedly.

'This has been a most enjoyable evening. It is gratifying to hear that the future King of England holds you in such high regard. I can just imagine Cornwall's wrath on learning the army will be under your command and not his.'

'He is a dangerous man and can cause a great deal of trouble, so I will not willingly cross him.'

'You are right but he will be shackled by his vows of allegiance to the crown and should he oppose you and Burnell, will stand in peril of being accused of Treason.'

'Bassett will be the counterbalance should such occasions arise. His will be the voice of reason.'

Maud leaned back against the large the downy pillows. 'But remember he is a man long in years and was there not talk of his sympathy with de Montfort?'

'As did many who were gulled by a persuasive tongue.'

'And paid the ultimate price for his failure.'

'Come, I can scarce keep my eyelids open we shall learn more on the morrow.'

The following day dawned damp and dismal which was too much for Maud who refused to leave the comfort of her lodgings.

'I have only just begun to feel my limbs again and will not sit all day in a saddle; my butt still bears its marks.'

'So what do you plan for the day?'

'To explore – on foot, the area and maybe do a little shopping.'

Maud was perfectly happy as she watched the party ride through the gateway; they planned to meet up with the Lord Edward for the day's sport. Turning to Martha, Maud smiled.

'Today, you and I will spend our time choosing fripperies and whatever takes our fancy, I feel we have earned our day of leisure.'

In the afternoon Maud and her maid returned, behind them were two pages bearing numerous parcels and bags. As Maud flung her cloak onto a trestle Martha gathered it up noting some muddy patches around the hemline.

'I will have this cleaned for morning my lady.' She hurried off whilst Maud went and lay down stretching her aching limbs. Upon Martha's return she went about her tasks in silence as her mistress had fallen asleep. She laid out the fine wool kirtle of rich blue and the silk over garment of paler blue; she placed the box with the headdresses beside the jewellery casket then, left to order hot water for her mistress to bathe before the evening feast.

By the time the hunters returned Maud had bathed and was busily choosing a matching coif and veil. Martha pinned a row of pearls around the chosen coif and the pair were admiring the effects in the reflector as Lord Mortimer entered.

'Did you have a good day my lord?' Maud turned as she spoke.

'The ground was heavy and the game was light, so my answer must be – not on a sporting level but enlightening on others.'

'That sounds intriguing!'

'Mmm! I will tell you more later but for now, I must go and lie in a warm tub and soak away my aches and pains.'

The evening proved to be a lively affair and the Lord Edward and his friends ate, drank and made merry. Maud noted that his elegant brother, Edmund, was far more circumspect and drank and ate less than his contemporaries but nevertheless appeared at his ease. During the evening Edward danced with Maud and smiled down at her, his bright blues eyes full of mischief.

'Your wife will surely hear of this my Lord.' Maud's tone somewhat tinged with feigned reproof.

'Eleanor is occupied breeding.'

'You keep her busy my Lord.' He noted the twinkle in her eyes as she spoke.

'I am merely an attentive husband.'

'Who obviously enjoys his marriage bed?'

Edward Plantagenet looked at his partner with undisguised amusement.

'And would happily demonstrate, if you would deign to join me one night, just how much enjoyment we could share my Lady Maud.'

'You flatter an *old lady*.' Maud laughed.

'But your beauty has not dimmed with time my Lady, and methinks you could still engage a man in a night of delight.'

'Ah! There you may be disappointed my Lord Edward for I have, nor ever would be, a man's object of trifling amusement.'

'You dash my hopes in a few short words; but do not deny me future attempts to entice you to my bed.'

'I have a distinct feeling if I ever indicated a change of mind you my Lord, would be the first to find an excuse and leave me totally embarrassed,'

'If you were ever to have a change of heart my dearest Lady Mortimer, I would never be so ungallant as to refuse myself such a pleasure,'

As the music ended he led her back to her seat and bowed deeply and then joined his male companions.

Edmund leaned forward as he spoke.

'The Lady Maud holds a special place in your affections, methinks.'

Edward nodded. 'She is both lovely and witty and I enjoy teasing her and she knows that full well.' A great smile spread across his face.

'Now let us drink and be merry.'

As the royal party continued to enjoy their evenings entertainments Martha made her way to the kitchens carrying two muddied cloaks, Lady Mortimer's and her own. A round faced young servants offered to help and when they had finished the girl, who was named Sybil, said as they were still damp Martha could leave them and she would ensure they would be left on two hooks in the cloakroom.

Martha went and turned down the rich covers of the bed and settled down to await her mistress. After finishing her duties Martha said God night and left. The following morning she rose long before the rest of the household stirred, as she had made her mind up to hear Mass at a local church. She found her way to the cloakroom which was all in darkness as the rush-lights had burned out and felt for her cloak. Without a sound she tiptoed out of the house and into the raw, misty dawn. It was only as she went to pull the hood of the cloak over her hair she realised in the gloom she had picked Lady Mortimer's cloak instead of her own. She hesitated but knew re-entering the house would cause a stir besides, it would make her late for the service.

On entering the church, Martha went and sat in the shadows as she listened to the priest and the choir and felt a sense of peace steal over her. After the service, she left the hallowed building and walked quickly along the narrow streets taking care to hold the cloak well above her ankles. Martha did not hear the figure creep up behind her, only felt the sudden pain rip through her body and in that instant knew she was dying. Blood oozed out of the wicked wound, for her assailant had twisted the thin, sharp blade, ensuring the death of his victim. Martha's body crumpled to the ground and as he bent to withdraw his blade he saw her face; for an instant he hesitated and cursed profanely under his breath as he wiped the blood off the weapon. A voice behind him shouted and he sprinted down a nearby alleyway heading for the River. A crowd quickly gathered as the traders and errand boys, who had begun to arrive for their days work, stooped to the see the identity of the murdered girl.

'She has to be some high born wench – look at her cloak.'

'Someone summon the Watch.'

A butcher's boy shouted, 'I'll fetch help from the big house they'll know what to do!'

In a matter of minutes one of the servants' from Robert Burnell's house, bent over the fallen form and gasped.

'She's Lady Mortimer's waiting woman.'

He quickly took charge and ordered one of the men to carry Martha to the Hall. They laid the body out on a trestle table and Lord Burnell was called for; in his usual calm way he took charge and ordered most of the pressing onlookers to depart with the exception of those who had been first on the scene.

'Did you see who did this?' His voice was quiet but firm.

'No my Lord.'

The butcher's boy croaked he had seen someone run down an alleyway in great haste.

'Can you describe this person?'

'He were bent forward but could see he were thin and darkly dressed. I think he were a tall 'un Sir.'

'You did well boy!'

Robert Burnell turned and whispered to his manservant who left hastily.

'The alleyway leads towards the River yer honour.' The boy continued.

'Thank you, pray remain, you may be of further service but the others can go but leave your names and addresses with my secretary and I shall see you will all be rewarded for your assistance.'

The boy and the thickset man bowed and stood to one side as the others left. Someone's unfortunate death would result in silver in their pockets. But the boy had felt pity for the pretty young woman who had died and he made the sign of the cross as he stood nervously by.

Upon learning of Martha's death, Maud felt sick but the feeling of nausea quickly changed into white rage when she heard that Martha had been wearing her cloak.

'Martha died because she was mistaken for me; didn't she?' Maud faced Robert Burnell. Her host nodded, for he had been fully apprised of the circumstances by his servant.

'It would seem there was no lights in cloakroom and your maid must have taken your cloak by mistake. Hers still hangs on the hook.'

'So who do you believe sent an assassin to kill me?' The question was almost a challenge.

Two names immediately spring to mind - De Montfort's and, Despencer's? He must have been watching the house. The girl lost her life because someone sought revenge on the House of Mortimer.' She hesitated. 'Poor Martha did not deserve to die like ....like that.'

'Hush my dear; we will do all we can to detain the villain and learn whose silver he took for such a wicked deed. I have sent word to the Watch to search the Riverside.'

She nodded. 'I will not rest until this cowardly cur is brought to justice. I will see his life cut off before me; or I shall not rest.'

'I hear your pain and understand the anger you must feel but, do not allow this terrible act of treachery steal your soul. It is my belief God will bring this perpetrator to his own justice. In the meantime, pray for the girl's soul and I will pray for you both.'

Maud was led back to her chamber and related the events to her husband who had only just awakened suffering from the effects of the previous night's carousing.

'So who do you believe is after my life?' She looked hard at the tousled headed figure fighting to grasp both the implications of the murder without complaining of his thumping headache. Mortimer struggled to remove his nightshirt and almost tumbled out of the bed in his effort to dress.

'Well we both know what the de Montfort's are capable of, especially young Simon, for he suffered greatly through his sense of guilt and will try and deflect his failure at Evesham onto anyone's head. You may have been chosen as an example. However, the Despencer's have to be included as it is well known they vowed vengeance on the Mortimer's - did they not?'

'Does this mean we must walk in fear of assassination from now on?'

Mortimer looked at his wife and nodded.

'I fear so!'

'Then I will choose the time and the place...........'

'Stop and do what you are always advising me to do, wait and see if they catch him and then consider the best course of action. Act in anger for the slaying of poor Martha and you may end up punishing the wrong person.'

For a long moment Maud stood perfectly still, her husband was uncertain whether she had heard him.

'You are right my lord, for I would act out of revenge and not out of cold facts.'

'But whichever way it is done, I *will* have this devil spore's life.'

She looked down at her hands and saw they were smeared with Martha's blood and she suddenly bowed her head and wept silently. The sight unnerved her husband who came and gently drew her into his arms.

'All the years I have known your Madam, this is the first time I have ever seen you openly weep.'

For once Maud allowed herself to be comforted and the couple stood for some time until her tears subsided. Later that day, news arrived that a boat had been seen drifting downstream. The following day there was further news; a body had been recovered from the River, that of a boatman whose corpse bore exactly the same wound as Martha's. The assassin appeared to have escaped, at least for the time being, and was leaving no living being in his effort to eliminate all traces of his identity.

By this time, the Lord Edward had been informed of the murder and he sent men all along the Thames to try and discover the whereabouts of the killer - without success. Finally it was agreed that Maud should return to Wigmore as soon as possible to make arrangements for Martha's funeral. The coffin would follow at a more dignified pace. The Lord Edward ordered a band of trusted guards to accompany Maud on her journey back to the Marches.

As soon as the riders reached the outskirts of the City even the seasoned company of soldiers admired Maud's horsemanship for she left no-one in doubt of her intentions to reach Wigmore in the shortest possible time, and the frequent change of mounts ensured that her wishes were fulfilled.

Upon her arrival Maud was grateful that Wigmore was ready to receive her guards and they were comfortably houses along with their horses. Errol ran forward to help her from the saddle. She strode into the castle and made her way to her own apartments with just the briefest of nods to her servants.

'Errol, will you see if Lord Rhys is well enough to see me?'

'My lady, he is waiting for you in his chamber.'

'This is a sad, sad business but we must not let it deter us from our duty. Whilst I am with Lord Rhys will you send for a light supper, and take it to my chamber?'

'I will my lady.'

Just as she was about to leave, a grey, shaggy form moved and sat before her.

'Gwayne!' Maud stooped and stroked his head.

'It is good to see you.' She bent forward and kissed the top of his head.

'Come, you shall accompany me.'

The three then made their way to the apartment of Lord Rhys.

'Thank you Errol I will be but a short while as I do not wish to overtax his Lordship.'

Errol bowed and left Gwayne to seek a place beside his mistress.

As she entered Lord Rhys rose and came and took her hands between his.

'There has been no further news from London.' He said then returned to sit in his usual comfortable chair; Maud moved to take her place before the fire; Gwayne joined her and laid his head in her lap.

'But, I do have word from Harwich that a tall, foreign merchant took passage on a ship bound for Italy, which points more to the de Montfort's than the Despencer's. Besides, I doubt they would be as stupid as to have you slain on these shores, it would be too obvious.' He paused before continuing. 'It is my guess the assassin will not travel directly to his homeland but continue his journey as far from the coast, and as deep into the Continent as he can; for as soon as his failure becomes known, it will undoubtedly result in his own death, if ever caught – by whichever side.'

He shook his head slowly. 'I do not think he will easily be found. He will have another identity somewhere, completely alien from that of an assassin, a merchant or, some other trade and one totally unconnected to violence.'

Maud looked thoughtful for a moment. 'You mean he will be a farmer or ....'

'Not a farmer my lady, but someone who is respected in his community a lawyer, maybe, or a notary, a profession that has need to travel from time to time.'

'That sounds very plausible but what you are saying is, he may never be brought to justice.'

'Oh! One day he will meet his end of that I am certain, his pride will dictate as much for he failed on this occasion but must prove to himself he is not a failure therefore.....' his words trailed off.

'Well at least it eases my fears for the time being.'

'On another matter entirely I know this may not be the right time to mention Martha's replacement but there is someone whom I believe would be ideal, and the girl in question is presently in dire need of help.'

'If nothing else you have awakened my curiosity. Who is this need-some person,'

'Her name is Ela and she is a former Mistress of Lord Devereaux.'

Maud's eyes widened.

'Will had a Mistress? You amaze me!'

'Indeed, the discovery is said to have caused consternation with his widow.'

'Do I detect the Giffard woman has sought vengeance?'

'To the point where the girl was found starving by the Sisters of Mercy.'

'Surely Will made provisions for her?'

'It would seem the girl gave it to the family who had raised her after her mother's death; they promptly rejected her after his lordship's death at Evesham.'

'How can we see a former friend's Mistress so misused? Besides, it will be a thumbed nose to Maud Giffard. I never believed Will deserted the king without pressure from her family. We shall see young 'Mistress' Ela and offer her a change

of circumstance and as Lord Mortimer has been granted
Lyonshall, together with many of Deveraux's lands, it must
be viewed as a charitable act to help the girl if she proves
suitable, don't you think?'

Now I am weary and must seek my bed; I fear my body is
not as supple as it once was and all this fast riding has taken
its toll. Until the morrow.' She rose and smiled wanly at her
aged advisor.

'As ever, you have brought me to an easier state of mind
with .... a little wicked pleasure to boot.' With that she left
accompanied by the ever faithful Gwayne.

CHAPTER XXVI

Summer of 1270
Wigmore

Maud stood and studied her image in the long reflector admiring her new kirtle. Ela nodded her approval.

'The shade is just right for your colouring, my lady.'

'I think you are right, green is much more flattering than the blue, which tends to drain the colour from my face. Clever of you to find it!'

'I have an arrangement with the merchant to let me see his latest stock so that I may bring samples for you to choose.'

'I applaud your initiative; it was a sad day which brought you into my service but, since that time, you have proved invaluable and count myself fortunate that Lord Rhys made me aware of your circumstances.'

Ela turned so Maud could not read her expression.

'You saved my life and for that I shall always be grateful. I had lost my self esteem and thought I would never again find peace and security.'

'In this instance some good did come out of ill and we must thank God for showing us his charity. Well, I think that gown completes the wardrobe I shall need for my visits with Lord Mortimer in his capacity as future co Regent. Now I must see what's amiss with Ralph.'

As Maud entered the Great Hall she was greeted by her eldest son and from his flushed face knew he was bursting with some good news.

'I have been elected as Deputy Sheriff for Shropshire and Staffordshire - which means when the current Lord Hugh's term is up, the position will be mine.'

'That is a great responsibility for one so young but, it will give you time to see exactly what the title entails.'

'Papa will be proud will he not?'

'For certain, as am I, as will all of your siblings.'

Maud was inwardly elated by her son's news and felt this important event was yet another step towards his future and prove beneficial one for the House of Mortimer. The times were still difficult and the backlash of the civil strife was ever present, as acts of violence, still erupted frequently throughout England and the Marches.

More recently, there had been added pressure as the extra taxes were imposed by the crown in an effort to bolster the funds for the Lord Edward's forthcoming Crusade. The latest property tax had been met with volatile resistance even though the church had donated a twentieth of their income, it was still insufficient. But this additional financial burden was not viewed as a stumbling block by Edward who was insistent that nothing would deter him from his mission. The latest intelligence had intimated that Edward, his wife and brother, with many of their adherents, would be ready to embark in a few weeks to join the pious French King Louis, on what was to be the ninth Crusade.

Throughout the kingdom Masses and prayers were said for the successful enterprise of the heir to the English throne and on the 20th of August, the royal party set sail on a journey many would never return from. There had been great sadness within the royal family at the parting.

In the Marches, with her husband and eldest son's frequent absences, the day to day administrations of the Mortimer lands fell to Maud who was kept busy from morning until night with countless claims; requests and complaints. There was also the never ending need for men and boys to be recruited into the army of the king, to fill the places of those accompanying the two Plantagenet brothers to the Holy Land.

In September, as the leaves were changing to their autumn hues, they learned that William Chillenden had been elected as the new Archbishop of Canterbury, but appointments in the church did not really have any immediate bearing on the lives of the people of the Marches. The furore of Edward's departure quickly faded as the biting taxes began to be felt in earnest, the effects were especially difficult during the hard winter months and many of the poor starved.

The year rolled on into 1271, and the Mortimer family were all kept busy in their new roles. Later that year they learned that Edward and his party had reached Acre but not before King Louis IX of France had died of the plague in Tunis; it left the Crusade in some jeopardy, and speculation ran rife as to what Edward would do now.

However, in late November Maud received a letter which struck her deeply, reviving the disturbing emotions she had experienced after Martha's murder.

'Damn those black hearted de Montfort's to Hell!'

Ela dropped her needlework at the vehemence of her mistress's words.

Maud face was a portrait of pure hatred and she stormed out of the chamber to the apartment of Lord Rhys. Without any warning she entered unannounced.

'May God forgive my fury but the Devil's spawn has struck again.'

'My Lady!' Lord Rhys had obviously been startled but quickly regained his composure.

The rage was now beginning to subside and tears burned in the green-grey eyes of Lady Mortimer.

'Pray come and sit, and tell me what has aroused your ire this time.'

Without another word Maud thrust her letter into the claw like hands of Lord Rhys. As he screwed his eyes up to read he let out a long sigh.

'They did not trust it to an assassin this time.'

She shook her head still unable to speak.

'Well this act of desecration and murder will leave the church no alternative but to excommunicate them.'

'But why Henry?'

'It says he was acting as a messenger on behalf of Lord Edward.'

In a voice cracked with emotion Maud sobbed.

'But what could have prompted such a vicious crime? Even in war, the messenger is usually given safe conduct. It says quite simply, Henry of Almain and his squire were murdered in a church in Viterbo, Italy, by Guy and Simon de Montfort. My poor cousin would have been unarmed; what an act of craven cowardice.' She paused before continuing. 'And if sacrilege was not crime enough - they desecrated his body. May their foul souls burn in eternal hell-fire?' She added. 'Henry was not even at the Battle of Evesham.'

'I suspect the Lord Edward had sent Henry to try and discover the identity of your would be assassin.'

'And died victim of the same hatred.'

'Their grudge is against Edward, the king, and the Mortimers'.'

She rose and paced up and down the chamber.

'Will it never end this........this insidious hatred?'

Lord Rhys rubbed his chin.

'Simon is already a damned soul; he can never forgive himself for not bringing support to his father in time to save the day. His former life, and that of his family, has been lost due to his ineptitude and from such dark place, he strikes out at all those he judges guilty of bringing about his current state. Guy, on the other hand has, by all accounts, married into a wealthy Italian family and this act of premeditated murder, must also reflect badly on them.'

'The Lord Edward will never rest, and will hunt the de Montfort's for the rest of their miserable lives. They have damned their souls to the eternal flames of hell and forfeited the church's support.'

Lord Rhys rose and poured a cup of wine and offered it to Maud who took it and sipped at the rich liquid. Grateful for the warming glow in her stomach.

'Forgive my dramatic entrance but I felt as though the blade had struck at *my* heart.'

'My door is ever open to you my Lady Maud.'

For some time the couple sat sipping their wine in silence, only the scratching at the door broke the spell.

'Your faithful companion.'

'Odd is it not, how much comfort that old hound gives me?'

'All that is left for me to do now are to send letters of condolence and have Masses arranged throughout the County.

It leaves me wondering, who will be the next to lose their lives to this vendetta.'

Lord Rhys rose and walked stiffly to open the door to let Gwayne enter.

'The young Plantagenet will see this act of treachery against his kinsman, as a direct challenge and I fear, his response will result in nothing less than a hideous execution for both brothers if they are ever caught. Let us not forget, he gave the command of *'no quarter'* at Evesham, which aptly demonstrated that he will brook no defiance against those foolhardy enough to take arms against their king.'

Maud stroked Gwayne's shaggy head.

'How could he forgive his uncle; a man who had forced his father to sign away his inheritance by making *his* son heir to the throne. The ambitions of de Montfort had outrun any family ties; quite simply, it was an act beyond forgiveness as far as Edward was concerned. Sadly, too many good men lost their lives for the pride and ambitions of two stubborn men. However righteous the cause; and I grant, it had some merit but, it is my belief that it was the underlying differences between the king and his brother-in-law which culminated in bringing this country into open warfare. The outcome; was to set brothers and fathers against each other at a terrible cost, and both protagonists claimed to be men of God; where was, and *is* their Christianity now? De Montfort is worm bait and Henry is ailing, but their legacy of hate continues.'

'I fear we are all guilty of seeking revenge at times, it is a human failing.'

Maud nodded. 'And so it will go on until Armageddon where all the sins of the world will be tried by God.' She crossed herself.

Lord Rhys nodded his agreement.

'Men have found reasons to fight each other since time began and will continue to do so. They deck it a variety of disguises; for God, for King and Country; give it a noble title but, invariably it is pride, power, religion and gold, which drives their ambitions and I fear the pattern will continue for as long as men walk the earth.'

Maud looked thoughtfully at the speaker.

'That is the truth which shape our lives and I suppose, I agree with my son Ralph, if I am completely honest, to fight for honour is sometimes necessary. But, we both know, many acts are committed in the name of honour which God must surely condemn, but still they claim to carry them out in His name. I freely grant the passions of youth frequently clouds good judgement. As you say, it continues from generation to generation, the lessons are sadly, never learned.' She rose and made her way to the door.

'Now, I have troubled you o'er long methinks. I will go and leave you to your books but your wise counsel has helped me to rein in my anger, for which I am ever grateful.'

She left with Gwayne padding along beside her.

Many weeks later the mangled remains of Henry of Almain were laid to rest in the Cistercian Abbey at Hailes. Maud was shocked to see the change wrought in the once arrogant and proud figure of Richard, Earl of Cornwall. He looked haggard, and his once powerful frame was gaunt and stooped; there was no denying the death of his son had broken the once fearsome spirit. She was therefore not surprised to learn he had suffered a stroke and died on the second day of April in the following year and was laid to rest close to his son. It was not the last royal death that year as Edward's young son, John had also died.

The year of 1272, continued to prove an eventful one: Pope Gregory set aside the appointment of William Chillenden as Archbishop of Canterbury, in favour of his own candidate, Robert Kilwardby, but the Mortimer family were also to suffer a loss, and one which left their eldest daughter, Isabella a widow. John FitzAlan, heir to the Earldom of Arundel, had died suddenly. Upon hearing the news, Maud immediately rode to join her daughter at Arundel.

Maud arrived to find the Castle busily preparing for the funeral. Isabella was distraught but with the aid of an efficient steward and his team of servants, the preparations were well in hand. Hastily, Maud made her way to her daughter's chamber and as she entered unannounced, Isabella upon realising who it was ran into the arms of her mother and the two women clung together in a long embrace. It was apparent to Maud,

Isabella had spent many hours weeping, for her eyes were red raw, and her lovely face, blotched and tear stained.

'How have the children taken the news?' Maud had led Isabella back to her seat.

Sobbing she murmured.

'Poor Richard is bemused and he is unable to accept his father is dead. Maud is too young to really understand.'

'Come Bella, you must show the world a brave face. Have a bath, put cold compresses on your eyes, for if the children see you thus, it will frighten them. I will go and visit them whilst you make ready.' Maud left her daughter and made her way swiftly to the nursery.

As she entered a little boy ran forward and clasped his arms around her legs.

'Oh! Grandy, Papa is dead.' She stooped down and gathered him in her arms.

He buried his face in her neck and wept. After a while he drew away and looked into her eyes.

'I knew you would come.'

Maud could not explain why this grandchild had stolen into a special place in her heart but it was an undeniable fact, he had.

'I will always be here for you Richard.' She said as she held him tight for a moment. Now, where is Maudie?'

By the time of the funeral Isabella, Lady of Oswestry and Clun, had regained her composure and although she looked pale and wan, she carried out her duties flawlessly. Maud kept close to her daughter and remained for a few weeks after the ceremony, leaving her husband and sons to travel back to Wigmore alone.

One evening as the women sat before a glowing fire Isabella took her mother's hand.

'There is something I wish you to do for me.'

'You know I will do all within my power to help you and your children.'

'It is the custom for the king to marry wealthy widows to his kinsmen.' She looked earnestly at her mother as she spoke.

'I loved John with all my heart and the thought of re-marrying fills me with revulsion. Would you ask Papa to purchase the license from the King, for I swear I would disobey such a command, and do not wish to dishonour our family name?'

Maud nodded as she squeezed her daughter's hand.

'I will also write to Robert Burnell, he is a family man at heart and if I explain your reasons, feel he will ensure your father will be successful in such a request.'

Isabella dropped to her knees before her mother, laying her head in her lap. Maud stroked the soft, pale cheeks.

' I will not lie to you my dearest Bella, the months and years to come, will be difficult one's for you, as grief will take you to a very lonely place. The only consolation is, you did have years of love and experienced a happy marriage which, gave you two beautiful children. You must now learn to become an independent woman in a world of men. But I have no doubt in my mind you have the mettle and the spirit to overcome any future problems. Besides, if you decide to reside at Oswestry or Clun, we are close at hand and you know you and your children are ever welcome at Wigmore.' She bent and kissed her daughter's forehead.

Mourning would be the key word, as later that same year, the long reigning King Henry III, followed his brother, nephew, and grandson to the grave, thus began the reign of the absent, Edward I of England.

Robert Burnell swiftly acted on behalf of Edward and sent for all the Earls and magnates to swear fealty to their new king in his absence. His powers of organization were carried out in a seemingly effortless manner. The funeral of King Henry, who was laid to rest in Westminster Abbey, went without a hitch and after the service; the streets rang with the age old chant of 'God save the King'.

'The new age begins!' Burnell murmured to Mortimer as they rode together in the lavish carriage. Although Edward loved his father, he was not blind to his faults. The title of King is not an easy one to bear, and the late King was not equipped to do it justice and his people suffered for his shortcomings. There will be radical changes made in the future but, one thing I have learned with Edward is, never demand, always seek his opinion; show him both sides of an argument and invariably, he will make the right decision, however, if he does not - do not rail against him. He is a loyal friend but a fearsome enemy.'

'You, my Lord Burnell know him better than most, so I will try and remember your advice in the future.' Roger Mortimer voice was earnest.

'Good, good, with the burial of the father let us pray for a brighter, more ordered future with his son. England is in sore need of a firm hand, as I am daily regaled with countless acts of lawlessness and many of the Sheriffs appear either, unwilling or, unable to hold any real control. This situation has to be addressed immediately, although I fear it will take time to bring about any significant changes.' Burnell looked across at Mortimer. 'I hear your son is soon to be elected as Sheriff of Shropshire and Staffordshire?'

'Indeed!' Sir Roger Mortimer spoke with pride.

'Then let us hope it will be the beginning of a new breed of lawmen. His reputation as an honoured knight will be of great help in his new position, no doubt! And it is good that the young ones learn to take responsibility.'

'Amen to that!' The rest of the journey was silent as the two men contemplated their future roles in this new Plantagenet reign.

When Edward Plantagenet finally learned the news of his father's death and he had inherited the title of King of England, he was nevertheless, determined to continue with the Crusade, even after there had been an attempt on his life. Sketchy reports had reached England as to the manner of the attack, but the assassin's knife had failed to kill Edward, even though the blade had reputedly, been dipped in poison, nonetheless, the news had caused Eleanor of Province, many sleepless nights.

The Crusade had been no cause for celebrations, there had been no great victories; disease had decimated the troops, and the pitiless heat, killed equal numbers of men and horses. When Edward and his wife finally left on their homeward journey, they did not head directly for England; in fact, to the watching world, the uncrowned king appeared in no hurry to return to his home shores.

Eleanor of Castile, his young Queen, had given birth to a daughter whilst in Acre, who was christened Joan, and the place of her birth was forever linked with her name. The royal family's journey was made in easy, unhurried stages, back to the Continent, eventually arriving in France, where they attended a colourful ceremony arranged ostensibly for Edward to pay homage to the young King Philip III.

Whilst Edward and his Spanish Queen were enjoying their time in France, Llywelyn ap Gruffydd, Prince of Wales, had once again begun to plague the Welsh Marches in a series of swift, but devastating raids. By 1273, he had begun to build a castle at Dolforwyn, much to the ire of Sir Roger Mortimer, who with his troops and other Marcher barons, were kept busy repelling and relieving the stricken outposts along the borders with Wales. He sorely missed the presence of his eldest son, Ralph, who had been duly sworn in as Sheriff of Shropshire and Staffordshire, and therefore could no longer ride at his side as his own duties were too pressing to join his father in the Welsh ventures.

The lawlessness, which currently ran rife throughout the kingdom, made the job of law enforcer, one of the most arduous of that era. It was due in part to the backlash of the civil conflict, men who had lost everything turned to plundering neighbours and travellers with virtual impunity. For those trying to maintain law and order in any County, town or, village, was viewed with suspicion, as it was well known, amongst these men, were those who took advantage of their positions of power and grew wealthy in the process.

However, for Ralph Mortimer, it was an honourable reputation he pursued, and endeavoured to demonstrate he acted as an impartial and fair handed official of the king's law. He spent countless hours in the saddle riding from place to place in an attempt to uphold order in the courts. His tireless efforts were applauded by his mother and she ensured he always travelled with well armed and trusted men, ensuring his protection from any possible attack. Maud realised that the responsibility of office had had a profound effect on Ralph, and it was one she felt most proud of, for he was an irresponsible boy no longer, but a man, and one worthy of his status as heir to the Mortimer name.

CHAPTER XXVII

1274

Wigmore was a busy hive of activity with the constant comings and goings; wagons loaded with the wounded had been a recent addition to Maud's problems and the Infirmary was full to overflowing. Nevertheless, she managed to encourage all the servants to help wherever they could and discovered a few were gifted healers.

Lulls in the fighting were times to be savoured and on warmer days, Maud and Ela, together with Carys and some of the other women, would sit and cut bandages or pick herbs and the flowers known for their curative powers. It was during one such day news arrived which was to have far reaching affects on the Mortimer family.

A dust grimed messenger was announced to the seated Maud, she could tell by his face the news he brought was dire and her first thought were that Mortimer had been slain but the words which danced before her eyes did not report the death of the head of the household, but that of her son and heir, Ralph.

For what seemed like an eternity Maud just sat and stared at the scroll.

'Where is he?'

'My Lady he lies at Shrewsbury where he fell ill.'

'Why was I not informed immediately?'

'It happened so suddenly, he complained of a headache and went to bed and was found this morning by his body servant, dead in bed.'

'This means, you have ridden hard and fast and for that, I thank you?'

The messenger dropped to his knee. 'I knew you should be told as soon as it was humanly possible, my Lady Mortimer.'

Maud turned to Carys and the rest of the women.

'It is with a heart full of grief I have to inform you that Lord Ralph has been taken from us, in the flush of his youth.'

The anguished cry from Carys echoed around the ashlar walls of Wigmore, then she dropped her basket of flowers scattering them far and wide, picked up her skirts, and ran back into the Castle sobbing loudly as she went.

Maud looked at those who remained in shocked silence.

'Lord Mortimer will be inconsolable when he hears the news.'

Maud spoke more to herself than to anyone else. Slowly she rose, dropped the partially rolled bandage into a wicker basket and walked back to the apartments of Lord Rhys.

A cup of wine was already poured.

'You know?'

'I heard Carys cry his name and guessed.'

Maud looked at the cup of wine and then took a long drink before she went and sat, stiff and straight in her usual seat.

'Maybe it's a punishment!'

'A punishment for what, my Lady?'

'When his young son Geoffrey died last spring, part of me was relieved.' She paused before continuing, trying to find the right words to explain herself.

'It had always troubled me the manner of his birth. Besides, he neither looked like a Mortimer nor acted like one. A little alien, a cuckoo in the nest, and God has seen fit to punish my uncharitable thoughts by taking them both.'

'You should not reproach yourself my Lady, the lad had a short but happy life and thoughts at least, can run unbidden even into forbidden areas of our hearts without committing any sin. You ensured he wanted for naught.'

'I still feel guilty of a betrayal to my son and grandson. I hope God will forgive me for I know I shall not forgive myself.'

'God has His own way of shaping our destinies and you should see it as such.'

Maud nodded but the old man could see her expression

of pain. Unlike many women, Maud did not wail and weep but he knew the grief she felt ran deep and would leave an invisible wound, a wound which would never truly heal.

'You must make arrangements in readiness for his Lordship's return; he will be in dire need of your support.'

'You are right of course and I must write to Edmund and tell him of his brother's death and that his days of study must now surely come to an end.'

'The wheels of Destiny turn yet again.'

Maud looked at the old man.

'On a path as yet unknown to any of us!'

'All we can do my Lady, is trust in God and pray for his guidance.'

The days that followed passed like a blur; the abiding memory for Maud was the expression on her husband's face when he rode through the gates of Wigmore. He looked older than the ancient oaks in Mortimer Forest. She stepped forward as he dismounted and embraced his hunched shoulders in rare demonstration of affection.

'I have written to the children and the funeral arrangements are all in hand.'

The stricken Mortimer merely nodded as they turned and walked back towards the Castle of Wigmore together.

'It is ironic is it not, that the king is due to return any day soon.'

Maud looked earnestly into his face.

'So you will be expected to be there to welcome him home?'

'Burnell has expressed his condolences but emphasised that as one of the surviving Regents, urges me to travel to London at the earliest as the Coronation will take place within days of Edward's arrival.'

'Then you must go!' She paused and added. 'Maybe it is for the best as it will give you scant time to dwell on your grief.'

The bitter look which crossed Lord Mortimer's face was one Maud had never witnessed before.

'I shall mourn my son for the rest of my life.'

'As will I my lord.' Maud's words were hardly more than a whisper but Mortimer did not hear them as he strode ahead leaving Maud to follow him at a slower pace.

The days which ensued were some of the most difficult ones of Maud's life but somehow her iron resolve got her though them. Just two days after Ralph's funeral, Mortimer and a small, but heavily armed troop, rode for London at all speed. Maud was thankful that at least Edmund was staying for a further week.

That evening as the sombre group sat before a crackling fire Maud drew Edmund aside.

'This sad affair could have an overwhelming affect on your life and I wish to know how you truly feel about it?'

'The truth is I am still in shock; Ralph always seemed so full of life, I know we did not always see eyes to eye on matters but nonetheless, I loved my brother.'

Maud nodded. 'I know! For all his youthful mistakes I felt he had turned the corner into manhood and was making a fair fist of it! I still can't believe the manner of his death. A headache! I could have accepted a wound, poison maybe but just ......' her words trailed off.

'It is possible it was a haemorrhage on the brain.'

'From a blow?'

'It could have been from a blow he received in battle or, at a tournament at some point.'

'We shall never know for certain but it does seem ironic that he fought through some of the bloodiest battles and apart from a few flesh wounds, appeared to have come through unscathed, only to die in his sleep.'

'It is a good way to go! Without fear or pain, just falling into a permanent sleep.'

'Your father has taken it very badly; Ralph was his favourite.'

Edmund took his mother's hand. 'So have you but you hide your hurt well Mama.'

She reached and pushed a lock of hair from his eyes.

'You were always the perceptive one but you still have not answered my question.'

'Well if I do not step forward it would mean young Roger would become heir, and we both know he is lacking in many areas required to uphold the duties and the title of Lord of Wigmore. I admit, I do not readily accept the situation but also am conscious that the name of Mortimer transcends any personal ambitions. You of all people know that better than most. I have often wondered what you would have wished for in your life had you been given a choice.'

Maud shook her head. 'We have been born into a privileged position with duties laid down for us by our families. Duties, they too had to uphold for the honour of their families. Vows, that are not always easily accepted; nevertheless we are not free to make our own choices and therefore must make the best of those made for us. I have devoted my life to the Mortimers' but, still do not really feel a part of the family. I have always striven to make things better for the next generation but..........' she hesitated; 'Wigmore has never been my true home.'

'I think I understand! I know you do not love my father in the romantic way but have been his dutiful wife. I often wonder who does hold your heart – if anyone.'

'Love certainly had no bearing during the first years of our marriage. Time teaches us forbearance and your father and I have learned to live together.' She smiled. 'Maybe not always amicably but we share similar aims; and over time I have grown to appreciate the soldierly qualities in your sire, he is a true Lord of the March and now fits his role well. However, I think this conversation has wandered away from its proper course and can I take it that you are ready to accept your position and will step into the role of heir to the Mortimer family?'

Edmund squeezed his mother's hand. 'I know you understand my reluctance but if Fate has cast me in the part it would be churlish to refuse?'

Maud let out a deep sigh. 'This change will be difficult for you in many ways not least; your father will compare you to Ralph, which inevitably must lead to friction between you. However, I am confident, in time, he will come to realise you possess a wealth of qualities of your own and accept you for yourself and not try and set you into a mould of your brother.

Now you must also adopt the life of a knight and all that entails not surreptitiously, as in the past, but in earnest.' She sighed. 'But for the present, we must inform young Roger his dreams of inheriting Ralph's position as heir, are forever dashed!'

It had been no understatement that the Lord of Wigmore was bereft at the loss of his eldest son. He attended the Coronation of Edward Plantagenet, with a heavy heart; Mortimer had sworn his fealty in person as did the ranks of nobles and magnates with one notable exception, the Welsh Prince, Llywelyn ap Gruffydd. It was an absence that Edward Plantagenet would never be forget and in the days which followed he took steps to ensure his old enemy was made acutely aware that as Edward of England, he was not about to forgive the Welshman's slight. The gauntlet had been thrown down and accepted, and Llywelyn was about to experience the fearsome nature of his opponent.

Whilst Edward began his life as King of England, Maud had been tirelessly writing a flurry of letters to the Archbishops of Canterbury and York and the King's chief advisor, Robert Burnell, in an effort to gain Edmund's release from his life of academia in Oxford. Although he had not taken his final vows of Holy Orders, he was nevertheless, within the jurisdiction of the church and as such needed to gain his release. Eventually, when the necessary legal documents arrived signed and sealed setting him free, there had been family celebrations. Edmund was now recognised as the legal heir to Sir Roger Mortimer, Lord of Wigmore.

Months later, Maud's words of caution regarding the relationship between father and son came to fruition. Whilst accompanying his father on one of the many Welsh raids an incident occurred which brought the matter to a head.

Late one evening Edmund galloped into Wigmore and Maud saw by the expression on her son's face all was not well but before she could speak to him his father, with the remainder of the troops, also thundered through the gateway. Edmund had gone directly to his own chambers with little more than a cursory nod. When Mortimer entered the Great Hall, Maud could see his mood was dark and angry as she waited for her husband to speak.

'Your son has disobeyed a direct order, and in so doing, has undermined my authority and I will not be subjected to such behaviour.'

The irony of his statement was not lost to Maud.

'How so, my lord?'

Just then young Roger burst in and joined in, his face red and agitated.

'Father ordered Edmund to put a village to the sword, but he refused.'

Maud could see by her husband's face that he was angrier than she had seen him for many years.

'There must have been a good reason.'

'Oh! Why am I not surprised you immediately defend his insufferable insubordination!'

'Because Edmund never acts rashly, which leaves me to question his reasons for refusing your command?'

Edmund entered, his face strained as he stood facing his accusers.

'To slay a village of farming peasants, mainly old men, women and children, was nothing short of murder and flies in the face of any knightly code of honour I have ever read.'

Sir Roger Mortimer's face was contorted with anger.

'So, you decide who lives and dies? I am both your sire and your commander and to override my orders is tantamount to treason in my eyes.'

Edmund moved forward from the doorway, his expression had not changed as he spoke.

'Pray tell me, exactly what will your barbarous attack achieve? Other than to incite Llywelyn and his people into reciprocating acts of barbarism?'

Maud stepped between father and son.

'I wish you both to consider well how this situation will affect your followers. Do you really wish to split your men into taking sides, and the family to do likewise?' She turned to look at her husband and son in turn to see the effect her question had prompted.

Edmund moved closer to his accuser.

'I would lay down my life for my father but will not damn my soul to Hell for heinous acts of senseless butchery.'

'You have spent too long with your dusty tomes and mealy mouthed clerics to understand the situation here in the Marches.'

'Those dusty tomes have taught me that warfare in the end, gains little, it is the might of the written word which carries the greater powers.'

'The truth is - you are gutless.' The words bit through the air like a well aimed spear.

Maud waved her hand. 'Enough! Edmund say no more and leave this to me!'

'No Mama, I will not stand by and allow my name and the name of Mortimer to be brought into disrepute for an act which, by all the laws of the land and the church, will be condemned out of hand.'

The air was electric as the two Mortimers' stood only a few feet apart. Sir Roger bristled with rage. Edmund, the taller of the two, looked pale but resolute, as he faced his sire.

'I have fought for more years, and spilled more blood, than you have lived and will not be spoken to in such a manner by my own son.'

'Maybe it is time someone gave you the truth. Ralph could do no wrong in your eyes and little good that did him; his arrogance and selfishness shattered many lives, especially where young girls were concerned.'

Maud moved to stand directly in front of Edmund.

'You have said enough Edmund, I urge you to go now for I do not wish to witness my husband raise a hand against his son and heir.'

Without another word Edmund turned on his heel and left. Maud noticed the movement out of the corner of her eye and grabbed at Mortimer's arm.

'No, my lord, let him go! Whatever the truth of the matter I will not see my family brought into a state of violence. Go; have a bath and a drink, and cage your rage for you may do something you will forever regret. It would result in a blow to our family as deadly as any Llywelyn could land.'

Maud called for Rufus and two of Mortimer's squires to escort her husband to his own chambers. She also instructed two guards to stand watch over Edmund. Her head was spinning this situation had caused a scene she felt could bring about a schism in her family which may never be resolved and one, Llywelyn would quickly hear about and use to his advantage. Slowly she walked to Edmund's chamber and knocked and entered without waiting for an invitation. Edmund was sat on his bed his head in his hands.

'Tell me in detail all that has transpired to bring about such a falling out!'

Haltingly Edmund gave the details of a deadly skirmish as a troop of Welshmen had swooped down on their party and killed a significant number of Mortimer men. Before they had been able to re-group as many of the Welsh fighters had melted away into the hills. Although they had given chase nothing could be found of their attacker's whereabouts. Eventually they had arrived at a small village some miles away. There had been no sign of any of the enemy or any evidence they had even passed that way but, his father had given the order for the village to be put to the torch and all the occupants killed. He had refused. Why a group of innocents should be made to pay with their lives merely because they were Welsh was, in his view little more than murder.

Maud held his hand. 'And your father?'

'Was too full of hatred to listen; and was egged on by young Roger.'

'Stay in your room; I have guards outside so that you will not be disturbed. I will go and seek the advice of Lord Rhys as I am too filled with anguish to think clearly.'

After Maud had recounted the events to her old advisor she sat and waited for his response.

'This is a serious business and not one which will be easily resolved. It was bound to happen, the two have such differing natures; one is a hardened soldier with an uncertain temper, whilst the other has been versed in the ways of the church and literature and thus, is far more self possessed and understands the far reaching consequences of such an action.'

He paused and rubbed his hands together before continuing.

'Your husband expects unquestioning obedience and therefore judges the refusal as a personal insult whereas your son, acted as a Christian in an effort to save his father's soul from damnation or, at least that is how he saw it.'

'Yes, yes, I am perfectly aware of that but how can we bring this situation to a peaceable conclusion?' She wrung her hands in distress.

'I cannot watch the House of Mortimer fall apart from the actions within the family. Edmund will obviously take a more measured stance on matters of importance, whilst we both know, how I have, over the years, had to struggle to contain my husband's more impetuous actions on many occasions.'

Lord Rhys nodded. 'First you must try to bring the pair together to discuss the issue which will not be easy but, it must be done or matters could deteriorate even further I fear.'

'I think to try and resolved the situation here at Wigmore, may be more difficult as Mortimer sees this as his ancestral domain and as such, he has the ultimate control whereas, on neutral ground he may feel less territorial and therefore be more disposed to listening.'

'There is merit in that idea. Where do you propose?'

Maud began to pace as her mind began to focus on the matter.

'Tetbury, it is my Castle and as wife and mother, I must be seen to be even handed in anything I suggest. Besides, I will feel more comfortable there should things go wrong.'

A frown played on her forehead as she spoke, but the former expression of anguish had eased somewhat.

'The next problem will be to get them both to agree to my suggestion.'

'May I suggest you take Edmund there directly and send word a few days later to Sir Roger, stating if he does not come and discuss matters, Edmund will travel directly back to Oxford and take Holy Orders and thus be lost to you both.'

There was a momentary pause as Maud considered his words.

'An excellent suggestion my Lord.'

Maud returned to Edmund's chamber and urged him to accompany her to Tetbury without delay as the whole situation had caused her to feel unwell and she wished to seek peace and quiet for a few days. She informed her husband of the plans to leave, and left him in no doubt, that he could not dissuade her. If Edmund suspected anything, he remained silent on the subject so on the following morning, he rode at his mother's side to her Castle at Tetbury.

Sir Roger Mortimer watched his wife and son depart and began to pace restlessly up and down for some time before calling for his horse to go hunting. As planned, a few days later a message arrived from Maud stating that Edmund was on the brink of renouncing his position as heir and return to the life of a churchman. The news had the desired effect and the Lord of Wigmore made hasty arrangements to visit his wife at Gloucestershire castle.

As Mortimer strode into the comfortable chamber, he saw Maud sitting before a table full of letters nearby, her lady-in-waiting, sat sorting a basket of silken threads.

'I'm glad you came, my lord.' Maud rose slowly replacing the long quill in its slot. She waved Ela away; and indicated for Mortimer to sit down as she called for refreshments.

'Am I too late?'

'I hope not my Lord. Edmund has gone to Gloucester Cathedral to speak with the Bishop but has promised to return here before making any final decisions.'

'And do you think he will return here?'

'Yes, Edmund will not break his word to me.'

'No doubt your health has improved.' She noted the sarcasm in his voice.

'It has given me time to think and regain my composure.' Her tone was cool and emotionless.

'And what conclusions have you come to over the matter?'

There was a long pause before Maud spoke.

'That as a father, you should have given him time to become accustomed to his new position as a warrior. He knows he can never gain the place Ralph held in your heart or, at your side in battle at least, not immediately. Pray cast your mind back; surely you can remember how you once felt inferior in the eyes of your father?'

Mortimer stared at his wife long and hard. She continued in low even tones knowing that she must present a measured argument, one without showing any personal emotions or all her well laid plans would be lost.

'How many times did we forgive Ralph's misdemeanours? And look how he blossomed.' She paused to allow her words to register. 'By the accounts I have gleaned, the situation became more untenable by young Roger's intervention and it is still my belief he has his eye on becoming your heir. All I ask is that you at least talk to Edmund without rancour.'

There was a knock at the door and Errol entered carrying

a tray of food and wine. Without a word he served the couple, bowed and left.

'You were right to leave when you did. It gave me time to calm down and you are also right about young Roger's motives, if I had listened, Edmund would have been disinherited there and then.'

'You and Edmund have been educated at the opposite ends of the spectrum and are very different in character but....' she hesitated as she offered him a sweat-meat; 'it does not mean you cannot work together in the future.' She sipped her wine then continued. 'Maybe you should attach Edmund to your brother's retinue; he and Robert have always got on well.' She reached across and held his sleeve.

'Pray do not place me in a position between husband and son. You of all people should know how hard I have worked at your side over the years. I urge you my lord, find a way to resolve this matter. We have enough enemies to fight without fighting amongst ourselves. Forgiveness may not be within your power to bestow at this time, but one day I pray you will come to it.'

Mortimer remained silent for what seemed an age.

'Some years ago you would have held a blade at my throat if I had not agreed to forgive your son.' His tones, acid.

'I have learned to fasten my tongue to my mouth on occasions. Many of my battles have been with my own temper and I have waged a dogged war with it, aware how important it was not just for me, but for our family. Besides, do not let your pride bring us down; if the king hears there is a rift within our family he may be less inclined to continue with his support, given the importance he attaches to family ties.'

By the expression on her husband's face Maud realised her reasoning had hit the target. Mortimer re-filled his cup of wine then looked across at her as he spoke.

'I accept you have a valid point my Lady.' He raised his cup to her and took a long drink.

'Do you realise this is the first time we have sat and talked alone for months.'

'Then maybe we should do it more often especially, if it achieves a satisfactory outcome.' Maud tried not to show the inner triumph she felt. For years she had played the part of diplomat mostly between bouts of physical exertions in their bedchamber; maybe today, was the beginning of a new era in their dynamic relationship.

It was a few days before Edmund returned and Maud ensured that the atmosphere remained one of calm and reflection, during that time.

Upon Edmund's return, father and son sat alone and talked for over an hour. Two days later, the Mortimer family rode back towards Wigmore together. Maud never knew exactly what the two had said to each other as their meeting had been in private but, she had felt a wave of relief when they had emerged from the chamber together, their expressions serious, but no longer angry.

CHAPTER XXVIII

1276

The years after Edward's Coronation, proved to be busy ones; and the agenda for the king was full and urgent. The continued lawlessness, which still ravaged the land, was a priority so too, the ancient enemy – Wales. Unlike his father, Edward was forthright in his leadership and he, and his trusted friend and advisor, Robert Burnell, set about bringing the necessary changes with the energy and foresight lacking in the previous reign.

The tenuous peace between Sir Roger Mortimer and his son was short lived, and within a few months after their reconciliation at Tetbury, Edmund had returned to Oxford. Before he left Edmund came and unburdened himself to his beloved mother.

'You know how hard I have struggled to embrace the life of a soldier but find I am neither physically fit nor, am I able to reconcile myself to the utter brutality of this war with Wales. I have given you my vow that I will not take Holy Orders or, step away from taking my place as heir but......' he hesitated. 'My heart and mind are not at ease with this sudden change and I must have time to learn the skills of a knight and accept all the changes Ralph's death has brought about. I cannot face being jeered at by my father's men-at-arms because I grow tired quickly and my sword arm has less power than that of a young squire. I have given this a lot of thought and can go and practice with de Vere's knights and squires, as he and Meg have connections in Oxford.' He rose and came and kissed Maud's cheek.

'Upon my return, you have my word, things will be different. I will be the one to test their metal, and thus silence the sneers and derision. One thing I have learned, men follow leaders they respect, and I have to prepare to fulfil that role both in mind and body.'

Maud smiled wanly but kissed his cheek.

'I know you will do the right thing Edmund and pray your transition from cleric to knight will be easier than you anticipate. As for your father's reactions .....' she shrugged. 'We both know he will blow like a storm over the sea, but I am quite used to such outbursts and as long as your decision brings about a successful conclusion then I am happy to withstand such tantrums. May God go with you, my dearest son?'

Without further ado Edmund made ready for his journey to Oxford before his father's return. It would be almost two years before he rode back to his childhood home to take up his rightful place as heir to the Mortimer family, but it would be a very different young man that returned to Wigmore than the one that left.

Roger Mortimer had scant time to berate his wife over Edmund's departure; his days were kept busy with recruiting and overseeing the training of men and horses for the king's venture in Wales. If Edward had believed he would bring about a swift victory, Llywelyn was about to teach him a very cruel lesson, and sent the royalist army back to England with a bloody nose. The humiliation so incensed Edward, his temper erupted like a volcano, and all who were close to him, picked their words very carefully in the days that followed.

Mortimer returned to Wigmore, also in a black humour.

'Maybe now Edward will be more willing to listen to his Marcher barons who have been waging this war for more years than he has drawn breath. Llywelyn is nothing if not canny and he knows his men and terrain better than any and uses them to the utmost advantage. It is not always brute force and numbers of troops which win in Wales but stealth, and often, instinct.'

Maud nodded.

'Then it must give you a sense of pride that Edward failed in the North and South, whereas you achieved success in Powys?'

'It was essential to regain Powys Castle even though Llywelyn left much of it in ruins.'

'Bye the bye, Bella has sent word she is at Oswestry and has recruited men from the area who should be ready to fight in the coming weeks. Apparently she has a young Constable who is proficient in training methods.'

Mortimer's face relaxed a little.

'The girl is proving herself a true Marcher, and has taken up the challenge with a will, worthy of any knight.'

Maud was heartened to hear her husband's praise for their daughter; she knew how difficult Bella had found the loss of her young husband had been to deal with but it appeared she was throwing herself into her role as Lady of Oswestry and Clun, in an effort to assuage her grief. There were frequent messages at first for advice, but as time passed they became less frequent and Maud knew Bella was becoming a proficient chatelaine. Under her instructions, work had begun in earnest on re-enforcing the walls at both Oswestry and Clun.

Whilst some of the Marchers were busy regrouping after their recent defeat, news arrived from court that Edward had set about drawing up ambitious plans for a string of castles to be built across Llywelyn's country.

'I knew it would stir up a hornet's nest. Edward will never let Llywelyn enjoy his victories for long.' He rubbed his chin as he spoke, 'but exactly what this will mean for those of us that live in the eye of the storm, is another matter entirely. We are the ones that lose more land and men. Your cousin, de Clare, built that castle at Caerphilly at great expense, but has it gained him aught but more expense? To my mind it only served to antagonise the Welsh.'

Maud remained silent she knew her husband was jealous of Gilbert's impressive castle in Wales. But she could not deny that the king's ambitions would involve a lot of silver which would be slow in coming from the treasury, given its poor state. The pursuit of power inevitably cost money and, given Edward's intractable nature, a small matter of lack of funds would not halt his ambitious plans, merely slow them down. This in turn would cause him frustration, and everyone was all too aware that Edward was very short on patience. She sighed. Undoubtedly he would impose more taxes to fund his building venture, and the effect would once more be felt across the land causing further hardships. The year was also notable for the elections in a short succession of three Popes. The first part of the year, Innocent V ruled, but was succeeded for just a few weeks, by Adrian V and subsequently, John XX1. Maud commented that the number five appeared to be unlucky for the churchmen but the changes to who became head of the Catholic Church would have little immediate effect in the Marches.

Whilst Rome settled to the new administration of its latest Pope, 1277, saw Edward was once more on campaign in Gwynedd. He ordered the castle at Builth to be re-enforced and improved; Aberystwyth Castle to be rebuilt, and the first of his stone castle to be built at Flint. By June, the expected demand for taxes came in the form of feudal levies, much to the chagrin of his nobles. In July, Edward and a troop of some 800 cavalry, together with 2500 Infantry, marched to Chester, before moving deep into Wales. Their progress was impeded by the thickly wooded terrain, but Edward, in his usual single-minded manner, quickly had a wide road built, guarded by fortified outposts along the route. Nothing it seemed would stop him from achieving his aim to bring Llywelyn to heel.

At Rhuddlan, by the crossing of the River Clwyd, Edward had the old castle reconstructed. He and his wife, Eleanor, also took time to lay the foundation stone for the Vale Royal Abbey in Chester, for the Order of Cistercians. Although he had inherited few of his father's characteristics, he was nevertheless, a devout Catholic so too, his Spanish wife, Eleanor of Castile.

In November, Edward's persistent efforts to subdue Llywelyn bore fruit as he finally defeated the Welsh Prince with the aid of his loyal friend, Sir Roger Mortimer, who had played a subtle part in bringing about the much needed victory by persuading some of Llywelyn's closest advisors to defect. The king demanded payment of £50,000 plus all Llywelyn's territories with the exception of Anglesey, for which he would receive a sum of £1000 per annum. His triumph culminated on Christmas Day when Llywelyn had no alternative but to swear fealty to the King of England, conscious that Edward held Eleanor de Montfort, to whom he was betrothed, prisoner.

Edward had left no-one in any doubt that his domination of Wales was no idle threat, and he was wreaking his retribution on Llywelyn for daring to refuse to recognise him as his liege lord.

At Wigmore the Christmas celebrations were rowdy as many toasts to Edward's success rang round the Great Hall, and to the Marcher lords who had played a significant part in the victory. The Giffards', LeStrange, de Lacys'. De Sayes' Cherlton and Cliffords' and many more, ate and drank with relish, and Maud presided with grace and good humour, when she was toasted as the Lady of the March.

Sir Roger stood and raised his cup of wine high above his head.

'Friends, we have just lived through a year none of us will forget in an age, and with the aid of our trusty swords we have done more than our fair share to humble Llywelyn's pride. So, raise your cups to God, and Edward our King.'

The Hall erupted as voices united in the toast. But as the men-folk celebrated with gusto Maud did not wholeheartedly feel their triumph; Llywelyn had bent his knee and appeared to have submitted but there may have been another reason for him so doing – Eleanor de Montfort. So, was the Welsh Prince playing a very devious game? The notion was one which would persist in the days to come but, it was one Maud would keep to herself, especially on this night of jollity.

As the year of 1278 dawned, Edward had set in motion plans for his friend and ally, Robert Burnell, to be installed as the Archbishop of Canterbury upon the departure of Richard Kidwardby, who had left for the Continent under a cloud. The position gave the secular authority of the Church in England to Burnell, highlighting the esteem in which Edward regarded him. Much of the powers of Chancellor had been for some time, in the hands of his friend, as the ailing Walter Giffard, became ever more frail.

The struggle for dominance between Edward and Llywelyn was at least for now, in the hands of the English king. He released Eleanor de Montfort from her confinement but kept her under close guard at court. Although Eleanor had been treated with the utmost care and respect, her brother Aumery, had not fared so well and was now imprisoned in close confinement at Corfe Castle, in Dorset.

By October, Edward and Llywelyn had signed the Treaty of Aberconwy, and on the 13th of that month, which was the Feast of St Edward, the King of England gave the hand of his cousin, Eleanor de Montfort, to Llywelyn ap Gruffydd, Prince of Wales, in marriage. The date was just another reminder of Edward's position of superiority and one which not lost on Llywelyn.

Maud had watched Llywelyn enter the great cathedral at Worcester, she was struck by the startling resemblance to her husband. Not so much in features but, in physique, even in the way he walked, there was no mistaking the two had been moulded from the same clay? She did not miss the look the cousins exchanged as Llywelyn made his way to the altar. Ironic that this magnificent ceremony was being funded by Edward, who had also invited the King of Scotland, attended by his closest retainers. No expense had been spared, no figure of importance ignored. It was rumoured that Edward had even made Llywelyn sign a pledge on that very morning forbidding him to detain any future prisoners. It was like pulling teeth; Edward was making the Welshman pay dear for his bride.

The voices of the great choir rose to fill the cathedral as Eleanor de Montfort walked down the aisle on the arm of her cousin. Her eyes were fixed firmly on the figure standing before the magnificent altar awaiting her arrival. Maud could see the tension in her pale face and knew this day must have been an enormous strain on the slender young woman. She would have been aware the cost Llywelyn had been forced to pay for their union. It was a strange feeling to watch the daughter of their erstwhile enemy, Simon de Montfort, be joined to another enemy, in marriage. Maud took a deep breath, what would this day's events bring forth? The answer - was hidden in the future.

At the feasting which followed the solemn ceremony, Maud sat beside her young grandson, Richard FitzAlan, who was full of questions and wanted his grand-dam to name the many nobles and barons, especially the ones he had never seen before. The diversion was a welcomed one as she enjoyed watching Richard's face as he watched the jugglers and fire-eaters; chuckled out loud at his side splitting laughter at the jesters which were making fun of one and all. Occasionally Maud's gaze turned towards the royal dais and noted the keen attention Llywelyn was paying to his new bride. The looks which passed between them was that of undisguised delight so, the Welshman had gained his prize, it would be interesting to see who had really won the battle; Edward, who was making a show to the world that he reigned supreme or, had Llywelyn played a canny hand and gained what he most desired – a wife?

As the night progressed Maud whispered in her husband's ear and warned him of drinking too deeply, without any opposition he obeyed, for she had urged him to listen to any rumours circulating around the gathering without giving anything of import away for others to dwell on. Maud remembered the advice Lord Rhys had instilled in her, watch, listen, and learn, but stay mute.

Throughout the evening Maud and her family were re-united with distant family members and when Gilbert de Clare, Earl of Gloucester, sauntered over she introduced him to her young grandson.

'The last time I saw you young FitzAlan, was when you were in swaddling clothes at your christening.' He grinned. 'You must come and visit me and bring your grand-dam.' He looked down at Maud and smiled: 'with this new peace we will all have more time for our families.'

Bella joined them. 'And what mischief are you currently in the thick of?' She teased her tall, flame haired kinsman. She turned to her son, 'listen, but do not emulate him, he will lead you into naught but mischief.' The laughter was unanimous.

'I would like to visit your castle in Wales.' Richard's face full of eagerness.

'Then I will arrange it!'

Maud bent forward and whispered to her kinsman.

'Do you really believe a few words scrawled across a page will bring this conflict to an end?' Although Maud's words were quietly spoken, there was no doubting their intensity.

Gilbert de Clare looked down at Richard as he spoke.

'Always listen to Lady Maud; she has more wisdom than an owl.' He continued. 'I give the lull in fighting at least a year.'

He suddenly grinned mischievously, 'Llywelyn will presently be paying more attention to his wife I dare-swear, than to acts of war at least, until she conceives a son.

Now pray excuse me, for I can see my wife looking somewhat agitated and I do not wish to upset her in front of so many distinguished guests.' With an elegant bow he moved back to his own table.

'His hair looks as though it's on fire!' Exclaimed Richard.

Bella chuckled. 'Be thankful you did not inherit the Irish locks.'

As the evening grew even noisier and the japes more lewd, Maud looked to see if the Queen had retired for she also wished to seek her bed. The day had been rich in pageant and symbolism but inwardly Maud felt choked by the hypocrisy of it all. Upon noting the absence of Queen Eleanor, Maud waited, then also excused herself, and headed for her chamber.

The corridor was cool and the flickering flames in the sconces, threw dark shadows along the walls and floor. A figure moved towards Maud, she would have passed with little more than a nod until he stepped into her path.

'The beauteous Lady Mortimer, is it not?' The voice was soft and mellifluous.

Maud looked up into the face of Llywelyn ap Gruffydd.

'You are leaving the festivities somewhat early?'

Maud looked into the dark eyes of the Welsh lord without flinching.

'I have passed the age where such occasions hold any true pleasure for me nowadays, my Lord.'

'Such a pity, I would have enjoyed dancing with my cousin's wife.'

'At the expense of upsetting your new bride?'

'Ah! Yes, you entertained her father on one occasion did you not?'

Maud's gaze did not falter.

'Indeed, I had that pleasure.'

'Maybe I can reciprocate at some time in the future and have your husband at the *head* of the table.'

Maud heard the inflection in his voice and the malevolence in his tone.

'So, the Treaty you so recently signed, appears to hold scant significance, my Lord?'

'The game of war is full of bluffs and counter bluff, as we both know.'

'Your word then is as false as the ceremony witnessed today?'

'My marriage is sacred whatever the circumstances but, the feud between Mortimer and Wales will not end so easily, there are too many old scores to be settled.' Without further ado he stepped to the side and as she was about to walk away.

He hissed. 'I promise, you *will* wear widow's weeds, Maud de Braose.' And with that he strode off back to his wedding feast.

Maud stood still for a moment until she heard quick footsteps, a breathless page stood before her.

'Do you wish directions my Lady?'

'Thank you, yes!'

The page turned and asked her name and then raised his lantern.

'Pray follow me your ladyship. My father serves in Lord Mortimer's troop, sadly I am too small to be a soldier but my brothers are training in Hereford.'

Maud was glad of the boy's chatter and as he stopped before the door to her chamber she turned.

'And what is your name?'

'Gyles, my lady.'

'Well Gyles, should you ever want to come to Wigmore you will be more than welcome to serve in my household.'

'Thank you my lady, it would be an honour, my father says he would stake his pension, that Lady Mortimer is the finest Lady in the March, if not the country.'

Maud smiled as she entered to find Ela laying out her nightshift.

'You are back earlier than I expected my lady.'

'The clamour became too much. Help me with my headdress then you can go and watch the spectacle, if you wish!'

'Thank you!'

As Ela left Maud shrugged off her rich garments and slipped the cool shift over her head and went to the great wide bed and lay down. She closed her eyes and re-lived the recent encounter with the Mortimer's cousin; there was no doubting his hatred but she knew she would not recount their meeting to her husband this was not the time to stir up more trouble, the Marches needed this interlude of peace. Lost in these thoughts Maud drifted off to sleep and some hours later, Roger Mortimer looked down at the recumbent figure and in the flickering rush-light, marvelled at how young she looked.

The following day the revels focused on a mock joust between the young squires of the many nobles households. Colourful, and noisy, with all panoply of a tournament but the weaponry was wooden but it did not stop the wagers or the enthusiasm of the company. Young Richard FitzAlan was feeling more than a little aggrieved as he had not been allowed to be part of the pageant and had to sit and watch full of envy and frustration, at the side of his mother.

'My dear, your day will come I promise, but for today, you have to act as my escort as we represent the Earldom of Arundel.'

Her words had only gone a little way to placate his ire and he sat with a disgruntled expression on his face throughout the afternoon's display. For his granddame, the spectacle was one she found unexpectedly moving. Ralph had been a champion of many tournaments and jousts in his short life and the day's events provoked memories she found painful. During the bouts, Maud's gaze would travel frequently to the royal dais and she noted the fond looks which passed between Llywelyn and Eleanor. Could their union have developed into a love match already?

On the final day of the festivities Maud hinted to Bella she would be glad when it was all over and they could return home. It was during a lull in the dancing Maud told Bella of her encounter with Llywelyn and the bitter words he had spoken.

'I tell you as a warning not, to become too complacent in the months ahead. This so called peace, does not sit easily with me. I remember the words of Lord Rhys who firmly believes that Llywelyn's Achilles heel is his youngest brother, Dafydd, a man who is all about treachery and misrule.'

'But isn't he in the pocket of the king?'

Maud smiled knowingly. 'He has proved a perfidious knave on more than one occasion and if he can cross his brother, do you really believe he will not betray an English king, without so much as a second's hesitation?'

Bella looked hard at her mother. 'It is well known that Dafydd is never satisfied with any lands or titles he has gained from either side.' She paused for a moment. 'Oh! Mama, I had hoped that when the time came for Richard to take full responsibility of his earldom, the Welsh wars would be over. Your words have aroused a great fear in me; I could not bear to lose Richard, he is my life.'

'I know my dear, but war, wherever it may be, is the destiny of many of our men, be they young or old. Your father is aging and no longer has the stamina he once had – although he would die rather than admit as much! The future lies with the generations of Edmund and Richard, our roles are as they have always been, to support, love and tend them.'

Bella nodded. 'And pray for them! I will have Masses said at Haughmond Abbey not only for the soul of John but, also for the safety of Richard and the Mortimer family.'

'I gain great comfort from the fact that even when faced by great adversity, as a family we have always managed to stand as a united front.'

Bella nodded she knew her mother was referring not only to the awkward relationship between her brother Edmund and his father, but also the wayward character of her brother, Roger.

As the Mortimer family travelled back to Wigmore, Roger informed his wife about the conversation he had had with Robert Burnell. Edward wished to have a record of all the land boundaries, families, the occupations of every man woman and child throughout his kingdom. For decades land disputes had strangled the courts and if William the Conqueror had discovered the wealth of his subjects in the book which had become known as *The Domesday Book,* Edward was going to be even more thorough and record every stick, cow, calf, hen, goose and duck, that was in the land and the name of who they belonged to, and the exact boundaries of every farm, wood, ridge and furrow.'

'The undertaking will be considerable but maybe, it will alleviate many hours every noble house has to sit judgement on each year. Although Burnell has given Edward the credit for such a venture, I can see his hand guiding the king's thinking in this!'

Mortimer nodded. 'One thing Edward has that his father never understood, was having the right men as advisors, and the right men to trust. A loyal friend but, a deadly enemy and that in a king, is exactly what England needed. The future looks full of change but let us hope it is for the good.'

The year 1279 saw Edward's commissioners begin the mammoth task of recording the boundaries of very Shire in the land. Also, during that same year, he had the mint begin to stamp new coins to replace the clipped ones which had also been the cause of so much contention and trials, especially implicating many of the Jewish moneylenders which had featured heavily during that period. It was an open secret, the king's mother, Eleanor of Provence, wished her son to banish the Jews.

At Wigmore, even though there was no outright war in Wales, there were many men still required to guard the stone masons and artisans who were busy building Edward's string of stone castles. It had not stopped the isolated incident of aggression or, the silent flurry of arrows that frequently claimed the lives of the unarmed builders and kept the forces of Roger Mortimer and the Marcher barons busy during the spring and summer of the year.

In late summer Edmund Plantagenet summoned Mortimer to Kenilworth and asked him to arrange a great tournament and pageant in celebration, and the theme was to be, the Arthurian legends of the Round Table. Mortimer, delighted at being singled out for the honour, turned to his wife for inspiration and together they organized what was to be one of the greatest spectacles of the decade. A time for all the nobles to gather in costumes of outstanding magnificence and splendour.

As the day dawned, Mortimer had made his mind up to announce his retirement from active service, a decision which had caused Maud some surprise. As the clarions blared as the contestants entered the arena; wagers were made, and for three days the king, his queen, closest friends and advisors, watched the daily performances. In the evenings, the feasting was enjoyed by the gallant knights and their ladies and the appreciative audience. In the final ceremony Edmund's beautiful wife, Blanche of Artois, with her little daughter who was the of the Queen of Navarre, handed Sir Roger Mortimer a silver horn filled with gold and silver in appreciation for his efforts in organising such a spectacular event.

The days which followed saw Mortimer and his wife bask in their success as they travelled back to Wigmore. Their joy however, would be short lived, but the memory would remain and talked about for the rest of their lives. The occasion had been momentous for their grandson, Richard FitzAlan, who had been among the youngest of the combatants and had covered himself in glory. Edmund, their eldest son, had also attended and had acted as a marshal, together with his brothers, Roger, Geoffrey and William.

After the event, Edmund returned to the Marches, not directly to Wigmore but to Oswestry to aid his sister at a time when her trusted Constable had suffered an injury, which although was not life threatening, did mean he would be incapacitated for some months. His arrival had proved a great change for young Richard, who began to dog Edmund's every move and was happy to emulate his uncle.

Since Edmund's return from Oxford, he had gained a reputation as a fit and skilled knight who had quickly proved to the Oswestry garrison, his ability as a leader of men. The Constable, although bound to his bed for awhile, was able to advise Edmund and the two worked together their objective, to keep the castle and its occupants safe from any sudden attacks. The experience of the injured Constable was invaluable through this period especially on tactics, and by using the right men to carry out the various scouting duties. It was just the grounding Edmund needed, and his judgement and innate abilities, made him both popular and respected by those he commanded.

Maud had also noted the change in his physique and demeanour at Kenilworth; her son was no longer a cleric, but a knight of authority and purpose. However, if the Lady of Wigmore held any hope for a lasting period of stability her husband was about to shatter that in a manner which would alter their relationship forever.

In late October, Roger Mortimer rode into Wales at the head of a small but heavily armed contingent of men their mission, to relieve Builth Castle. On his return journey, he encountered a young woman who it was obvious had walked many miles. She begged to be taken to the commander and what she told him caused him to ride back with her to a small village he had stayed at some six years before. In the back room of the Inn, lay a young woman, obviously labouring to breath with the pallor of death on her once pretty face. Beside her sat a little girl with thick tousled hair, a sharp pointed chin, and eyes as black as coals. The woman who had begged his aid now spoke quietly.

'Kate, is this the one?'

Unable to speak, the gasping figure nodded.

'Sir, you can see for yourself the situation here. The girl is not expected to live through the night and her only wish is to see her daughter is cared for. I have a family and my husband refuses to take the child. This is a poor village and we all struggle to survive; an extra mouth can mean the difference between life and death for all.' She paused to watch the reaction of the nobleman.

'Kate swears the girl is the daughter of a commander of a Mortimer company who stayed here six years since. All she wants is to die knowing she has secured the future of the child.'

Mortimer stood for sometime in the fetid air of the cramped room. His expression was stern and serious. He remained motionless for some moments before he spoke.

'Your friend has indeed proved true and the coincidence of our meeting has not gone in vain.' He paused before continuing. 'I came here during that time and indeed, enjoyed the favours of a pretty girl who, it appears has fallen on hard times.' He bent towards the pale faced figure. 'Have no fear Kate, I will take the child and raise her as my own.'

He turned his gaze on the seated child.

'Pray what is your name?'

The dark eyes were full of tears.

'Answer his lordship. I haven't walked the soles of my shoes off for you to play dumb; you usually have more than enough to say for yourself.'

'Iseult.'

'Most would pronounce it Isolde.'

Their conversation was interrupted by the struggles of the dying woman. She reached up to Mortimer and made the sign of the cross then slumped back dead.

Her friend covered her face and pulled the girl to her feet. 'You must go with his lordship. I will take care of your Mama. Now go!'

Mortimer reached into his pocket and drew out a number of silver coins.

'See she is buried in the churchyard and have masses said for her soul. If you do this, I will ensure your village will not suffer further poverty – do you understand?'

Bess Tucker could only nod her head, she was overcome with emotion; relief she had found the father of Kate's child, who had accepted without a word, the paternity of Iseult. Later, when she had time to reflect on the events of that night, she could see why the Lord of Wigmore had acknowledged his bastard daughter; the dark mass of unruly hair, the black eyes the and the way the child held her head she had undoubtedly inherited those from her sire.

'Come! We have a long way to ride before we can sleep.'

The child went to the bed and held the hand of her dead mother for a moment then turned and followed the powerful figure of her father out into the night. He mounted his great horse and his squire lifted Iseult up and placed her at the front of the high pommel. Without further speech Mortimer rode away into the gloom knowing that this child would cause consternation to his wife and family. The rest of the journey was made in virtual silence with only the child's piping requests to relieve her-self, punctuating the long ride.

During the late morning the company of riders had been spotted by Maud, who informed both Bella, and Edmund, who had been visiting, to join her in greeting the return of the Lord of Wigmore. The scene which ensued, however, was one which would mar the lives of many at Wigmore for years to come.

Lowering the child into the arms of the waiting servant, Mortimer said loudly.

'Take my daughter to the nursery and see she is well cared for.' He dismounted before he strode into the castle leaving his family standing with looks of undisguised amazement on their faces. It was Maud who moved first and hastened after Mortimer's retreating figure.

'What do you mean? Your daughter?' Her voice was full of anger.

'Her name is Iseult or Isolde and I have brought her to be raised at Wigmore, due to the death of her mother.'

'I care not a jot what the wench's name is but the manner in which she arrived. Pray, why did you not send word? Surely even *you* must have realised what a sensation her arrival would be! Besides which, you have shamed me before my children and household.' Her green-grey eyes burned with fury.

'I swear you will rue this day for the rest of your life!' With that she turned on her heels and stormed out. Mortimer stood for a moment then called for a cup of wine and drank it down in a single gulp. The die was cast, the act was done, and they would all have to accept the fact however much they railed against it.

As Mortimer was left to ponder on events, Maud almost ran up to the nursery where she found the little girl standing in the centre of the room with a look of defiance etched all over her sharp face.

'No, I will not take a bath. You shall not take my clothes.'

'That is where you are mistaken miss, if you are to remain here at Wigmore, you will do as you are told! I am mistress here and anyone who disobeys me or disrupts the routine of my household, is punished severely – is that understood?' Maud turned to Carys, 'feed her, clothe her but, if she refuses anything then leave her naked and without further food until she does. Is that understood?'

Carys nodded she had never seen Maud in such a white hot fury. Maud turned to the girl again, 'do not try and oppose me or I will have you sent into a silent order of nuns far from here; is that understood?' Maud did not wait for a reply she walked swiftly back to her own chamber.

Bella knocked and entered, she could see her mother was still in a rage.

'I have expressed my disapproval to my father and Edmund is with him now, so have no doubt he will add his own feelings of ....'

Maud just raised her hand, 'I shall leave for Tetbury on the morrow and leave the *Lord of Wigmore* to deal with the daily problems.' The words were said in scathing, bitter tones. 'If he wishes to dishonour me then he will quickly learn he has taken on an adversary than can cut him down to size in a variety of ways.'

'Mama! Please don't distress yourself further by all means go to Tetbury until you feel ....'

'That's enough Bella, I am perfectly able to deal with this matter if I so choose but,' she paused, 'do I choose? Now, go and get acquainted with your new sister but show her she must be subservient or, be discarded by the Mortimer's and banished to a nunnery.' With that Maud turned her back on her daughter and walked to the casement to gaze with unseeing eyes at the familiar view.

Some time later Edmund entered and without a word went to where his mother stood and folded her into his arms.

'A fearsome storm over Wigmore.'

Maud remained for some minutes finding comfort in the warmth of her son's arms.

'I told him he had shown a serious lack of judgement in his handling of the situation which has severely damaged your relationship.'

'And do you believe that will worry him over much?'

Edmund sensed her fury was a-baiting.

'Maybe not right now, but he will have cause to remember in times ahead. When he comes to realise the loyalty everyone has for you, that you are the one to whom they come when they need help, for he is so frequently away in Wales or at court, his estates are mainly administered by you, and then he will feel the cold wind of disapproval begin to bite.'

'That comforts me somewhat. Although at this moment I could happily strangle the pair of them.'

Edmund bent and kissed her brow. 'Your humour returns. Little Maudie's comments may amuse you! She asked if grandfather had to buy another daughter, why he had he not purchased a cleaner one!'

Maud gave a wry smile. 'Well children often speak the simple truth.'

She reached up and kissed Edmund's cheek.

'Now I will go and pray for God's forgiveness in losing my temper and for strength to deal with our 'little problem' in the future.'

She turned at the door. 'I shall leave for Tetbury on the morrow; let your father deal with the commissioners and his new offspring, see how he enjoys the disruption.'

CHAPTER XXIX

Wigmore

It was a week before the start of Advent when Maud returned to Wigmore; there had been a rush of activity to get the place cleaned and in order for her arrival. On the first morning she sent Errol to collect reports from all quarters of the castle to learn of their progress but, it was to Carys she paid her first visit of the day to hear details of how the 'new arrival' had been behaving since her departure.

'All I can truthfully say is she pushes the boundaries of obedience to their limits without actually stepping beyond them. Her manner is sullen and belligerent although, the tutor did state she has a quick intelligence when she chooses to use it! I am still waiting for this event to begin. She has now realised she is a Mortimer, and did for a time, try to adopt a haughty manner but was quickly brought down to earth and that is how things stand at this moment.' She paused then continued. 'She is a child that is not easy to even like but, I do believe she hides her grief and loneliness behind this shield of defiance.'

'Does his lordship visit her?'

Carys cleared her throat before answering.

'Only occasionally.'

'And what is their relationship like?'

'Stilted, awkward for both of them.'

'Mmm! I will speak with Master Farron and hear his views on her progress. Thank you Carys and, I am sorry you have been burdened with this problem.'

The Yuletide celebrations were not the usual easy going event of previous years. Bella and her son, together with Edmund, had declined the invitation on grounds of poor travelling conditions. This applied to her two younger sons, Geoffrey and William, only Roger was close enough to attend. However, although the tension between the Lord and Lady of Wigmore was obvious, one member of the household was transformed by the whole occasion– Isolde.

Maud had found an old kirtle of Bella's and asked Ela if she would cut it down and make one for Isolde. Unwittingly, Maud had brought together her reserved lady-in-waiting, and the rebellious little 'by blow', and marvelled at the transformation this request was to make on both Ela and Isolde. Whilst taking the girl's measurements, Ela had offered to style the mass of wayward hair and had, at first, been re-buffed but when she explained that having fine clothes and messy hair would spoil the effect, Isolde reluctantly allowed her to brush, comb and plait the thick braids. Slowly, the two began to talk to each other of all manner of things and over a few weeks the little girl had opened her heart to Ela and to everyone's surprise, the normally quiet lady-in-waiting had unwittingly, discovered the key to the heart of the lonely child.

During one the fittings for the garment, Maud whispered to Carys: 'an odd pairing but, maybe Ela has found the child she may have wished for!'

'Let us hope this is the beginning of better things for all our sakes!'

'Amen to that!' Maud smiled and patted Cary's arm.

When Ela lead Isolde into the Great Hall that Christmas, the wonder and excitement the child felt was plain to see for it was etched all over her face. The jesters ran around causing their usual mayhem. Minstrels strummed their lutes and sang songs of happiness and joy, and the smell of the food, which filled the tables, was quite simply, mouth watering. All around the walls there were boughs of holly and ivy and some of the bunting saved from the Kenilworth tournament, lit by so many candles. it set the scene ablaze with light.

'Oh! Ela, I have never seen such a beautiful sight.' Isolde's eyes widened when her gaze fell on the heaving table of food and for the first time since her arrival, she clapped her hands and the pale, sharp face, was softened by a beaming smile. Ela took her to where her father sat at the head of the table and with a mock expression of amazement, he opened his arms and said; 'My, who is this vision of happiness, pray?'

'It is only me, Papa!'

Eyes turned to see the expression on Lady Mortimer's face but she sat straight backed betraying nothing of her inner emotions. Then she clapped her hands for the attention of the company; 'Everyone, pray take you places and we will say Grace before partaking of this delicious feast.' Everyone obeyed and took their allotted place and in unison said Grace – and then the Christmastide feasting began in earnest.

Maud was glad to sit back and let everyone enjoy the evening's entertainment but she did note the frequent summons for wine made by her husband. Their personal estrangement did not extend to public appearances but their last conversation before her departure to Tetbury had left Mortimer in no doubt that should he try and bestow a single perch or rood of land to Isolde from the Marshal estates, she would personally sue him and bring the name of Mortimer into disrepute. The Lord of Wigmore had been left in no doubt that even when Maud's rage cooled, she would never accept the child.

The twelve days of celebrations quickly passed and the harsh winter winds brought heavy snows, which held all but the most foolhardy close to their homes. At night, the haunting, howling of hunting wolves could be heard, causing the efforts of shepherds and stockmen to be doubled in guarding their flocks and herds from attacks. As the weather had curtailed any travellers or messengers, time at Wigmore was spent in a variety of activities. Squires were kept busy practising their sword and fighting skills, punctuated by dancing lessons and courtly etiquette. Young grooms, cleared a series of circles and laid straw to enable the senior grooms to lunge the many great destriers and chargers in their care. The kitchens were kept busy being inventive in making the rations extend as far as possible, until the thaw came. The womenfolk, spun, wove or, sewed, whilst Ela taught her protégé how to make fine clothes.

It was a time when all the broken harness and saddles were stitched and mended; weapons sharpened, chainmail re-furbished and new swords and blades forged. If the weather held the occupants of Wigmore as tight as prisoners, it certainly did not imprison their skills.

By the time the first thaw began the knights, squires and troops were all well equipped for any eventuality. It was good to see the first wagon full of provisions rumble into the castle grounds and messengers from all directions began to arrive. Life was once more beginning to return to a more normal pattern and the promise of spring, lifted the spirits of one and all.

During the year the Mortimer's were kept busy with matters relating to the new legal commissioners compiling the Hundred Roll. Maud visited Bella as soon as the roads were deemed fit enough, and was relieved to be re-united with her daughter, son, grandson and granddaughter. Bella was full of questions about Isolde, and promised to visit in late spring.

It was also decided that Edmund should return to Wigmore with his mother as Elwyn, the Constable, although lame, was now strong enough and mobile enough to resume his full duties. Maud felt a sense of relief, she hoped with Edmund's presence it would help ease the strained relationship between herself and her husband. She had not failed to note how much Richard had grown during the past months and how he shadowed his uncle's every move. Edmund had spent time discussing many of the issues of the day with him and selecting books he knew would be of benefit to his education.

'Edmund will make a good father one day.' Bella looked across at her mother as she spoke.

'Yes, but somehow I do not think the time is quite right given the circumstances. I cannot explain why I feel like this, but I do! Maybe the family is a little at odds just now and it would hardly be fair to bring in a stranger which could confuse matters. Besides, Edmund strives for his father's approval but the shadow of Ralph is ever present I fear.'

Bella's smile had a trace of wistfulness. 'Well, I am just glad that Richard is not losing out on not having a father to guide him at this important period in his life, and there is no-one I trust more than Edmund. He is so patient and even tempered. I often wonder which side of the family that comes from!'

Maud looked thoughtful as she replied: 'his great grandsire, William Marshal, is my belief. Look how he negotiated his way through a turbulent life and the reigns of five of the most diverse characters of their age, and still rose to prominence. I would say that took a level head, cool courage, and a velvet tongue.'

Bella sighed. 'You may well be right. All I hope is that Richard has inherited some of those attributes.'

Maud grinned mischievously, 'be grateful he has not inherited my temper.'

Bella reached and squeezed her mother's hand; 'maybe not her temper, but her courage.'

When Maud returned to Wigmore she was accompanied by her son, and grandson. The March winds tugged at their cloaks and blew into their faces, making it a very unpleasant journey. Speech was nigh impossible as the words were snatch from the lips and lost in the howl of the wind. It took skilled horsemanship to steady fractious mounts as they shied and sidled as a variety of objects were blown around them as they rode.

Upon Edmund's return, the Lord of Wigmore showed him far more deference than either Maud, or her son expected. Maybe it had been Richard's outpourings of praise that had stemmed any scathing comments by the senior member of the Mortimer family.

As the first days of May arrived, following a showery April, so did Bella with her daughter, Maudie and their timing was quite propitious for Meg had also made the journey from Hedingham, on a rare visit. It was the first time the two sisters had been together informally since Meg's marriage. Maud was overjoyed at having her beloved daughters at Wigmore again and the family reminiscences frequently found them laughing and teasing one another in the ensuing days.

However, one member of the household was not at all pleased by the intrusion, Isolde. Her first introduction to Bella's daughter, Maudie, had been quite an awkward one.

'So, Mistress Carys, is this my grandsire's bastard?' Maudie's voice held no spite, merely an inquisitive note. The statement caused Isolde to rush headlong at the speaker who neatly side stepped the onslaught, putting her foot out, deftly tripping her attacker.

'My, what a fuss; surely you must know that is what people refer to you as?' Maudie went and bent over the prone figure and offered her hand.

'Oh! Come now, it was said without rancour – besides, you must not let anyone show how such words affect you, it would be seen as a sign of weakness and used to taunt you! Let me help you up, you are a Mortimer now, and I do believe my step aunt, is that not amusing, as you must be younger than me?'

For an instant Isolde remained where she had fallen and glared angrily up at the speaker.

'Then if I am as you say, your something aunt, you should show me more respect!' Suddenly the two girls laughed and Isolde took the proffered hand.

When Carys recounted the incident to Maud appeared satisfied at the outcome of the girls first encounter.

'Well at least it demonstrates Maudie is no snob, and feel heartened by her attitude towards the newcomer.'

'Children find their own level, all we can do is discover their strengths and weaknesses and try and help them overcome any shortcomings.'

Maud nodded her agreement, 'and what do you make of Meg?'

Carys looked thoughtful at the unexpected question. 'From my first impressions, I believe, she feels somehow failing in her duty by her frequent miscarriages. Poor Meg, I fear she has not inherited the Mortimer thick skin, or her mother's constitution.'

'She was ever the more sensitive soul, and de Vere is no easy character to live with, by all accounts.' She paused: 'but I would know your opinion, of our young *'cuckoo'*?'

Carys bustled about the nursery before she replied.

'Oh! I think that one is a tough little nut but, she is still feeling vulnerable as yet! Meg on the other hand will never be as resilient as you have been my lady. Maybe we should try and build up her strength whilst she is here, and also persuade her that she should not feel she has failed in any way by not having a baby, yet! If the mind is uneasy it often has a detrimental effect on the body in my experience.'

'I think you could be right but it cannot be easy when you have a husband as serious and dominant as de Vere!'

Maud looked at the speaker intently as she spoke.

'I hope he is kind to Meg, for if ever I discovered otherwise ....' She did not finish her sentence but Carys knew that Robert de Vere, would experience the full force of Maud's anger should that be the case.

'I do not think he is cruel, merely pedantic on every level. If gossip is to be believed, he does not invite friendship too easily.'

'Maybe Meg feels isolated, this is the first time she has ever visited Wigmore since her marriage. He probably feels her place is at his side at all times. Heavens! What a stifling relationship if that is the case.'

Maud made sure she acted upon the advice of her trusted servant and was insistent that Meg should have a full health check during her stay. The physician had prescribed a remedy of herbs and root extracts, and insisted they should be taken each night and morning for a week, to see what effect it would have on her health. Although it caused Meg to wrinkle her nose when taking the prescription, she followed the instructions to the letter and by the seventh day it was obvious there had been a great improvement; the colour had returned to her cheeks and she was far more energetic than when she had first arrived. She no longer had to seek her bed by mid evening but remained to talk and sew with her sister Bella, her mother, Ela and Carys.

The visit of Bella and her daughter came to an end far too quickly for all the Mortimer women, and when Maudie asked if Isolde could return with them to Oswestry, it was agreed as the two girls had discovered a new found friendship. Besides, Maudie could hardly believe that Isolde had never learned to ride and promised to teach her on her own pony. Maud also agreed to allow Ela to accompany her young protégé, helping to maintain their bond.

As the party rode through the gateway of Wigmore Castle, Maud sighed as she waved them goodbye. She turned to Meg, 'and now young lady, we shall enjoy the rest of your stay undisturbed. I promise to spoil you utterly.'

Meg laughed nervously. 'Well, I really feel I also should return to Hedingham.'

'Oh not for a few weeks yet, methinks! Too many miscarriages are harmful for both you and any future pregnancies; you need to continue to re-build your strength before returning to your marriage bed. We will visit a little church close by, and the stream that runs at its boundary is reputed to have healing properties. It can do no harm, now can it? Besides, we have never had any time alone before, and I should like you to stay, if not for your sake, then mine.'

Meg looked surprised. 'What can I do for you Mama, when I am unable to help myself?' Her daughter's note of uncertainty did not go unnoticed by Maud.

'You can help me by just sharing these precious days together. I have felt at odds with your father since the arrival of Isolde. I admit, it is not easy to find myself living under the same roof under such circumstances. But .... I am not about to forgive his behaviour or, the manner he brought the child to Wigmore.'

Meg looked shyly at her formidable mother. 'Are we not obliged to honour and obey our husband's?'

'If they honour us! And there was no honour shown to me, in the manner of her arrival. If only he had sent word ahead, I could have.....' she waved her hand. 'It is too late to dwell on the matter now for what is done is done but, just because we are married, it does mean we lose our own self respect. Husbands are not entitled to take that away from us whatever the circumstances, and if we do not respect ourselves, then how can we be expected to hold the respect of others?'

Meg looked down at the floor, not wanting her mother to see her expression as she absorbed the full meaning of her mother's impassioned statement.

'I do not possess your cleverness, or strength of character Mama.'

'Rubbish girl! You are the great-granddaughter of William Marshal; you are related to some of the most important nobles in England, so you should neither bow your head or your will, without a perfectly good reason! Men can try and impose too much control over their wives but...' she hesitated, 'only if they are allowed to do so! Can you understand what I am trying to make clear to you Meg?' Maud knew her word had unnerved her daughter.

'Your husband has a reputation for being taciturn and humourless, and I am not suggesting you openly defy him but, there are ways of making yourself less subservient without causing a confrontation. Use your guile, you mean a great deal to me, and I will not meekly stand by and see your future well being, trampled by *any* man. Promise me you will at least try and find a way to assert yourself more in your marriage.'

Meg nodded, but would not meet her mother's intense gaze. Maud reached out and took Meg's hand and squeezed it; imagine how I would deal with him and see if that helps.'

A nervous smile crept across Meg's face. 'Like you did with my brother Roger, when he used to tease Bella and me?'

'Yes, but suggest you omit boxing de Vere's ears.'

The two women laughed and Maud knew her daughter understood her concerns but whether she would act on it may be another matter. The rest of the visit was spent in pleasant banter and pastimes, and Maud felt happier now she saw how Meg had finally been able to relax.

On the morning of her departure Maud noted the slight frown which played on Meg's face.

'Remember my advice, do not forego your Marshal forbears and do not allow yourself to be browbeaten, especially by your husband.' Her words were whispered.

'I shall miss you so much Mama. This visit has been the happiest time I have known for years and to spend time with Bella and Edmund is a memory I shall treasure always.'

'May God go with you my dearest child, and remember, you are always in my prayers.'

Maud knew it would be many months, if ever, before she would see her daughter again. The number of miscarriages Meg had experienced over the past few years did not bode well for any future pregnancies, and had definitely proved detrimental to her health. As she turned back into the castle her thoughts were heavy but Maud threw herself into the pressing matters of the day and tried to suppress her growing feelings of foreboding.

The days passed quickly and Maud was frequently left to deal with the issues of the numerous estates as her husband and Edmund, were kept busy at court. She was alarmed by the growing list of complaints against her son, Roger, whose aggressive actions caused a great deal of bad feeling in the district. She had hoped his marriage to Lucy le Wafre, would have had a calming influence but this sadly, did not appear to have been the case. Maud mused over the thoughts of her daughter-in-law; Roger had never shown any signs of tenderness or kindness, even as a child, but this lack of emotion as a husband, did not bode well for his wife.

Maud made a mental note that she would visit Lucy as soon as she was free in an effort to try and discover more about her son and his disreputable behaviour. She was determined to discover whether Lucy was also a victim of her son's more violent excesses. Adulthood had not brought about any of the hoped for changes to her problem son. He was fast gaining the reputation her father once held, and the thought disturbed Maud more than she wished to admit – even to herself.

As she went about her never ending duties, Maud pondered on how many of her family she was concerns for, but the one closest to her at present, was of course Isolde, and although the visit to Oswestry had certainly had a profound affect; to make a lady from the wayward child, was never going to be an easy task. Thankfully, the relationship which had grown between Ela and the little girl was bearing fruit and Maud was willing to overlook many of her shortcomings, if she now applied herself to her lessons.

There was a glimmer of light in her education which began to emerge when Isolde was allowed to watch the dancing lessons Maud took two afternoons a week for the young squires. Where music was involved, Isolde would be drawn like a moth to a flame. Musicians frequently found her hiding as they practiced and whenever she had a chance, she would pick up and pluck the strings of an abandoned lute or harp, only to be chased away upon the return of its owner.

It was Ela who brought Isolde's interest in music to Maud's attention and upon this observation she invited the girl to join in the next dancing lesson. It was obvious by the delighted expression on the child's face from the onset, that this had been an inspired move. At first, some of the squires, who felt awkward and self conscious, voiced their objections that their efforts were being watched by an outsider, but Maud quickly dismissed their complaints and let Isolde clap in time to the music. Slowly, she began to include her and showed her the steps to one of the slower dances. It was easy to see Isolde had an ear for the music, as she quickly picked up the tunes and also the graceful movements of the dance. Soon, the whole company joined in the clapping and teased each others' efforts when they made mistakes. After one of the lessons ended, the squires all applauded Isolde's achievements and their former objection evaporated. The 'dancing days' were the highlight of the girl's week and Maud promised to have a small lute made for her name-day present. She was heartened to see the delight her words had had on her protégé.

The year moved inexorably through the seasons with all its trials and tribulations that entailed. A fever ran through the village just as the harvest ripened, leaving those unaffected to work even harder than usual to get the grain and straw in before the weather broke. The troubles only worsened when a murrain infected some of the best cattle and Maud knew this would mean extra expense buying in the shortfall beef for the winter.

Yuletide that year was a more restrained affair than normal as there had been a number of deaths, which included many of the servants. Only Isolde seemed oblivious and practiced for hours on her miniature lute. One of the travelling musicians had taught her the basic notes and it was not long before she could play a tune without faltering. Ela was also teaching her needlecraft as Maud had never conquered the art. Few in the household had any premonition of how life was about to change for the Mortimer family and those that shared their lives. Only the Lady of Wigmore, who had long held a niggling fear, was not wholly surprised when Fate once more took a hand in the events of the Marches.

CHAPTER XXX

1282 Wigmore

As the fierce March winds began to ease and the promise of spring filled the air, a hard riding messenger galloped through the gates of Wigmore Castle. The news he brought was about to set the Marches alight once more as the Welsh had begun to attack the castles occupied by Edward's troops.

Sir Roger Mortimer heard the commotion as he poured over the new boundary maps; he paused and waited for the breathless messenger to be shown to his study. Without preamble he thrust the crumpled scroll forward as he dropped to one knee.

'My Lord, it is Dafydd ap Gruffydd, he has attacked Harwarden Castle in Flint. Lord Clifford has been captured; his life spared, but many were slain. Wales is marching to war again.'

'God's blood! Is it only Dafydd that has broken the Treaty?'

'My intelligence is that Flint and Rhuddlan were also attacked; as yet the fate of their commanders is unknown.' He looked nervously at the glowering features of the Lord of Wigmore.

'Oswestry has also been hit hard my lord so too, Ystrad and Englefield.'

No-one heard Maud enter, but she knew immediately from the expression on her husband's face the news was dire. When he told her of the attacks her first thoughts were for Bella.

'Is Bella still at Oswestry?'

'Aye my lady, but Lord LeStrange had wind of the rising and sent more men to relieve the castle; I believe her ladyship has been taken to safety.'

Without speaking she moved to the table and fingered the discarded maps. She remembered the words of Lord Rhys, who had long held the belief that – Dafydd would eventually be the cause of Llywelyn's downfall. However, she kept such thoughts to herself.

'Has Llywelyn featured in this uprising?' She turned to look at the messenger who had risen to his feet.

'Nothing is clear my lady, no-one is sure who has remained loyal to the king and who are among the attackers.'

'Where is the king presently?' Mortimer began to pace in his agitation.

'Sir, I am not certain, I have ridden from Shrewsbury and brought the news from Wrexham, exactly where the king is now, I cannot say for certain'

'Right, you go and get refreshments; do you have further to go?'

'Aye, my lord, Hereford but will need a fresh mount.'

The following morning Sir Roger and his son, Edmund, with a well armed company of troops, rode towards Chester. A few days later Maud learned that Aberystwyth Castle had also been attacked with much bloodshed. Rumours began to run like wildfires throughout the March and what Maud could deduce, was that the heavy handed tactics of the king's officials, had prompted the uprising. However, she had no way of knowing if this was the truth or, just excuses for the Welsh to lay blame elsewhere.

It was still not clear whether Llywelyn had in fact joined his brother or indeed, if the attacks had been instigated by him. What she did learn was that Eleanor de Montfort, Llywelyn's wife, was expecting their first child in June; this piece of news, she felt may hold the key. Would a man who had always shown a shrewd grasp of his position put both his wife and his nation at risk at such an important moment in his life? Llywelyn had been willing to lose much to gain his bride – therefore, would he have freely called for the onset of hostilities just at such a time in his life? Maud struggled with her doubts and could not dismiss the thought that it had been his younger brother who had made this unexpected move to war.

Lord Rhys had always voiced his condemnation of Dafydd's lack of loyalty to Llywelyn but, the fact was that however many times he had proved treacherous; the bond of brotherhood had proved stronger in the older man. How could Llywelyn have forgiven Dafydd's plot to murder him? This had been an irrefutable act of perfidy only averted by a heavy snow storm, which had saved him from an assassin's blade. What right minded man would forgive such a terrible sin? One thing Maud felt deeply was that Dafydd was playing a very cunning game of his own. It may prove beneficial to the king, but deadly to the Welshman who was styled, the Prince of Wales. Whatever the truth of the matter, all she could do was to ensure that Wigmore and the castles closest to her, were well provisions and guarded. The thin trickle of wounded had already begun to return and so the days were busy and each night, when Maud and her women gathered for an hour before bedtime, they would all give an account of their day's activities.

It was a few months later when the Lord of Wigmore returned for a brief respite. Maud noted how weary he looked, she felt it was ironic that the king had ignored Mortimer's so called retirement but she made no comment it would not help to make him aware of either fact at this point. Their relationship had, over the months, eased somewhat.

As he sat sipping a cup of wine, Mortimer glanced up at his wife.

'Well - you were right about Edmund!' He looked to see his if his wife's expression had changed but felt cheated that she did not even hesitate from her task of folding bandages.

'He has already earned the respect of the men and the regard of the king, and his advisors.'

Maud still made no comment.

'I thought you would crow in triumph!'

'My faith in Edmund has never wavered; he has the wit many lack, so why should I crow pray?'

'By God's breath, you are the most infuriating woman!'

A smile flickered at the corners of her mouth.

'You should not upset yourself; surely it is good news, is it not?'

Mortimer downed the rest of the wine, rose and stormed out of the chamber. He had failed to provoke his wife into any sort of retaliation and that he felt, was a victory for her. During the evening meal Maud turned to her husband; 'I thought you would have gone to see Isolde before now!'

He looked up from his trencher and glowered at her.

'She was at her lessons.'

'I'm sure Master Fenton would not have minded a short interlude.'

Mortimer felt discomforted at her words, when Maud chose to, she could always knock him off guard, especially in the game of words.

'As long as she is well and cared for, I do not see any pressing reason to see her.'

Maud looked hard at him. 'The child needs to know that you are interested in her; she lost everything when her mother died and was whisked away into a life and surroundings totally alien to her. Surely, even you can appreciate that!'

Mortimer grunted. 'Wenches, they are the bane of men's lives from the moment they draw their first breath until they breath their last.'

'Come now my lord, you have little to complain about for it was a '*wench*' was it not, who brought a great deal of wealth and estates to the coffers of the Mortimer family and is a '*wench*' who has stood at your side through all the adversities of life?'

'Aye, but not without its consequences. Remember you are the daughter of a felon hanged for............' His words were cut short as Maud picked up a jug and hurled it at his head.

'How dare you!' The jug just missed its mark and clattered to the floor; a servant rushed forward to mop up the mess.

'You can hardly condemn my father for doing what almost everyman does, take his pleasures where he pleases. The child in the nursery is a living example of *one* your indiscretions, heaven alone knows how many more of your bastards roam the earth.'

'Ha! So, this is what it is all about, your peevish jealousies.'

'Never! But I will not meekly stand by and listen to you malign my father for acts you are also guilty of! I could have easily had your little bastard disposed of but saw no reason to punish the child when she was merely the result of your fornication. She will be raised as a 'lady' but be assured, when she is of an age to understand, will be told about the sin of adultery.' Without another word Maud rose and stalked out of the chamber.

'By all the Saints and Martyrs in heaven, I have never known a more contrary woman in my life!' He reached for the wine and drank the contents of his cup down in one; then rose and went to his own chamber.

Later that evening however, Roger Mortimer did make his way to the nursery to spend time with Isolde. She happily showed him her needlework and chattered on about her dancing lessons with the youngest squires, as the older ones had gone to join in the wars in Wales. She ended the visit by proudly demonstrating her prowess, by playing him a pretty tune on her lute.

A few days later Bella arrived; Maud noted the air of distraction and knew there was something bothering her daughter and she was not left pondering for long. After the greetings were over Maud invited Bella to her chamber intent of discovering what was at the root of the worried expression which was so out of keeping with Bella's normal demeanour.

'Mama!' Bella hesitated and began pacing around the chamber liked a caged cat. She stopped and searched for the words to continue: 'would I be deemed a coward if I handed the responsibility for my authority in the March to Edmund?' She looked anxiously at her mother.

'Why? What has brought this about?' Maud moved to stand in front of her daughter as she reached for her hand.

'I .....I just do not wish to shoulder the responsibility anymore. I am........tired – so tired. Every day brings no respite and .... and... I awoke one morning and could no longer visualise John's face.' She bowed her head and wept softly.

'Come now!' Maud put her arms round her daughter. 'No-one can ever accuse you of being a coward. You have proved over the years the courage and fortitude lacking in many men. I think you need to speak with your father and Edmund, no doubt they will advise you in the matter and as for feeling any betrayal towards John – it is merely nature's way of telling you your grieving is at an end.' She paused. 'Bella, it has been a decade since he died and I think it is time for you to embrace the future, not keep your emotions locked in the past.'

Bella gave a deep sigh of relief then hugged her mother. 'You will never know how long I have carried these fears; so many sleepless nights, so many stressful days.'

'Then put your fears aside and tell me what you propose to do in the future.'

Bella wiped her eyes as she moved towards the window; slowly she began to tell Maud of her dilemma.

'I have received complaints about how the Arundel estates in the south are falling into wrack and ruin because there has been no overlord to maintain any real authority. From what I can glean from the many letters, there are some of the sheriffs taking revenues for themselves which are meant to maintain these lands. Richard will soon be old enough to take his place at the head of the house of Arundel and I would not wish him to feel I have been neglectful of his southern lands by focusing on the struggle in the Marches.'

Maud patted her hand: 'This sadly is what tends to happen when there is a woman left to fend for herself. You have had difficult decisions to make over the years and wars take up so much silver to maintain troops, lands, castles, there is no wonder there are rogues who have taken advantage of your situation and made merry at your expense. Your father and brother will understand your position.' She smiled wryly. 'I have recently had a spat with your father concerning the problems of 'wenches' as he dubbed us!'

'You and Papa were ever at odds about one thing or another but nevertheless, you work as a good team on all else but the personal level. Have you forgiven him and Isolde yet?'

'My grievance was never *with* the child but the manner in which she was brought here. I cannot say in all honesty that I have forgiven him on that score and think it will take a while longer before I can truthfully engage in the words of forgiveness. Believe me, I search my heart and conscience frequently but.........' she waved her hand. 'No doubt time will heal the hurt eventually. I know it is my pride which is the stumbling block but nevertheless, I have to remain true to my own conscience.'

Bella noted the rueful tone of her mother's voice.

During the evening meal Bella raised the subject which had plagued her mind for some months and was heartened at the understanding response from both her father and brother. She sat back and listened as they discussed the best plan of action regarding Oswestry and Clun, and all the Arundel lands which lay within the March. The sense of relief was such that she slept late the following morning.

A few days later the Lord of Wigmore and his eldest son rode through the gates of Wigmore heading once more to Wales and the conflict which continued to rage throughout that mountainous land. Maud and her daughter were left to enjoy a short sojourn before Bella, also made ready to leave. As mother and daughter embraced Bella said softly: 'I am sorry to go - this has been a short but beneficial visit. Once Edmund has sought permission from the king, I shall be free to return south and begin the process of reclaiming the control of those estates once more.' She looked into her mother's green-grey eyes. 'Do you think this war in Wales will ever end?'

Maud nodded: 'Yes, I do, one day! Llywelyn has been placed in an untenable position by the actions of his brother. Family loyalty can sometimes overrule personal decisions. Lord Rhys has always felt it would be Dafydd that would bring about the downfall of Llywelyn. Who knows, he may be proved right. All we can do is pray and continue our unstinting support for our men-folk.'

The days after Bella's departure Maud was kept busy but went each morning to her private chapel to pray for the safety of her family. Messengers began to arrive and although her husband's letters were somewhat garbled, she managed to grasp the gist of what he was trying to convey. The command of the king's army had been divided into three and he was head of the central force. Gilbert de Clare had caused an upset when he had demanded to take command of the south. She smiled as she read those words and could well imagine his reaction upon learning of young Gloucester's rash act. Poor Gilbert, he had never learned to control his temper or his pride, and it had lost him many friends through the years. She knew her husband's relationship with her kinsman was a difficult one and had been since their victory at Evesham. Now it seemed no-one was certain where Llywelyn was or, if indeed he was fighting on any front.

However, in late June a message arrived bearing the news that Llywelyn's wife, Eleanor de Montfort, had died soon after giving birth to a daughter. It answered the many questions as to the Prince of Wale's whereabouts; he would probably have stayed close to his wife during the final days of her pregnancy. Maud could not assuage her feeling of pity. Even though he was the sworn enemy of the Mortimer's, he shared their bloodline and such a devastating loss would have a great affect on the Welsh leader. Maud made the sign of the cross; was Eleanor's death the fatal blow which would finally bring about the end to this war? All she could do was pray and hope, but mused how the Fate of England and Wales had been so entwined with the de Montfort family over the decades.

Subsequent letters which arrived only detailed some of the hand to hand fighting and she was proud to learn that the bowmen trained at Wigmore, had proved to be a great asset in the campaign and had achieved many successes for her husband's command. In a far more lucid account sent by Edmund, she learned her kinsman, Gilbert de Clare, had been heavily defeated at a Battle near Llandeilo and had lost a great number of men, including the son of William de Valence, the Earl of Pembroke, who had subsequently been given the command of the south. Gilbert had left the field of conflict in high dudgeon but nevertheless, she could imagine his chagrin at his ignominious defeat.

Through the summer, the crops ripened and in early September the long scythes began the slow rhythmic task of cutting the corn. Horse drawn wagons filled with golden grain, arrived to fill the barns with the precious cereal. Women and children helped to stack the sheaves of straw to dry, ready to build the ricks for the winter. Fruit was picked and preserved; vegetables stored; and logs cut and brought into the fuel sheds, in readiness to feed the many fires of the castle, and its farms and cottages against the icy chills.

In early October, as Maud was inspecting the shelves of preserves, a messenger arrived bearing a letter with the familiar seal of her son, Edmund. She wiped her hands and began to roll down her sleeves when she noticed how agitated the young man was: 'What ails you? Pray take a sip of fruit juice it will ....'

But as she read the familiar hand of Edmund was soon struck by his words; Lord Mortimer has fallen ill and the field surgeon has advised his immediate removal back home. Maud looked at the messenger. 'Where is his lordship now?'

'They were preparing a litter to transport him back from the front line. Lord Edmund said he would send word as soon as they were sure Lord Mortimer was strong enough to travel.'

'It says illness not wounded - what manner of illness?'

'A virulent fever which has begun to affect his lungs, my lady.'

'You look done in, how far have you travelled today?'

'Nigh on fifteen leagues.'

'Mercy! Not on one horse I hope.'

He looked up: 'No your ladyship - I managed a change of horse some six leagues hence; the other mount was done and fear may never recover.'

Whatever the situation was with her husband she knew at this moment there was nothing she could do so, she did as she had done throughout her life, concentrated on matters she could have influence over.

'Take some refreshments, I will send a groom to collect your gallant steed and see if we cannot help the poor animal.'

He nodded and she could see by his face he was too filled with emotion. The crucial role of the messengers depended on their horses and it was only natural for them to develop a strong bond as often, it was only their swiftness that saved the lives of the riders who played a vital link, carrying news throughout the country.

Maud made for the study and found Arthur busily scratching away with his quill, piles of ledgers and scrolls were spread around him. Without any preamble Maud told him of the message she had received and asked him to write to Bella and Meg immediately but not phrased to alarm them. Arthur knew his mistress well and how best to serve her. She was never one for histrionics but always took the realistic actions to whatever situation arose. He was proud to have risen to become her chamberlain now that Lord Rhys was no longer well enough, as his health deteriorated with each passing day and it was only a matter of time before he passed into Eternity. Although Arthur knew he could never aspire to the special relationship that had existed between the Lady of Wigmore and the old Welshman, nevertheless he would always strive to serve the woman he most admired.

In the following days messages continued to arrive keeping her informed of the condition of her husband whose slow progress brought him ever closer to his family home. Until finally, she received one which stated that he had grown so weak they would have to stay at Kingsland; without hesitation Maud began to make arrangements to leave immediately. With a small, but well armed band of men, the Lady of Wigmore spurred her horse through the gates, thankful that their journey was not too far. Errol rode on her right hand side, and a squire to her left. Maud failed to notice the icy wind that whirled around their heads and tugged at their heavy riding cloaks, but she had noted Hal had laced a sheepskin to her saddle, which made for both warmth and comfort on that frantic journey.

Some hours later, the group arrived at Kingsland, horses, sweat streaked, their sides heaving, but all were still sound. Handing her reins to the groom Maud hurriedly made her way in through the studded door of Kingsland castle to be greeted by Edmund; his grim expression told her everything.

'I must warn you Mama, there is no hope – in fact the physician is confounded by his tenacious hold on life.'

'Your father has the constitution of an ox that is why!'

Maud followed her son into a darkened chamber where the rasping breathing was the only sound. There she found her husband propped up in bed; Rufus bending over him bathing his face. A look of total exhaustion was etched across his once handsome face.

'Go and rest I will see to him now!' She took the damp sponge from his grasp. 'When was the last time you slept Rufus?'

He shook his head and shrugged his shoulders. Edmund whispered: 'he has not left father's side since we arrived yesterday morning and has sat every night with him, on the journey.'

The physician stepped out of the shadows. 'I'm afraid the end is very near my lady. His hold on life is a strong one but no-one can deny the inevitable.'

Maud leaned over the prone figure: 'can you hear me Roger?' There was a gurgled choking cough. 'Maud?'

She reached and took his hand which was hot and clammy. 'Aye, my lord I am here now, so you can rest easy.'

With great difficulty he whispered: 'am.....I.....forgiven...... now?'

The effort left him panting; each breath was an agony, his face was contorted and a ghastly shade of grey.

She squeezed his hand gently. 'You have my forgiveness and my blessings, my lord.'

No longer able to speak he just nodded then a bout of dreadful coughing took hold. The physician indicated for Maud and Edmund to leave.

'His lungs are full of the bloody flux.'

Edmund grasped his mother's arm and led her from the chamber.

'I should stay with him!'

'No Mama, he is drowning in his own blood and would not wish you to witness such a scene. It is only God's indulgence that has saved him for your arrival.'

'He would not die without my forgiveness.'

For what seemed like an eternity the two stood silent both lost in their own thoughts when eventually the door opened and the physician came out his hands still covered in blood.

'I'm afraid Lord Mortimer has passed into God's domain now.'

Maud walked through the still open door and went and stood at the side of the bed.

She made the sign of the cross over the body then crossed herself, but she said not a word.

A shadowy figure moved towards the other side of the bed.

'I shall never meet your like again my lord, and am proud to have served a true Marcher knight. God give you eternal peace.'

Rufus stood, with tears coursing down his face.

'Oh! Rufus, you have been the most loyal friend and servant over the years and for that I thank you. Words are never enough on such occasions, what we carry in our hearts can only be known by God.'

She walked slowly round the bed and put her arms about the grieving man and they stood not moving for several minutes.

'We must make arrangements to return to Wigmore and inform the king of the passing of his most loyal servant.'

As Maud lay in her bed that night her thoughts ran backwards and forwards like a busy shuttle, remembering from the time she had first met Mortimer, until his final hours. A life so full, so crammed with memories, so many heartaches, so many emotions but one thing she did feel, was pride. She had done her duty by him, and done it with all of her strength and fortitude she possessed. Whatever happened next she could face the future with a clear conscience. In the darkness she prayed for his soul and for the courage to aid her son as he began his life as the Lord of Wigmore.

CHAPTER XXXI

Wigmore Abbey
Nov 1282

On an icy morning, the Abbey at Wigmore filled to capacity
with dignitaries and noblemen and women who had travelled
from far and wide in order to pay their final respects to the
Lord of Wigmore, Sir Roger Mortimer. Maud walked towards
the altar between her sons, Edmund and Roger closely followed
by their younger brothers who escorted their sisters. She noted
the tall figure of Edmund Plantagenet, the Earl of Lancaster,
the representative of the royal family.

The Requiem Mass was a long service but Maud remained
straight backed, with her face hidden by a fine black veil. She
could hear the sobs of her daughters but made no sound herself.
The eulogies were lavish and many, all extolling the virtues
of a man she knew in her heart, deserved the many words of
praise for his long service to the crown. When she and her
sons walked to stand by the coffin, she reached out to hold
Edmund's arm, the only outward sign of the great strain she
had felt since the death of her husband.

Finally the ordeal was over and the family and mourners
returned to Wigmore Castle. Still flanked by her sons, Maud
received the condolences with a set expression, merely nodding
and thanking each one as they moved passed her. It was only
when the royal Earl, stopped and clasped her hand did the
iron resolve falter.

'My brother sends his deepest sympathy. Your husband is
a great loss to all who knew and understood his true worth.
His courage was legendary, and his loyalty, unstinting. I am
proud to have called him friend.' He took her hands and

kissed each in turn and felt the tremor that ran through her. Maud could not speak and just inclined her head. Edmund and Roger dropped to one knee in deference.

'It is with regret I must leave almost immediately. I'm afraid the war does not wait and my brother is set on victory. Besides,' he indicated for the Mortimer brothers to rise: 'Giffard will need reinforcements I'll warrant, and you will be happy to learn that LeStrange appears to be gaining ground!'

Edmund spoke softly. 'We will return to the fight as swiftly as possible, my lord Earl.'

'You must ensure your mother is not left unprotected, Llywelyn may strike knowing that grief can often cause us to drop our guard.' He bowed, and the elegant Earl walked back to his waiting attendants.

Maud murmured: 'Do not fear for Wigmore, we have withstood too many raids not to have learned how to defend ourselves should the Welsh reach us. Your place is with your king and to avenge your father's death for, he died from a battlefield sickness brought about by the constant deprivations of war. Now, I have to comfort Bella and Meg, as they appear to be somewhat overwrought by the occasion'

As Maud moved away Roger looked at his brother. 'I swear our mother is cast in Toledo steel, as hard as any weapon made by man.'

Edmund just nodded. 'Let us hope we have inherited some of her strength.'

They both watched as Maud joined her daughters and saw her shake her head.

'Come; this is no way to mourn your father, you know how he hated tears.' She called for two cups of wine and insisted her daughters drank the intoxicating liquid. 'Now, straighten your backs, catch hold of your resolve, and mingle with the guests.'

Later that evening Maud left her guests and hurried to the nursery. Isolde was sitting on the floor rocking to and fro with Ela looking helplessly on.

'She has been like this all day, my lady.'

'Come Isolde, tell me what ails you?'

The defiant expression had returned.

'I won't go to a nunnery. I shall run away.'

'And why would you think you are bound for a nunnery, pray?'

The black eyes flashed a questioning look.

'But.........you.....now......my father is dead!'

'And you believe because your father is dead you will be banished to a nunnery?'

The child nodded.

'You are a Mortimer Isolde, and shall continue to live here until you are all grown up and we can find a good husband for you like all young noblewomen, that is what your father wanted and that is what will happen.'

'But why have both my mother and father died and left me alone?'

'That I cannot truly answer, we have to trust in God, the keeper of our Destiny, for only He knows how we feature in the great scheme of things.'

'But why is he always taking away my ......' she could not finish as she began to sob and weep violently.

Maud stooped and went to pick her up but was pushed away.

'Isolde, God has not abandoned you! Look around, you are not in a gutter, you are not forced into service, you have fine clothes, good food and a warm, comfortable bed and you have Ela, who loves you!'

The weeping began to subside slowly. 'And I will not be left again?'

'Ela will not leave and your home is here! It is up to you to make the best of your life and the chances it has given you. Besides, you don't see me weeping and wailing and your father was my husband of many years.'

The little girl raised her head and looked deep into Maud's eyes.

'But you *are* sad deep inside?'

Maud nodded. 'Your father was a brave knight who fought many battles. He served his king and country with honour and would wish you to work hard and become the fine young lady he knew you were capable of becoming; that is the legacy he left you. Now, be a brave girl and show us all you are truly the daughter of a great lord.'

For what seemed like a long time, Isolde remained motionless then; she suddenly stood up and faced Maud. 'Can Ela stay with me tonight?'

'Ela can stay with you all the time.' Maud looked across at Ela as she spoke and nodded. 'Now that is settled shall we try and help each other through these sad times?'

Maud drew Ela to one side. 'Carys is too old now to deal with a troublesome child on a daily basis and I think as the child appears to have given her affection to you it seems only sensible for you to be attached to the nursery from now on!'

Ela nodded. She would do anything her mistress wished for she never forgot the debt of gratitude she owed to the Lady of Wigmore. When Maud walked back to her own chamber that night she was exhausted. She had called for a hot tub and lay in the sweet smelling waters mulling over the events of the day and what the future may hold. One thing she was grateful for was that Edmund would now assume the lordship of Wigmore and once he had taken a wife then her role would become easier. But did she really want that? All her life she had been at the centre of conflict and wars; would a time of retirement really suit her? Although the years were beginning to quell her boundless energy, she could still ride a spirited horse, work all day at whatever task was to hand, true, she had gained a few aches and pains over the years but nothing that caused her too much stress. She mused as she soaked; she was like an old war horse who still charged round the paddock when he was passed his best and squealed and bucked when he saw the chargers going off to war. Well, for the time being at least, Edmund had no wife and therefore, her role would scarcely alter, she would remain Lady of Wigmore awhile longer! Comforted by such thoughts she stepped out of her bath, rubbed herself dry, and began to consider who would be her next waiting woman.

However, it was the continuing conflict in Wales which would take immediate precedence over her life. Just a few days later Edmund and Roger returned to re-join their men; Edmund sent word that English agents had discovered a plot to seize Radnor as it was a vital route used by the royalist troops to get provision through to reinforce those fighting in the central regions. Without delay Maud called for men and equipment to be made ready to strengthen the garrison at Radnor and on a whim, decided to take personal control by accompanying them. No amount of arguments would dissuade her from her resolve and within days she rode out at the head of contingent of well armed knights, squires, and bowmen.

The weather had turned icy and the trees looked as though they had been decorated in readiness for the approaching Yuletide but Maud was in no mood to appreciate the beauty of her surroundings. Even as they travelled they met a messenger bringing word of a terrible defeat at Moel-y-don, in Anglesey. Luke de Tany, had taken the decision to attack Llywelyn's fertile lands, their main source of cereals and forage, but they had been faced with strong resistance and a disastrous outcome ensued. Many of the English forces had been killed or drowned as the bridge had collapsed under the weight of the armoured knights. This catastrophe only hardened Maud's resolve that Radnor would not fall to her Welsh enemy. The Mortimer standard would be raised in defiance against her husband's lifelong enemy.

Upon arriving at the castle it was obvious that morale was at its lowest and Maud was all too aware that a disheartened force was an ineffective one. Fear, was a weapon which would aid their enemies and Maud, Errol and the new captain, set about bringing discipline back to the Mortimer stronghold. Tactics were the key, and every company of men was set a task which entailed hours of drilling. Archers, knights and squires, all practiced hard during the days. Destriers and chargers were schooled, leaving no-one time to even consider the possibility of defeat.

The one lesson Maud had learned from Lord Rhys, was to keep your agents busy gathering intelligence, in order to keep abreast of your enemy's movements. This she did to good effect during the weeks before Advent. Any useful information she received, she sent directly to Edmund so when an exhausted messenger arrived, bearing the momentous news which would affect each and everyone who lived and fought along the Marches; Llywelyn ap Gruffydd had been slain. Upon reading these words Maud sank to her knees and offered up a prayer of thanks. As she continued to read was elated to learn that her sons had been instrumental in bringing the Welsh Prince to his end.

However it had been accomplished Maud knew it would only enhance the reputation of her sons. The details she would learn later, the important thing now was to forward this news back to Wigmore. Edmund had sent Roger with Llywelyn's head to the king at Rhuddlan. The season's festivities would have a note of celebration after all.

However, fighting continued, as the role of Prince of Wales had been assumed by Dafydd ap Gruffydd, but Maud knew that he did not have the unquestioning loyalty of his troops, nor did he possess the shrewdness to use the tactics adopted over the years by his dead brother.

Through the long winter, Maud maintained her post at Radnor but by spring she left a revitalised garrison in the hands of the young, energetic Constable, named Roland, and returned to Wigmore. By June, the royalists had captured Dafydd and the rest of his army had either, surrendered or melted away to fight and harass the English forces wherever possible. Maud ordered a great feast to celebrate the return of her sons, and Wigmore resounded to voices filled with joy.

§

Edmund Mortimer stood looking out of the window of his mother's chamber; his face was set in a stern expression, as he gazed with unseeing eyes at the scene below.

'We both know Dafydd's execution will not bring the fighting to an immediate end.'

'No! But.......' his words trailed off before he turned and came to sit before his mother.

'Yesterday, in Shrewsbury, I witnessed the brutal torture and death of Dafydd ap Gruffydd, and through all of the barbarous cruelty, he uttered not a murmur.' He paused again and Maud could hear the emotion in his voice.

'For the space it took to torture and execute him, Dafydd truly deserved the title of Prince of Wales. Such a death will inspire others to seek revenge, if not in open warfare, then by stealth and surprise.' He reached across and took her hands.

'Roger and I were the ones to bring about the fall of Llywelyn, so must stand as prime targets, therefore our watch word must be caution and on no account, can we drop our guard. I know you will agree on that score. I have sent word to all our outposts to be on the alert.'

Maud squeezed his hand.

'After all these years of conflict I have already learned that important premise. Have you sent word to your brothers yet? I will write to Meg and Bella. It is somehow prophetic that Dafydd's execution is in October, almost a year since the death of your father.'

'At last he can lie easy in his grave knowing his enemies have been vanquished.'

'Amen to that! Methinks you witnessed the closing of an important chapter in the history of Wales yesterday, a chapter in which the Mortimer family played an important part but now the focus must be on the future.'

Some months later a small company of riders entered the gates of Wigmore and their leader sought an audience with the Lady of Wigmore. As she entered the chamber Maud's usual self control deserted her for an instance as she recognised the taller of the two men.

'My Lord, you are most welcome here at Wigmore.'

As he stepped forward Guy de Longeville bowed and took her hand and kissed it.

'I have come to offer my services.'

Maud's quickly recovered her composure and merely smiled, as she politely thanked him for his offer.

'I cannot imagine how you have managed to extricate yourself from the services of Comte de Vivonne.'

'The Comte died last summer; soon afterwards I set about putting my affairs in order and made arrangements to return to my homeland. My son is a Frenchman through and through and will serve their king without a divided loyalty.'

'Through all of your years of living and travelling for France, to call England your home sounds a mite contrary. Surely, after so many years in service, freedom must feel sweet?'

'Freedom is a state of mind my lady but, at least now I can choose whom I will serve.'

'Then I would be churlish not to accept you gracious offer.'

The looks exchanged between the couple spoke far more eloquently than their words.

She called for wine and refreshments and as they sat relating the events of the intervening years, they both realised their long held feelings of love had not dimmed during the long period of separation and it soon became clear to them both, that whatever life had in its vast store of surprises, they would face the coming years as one.

'Long ago we made a vow that if we ever had an opportunity to be together we would not allow anything to stand in our way. Does that vow still hold true?'

Guy de Longeville looked deep into the green-grey eyes which had haunted his dreams for decades.

'My heart is, and always has been yours, and I solemnly promise to fulfil that vow for as long as you desire it.'

He gathered her in his arms oblivious to the robin's trilling song outside or, the sounds of everyday life in the castle. Life had finally brought them full circle and they could both enjoy this reunion in the full knowledge they had been true to their family duties and now it was their time go forward in life - together.

Next morning Maud rose long before the household stirred and made her way to the stables knowing there was always a groom on duty. She put her fingers to her lips as the young groom was about to bow.

'Kindly saddle my horse and accompany me, we will not be away long.'

Maud stared at him: 'surely I know your face?'

The boy looked flustered but answered with a shy smile. 'It's me your ladyship, Gyles.'

'Ah, yes! But what are you doing in the stables?'

He chuckled. 'I prefer horses my lady, and when my brother told me of a vacancy here, I ran away and applied for the job.'

'Good! Then tend me and my horses well young Gyles and you will go far in my service.'

He nodded nervously as he went about his task with quiet efficiency as he had been taught by the aging head groom, Master Hal. Once mounted, the two riders left through the gate leaving a startled and bemused guard watching them as they disappeared into the wreathing mist which curled around the horses and their riders, giving them a ghostly appearance. Maud pulled the deep hood of her heavy riding cloak further over her head, hiding her face. As they reached Wigmore Abbey she dismounted, and handed the reins to the young groom ordering him to remain.

Just as the first fingers of dawn began to break through the mist, Maud reached the place of the Mortimer family burial plot. She went and knelt beside the impressive sandstone tomb.

'I pray you have found peace my lord and have been re-united with Ralph. Your enemies have been vanquished; your name and deeds are spoken of with respect.' She paused before continuing. 'We travelled the road of marriage together, faced all of its trials and pitfalls but know, I never once betrayed you. I will ensure Isolde fulfils your wishes for her future and to be acknowledged as a true Mortimer, and will never forego my duties as mother to our children. But I now absolve myself from the vows I took so many years ago when I became your wife. From this time forward, I intend to go into the future unfettered by duty to you, and for whatever years I have left, will live them as I see fit. I will keep you in my prayers and Masses will be said for your salvation – God keep you and may your soul be at rest. This is my final farewell to you Sir Roger Mortimer, Lord of Wigmore.'

She leaned and touched the headstone and paused as she made the sign of the cross. Then, without a sound she rose and walked slowly back to the nervous groom. In silence they rode back towards Wigmore and as they entered the arched gateway, the sun broke through the clouds and the mist began to thin.

'I think it will be a fine day Gyles!' She said as she smiled at her young attendant.

'Aye, my lady.'

A tall figure walked towards them and came and took Maud's hand. Neither conscious of the quizzical stares they attracted as they walked back from the stables.

THE END

EPILOGUE

Maud de Braose [Mortimer] lived for many more years, although the exact date of her death is unknown, in almost all of the references it states, she was dead by March 1301.

There was one amusing anecdote which sounds perfectly in character, that upon deciding to occupy Clun Castle, Maud ejected the sheriff who vowed to complain to the king. Maud dismissed his threat and upon hearing of her audacity, the king is said to have chuckled and taken no further action. Maud was, after all, a heroine in Edward's eyes and would remain so for the rest of her life.

Maud's exact whereabouts during the years after Edmund's marriage is not certain but upon a visit to Radnor church some years ago, a well worn sandstone effigy of a woman dressed in medieval costume of the 13th century, is thought, by Paul Martin Remfry, to be that of Maud Mortimer; he also believes she became the Constable of Radnor sometime after her husband's death.

In Kingsland church, there is a window displaying the heraldic coat of arms of the de Braose family and as Sir Roger Mortimer [d: 1282], died there, so it is highly likely Maud would maintain the connection with the church,

The Castle at Presteigne also played a part in the life of the Mortimer's and many believe Maud may have spent some of the years of her widowhood in this beautiful part of Herefordshire. The peripatetic lifestyle of the medieval period lends weight to Maud being involved with many of the castles in the location of the Mortimer and Marshal lands.

You can well imagine that Maud would certainly have instilled in her grandchildren, the pride of their Marshal ancestry and that they were a direct descendants of the knight, dubbed, 'The Greatest Knight in Christendom', William Marshal. Young Roger Mortimer's advantageous marriage to Joan de Geneville could well have been at the instigation of Maud. During his early life, her grandson, Roger Mortimer, who would eventually become the [Ist Earl of March], demonstrated his loyalty and knightly qualities that is until Hugh Despencer, became the favourite of Edward II, and successfully blighted the Mortimer name. This appears to have unleashed the traits of his great grandfather, William de Braose [Gwilym Ddu], who had been re-known for his cruelty..

Maud lived through one of the most defining periods of English history and proved without doubt she was a woman of her time; fearless, loyal, described as beautiful, and witty. She saw a man hailed as the corner stone of democracy, Simon de Montfort, crushed by a young prince who upon gaining the throne, began to implement many of the changes in law instigated by de Montfort and the Magna Carta.

As a Marcher, Maud understood the unique position held by the lords of that region; they stood like a shield against the almost continuous onslaught of the Welsh and held the Standard of England high against their enemy. They were a tough, resourceful, independent breed of men and women, who should never be forgotten for their efforts, and tenacity who earned their place in the history of the March.

AUTHOR'S NOTE

Bringing Maud to life has been a fascinating experience; the era in which she lived has to be deemed as one of the most significant periods in English history. Not only dominated by civil war and the wars in Wales but also, by the battle of wills between two men who shared nothing in common but the sin of pride, Henry III, and his brother-in-law, Simon de Montfort.

The title 'The Twisted Legacy' was prompted by Maud's maternal and paternal lineage. Descended from both the noble and legendary, William Marshal, Earl of Pembroke, her grandfather and her father, who was loathed, hated and feared by the Welsh, William de Braose [Gwilym Ddu], hanged for the adultery with Llywelyn ap Iowerth's wife, the Lady Joan. The shame of her father's execution must have conflicted with the pride of being related to a legendary hero and therefore, feel it could have had a profound effect on the mind of a young girl. Honour, respect, chivalry and faith, were the codes by which medieval society lived by.

Betrothed when she was still only seven to the infant, Roger Mortimer, Maud would have been a young woman of twenty three by the time they eventually married. The age difference may have had some bearing on their relationship and I am of the firm belief, that if Maud was the beauty she was purported to have been, somewhere in her life she would have been wooed by someone nearer her own age. After all, love and romance, were read and written about and like all young girls, the notion of 'true' love is as valid today as is was in medieval times. Thus, it gave me the chance to weave a fictional relationship with Guy de Longeville.

However, the notable events which occurred throughout Maud's life, I have endeavoured to remain as close to the facts as my research has led me. The complex relationship between Henry III, and Simon de Montfort, is at the heart of the civil war. Whatever noble motives have subsequently been placed on their quarrel; these two deeply religious men, were set on a collision course in a test of personalities at a time when there was strong opposition to a king, who persistently refused to uphold the rights of his nobles, laid down in the 'Magna Carta' in 1215. There is no doubt; De Montfort was a character burning with moral indignation, ambition and religious fervour. His true aims are forever obscured by time and speculation. In the beginning, when he emerged as spokesman for the 'Barons Party' he was seen by many as altruistic, but somewhere along the line, it appears his ambitions blurred those original goals, and he fell foul of more baser instincts.

It was during the 'Battle of Evesham' that the Mortimer name would be forever linked with that of de Montfort. A battle where the young Lord Edward, demonstrated his might, when he nailed his colours firmly to the mast - *follow me or die!* After his loyal adherent, Roger Mortimer slew de Montfort; Edward gave his permission for Mortimer to send the severed head, draped with the testicles, to Lady Mortimer at Wigmore, the *prize* of victory.

Although the civil strife featured greatly during the years of 1264-5, it was the long conflict with Wales where the Mortimer family faced their perennial enemy. Ironically, the man who took up the cause when Llywelyn ap Iowerth's son Dafydd died was Roger Mortimer's cousin, Llywelyn ap Gruffydd. Their bitter struggle is at the heart of this story and how Maud's loyalty to her husband never wavered.

Myth and fact are woven together to bring to life the chaotic years of the thirteenth century, as seen through the eyes of Maud de Braose. The Focus of the story is based mainly in the Marches of Wales, where the continuous wars affected so many lives. How the loyalties of the Marcher barons were tested, as they fought to uphold their rights, during the reign of Henry III, a king whose intransigent position, ultimately ended in outright civil war. How friendships and families, can at times, be divided by differing beliefs. But it is also highlights the role of the Marcher wives, mothers and daughters, women who also played a significant part in the history of the Marches, their courage is rarely written about. So, I hope in some small way, 'The Twisted Legacy', has acknowledged their true place on the pages of history.